The
Greatest
of These

The Greatest of These

Cheryl Fehrmann Okimoto

*To Tom & Marie,
I love you all so much! You are awesome friends, and I pray God blesses you richly.
Love,
Cheryl*

The Shepherd Series:
Seasons of Change
A Gilded Sky
After the Storm
Always a Sunrise
The Blessed Winter

Hilo Suspense:
Shadows In Light
Flames of Hope

Historical:
By Any Other Name

The Ohana Project:
A Cord of Three
Living Stones
A Piece of Dust
Foolish Things
Secret Righteousness

The Greatest of These

© 2020 Cheryl Fehrmann Okimoto

All rights reserved. No portion of this book may be reproduced in any form, stored in a retrieval system, or transmitted by any means – electronic, mechanical, photocopy, recording, scanning, or other – without the prior written permission of the author. The only exception is brief quotations in printed reviews.

This is a work of fiction. Names, characters, places and incidents are either the product of the author's imagination or are used fictitiously. Any resemblance to actual persons, living or dead, is entirely coincidental.

Unless otherwise noted, all scriptures are taken from the *Holy Bible, New International Version*®. Copyright © 1973, 1978, 1984 Biblica. Used by permission of Zondervan. All rights reserved.

Cover art:
    Bouquet by Sandy White, Owner and Designer, Beehive Florist and Gifts, LLC, Salem, Missouri
    Photo by Leslie Fore at Fore Photography LLC, Salem, Missouri

ISBN 978-1-67810-617-1

Printed in the United States of America

Visit www.cherylokimoto.com

Love never fails. But where there are prophecies,
they will cease; where there are tongues, they will be
stilled; where there is knowledge, it will pass away.
For we know in part and we prophesy in part, but when
completeness comes, what is in part disappears. When I
was a child, I talked like a child, I thought like a child,
I reasoned like a child. When I became a man, I put the
ways of childhood behind me. For now we see only a
reflection as in a mirror; then we shall see face to face.
Now I know in part; then I shall know fully, even as
I am fully known. And now these three remain: faith,
hope and love. But the greatest of these is love.
1 Corinthians 13:1-13

I deeply appreciate Sandy White and Leslie Fore, who not only helped with the artwork for this book, but also encouraged me with thier enthusiasm for the project. Both of you have been a great blessing to me.

I also owe a deep thanks to Emi Ayau, whose editorial skills are priceless.

The Ohana Project is the name of the ministry first envisioned by Greg Shepherd in *A Gilded Sky*. Its primary purpose is to give orphaned adults families. Ohana is Hawaiian for "family."

This is the sixth book in the series. While each novel can theoretically be read as a stand-alone book, you will enjoy them much more if you read them in order. You can follow the list in the front of the book.

Characters from previous books reappear in this novel. In the back of the book, you will find a list of characters for when you don't remember who's who.

Chapter 1

"Tim, are you coming out sometime tonight?" Brandon Wolfe called from the main room.

Tim Shepherd scowled at the mirror, frustrated by his tie and his brother.

"Why do I have to wear a tie?" he snarled loudly.

"Because Joylynne told you to," the laughter in Brandon's voice came through loud and clear. It was also clear that he was coming toward Tim's room.

"Then why isn't she here to tie it?" Tim complained.

"Because you aren't married yet," Brandon said drolly as he crossed the room. "She's not dressing or undressing you until after you are."

Tim felt heat rising in his face.

Brandon was working on his brother's tie, so he didn't see Tim's already dusky skin get darker, nor did he notice Tim looking down and away from him. But he did realize that the silence had suddenly gotten very loud.

He looked at his brother and was alarmed by the signs of shame that he saw.

"What did you do, Tim?" he sighed sadly.

This was one of the hardest parts of being in Norman, Oklahoma with his "little" brother. Tim was nine years younger, but considerably larger than Brandon's six foot one. At one inch shy of seven feet, Tim had speed and an extended reach that made him one of the best wide receivers to play college football in many years. That ability was enhanced by the toughness he'd learned wrestling with his older half-brothers for as long as he could remember. Luke and Greg were also very big men, and Tim had learned that even when he was hit, he didn't have to go down. When he was on the field, until he heard the whistle, he was pushing for the goal line.

With his size and athletic ability, he didn't need good looks to have his pick of women. But he had the looks in abundance – dark wavy hair, hazel eyes that leaned toward a golden hue and skin perpetually tanned from a diverse heritage – African, Japanese, Hawaiian, English, Mexican, Irish, Cherokee, Filipino and Italian. That heritage had combined to give him unique features that lent him an air of mystery since no single ethnicity came through enough for him to be categorized. Women fairly swooned over him.

But Tim had also been a committed Christian since he was a boy. He tried to live his life in a God-honoring way. He believed that sexual purity was part of honoring God, and he'd long ago chosen to follow his big brothers' advice on keeping sexual purity as a single man – don't look for it and flee temptation.

That was why he'd never noticed the women who swooned over him. The woman he was now engaged to, Joylynne Quintanilla, had never swooned a day in her life. She was also a Christian who wanted to honor God by remaining sexually pure. Since they'd gotten engaged three months ago, they'd had some struggles in that direction. With the wedding only three weeks away, Brandon would hate to see them fumble so close to the goal line.

"Tim?" Brandon gently prompted his brother.

"We didn't go all the way," Tim turned from his brother without raising his eyes. He dropped down on the bed, propped his elbows on his knees and dropped his head in his hands. "But we went too far. My shirt was off and hers was well on the way."

"What stopped you?" Brandon asked curiously, dropping down on the bed beside his brother. He wasn't going to stand over his brother or scold him. He was trying to help him, not judge and convict him.

"That silly alarm you suggested we put on our phones," Tim glanced sideways at his brother without lifting his head from his hands.

Brandon grinned. When Tim and Joylynne had wanted more private time than double dating allowed, he'd talked to his brother about how they could do it and still stay on the straight and narrow. One of Brandon's suggestions had been an eleven o'clock alarm on both their phones. The alarm would go off even if the ringer was set to silent or vibrate. They also used songs instead of the regular alarm tones. Tim's was the chorus of "God is Bigger Than the Boogie Man" from VeggieTales and Joylynne's was DC Talk's "Jesus Freak." They were both raucous enough to douse flames of passion, especially going off at the same time. If Tim and Joylynne ever did manage to ignore the opening measures, the messages of the songs would soon bring them back from the brink.

"Was that the first time you needed them?" Brandon asked.

"Yeah," Tim nodded.

"That's good," Brandon nodded too. "What're you going to do differently so you don't need to use them again?"

"I don't know," Tim growled. Part of him didn't want to care. Touching Joy and being touched by her felt so good. He really wanted to do it again, and go even farther. But he knew that was his sinful flesh rising up. God asked his children to keep sex for marriage only. Tim wanted to obey God more than he wanted to please his flesh, but it was still a struggle.

"What did you do wrong this time?" Brandon asked patiently.

"I don't know," Tim answered rather petulantly.

"Why don't you know?" Brandon asked with a small smile.

"I hate it when you do that, *Dad*," Tim glared at his brother.

"I am my father's son," Brandon said solemnly.

Tim's reply was to launch himself at his brother.

Brandon was the only one of Joshua Wolfe's sons who was biologically related to him. He looked and sounded remarkably like the Colonel, who had a penchant for asking questions more often than giving advice. Of course none of his six sons and three daughters appreciated that when they were on the receiving end, but after four years with the Colonel, they were all learning to dish it out pretty well.

At the moment, Tim resented Brandon's ability to not just question as their dad did, but look and sound just like him. The only logical response was to hit him.

Unfortunately, Tim failed to anticipate his brother, who had an almost psychic ability to accurately anticipate his much larger brothers – Greg at six five and two hundred fifty pounds was the closest to Brandon's six one, one hundred ninety pounds. His hand-to-hand combat training as a Marine had kicked into high gear, gone into overdrive when he'd gained a very large family after leaving the Marines.

As soon as Tim started moving toward his brother, Brandon was moving too. Instinctively he knew he wasn't going to totally escape his brother's grasp, so he needed to minimize contact and turn the tables on Tim.

Brandon dropped his shoulders to his left, away from his brother. He also brought his legs up and to the right, flattening himself on the bed. His hands were up at his chest when Tim's body hit his, and he pushed with both arms, rolling his body toward the side of the bed.

They both hit the floor, but Brandon was on top, pressing his forearm against Tim's throat.

"Does this mean you don't want to talk about this now?" Brandon calmly asked with a highly arched eyebrow.

His affect was so out of line with their current circumstances that Tim had to laugh.

"Get off me, you jerk," he pushed Brandon who rolled smoothly off him, offering Tim a hand up.

Brandon didn't repeat his question, but when he didn't say or do anything else, just stood and stared at his brother, Tim knew he was going to have to answer, and a simple "no" wouldn't be sufficient. It would just lead to other questions. He knew where the questions would end up, so he could either go ahead and answer them before they were asked or face Dad's doppelganger.

"No, I don't want to talk about this right now," Tim straightened his tie and checked to make sure his shirt was still properly tucked as he answered. "I do want to talk about it later. I think I'll talk to Joy about it before she leaves tonight, then you and I will talk again, before Joy and I have a chance to get in trouble again. Is that okay with you brother-dad?"

"That's fine with me," Brandon grinned and nodded. "Are we talking tonight before we go to bed?"

"Yes," Tim growled then reached for the suit coat hanging in his closet, grumbling to himself. "I didn't have enough big brothers, God? You had to give me more? Why couldn't you give me another little brother?"

Brandon wasn't bothered by the complaint. He knew Tim loved him, and was very glad that they were not just brothers, but also friends.

"It could be worse," Brandon threw over his shoulder as he headed for the door. "God could've given you more big sisters. Still might if you keep complaining!"

Tim groaned and followed his brother. Brandon was too right. Tim loved his sisters, but they could be very bossy, especially Heather.

He actually was very glad that Brandon was also living in Norman. All his older siblings were in Missouri, and Robert, the baby of the family, was in college in Hawaii. Brandon had moved from St. Louis to Norman at exactly the right time as far as Tim was concerned. They'd shared many experiences, the highlight being Tim's proposal to Joy. Brandon had worked with him for the better part of the summer, preparing for Tim to ride in on his white steed and sweep Joy off her feet.

When she'd accepted Tim's proposal, things had started to heat up pretty quickly between them, and Brandon had been there to help Tim keep things under control. Then, when the semester ended, Brandon had suggested that Tim move into his two bedroom cabin on the Living Stones Ranch, the Vogt farm that was now part of Living Stones Ohana Foundation. That was the ministry Bill and Reylynnda Vogt had set up and connected with Tim's family's ministry, The Ohana Project.

Tim agreed to move in with Brandon because it made sense. Since he and Joy had set their wedding date for the first Saturday in January, he wasn't going to be living in the dorm next semester, so he needed somewhere to stay. But he certainly didn't need to be living alone in the house they were going to be moving into after their honeymoon. The temptation to spend some alone time there would be too great, even though the house was only two doors down from Pastor Charles and Stormy Brown's house, Tim's cousin and her husband. It was still way too private for an unmarried couple who wanted to be sexually pure.

Tonight, the location of Brandon's cabin was very convenient, just a few hundred yards from Mama Rey's home where they were having dinner. Tim was very nervous about that dinner because he was going to be meeting Danita Quintanilla, his fiancée's mother. He was nervous because he knew he was already predisposed to not like her. He'd had a hard enough time with his own sister when she'd left her husband for almost two months. Danita Quintanilla had been separated from her husband for six years. The fact that Joy was still hurting over her parents' separation made matters worse.

On the other hand, Joy loved her mother very much which gave Tim motivation to like Danita. That was one of the things Brandon had helped him with in the six months that he'd been in Norman. Brandon's biggest reason for fleeing St. Louis had been his suddenly too intense attraction for Cari O'Phelan, whom he'd actively disliked for the better part of fifteen years. They had talked a lot about how Brandon had lost his long-term animosity to Rachel's best friend, and about how Tim could bury the antagonism he felt toward Joy's mother. Tim had come to realize that he had to get to know the real woman, not judge her based on the hurt she'd inflicted on her daughter.

He knew he had a good foundation to work with, so he was pretty sure he would be able to find some liking for Joy's mother, but he was nervous because he wasn't one hundred percent certain. In fact, he probably wasn't more than seventy percent sure. That thirty percent really bothered him because the stakes were very high. Danita would be his mother-in-law soon, so she was going to be part of his life whether he liked her or not. It would be much easier if he liked her.

TIM DUCKED THROUGH the door of Bill and Mama Rey's house and his heart did a now familiar flip-flop. Joy was already there.

His fiancée was incredible. She was very tall for a woman, but almost a foot shorter than his six eleven. Her red hair and green eyes could have made her a quintessential Irish woman, but she was also Mexican and Choctaw, so her skin was too dark to have very many of the requisite freckles, and her hair was a dark red rather than an Irish red.

She was smarter than anyone Tim had ever met, except maybe his brother Greg, but that would be a very close call. She was confident about where she was going in life, and she moved and talked in the strength of that confidence. Best of all, she loved God passionately.

As soon as he saw Joy, Tim only had eyes for her. He quickly crossed the room and brushed a kiss on her lips before giving her a hug.

When he reluctantly dropped his arms and stepped back, Tim saw that in spite of the fact that his fiancée was very happy to see him, she was also distraught.

He looked around the room and almost snarled. He knew Joy's dad, Al, very well, but he'd never seen such sorrow in the man. The cause of that sadness had to be the tallish elegant older red-headed, green-eyed woman who was approaching Tim from the other side of the room.

"You must be Joylynne's Tim," as she offered her hand to him, Danita fairly purred with a barely perceptible Southern accent.

Tim glanced briefly at his brother. Brandon's stony mask of indifference told him that the woman made his hackles rise too. She was very much like the ice princess that Cari O'Phelan had presented to Brandon for many years.

Long before Brandon had ever suspected that a very different woman lurked beneath the cold façade, Tim and the rest of the Shepherd-Wolfe clan had seen that other woman in Cari and liked her. Maybe a similar woman lurked beneath Danita Quintanilla.

Tim immediately decided that he was going to try to find that woman. As he accepted his future mother-in-law's hand and bowed deeply over it, he dropped his resentments in a rubbish bag, tied it tight and threw it in a dumpster.

"I'm very pleased to meet you, ma'am," Tim said with an open friendly aspect that his pastor-brother Greg would be proud of. "I see where Joy gets her beauty."

"And I now see how Joylynne got caught," Danita smiled slyly. "Not only are you as handsome as the day is long, but you're quite the charmer too."

"Charmer?" Tim laughed cheerfully. "Oh no, ma'am. I'm no charmer. I'm sorry to say that my brother Greg took all the charm God allowed our family. If I appear a charmer to you, I guess you just bring out the best in me!"

Tim knew that everyone in the room was watching them, but Brandon was the only one he could see enough to judge his reaction to him and Danita.

Tim saw Brandon's left eyebrow wing skyward, then a slow smile lifted his lips. Brandon nodded slightly when Tim's eyes briefly met his.

That all happened in the space of two breaths. Tim focused his attention back on Danita, but he was confident in his course. Brandon had realized his intent and approved.

With a merry laugh, Danita quickly covered her surprise at Tim's declaration.

"Your brother Greg should check his charm bucket, Timothy Shepherd," Danita declared. "I do believe you've swiped some of his supply."

"I'm sure he hasn't, ma'am," Brandon said as he joined them. "My big little brother has never been long on charm before, so it has to be your presence that makes the difference."

"Brandon, I'm pleased to introduce you to my future mother-in-law, Danita Quintanilla." Brandon took Danita's hand and bowed politely. "Mrs. Quintanilla, I'm not quite as pleased to inflict you with my little big brother, Brandon Wolfe."

"Oh please, there's no need to stand on formality," Danita scolded. "You must call me Nita, all my friends do."

"Alright," Tim said hesitantly, "but I hope you'll let me call you Mom after the wedding."

"I'll be pleased if you do," Danita agreed with an amazed smile.

"I'm going to have to let my brother enjoy your charm without me for a bit," Tim said reluctantly. "I do have other friends to greet, but promise me you'll sit by me for dinner?"

"It'll be my pleasure," Danita nodded.

"And you'll be on my other side," Tim turned toward Joylynne. He almost stepped back in shock.

Joy shone with love and approval.

No, that was an understatement. The love flowing from her toward him was like the winter waves on the North Shore of Oahu, huge and thundering boldly but beautifully.

Apparently she too had divined his intention, and approved heartily.

He needed to have that conversation with Brandon as soon as he could figure out a reason for them to step outside.

Tim gave Joy the briefest of kisses, then stepped over to greet her father.

"Good evening, sir." They shared their customary handshake and half hug. "Any fascinaing new cases this week?"

"One in particular I'm sure you'll be interested in," Al nodded. "I met with a young couple who recently came into a rather sizable fortune and now they want to turn their bakery into a non-profit training facility, but they still want to run it as a business, so that they can do training in business management and sales, not just baking."

"That is interesting," Tim exclaimed. "That's what my sister did with her auto repair shop!"

"She did? Were you involved in it?" Al was also excited.

"Kinda," Tim shrugged. "I was still in high school, but I helped out some. Who are they thinking about training? They looking at abused women, at-risk kids or ex-convicts?"

"They mentioned at-risk kids, but they might be open to helping others too."

"At Heather's shop, they train ex-cons in the morning and at-risk kids after school."

"That makes sense," Al mused. "You sure wouldn't want to pull already at-risk kids out of school, but the shop shouldn't sit idle during school hours either."

"But don't bakeries do most of their baking way early in the morning?" Tim asked.

"I think you might be right, but I didn't ask that. We just had our initial consultation this week."

"So you don't have many details yet," Tim's eyes suddenly lit up. "Hey, do you think they'd mind if I work with them too? Not legal stuff, of course, but it'd be great to practice my business education in a real-life situation."

"I can ask," Al cheerfully said. "I think they'd be thrilled, especially since you already have some experience with what they want to do."

13

"We'll talk more later, sir," Tim nodded. "But right now I've got to go say hi to Bill."

Tim glanced at the older man, then turned back to Al and whispered loudly. "Hey, did you know that your mom's husband is an incorrigible flirt? Keep an eye out. Don't let him get too close to your wife."

Chapter 2

*J*oylynne watched her fiancé with undisguised adoration. No one should be surprised by it, not since she was marrying him in three weeks. No one would know that her love for him had just taken a quantum leap forward.

No one liked her mother. Danita had always been a rather difficult woman, so she'd never been anyone's favorite even before she left her husband six years ago. Since then every reluctant trip she'd made to Norman, Oklahoma had been a miserable affair. The best Danita Quintanilla ever got was being ignored, the worst was open disdain.

For some reason that she would have to ferret out later, Tim had made an instant but very firm decision to love Joy's mother. She knew it was spur of the moment because just last night he'd been whining about not wanting to meet her. After he'd kissed Joy this evening, he had been angry, probably because she was upset about the frozen wasteland her parents had once again placed her in.

Somewhere between that kiss and shaking Mom's hand, Tim had decided to change the climate in the room. He'd charmed her mother then turned around to reaffirm his friendship with her father, and challenge him to reclaim his relationship with his wife. Now he was moving on to Bill Vogt, Joy's stepgrandfather.

"How you doin', you old coot?" Tim greeted his dear friend with a handshake and hug. "Saw you out in the corral with that ornery old mare this afternoon when I got back. Were you missin' Mama Rey while she was gone on her shopping trip?"

"I'll make you wish *you* were missin' me, you young whippersnapper," Mama Rey shook a fist at Tim, but she didn't get the chance to use it before she was wrapped in a hug.

"What I'm missing is your cooking," Tim whined plaintively. "How come you aren't in there getting it ready? I'm hungry."

Joy heard Brandon's quiet snort. She glanced at him, her eyes wide in alarm.

Brandon caught her eye and burst out laughing.

Bill and Mama Rey were also chuckling, so Brandon had to explain to Danita and Al.

"I think your daughter just realized her fiancé might not be as calm and serious as she thought he was," Brandon snickered. "The way Tim just talked to Mama Rey, both the words and the tone, were exactly like our brother Greg."

"I don't know what you're talking about," Tim crossed his arms and glared at his brother.

Joylynne fled the room!

She darted across the dining room and into the kitchen. She sank into a chair both laughing and crying.

Tim had looked and sounded just like his big brother, but Joy wasn't surprised. She knew he had it in him, and so did everyone else who knew him well. But he was only that silly man when he was completely comfortable with people he knew and liked. She'd been surprised to see him open up that part of himself in front of her mother.

"Why I gotta help in the kitchen?" Joy heard Tim's loud whine. "I thought I was the guest of honor tonight."

"Honor?" Brandon hooted with laughter, but whatever else he was going to say was cut off, probably when the door to the dining room swung shut.

Joy jumped to her feet and ran back toward the kitchen door just in time to jump into Tim's arms as soon as the door swung open.

"I love you!" She squealed happily. "Will you marry me?"

Tim stared at Joy in surprise. She wasn't a squealer. Her three best friends were, but not Joy.

He grinned broadly. Obviously Joy was pleased with his plan, and his method. He hugged her much more briefly than he wanted, but longer than was prudent, then set her back on her feet.

"Are you trying to get my son and daughter-in-law back together?" Mama Rey stared at Tim with her hands on her hips.

"Yes ma'am, I am," he said firmly.

"Praise God!" Mama Rey threw her hands in the air. "I think you'll do it too!"

"I'm not complaining," Joy said, "but what made you decide to do this?"

"Well," Tim shrugged, "since Texas won last weekend, we're out of the bowl games, so I need something to do with my time the next three weeks."

Joy stared at him a moment. "That's not all, is it?"

"No, but that's all that matters to you right now, so let's leave it at that," Tim said firmly.

"Will you tell me sometime?" Joy asked. She was okay with it if he kept his other reasons a secret, but it would take awhile to get over her intense curiosity.

"After I talk to someone else, I might," Tim nodded once.

"Well, if you can get Al and Danita to even be civil around each other by the day of the wedding, I'll love you forever," Mama Rey promised.

"You'll already love me forever," Tim laughed.

"Well then I'll, … I'll, …," Mama Rey frowned thoughtfully then smiled brilliantly. "I'll give your fiancée my secret pound cake recipe!"

"You better make it happen!" Joy threw her arms around Tim again.

One look at that joyous face and Tim couldn't help himself. He had to kiss her.

The kiss went on.

And on.

"Let her go, you oaf!" Mama Rey pulled on his arm with her tiny hands.

Tim reluctantly dropped his arms and stepped back, though he didn't take his eyes off his fiancée.

"Right now we better make dinner happen," Mama Rey turned Joylynne toward the stove. "Check the dinner rolls. They should be done. Tim, make yourself useful and get the platter from on top of the hutch so I don't have to drag out my stepstool."

Mama Rey ordered them around like a general directing her troops. They soon had everything ready, so Mama Rey sent them out to get the others up to the table.

Tim wasn't surprised when Bill asked him to pray for the food. He'd prayed many times at this same table, but so had Bill, Mama Rey, Joy, Brandon and anyone else who professed Christianity and sat in the Vogt's dining room more than once. He looked up and raised his hands, as was customary in his family.

"Jesus, thank you for bringing us all together tonight. I for one am very happy to have both Al and Nita together for fellowship because I hope to pry many embarrassing stories about Joy out of them. I've gotta 'cause when my crazy family gets here in two weeks, they're gonna tell her lots of stories about me, most of them greatly embellished. Thank you for Mama Rey and her great cooking, and please help me get her top secret pound cake recipe. Amen."

When Tim looked down, Al was staring at his plate with a bemused frown, Mama Rey was humming softly, Bill was grinning broadly and Brandon was intently focused on the platter of fried chicken that he quickly picked up. Tim couldn't see Joy or Nita's face because they were sitting beside him.

"You are not funny, Timothy," Joy pouted. "Ignore him, Mom and Dad. He's already heard everything he needs to hear."

"Oh, I think not. young lady," Al snorted then looked right at Danita. "Dani, I think you should tell Tim about camping with Joy."

"Daddy!" Joy gasped in serious distress.

"The whole thing?" Danita giggled and smiled at her husband. "Including the …?"

"Mother! Don't you dare!"

"I think you should, Nita," Mama Rey nodded firmly. "You tell it so well."

"Yes, you do," Al smiled at his wife. "I'd love to hear you tell it again."

"You should know, Tim," Danita looked up at her future son-in-law, "that your fiancée loves to go skinny dipping."

"Mom!" Joy wailed and buried her face in her hands.

"She does," Danita nodded solemnly. "Much to our chagrin we found that out when we went to a family church camp the summer she turned three. Each day for two hours in the morning and two hours in the afternoon, there were activities for the children which allowed the parents to go off and do something on their own.

"Al and I went out on the lake in a canoe, thinking Joy would be fine swimming with the other children. We knew she wanted to because she'd been walking around singing 'Swimmy, swimmy, swimmy,' ever since she'd seen the lake when we'd arrived the night before. Unfortunately, we were frantically waved down as soon as we got close to the camp on our return trip."

Danita drank some water then shared a smile with her husband before she continued.

"Joy was in the water no more than five minutes before she started peeling out of her swimsuit! When the camp counselors tried to get her to stop, she threw a temper tantrum. When we returned from our canoe ride, Joy was running through the camp, stark naked, screaming, 'Swimmy, swimmy, swimmy!'"

Tim glanced over at Joy with a huge grin. She sank down in her chair, staring steadily at her plate. She knew this wasn't over yet. Part of her wanted to scream in frustration that Mom and Dad were telling her wonderful fiancé such a horrid little story, but part of her was dancing for joy – Mom and Dad were laughing together!

"So the next day," Danita ate a few bites of food before resuming her story, "we took Joy down to the playground, thinking that was safe."

"I bet it wasn't," Tim snickered.

"You'd bet right," Al shrugged in mock sorrow.

"Once again we were called to the 'principal's office' when we got back to camp," Danita shared another smile with Al. "This time Joy had been chasing down boys and kissing them, then she would scream, 'Frog!' and punch them."

"She hasn't done that to me yet," Tim said solemnly, though it took great effort to not bust out laughing, "so I guess she got over that."

"That afternoon we were down at the stables waiting for our horses, when suddenly she pounced on something on the edge of the weeds," Danita was again smiling happily at Al. "She squealed 'Prince!' Al was fast enough to snatch that toad out of her hands just before she kissed it!"

"Apparently, she was kissing the boys to turn them into frogs so she could kiss them and find a prince!" Al grinned at his wife then glanced at Joy who had her face buried in her hands.

Tim laughed and wrapped his arm around his embarrassed fiancée.

"No worries for me then," he said cheerfully. "She's done with the punching 'cause she already found her prince."

Brandon snorted loudly, but Mama Rey beamed happily.

"That's a hard one to argue with!"

Bill and Brandon both snorted at that, but Tim quickly changed the subject. He'd gotten Al and Nita to join each other and enjoy it. He wanted to keep that going. This time hopefully it wouldn't embarrass Joy. They would get back to that later.

"I've been curious about something," he included both Nita and Al in his glance. "Joylynne is a beautiful name, but very unusual. Where did you get it?"

"It's a combination of factors," Al looked at his mother as he answered Tim's question. "I guess you know that we're descendants of Edwin Anderson. His wife, Keanna, had been orphaned when she was sixteen. She loved her parents very much, and when their first daughter was born, Keanna named her after her parents, Ray and Lynne. Of course she changed the spelling of Ray to the feminine form, with an 'e' – Reylynne. When Reylynne had children, she named her daughters Reyanne and Lynnella. Since then all the girls in the Anderson family have some variation of Rey or Lynne in their name."

"That's why Reylynnda and Reylene," Tim frowned slightly and looked at Mama Rey. "But isn't Christmas Baldwin your cousin on the Anderson side?"

"Yes," Mama Rey shrugged. "Her father was the only boy, and he was rather spoiled, especially since Grandma and Grandpa had three girls before he was born. Unfortunately, when he didn't inherit the bulk of the Anderson estate, my mother did since she was the oldest, he was rather petulant about it. He didn't disassociate with the family entirely, as you know, but he did drop the Rey-Lynne tradition. Since his oldest daughter was born on Christmas Day, he had a good excuse for doing it but he didn't pick it up again seventeen years later when they had another baby girl, though he did let his wife get close when she named her Belinda."

"Who did resume the tradition when she named her only child, Reylene," Al added.

"But of course Christmas didn't pick it back up again with her daughters," Bill growled. Christmas Baldwin was one of his least favorite people, especially after the way she'd actively tried to break up Charles and Stormy Brown when they were first dating.

"Speaking of Christmas' daughters, well, her granddaughter," Tim knew the conversation could easily go in the wrong direction because Bill wasn't the only one who strongly disliked Christmas. He was determined to keep it headed where he wanted it to go. "Why do Joy's friends stay well away from her whenever she has scissors or a knife in her hand?"

"Because she scalped her brother," Al replied casually.

"I did not!" Joy glared at her father.

"Scalped is a rather strong word, Alfred," Danita scolded her husband, but it was with a fond smile.

"Not by much, Dani," Al's eyes twinkled though his countenance was very serious. "The boy had abrasions on his head."

"Please tell me the story," Tim begged.

"You take this one, Al," Danita shrugged. "I think you'll tell it better."

"I think he won't," Joy grumbled.

"Sean was only eight and it was right at the beginning of the school year, so it was very traumatic for him," Al started his story with a sad sigh. "His hair was quite wild, and Dani had been observing for a couple weeks that she really needed to cut his hair. One afternoon Joy decided to help out.

"She'd watched her mother cut the boys' hair many times, so she knew exactly what to do, or at least that's what she told Sean. Unfortunately she forgot to put the cutting guard on the clipper –"

"I didn't forget," Joy grumbled. "It broke."

"Whatever," Al shrugged and continued the story. "Those blades were right against that poor boy's head! He had a long furrow right down the middle of all that dark curly hair. There was nothing to do but finish the job."

"Sean didn't talk to his sister for a month!" Dani laughed.

"And no one has ever again let her get close to them with cutting devices," Al added with a warning look for Tim.

"I'll remember that, sir," Tim nodded solemnly. "Anything else I should know?"

"Well," Danita thought carefully. "Did Joy tell you that she's been married before?"

"Mother!" Joylynne wailed.

"More than once," Al nodded sadly.

"She was quite an accomplished flirt when she started kindergarten," Danita began the story but Al easily joined her.

"The poor boys in her school didn't know what hit them."

"The first one we didn't even know about."

"But when she tried to kiss the second one, we got called to the principal's office," Al sighed sadly.

"She convinced Reylene to be the preacher when she decided she wanted to marry Billy Perkins."

"Terry Barnes was the boy she tried to kiss."

"Danny Teater was the next, but she didn't try to kiss him," Nita said with silly solemnness.

"If she tried to kiss Matt Ernst, we never knew."

"She introduced us to Davy Knudsen in church, but only after she was married to him."

"Regular as clockwork Joy got married," Al shook his head sorrowfully. "Once a month all the way through kindergarten and first grade."

"Thankfully in second grade she decided that she wanted to be the preacher," Danita sighed in relief.

"Thankfully for us but not for everyone," Al amended her statement. "She started with her poor cousins and she made them marry her ex-husbands."

"After Sally and Reylene, Kendra was next, then Joy moved on to her other friends."

"She started with just once a week, but soon she was doing it two or three times a week."

"We got called to the principal's office *again* when she was making other kids get married two and three times a *day*," Danita sighed dramatically.

"She had gone through all the second graders and was working on the kindergartners and first graders," Al said with great shock.

"We had to stop her before she got to her little brother!" Danita's eyes were wide with horror.

"Who knows where it would've gone if we hadn't threatened to send her to boarding school?" Al leaned toward Tim and whispered loudly. "She was turning some of the kids into bigamists!"

"So all her exes are remarried?" Tim asked with very commendable seriousness.

"More than once," Dani nodded, equally solemn.

"Good," Tim sighed. "Then I guess I don't need to worry about any of them popping out of the woodwork and challenging me to a duel."

"You're not funny," Joy popped him on the arm.

"But you might want to hedge your bets," Brandon frowned thoughtfully. "I'll have to teach you fencing."

"I know just the place," Bill quickly offered his help.

And so it went. For the rest of the evening Joy endured an enjoyable blend of mortifying stories and growing delight over how well her parents were getting along.

She would have suggested some stories herself, just to see her parents laugh together for the first time in many years, but she didn't need to. Grandma, Bill and Brandon all got onboard and kept the ball rolling. Her mom and dad didn't stand a chance with all those wonderful people pushing them to remember the love and happiness they'd once shared.

A tiny part of Joy was bothered by the course of action Tim had set himself upon. If he wasn't successful, if the Siberian freeze returned, would it steal some of the joy of their wedding day?

Chapter 3

By the time Joy and her mother finally left the Vogt's house, Tim was almost desperate to get out into the cold night air. His entire body thrummed with desire for Joy. His plan to bring Danita and Alfred Quintanilla back together might be a productive use of his time, but it wasn't going to help control his passions.

During dinner, every time Joy had moaned, groaned, wailed or whined about a story that her parents were telling, she'd also touched Tim. Sometimes she leaned her head on his shoulder, sometimes she hid her face behind his back. She pressed her knee against his, laid her hand on his arm or thigh, and subtly hooked her pinkie through his.

She didn't usually touch him like that, so Tim realized that she was doing it to reassure him that she wasn't really upset. In fact, she was quite pleased, at least about her parents being more than civil to each other. He hadn't needed her reassurances, not after her greeting in the kitchen.

Joy and her mom were staying at Mama Rey's house in town, where Tim and Joy would live after the wedding, so of course they left together.

As they rose to go, Tim gave his future mother-in-law a hopeful smile, "You'll come to church with us tomorrow won't you? It's only half a block from the house."

"I guess since Joy's going, I might as well," Danita agreed, but rather hesitantly.

Tim accepted it as fact and turned toward Al who was also rising.

"Will you come too, sir? I'd love to be surrounded by family in church again," Tim sighed, not needing to embellish even a tiny bit. "It's one of the things I miss a lot, being in church with my own family. Brandon's great, but there's just him and me here in Norman."

"I guess since I've got to get the boys up anyway, I may as well," Al was only a little less hesitant than Danita, but Tim smiled happily anyway.

"That's great!"

He turned toward Danita who was reaching for her coat. Tim easily reached over her and got the coat before her. He almost absently handed Danita's coat to Al who had walked with them to the coat closet by the front door, then Tim claimed Joy's coat.

Joy watched her father hold the coat as her mother slipped her arms in it. As soon as she was ensconced in her own coat, she turned and flung her arms around Tim's neck, pulling him down for a kiss.

"I love you! Please take me home," Joy whispered in his ear.

"Not a chance, sweetheart," Tim whispered back. "I need to get some distance from you!"

"Oh!" Joy's eyes went wide in surprise. She dropped her arms and smiled sweetly up at him. "Then I'll see you at church in the morning."

Al was already putting on his coat, so Tim went ahead and grabbed his and Brandon's. They all gave hugs and kisses to Mama Rey with thanks for a wonderful meal. Bill got hugs too, but kisses from the women only.

Al walked Danita to her car and opened the door for her. On the other side of the car, Joy once again threw her arms around Tim in a fervent embrace. Tim only bent his head far enough to kiss the top of her head.

"See you in the morning," he said as he opened the car door.

The three men silently watched the women drive away.

"I've been trying to get that woman to talk to me for six years," Albert suddenly said, still staring down the road where his wife's car had disappeared. "I don't know for sure what happened tonight, but I can guarantee you that I'm going to be in church tomorrow morning."

He didn't wait for a reply. He simply turned and walked to his car.

Brandon and Tim started toward their cabin.

"I'm going to walk for a while," Tim said after a few moments of silence.

"What did happen tonight?" Brandon stayed with his brother when he turned toward the corral. "One minute you're dragging your feet because you don't want to meet Joylynne's mother, and the next you're loving on her almost like she was our mom. What happened?"

"Maybe it was divine revelation, maybe it was a brilliant deduction," Tim shrugged.

"What was the part that might be a brilliant deduction?" Brandon asked.

Tim didn't want to tell his brother. He knew that Brandon still acutely felt the pain of his loss. It hadn't even been two weeks since Cari had told him that she'd moved on. She had chosen to see Brandon's move to Oklahoma as abandonment of her, not a stratigic withdrawal to make sure his relationship with God was strong and true before getting into a romantic relationship with Cari. He had realized that he had wasted nearly fifteen years wallowing in self-pity and bitterness, and he was afraid that man wasn't far enough gone yet.

Tim's brother also still felt shame whenever he was reminded of the man he'd been. If he told Brandon about his "brilliant deduction," it was going to hurt his brother. He did not want to do that.

The silence stretched on.

"I guess I'm not going to like this," Brandon finally said with a sigh.

Tim shrugged and nodded slightly.

"Please don't make me try to figure it out, Tim," Brandon pleaded sadly.

"I was ready to give Nita the cold greeting that she deserved," Tim confessed just as Brandon was going to nudge him again. "Then I glanced at you and saw that same stony indifference that you used to give Cari. I realized that Nita was approaching me almost exactly the way Cari used to address you. I immediately knew that there's a hurt woman under that mask. I wanted to find that woman. I knew I could because you found the woman under Cari's mask."

As Tim talked, Brandon did feel pain and shame, but with Tim's last sentence something wonderful blossomed in his heart.

"Wait," he stopped walking. Tim turned to face him. "Are you telling me that your masterful performance tonight was because of something I did?"

"Yeah," Tim shrugged and casually resumed his walk. "I didn't really think about it, but I knew that if I followed your lead I would help Nita and Al."

"What lead?" Brandon asked, genuinely puzzled. "You weren't in St. Louis to see what happened. And I certainly didn't do something that spectacular."

"No," Tim mused aloud. "But that was because you were fumbling in the dark, and you were still pretty hurt yourself. But you've talked a lot about how you changed and how you finally found the real Cari."

Brandon shook his head. "I had nothing to do with what you did tonight."

Tim suddenly laughed heartily.

"What's so funny?" Brandon glared at him.

"You!" Tim gasped. "You are so much like Dad and Greg."

"Am not," Brandon grumbled though his lips twitched.

"I don't understand it," Tim shook his head as he turned and started back toward the cabin. "How can you guys so quickly see how God uses other people's mistakes for his glory, but you don't think he uses yours? Why does it take you so long to let go of your shame?"

"Good question," Brandon thought about it for a moment. "I think it's because of unrealistic expectations. I have a subconscious expectation that I shouldn't make those kinds of mistakes because I should know better."

"Do you think Dad and Greg shouldn't make the mistakes they make?" Tim asked with a puzzled frown.

"No," Brandon quickly said. "For all their godliness and maturity, they're still just men, and they will make mistakes."

"So you think you're better than them!" Tim stopped and stared at Brandon in bewilderment.

Brandon stared back, slowly shaking his head.

"I am so dumb," he finally muttered. "Of course I'm not better than them. And I get so frustrated with them, especially Dad, when they go off on guilt trips."

"I gotta say this, Brandon," Tim said seriously. "I promise I won't ever bring it up again, but I will talk about it if you want. You may have been a selfish, self-centered, arrogant jerk, but you wanted to be a good man. As soon as you were confronted with your own ugliness, you very deliberately changed, looking to God and family and friends to help you. If Cari O'Phelan doesn't see what she gave up, then maybe she isn't worthy of you. You've been seeking God, growing and serving since you came here. You're a much better man than you were six months ago, and you were already a good man then."

"Thank you, Tim," Brandon said softly. "It means a lot to me, hearing you say that."

"Don't let Cari keep you from finding love, Brandon," Tim urged.

Brandon shook his head as he started walking again. "I'm not, Tim. But I'm also not letting go of my love for her until the Lord tells me it's time."

"Fair enough," Tim nodded. That was as it should be. Any love that didn't come from God wasn't worth holding onto, and even a wounded love was worth clinging to as long as it was in God's will.

"YOUR MOM AND dad are both here!" Sally squealed softly as she bounced up to Joylynne in the multipurpose room after church the next morning.

"Yeah, I noticed," Joy muttered sarcastically. "They were sitting with me."

"How did that happen?" Reylene was fairly bursting with excitement.

"Tim," Joy sighed as her eyes found her fiancé across the room talking to her dad. "He invited them."

"Just like that?" Sally harrumphed. "It wasn't that easy!"

"It was after he had them laughing together for two hours," Joy grinned.

"How'd he do that?" Reylene's eyes were wide.

"He asked them to tell him embarrassing stories about me," Joy sighed happily. "You should've seen them laughing at me. It was wonderful!"

"How many stories?" Kendra asked in astonishment. She had first-hand knowledge of some of Joylynne's embarrassing moments. She could hardly believe that her friend would be happy about hearing them told to her fiancé.

"All of the most embarrassing ones," Joy's slight grimace did nothing to diminish her pleasure.

"Of course they laughed together!" Reylene gasped. She was as familiar with Joy's escapades as their friend was. Her cousin was five months older than her. When they were little, Joy had often roped her younger cousins into her crazy adventures.

"Is Tim trying to get them back together?" Sally whispered.

"Not just him," Joy grinned and pointed toward her grandma. "Watch."

Mama Rey sailed up to Tim and Al. She said something that made both men laugh, then she turned Al toward the outside door. Al waved toward his sons.

Meanwhile, Tim was sauntering over to Danita.

"Mama Rey's going to get Dad down to Pastor Charles' house for dinner," Joy nodded her head toward Tim. "And he's going to get Mom down there."

"Awesome," Reylene bounced happily. "Do you think it's going to work? Will Tim actually get them together again?"

"I wouldn't bet against him," Kendra sighed happily. "He's doing a pretty good job with me and Derek."

"What do you mean?" Sally tilted her head with a puzzled frown.

"You never realized that Tim finds a hundred reasons to get me and Derek together?" Kendra laughed softly.

"He does?" Reylene was also surprised.

"Back in October, that first weekend that Derek was here, Tim decided they were perfect for each other," Joylynne nodded firmly. "He told Brandon and offered a bet that he'd have them engaged before Christmas. Brandon said, 'No bet. I really like the idea of Derek and Kendra, so I'm not betting against it.'"

"We aren't engaged yet," Kendra sighed.

"But you will be, maybe not by this Christmas, but I'll bet you're married well before next Christmas," Joy said confidently. "Did you know that Derek's looking at land for sale here in Oklahoma?"

"He is?" Kendra asked with wide eyes.

"Maybe I shouldn't have said anything," Joy groaned.

"Why would he move to Oklahoma?" Sally teasingly asked Kendra.

"I'm sure I don't know," Kendra said with aggrieved innocence, though she couldn't keep a smile from twitching her lips.

"I know I'm going to go down and help Stormy and Charlotte get lunch ready," Joy laughed happily.

"I think I'm going too. Daddy didn't have plans for today. I bet he'd love to get in on the action with Al and Nita," Reylene immediately invited herself. Her dad, Festus, had been childhood friends with Al, a bond that had been made firmer after he married Al's cousin.

"I wish I could come too but we're going to my grandma's today," Sally sighed. An afternoon with Mama Rey's family was a thousand times better than one with Christmas Baldwin.

"Come on over when you can get away," Joylynne suggested. "I'm sure we're going to be there well into the evening. What about you, Kendra? You want to come?"

"I think I will," Kendra grinned happily. "It sounds like fun."

It was lots of fun. After lunch, Stormy brought out games, all of which required teams. Of course the team captains, Charles and Brandon, made sure that Al and Nita were on the same team, but they split up Tim and Joylynne. Tim was on Brandon's team with Al, Nita, Stormy, Kendra and Joy's middle brothers, Sean and Heath. Joy had her grandma with her on Charles' team along with Charles' daughter Charlotte, Reylene and her dad Festus, and Joy's youngest and oldest brothers, Chavis and Taggart. With an odd number of people, Bill decided he would be the referee.

When they played Pictionary, they discovered that Tim was the best artist in the bunch, but Encore assured them that he was the worst singer. They didn't need a game to tell them that Stormy was the best singer, but Al, Charlotte and Heath were surprisingly good. Danita and Chavis were almost as bad as Tim.

Towards evening, the board games were put away but everyone wanted to continue the fun, so they decided on the good old reliable Charades. Joy and Kendra were bright stars while Brandon, Tim and Al were declared to be the Three Stooges.

When Sally arrived shortly before dinner, Brandon immediately claimed her for his team. Of course, that meant that Bill had to join Charles' team. Tim suggested they do some improvisation, a game at which Bill turned out to be a master. Everyone laughed so hard their sides hurt. Their enjoyment was multiplied when Danita and Al had to hold each other up more than once.

Charles finally kicked everyone out around ten.

"Best day ever!" Chavis, Joy's youngest brother declared as Al and his sons were leaving.

No one argued.

Chapter 4

*T*he Tuesday before Christmas dawned bright and fair. Since the forecast was for a balmy seventy degrees, Tim called Nita and asked if she would like to go horseback riding. His purpose was two-fold. He really did want to get to know his future mother-in-law better, but he also needed to avoid Joy as much as possible. After their Saturday evening dinner with her parents just over a week ago, he'd reluctantly conceded Brandon's assertion that the only sure way they would stay sexually pure until the wedding would be to keep their distance from each other.

In the big scheme of things, their virginity wasn't that big a deal. They were going to happily lose it on their wedding night, but sexual purity was a lifelong goal. Keeping their virginity but tossing sexual purity before the wedding wouldn't be God-honoring. Sure sexual purity could be restored, but Tim knew it was wrong to go ahead and sin because he knew God would forgive him. Once they got started on that road, it would be hard to get off it. If Tim didn't do the difficult thing and stay sexually pure these last couple weeks before his wedding, how was he going to handle it if God put him in more challenging situations down the road?

Danita was delighted to go riding with her daughter's fiancé. Not only was he a wonderful young man, but she felt like he was the only person in the whole state of Oklahoma who might love her without judging her.

In the past week, she'd seen Tim almost every day, and her family nearly as often. Of course she saw Joy every day since they were staying together in Mama Rey's house. It hadn't been an unpleasant time. She no longer felt like her life was as cold and barren as the landscape. Unfortunately, it was still like picking blackberries in the wild. There was a lot of pleasure in her time with her family, but Al and the children were still too likely to scratch her with anger, distrust and wariness.

When Tim was around, it was as if she was in a lush, well-loved, well-tended garden. Sure the thorns were still on the blackberries and rosebushes, and there were other hazards too, like bees and snakes, but they weren't densely packed. In fact, they were quite easy to see and avoid. Being with

Tim while she was with her family was beginning to make hope blossom in Danita's heart.

Maybe she could trust Tim enough to talk to him about the mess she'd made of her life. When Joy had told her mother about her new friend whom she'd met at the beginning of her freshman year, Danita had detected unusual interest for the young man. Her daughter had never talked about a boy so enthusiastically, so Danita had checked out Tim Shepherd and his family on the Internet. She was fascinated by his brother, the big preacher. Tim seemed a lot like him, and Pastor Greg seemed to be the real deal, living his faith openly, boldly and lovingly. If she had someone like that to talk to, maybe she could figure out how to make things right with her husband and children.

As soon as Tim had his date with Danita confirmed, he headed up to the big house to see Mama Rey about a picnic lunch. He was a lot like his sister Heather, almost as good with art and cars as she was, and just about as bad in the kitchen. After nearly four years on his own in Oklahoma he could consistently make a decent pot of rice in his rice cooker, but that wasn't going to help him today. Even if Nita liked it, he couldn't make sushi or Spam musubi once he had a pot of rice.

"You're out and about early," Mama Rey greeted him cheerfully.

Tim wasn't by nature an early riser. On days when he didn't have to get up for classes or football practice, he was rarely out of bed before nine, and he didn't emerge from his den before eleven. This morning it was nine-thirty and he was fully dressed, ready to face the day and standing in Mama Rey's kitchen.

"I didn't know if you were going anywhere today, so I wanted to get here early, at least for me," Tim grinned ruefully.

"What are you wanting from me?" Mama Rey asked cheerfully.

"Just a picnic lunch."

"For you and your beloved?"

"Not a chance," Tim said firmly. "Not until after we're married."

"That's good to hear," Mama Rey smiled proudly. "I'm glad you're not planning on disappearing into the wilds for a few hours with Joy. Is this lunch perchance for your future mother-in-law?"

"How'd you guess?" Tim grinned.

"I'm so proud of you!" Mama Rey reached up to give him a hug. Tim obligingly ducked to receive it. "I think if anyone can find out what happened six years ago, it's you."

"Greg would already know," Tim shrugged humbly.

"But your brother isn't here, you are," Mama Rey knew better than to argue, especially since the young man was probably right. There was a reason his brother was a very successful minister of the gospel.

"So, you'll make that lunch?" Tim pleaded.

"You just tell me when you need it."

"Nita will be here about eleven. We're going riding."

"Then get on out there and find out who's too frisky today, and if that beast of yours is going to need a good workout before your ride," Mama Rey gave him a little push. "You want horses calm enough for you to talk while you're riding. Nita's a good rider, but not like your Joy. I don't know how much she's ridden in the last few years. You better talk to Bill and make sure you get a good mount for her."

Tim happily followed her advice, especially since he'd already intended to do precisely what she suggested.

His big white gelding, Kai, was half Percheron, half Quarter horse, broad and tall enough to carry Tim's weight. If he was going to be able to talk to Nita while they rode, she would need a mount who could keep up with Kai's long-legged stride. Bill decided they would longe both of his Fox Trotters and see which mare would be calm enough for Nita.

By the time Nita arrived, Kai and Sunny, the beautiful palomino mare, were saddled and ready to go, with the picnic basket already strapped behind Tim's saddle.

Mama Rey had made Bill take her into town, so there were no greetings to delay Tim and Nita's ride, and they were soon on their way.

Because his primary purpose was to have a fruitful conversation with Danita, Tim had chosen a trail that would allow them to ride side-by-side most of the time. For the first few minutes they talked about their horses, the weather, and the beauty of the land. Then Tim decided to get to more important matters, the family Danita had abandoned.

"When I asked about Joylynne's name at dinner the other week, Al said it was a combination of factors. He told me how you got the Lynne part, but where did 'joy' come from?" Tim asked.

Danita sighed. She now knew for sure that she was going to bare her soul to this unusual young man. How had he so quickly found the road to her hurt places?

He was waiting patiently for her answer, so she went ahead and dove in head first.

"I guess you know Al and I used to be church people," she said sadly.

Tim nodded. He did indeed know. It was one of the things that Joy ached over. He also knew that God was working in Nita's heart. She'd said "church people" not "Christians." Sometime in the last six years she'd discovered that there was a difference. She was already on the road to healing even if she didn't know it.

"I wasn't always," Nita continued. "I suppose Joy's also told you that I was an orphan."

Tim did know that, but he didn't like the way she phrased it.

"You still are, Nita," he said softly. "The loss of your parents didn't end just because you became a wife and mother."

"Of course you would say that," Nita was both surprised and awed. "I know about your family's ministry. It intrigues me."

"That doesn't surprise me," Tim smiled, but he wasn't going to let this conversation drift toward The Ohana Project. "Being an orphan weakened the foundation of your life. How does that fit in your story about Joy?"

Danita smiled. She liked the way he said that. She knew when he said "Joy" he meant her daughter, but he could very well mean "joy" as in a state of being.

Maybe the double entendre was deliberate.

"I grew up being shuffled between relatives. None of them went to the same church and many of them didn't go to church at all. I didn't have a family or faith foundation, not until I met Al. I guess that was one of the reasons I fell in love with him. He did have a solid foundation, in both family and faith.

"I wanted to have a big family, lots of kids," Nita sighed. "But I didn't get pregnant. Not in the first year or the second. Our third year of marriage was drawing to a close when I finally found out I was expecting.

"Since I'd started going to church with Al, I started reading the Bible too. Of course I paid particular attention to the stories about pregnancy and birth like when Leah and Rachel were competing for Jacob's favor. I knew that in the Bible children were often named based on the feelings of their parents. I told Al that if our baby was a girl, I wanted to name her 'Joy' because God had given me joy beyond measure."

"That's an awesome story," Tim smiled in wonder. "I see why Joy loves her name."

"But God took my joy back," Danita said sadly. She may as well get right to the heart of the matter. She suddenly knew without a doubt that Tim was determined to do everything within his power to heal the breech between her and her husband.

She also knew she wanted Tim to be successful. Since she was the initiator and primary upholder of the breech, he probably would be if she cooperated.

"You mean your Reybeka," Tim said sadly.

Danita wasn't surprised that he would know. Of course Joylynne had told him about her little sister.

"She was so full of life and laughter," Danita felt tears slipping down her cheeks. Seven years later it was still raw. "Why did God take her?"

Tim didn't try to answer her. Instead he prayed.

They rode for a few minutes with the question hanging between them.

"My niece had leukemia," Tim finally broke the silence.

"I didn't know that!" Danita was surprised.

"It's been in remission for three years," Tim nodded. "We're all praying fervently that she'll pass that crucial five year mark. It scares me to think that we might lose her."

Nita thought about that, and some of the other things she knew.

"Your family's seen more than your fair share of suffering," she acknowledged. Tim's niece might have survived cancer, but his father hadn't. His sister was a wounded war hero, and the hero of a foiled school shooting during which she'd again been shot. His brother had been abducted and seriously wounded.

"More than you know," Tim said sadly. "I don't know if I told Joy outright, but we did talk about it. You remember the airport hostage situation a few years back?"

Nita nodded slowly. "That was just before Joy started college."

"The woman is my cousin."

Nita stared at him in shock. She didn't need to ask which woman. He meant the one from Hawaii, the newlywed who was on her way home with her husband when they became the object of a ghastly real reality show.

"You watched too?" Danita hadn't been able to turn away, even though she was horrified to see that poor man suffer.

"I couldn't not watch," Tim shrugged sadly. "I hated to see them suffer, but I kind of felt like if I turned away, I was turning my back on them. If I stayed with Brian and Cait and prayed for them, then I was helping them get through it, even if they didn't know I was with them."

Danita nodded. She understood that a little.

"She's quite a bit older than you. Did you know her well?"

"She's eleven years older, but she was my first crush," Tim grinned and shrugged. "Actually I don't remember a time when I didn't adore Cait. We visited Hilo at least three or four times a year, and we always saw the Kurokawas. Cait played with us kids, but not like we were kids and she was just tolerating us. She really played with us, like we were her best friends. She went to college on Oahu, and we saw more of her for those four years. When Cait visited with our family, she always spent more time with us little kids than with our older family members.

"Brian moved to Hilo when I was just starting high school. I didn't know him really well because I only saw him at church when we were there, but I liked him a lot. He always treated me like a man. Watching them that day, I felt every blow that hit Brian."

Danita thought about what Tim said. She thought about why he'd told her. It wasn't just casual conversation. He was telling her something deeply personal.

"You've seen a lot of suffering," she finally said. "How did you keep your faith through it all?"

"I'm going to answer that," Tim said cautiously, "but first I need to ask you a question or two if you don't mind."

"Okay," Nita hesitantly agreed.

"It's just that the Bible makes it very clear that things of faith are almost impossible to understand if you're on the outside looking in," Tim quickly explained. "So I need to know, do you have a real, personal relationship with Jesus Christ? Your answer will guide my answer to your question."

"At one time I would've said, 'of course!' but now I'm not so sure," Nita said sadly. "I know I don't have what you and Joy have."

"What do you see in Joy and me that's different from what you have?" Tim asked thoughtfully.

"Peace, and confidence but not a cocky confidence, more like really knowing who you are, and … I don't really know how to describe it," Nita pondered the problem. "It's kind of like you're rich kids, but not the spoiled kind, or the tragic ones. You're the kind of rich kid who knows his parents are wealthy and powerful and they can protect him from anything, but doesn't let that be a license to do stupid things. He loves them too much to do anything that would put them to shame."

"Thank you, Nita," Tim said in amazement. "I often doubt if I really do live the Christian life well, but you've described it wonderfully."

"How can you doubt that you're a good Christian?" Nita was truly puzzled.

"I know how many mistakes I make," Tim said wryly, then sighed. "I can be very sinful. That's one of the reasons why I'm with you today instead of with Joy. We've already done more than we should. Enough that I'm relatively certain that I won't be able to stop if we get … too passionate again."

"Oh," Nita was astounded that he had confessed that to her, Joylynne's mother. On the other hand, "But don't you see that's exactly why you are a good Christian?"

"Because I almost had sex with your daughter before we're married?" Tim was so shocked that his gelding did a little hop-skip, unsure what his master wanted him to do.

"No! That makes you just an ordinary young man," Nita laughed. "What makes you a good Christian is that you saw your sin and corrected course!"

"You do have a point, ma'am," Tim laughed at himself. "I guess I am my father's son."

"What do you mean?"

"It's a bit of a family joke," Tim explained. "Dad has a bad habit of seeing the worst in himself while everyone else sees the good."

"He should stop that and so should you," Nita said firmly.

"Yes ma'am," Tim nodded. "We both should, but old habits are hard to break."

"That's the truth," Nita sighed.

"But we got sidetracked. We were talking about what you're missing."

"How did you get to know God like you do?" Nita asked. "I went to church for more than a decade and I didn't learn even a small fraction of what you know."

"Well, that's because being a Christian isn't about doing things and knowing things, no matter how good those things are," Tim said.

"So Christians don't need to go to church?" Nita was puzzled.

"That's not an easy question to answer," Tim shook his head. "We've got to start with 'go to church.' If you meant to ask 'Do Christians need to go to a building on Sunday morning, sit through a service, hear a message preached at them and then eat some donuts and drink some coffee while saying hi to the other church-goers before going home and repeating the whole thing over again next Sunday?' then the answer is an emphatic 'No!' That's not what the Bible means when it talks about church."

"Then what is biblical church?"

"Biblical church is living life together, not just studying the Bible together, though that's part of it. It's being in each other's lives, sharing each other's burdens, correcting each other, encouraging each other, and not just on Sundays. It's gathering together regularly to worship God in unity. And by worship, I mean all those things I just said. Worship isn't just what we do on Sunday morning. It's living life together, serving, and, well, doing all the things God says we should do."

"That doesn't describe the church Al and I were going to," Nita mused. "Does it describe your church?"

"Well, we're not perfect, but we do have many of those elements," Tim said thoughtfully. "The thing is, Nita, whether or not you're part of a church isn't so much about the organization you belong to as it is about the person you are."

"How do you figure that?"

"My brother Brandon just joined Living Stones about six months ago. Even before he got here, he intended to truly be part of the church. He wanted to grow in Christ, and he wanted the people of Living Stones to help him do that. He was honest about his questions and struggles. The more he shared, the more he encouraged others to do likewise. He grew and people began to learn to trust him and share with him. In trying to help them, he grew even more, which made people trust him more and turn to him for help more, which caused him to grow more. That's what church really is, a continuous cycle of trials and growth experienced in community. Brandon didn't try to, and he would deny that he's done it, but he has ramped up the unity, the biblical churchness if you will, of Living Stones, simply by choosing to live as if the members of the church were indeed his Christian brothers and sisters."

"An interesting perspective," Nita sighed heavily. "So you're saying that I missed what church really is because I didn't share my struggles and seek to grow through them."

"What church is, yes. That's probably as good a statement as any," Tim shrugged. "But you haven't asked the question that's foundational."

"What's that?"

"How does a person become a member of a biblical church?"

"I'm going to go out on a limb here and say that simply attending services doesn't make you a member of a biblical church," Danita said facetiously.

"That's a mighty strong limb you're on, Nita," Tim laughed.

"Then let me test a different limb since I'm already up the tree," Nita smiled wryly. "Becoming a member of a biblical church has something to do with knowing Jesus Christ."

"That's an exceptionally stout limb you're testing," Tim grinned broadly.

"This is going to sound like a really stupid question, but I've got to ask because I'm confused," Nita sighed. "If someone told Jesus that she was sorry for her sins and that she wanted him to be her savior, would that make her eligible to be a member of a biblical church?"

"Yes, Nita," Tim said firmly. "That would make her a true believer, a Christian."

Nita was thoughtful for a while.

"I was going to ask, 'Then why wouldn't she be different?' but I think I'm going to try another limb, if you don't mind."

"Not at all!"

"If a woman is a new Christian, but she keeps it to herself because she doesn't want anyone to know she hasn't been a Christian all her life, then she's choosing to not be a member of a biblical church."

"Another incredibly fine limb!"

"If she reads her Bible but never talks about what she's reading, never seeks to really understand it, she isn't being part of a biblical church."

"I think you've found a tree worth climbing around in, Nita," Tim smiled softly.

"That would be why, when storms came, her foundation wasn't strong enough and her faith ended up in ruins," Nita sighed sadly.

Tim didn't say anything. He was too busy praying.

God told him to wait and listen.

When the silence stretched on, Nita knew she had to fill it.

"When Reybeka died, I blamed myself," she sadly began her confession. "I hadn't wanted another child. Neither had Al. In fact, he got a vasectomy. But when he went in for his two week checkup, I went to see the doctor too, thinking I had a stomach bug. I was already six weeks pregnant.

"Al was happy, but I wasn't. I never even thought about an abortion, but the way I hated being pregnant, I may as well have. I was angry the whole time. Feeling the baby move didn't ease my anger. I didn't take care of myself, didn't eat right, did too many things I shouldn't, but still, when Reybeka was born, she was perfect.

"I didn't love her. I barely tolerated her, but she really was a perfect baby. She hardly ever cried, slept six hours straight every night by the time she was a month old, and she laughed a lot. She was never demanding. Everyone loved her. By the time she was six months old, she was the center of my world," Danita sobbed and her voice dropped to a whisper. "There were times I wished I'd waited and named her Joylynne."

Tim was deeply disturbed. It was almost as if Danita had wished his Joylynne hadn't been born. No wonder Nita felt guilty.

"When she was diagnosed with Ewing sarcoma bone cancer, I prayed so hard," Nita continued her story. "She died before her fifth birthday, and I knew it was my punishment. God was punishing me because I had hated my baby, then when I grew to love her, I shut out the rest of my family, loving her above all of them, wishing she was the only child I had. God had to take her because she became my idol."

They rode in silence for a while.

"You know that isn't what really happened, don't you?" Tim asked gently.

"I do now, but I didn't then," Nita confessed. "The poisoned love I had for my baby became hatred of myself. I wouldn't be comforted. I shut Al out. When I started breathing again almost a year later, I wanted to be loved, but I'd already pushed Al so far that he couldn't love me like I needed when I needed it."

Nita hung her head and closed her eyes, trusting her horse to keep walking beside Tim's. She struggled to go on, to continue her confession.

Tim prayed for wisdom to help Nita. He suddenly knew where this story was headed.

"You had an affair," he finally said it for her.

"Yes," Nita sobbed. "It was very brief, just a couple weeks, but when it was over I knew that I'd destroyed my marriage, my family. They were better off without me. I went back to Tucson where I'd spent most of my childhood, and that's where I've lived the last six years."

"You'd like to stay here in Norman now, wouldn't you?" Tim asked after another prayerful pause. "You'd like your family back."

"Yes," Nita agreed in a hoarse whisper. "I miss them so much. It's a kind of living death, being separated from them like this."

"Then why don't you go home?"

"It isn't my home anymore."

"Why do you say that?" Tim asked with a puzzled frown.

"Because I walked out on them."

"That doesn't undo it being your home."

"How do you figure that?" Nita said bitterly. "I betrayed my husband and my children."

"Why didn't you file for divorce?" Tim asked.

"Because I didn't want to," Nita was bewildered by his change of direction.

"But you don't want to be married anymore," Tim infused his voice with confusion.

"I do too! I love Al!" Nita exclaimed.

"I wonder why Al didn't divorce you?" Tim immediately wondered aloud.

Nita rode in stunned silence. That question, coming immediately after her declaration, suggested something she was afraid to hope for.

"Al couldn't possibly still love me," she finally whispered.

"I don't see why not," Tim shrugged.

"How could he after what I did?"

"I can't answer that, only your husband can, but I can tell you one thing for certain," Tim said firmly. "Al does indeed love you. I see it in the way he looks at you, how he wants to be close to you. He's very sad without you."

Again they rode in silence. Nita couldn't argue with Tim's declaration, but she couldn't agree with it either.

Tim finally broke the silence.

"The real thing that needs to concern you, Nita, isn't how to restore your marriage. It's what are you going to do to become the woman God wants you to be?"

"At one time I'd thought I was doing that, becoming the woman God wanted me to be. Now I realize that I was only becoming the woman I thought he wanted me to be," Nita answered cautiously. "I guess I don't know what I'm supposed to do to become the woman God truly wants me to be. I'm going to have to pass the question back to you, Mr. Wide-Receiver. What do I do to become the woman God wants me to be?"

"Don't worry Nita. It's not a Hail Mary pass!" Tim laughed.

"It feels like one," Nita sighed.

"That's only because you've lost track of where you are on the field," Tim grinned. "You're huddling up near that big, bold 20 and you think you're in your own territory, but you aren't."

"You mean I'm already past midfield?"

"You're in your opponent's territory," Tim nodded.

"What down is it?" Nita easily kept up the analogy.

"First and goal," Tim's grin was very broad.

"Then maybe I should hand off to the running back."

"A quarterback sneak might be a better option."

"The quarterback's a little battered after a hard game," Nita sighed. "The o-line better open up a hole for her."

"Call for the snap. There's gonna be a hole the size of a Mac truck, guaranz ballbaranz," Tim said confidently.

"How can you know for sure?" Nita challenged him.

"Have you been watching football since you were a kid?" once again Tim seemed to change the subject.

"Growing up, it was on TV a lot, but I didn't really watch it," Nita shrugged. "I was usually reading a book in the corner. It was pretty much the same after

I married Al, but then I didn't read very much because I had so many things to keep me busy."

"When did you start watching it?"

"Just over three years ago when my daughter became enamored with a football player," Nita happily confessed.

"You've sure learned a lot in just four seasons," Tim said in surprise. "You didn't watch just our televised games, did you?"

Nita shrugged. "I decided that if I was going to have a son-in-law who was playing football, then I wanted to really understand the game. I watched lots of football, college and pro. I even went to some high school games. And I read about it too. I even went to sports bars to watch games so I could learn more. It's amazing how much a woman can learn when she asks a guy to explain football. As long as she waits for a commercial break."

"In four years, you learned enough that you understand more than many people who've been sitting in front of the TV for years, watching and enjoying, but not really getting to understand the game," Tim laughed happily. "Oh, Nita, I think you do know what you need to do to become the woman God wants you to be!"

Nita stared at him in astonishment. "Maybe I do."

Tim pointed to a small, sunny hill just off the trail.

"There's our lunch table."

Chapter 5

*T*im and Nita directed their horses off the trail. After they took care of the animals, Tim retrieved the picnic hamper. Together they unpacked it.

Nita wasn't surprised to see Mama Rey's fried chicken just beneath the blue-checkered tablecloth, but amazement grew as they opened the other dishes.

She loved Mama Rey's pickled onions and cucumbers. German potato salad was one of her favorites even though it wasn't standard fare at picnics anymore. The fresh salad was all green – lettuce, spinach, broccoli, cucumber and green peppers, just the way Nita liked it, and with sweet onion dressing. Strawberries and clotted cream were obviously their dessert.

It was almost as if Mama Rey had packed the lunch for her, Danita, not for Tim, but that didn't make sense.

Suddenly Tim laughed.

"She thought of everything!"

Nita glanced over and saw that Tim was holding a Bible.

She gave him a puzzled frown.

"Mama Rey loves you very much," Tim answered her unspoken question. "She prepared this for *you*, not me. She obviously had great hope that by the time we got here, you would be ready to hear the word of God again."

"She can't love me," Nita reached for the Bible and hugged it to her chest.

"Why not?" Tim sat cross-legged on the edge of the tablecloth, facing Nita.

"I led her son astray."

"How do you figure?" Tim was now totally in the dark. He couldn't even hazard a guess at where this was going, and God didn't give him a revelation.

"I'm the one who wanted to find a different church after we got married," Nita sadly traced the letters on the cover of the Bible. "I'm the reason Al doesn't go to her church anymore."

"You guys going to a different church didn't bother Mama Rey!" Tim exclaimed in relief, happy to easily help Nita see her wrong thinking in this area. "It bugs her greatly that in the last few years Al hasn't been going to church at all, but she's always thrilled and delighted to see her children and grandchildren begin to seek a relationship with God without her direct influence."

Nita just frowned at him.

Tim thought for a moment.

"Let's say you and Al are still living together," he finally said. "Would you want Joy and I to move in with you after the wedding?"

"No," Nita looked at him as if he was crazy. "Maybe for a few weeks if you didn't have a place of your own yet, but y'all need to start your own lives, separate from ours."

"If we stayed with you and Al, how easy would it be for us to grow together as a couple?" Tim asked.

"Not very. Al and I would have to work very hard to stay out of your business and let you work things out on your own."

"Mama Rey thinks like you do," Tim said. "But she takes that same type thinking to the spiritual part of marriage too. If you and Al had simply gone to church because it was the one Mama Rey and Niguel went to, then you wouldn't have been building the spiritual dimension of your marriage on Christ. You would've been building it on Mama Rey and Niguel."

"We probably would've been better off if we had," Nita said bitterly.

"You don't know that, Nita," Tim gently scolded her. "Like Aslan told Edmund, it isn't yours to know what would've been. Let that go. We weren't talking about that anyway. We were talking about Mama Rey loving you."

Nita stared at the Bible. Warmth flooded her soul.

If Mama Rey could still love her, maybe Al did too.

Maybe God still did.

"So what did she hope we would do with this?" Nita offered the Bible to Tim.

He took it tenderly.

"Read it, of course."

"Why?"

"Why do you think?"

A smile twitched Nita's lips.

"Do you know you have an annoying tendency to ask questions instead of answering them?" she asked tartly.

"I am my father's son," Tim answered solemnly.

Nita was looking forward to meeting Tim's father and getting in on the family joke, but it wasn't important now. She ignored Tim's comment and answered his question.

"One of the big reasons that I failed in the first quarter of my walk with Jesus is that I didn't really read the Bible and study it," she said quite confidently. "Mama Rey was hoping I would give you the opportunity to begin to show me how you study the Bible."

"I see why Joy's such a smart person," Tim said happily.

"Trust me, she gets most of that from her father," Nita snorted.

"I think not, but let's not argue that," Tim looked at the feast Mama Rey had prepared. "How about we eat and read in shifts? I'll start reading while you start eating. When you have a question or a comment, just interrupt me, okay?"

"Okay," Nita picked up a plate. "What book are you going to read?"

"John," Tim opened the Bible. While Nita fixed her plate, he began to read. "'In the beginning was the Word, and the Word was with God, and the Word was God.'"

"Wait," Nita interrupted him. "That's how Genesis starts, 'In the beginning.'"

"Excellent observation!" Tim smiled proudly. "John did that very deliberately, quoted Genesis. See, his original audience knew that the words 'In the beginning' were the start of Genesis – 'In the beginning God created the heavens and the earth.' He wanted his readers to think, 'Genesis' because it would get them on the right track for what he was going to say next – 'the Word was with God, and the Word was God.'"

"John tells us that Jesus is God and he existed with God from the very beginning," Nita said thoughtfully.

"Exactly, but there's more," Tim looked back down at the Bible, though he didn't really need to, not for this part. He knew it by heart. "'In the beginning was the Word, and the Word was with God, and the Word was God. He was with God in the beginning. Through him all things were made; without him nothing was made that has been made. In him was life, and that life was the light of men. The light shines in the darkness, but the darkness has not understood it.'"

"So Jesus wasn't just 'in the beginning,'" Nita again interrupted Tim. "He's also our creator, so he was before the beginning, just like God the Father."

"That's right. That part about Jesus being the light that shines in the darkness, that underscores his presence and action in Genesis," Tim nodded, then recited from memory. "'In the beginning, God created the heavens and the earth. Now the earth was formless, and darkness hovered over the deep. And God said, "Let there be light." And there was light.'"

"I like that," Nita smiled in wonder. "I never saw that, though I've read both Genesis and John more than once."

"That's the difference between reading and studying," Tim said with a slight smile.

"So," Nita said then took a bite of food and chewed thoughtfully. "It almost sounds like Jesus is in creation."

"Yes and no," Tim thought carefully too. "If you're talking about something like God is in everything so everything is God, that's not right. But the Bible does show us that Jesus is very active in his creation. In Colossians, Paul tells us that Jesus not only created the universe, but he holds it all together. So, in that sense, yes, Jesus is in creation. We also know from many different passages that God is everywhere, in everything – if I go to the deeps he is there, that kind of stuff. That's what we call omniscience – God is present everywhere."

"I understand that," Nita nodded slowly. "I'd heard that kind of stuff before, but I never looked for it in the Bible myself. I think I want to see those other verses you talked about, but later. Go ahead and read more in John."

Tim turned back to the Bible.

It was very slow going. Nita had lots of comments and questions. They talked about the John who appeared in the book, that he wasn't the same John who wrote it, that Luke talked about his birth, that he was a prophet whom Isaiah had foretold.

They discussed how "The true light that gives light to every man was coming into the world. He was in the world, and though the world was made through him," once again showed that Jesus was God and creator. They talked about what it meant to be children of God, to be born because of the will of God.

As Tim read, Nita was intrigued by how much she understood. Some of it was because of their discussions today, like when John the Baptizer talked about who he was and who Jesus was, but some of it was coming from much farther back in her past. Apparently she'd been learning something even though she hadn't been approaching the Christian life the way she should have.

When Tim finished the first chapter of John, he passed the Bible to Nita and picked up his own plate. Nita didn't stop once as she read through the story of Jesus turning water into wine at the wedding in Cana. Tim knew that there were many subtle nuances in that story that the original readers knew but American readers missed. Exploring them gave deeper richness to the story but that was something Nita would be able to discover later. Now it was important to let her lead the way in the study, to discover how much she could learn simply by reading with the desire to know more.

Nita had questions about Jesus in the Temple, starting with why was he so angry? His reaction seemed extreme. Tim told her about how the Temple was set up. He explained that the sales business that was going on was not necessarily bad, and told her about the laws God had given that required buying and selling sacrifices for the Temple. If the sellers were not giving a fair price for their wares, that was wrong, but the greater problem was where they were doing it. They were doing their business in the outer court, the Court of the Gentiles.

That meant that they were hindering the Gentiles from approaching God. Tim showed Danita that in the similar story in the synoptic gospels, Mark quoted Jesus as saying, "'My house will be called a house of prayer for all nations'? But you have made it 'a den of robbers.'" That underscored that one of Jesus' primary problems was that they were robbing the Gentiles of their way to approach God.

By the time they were done with that discussion, Tim had finished his lunch, so Nita passed the Bible back to him. He started reading in the third chapter.

He noticed that Nita was listening carefully. She didn't stop him while Nicodemus and Jesus were talking about being born again, but shortly after, she frowned and held up a hand.

"Wait, that's John 3:16," she said, "but that can't be right. It doesn't make sense."

"Why not?"

"Well, why is it there? What's that verse about Moses all about? They have to connect because John used the same idea in both – everyone who believes will have eternal life."

"You're right, they do connect, and the verses right after verse sixteen do too," Tim nodded. "You've discovered one of the most important things to know when you're studying the Bible – what does the context of the passage itself tell us about any verse? Verses lose much when they're taken out of context."

"But isn't John 3:16 the gospel in a nutshell?" Nita asked. "'For God so loved the world that he gave his one and only Son, that whoever believes in him will not perish but have eternal life.'"

Once again Tim thought carefully before answering.

"Okay, John 3:16 is the gospel in a nutshell," he finally nodded. "So what? How does that give fullness to life?"

"I don't get your question," Nita shook her head.

"Wait a minute!" Tim jumped up and ran toward the woods.

Nita watched in bemusement as he disappeared, then a minute or so later reappeared, running back toward her.

"Here," he dropped down and held out his hand. "I knew there was a pecan tree back there. Here's your nutshell."

Nita held out her hand and Tim dropped a single pecan into it.

"What are you going to do with that?" Tim asked as she stared at the nut.

"By itself, not much," Nita grinned, getting Tim's point. "I'd be much better off going back to the tree and picking up some of the other nuts. Then I could make a pie."

"Or a pecan log," Tim moaned in pleasure at the thought. "That's how it is with the Bible. You can get something out of a verse by itself, but it's just a little taste, a tease, of what God is trying to tell you."

"So," Nita bounced the nut on her palm. "This nut needs another nut or two or forty, just like John 3:16 needs John 3:15 and 17, and a whole lot more."

"Exactly," Tim nodded.

Nita thought again. "So a good place to start would be finding out what Jesus was talking about when he mentioned Moses and the snake."

"That would be an excellent place to start!" Tim said happily, then shrugged ruefully. "But I think that's going to have to be a study for a later time. We should be heading back."

Nita was shocked to realize that the shadows were growing quite long. Their sunny little knoll would soon be in the deep shadows of the setting sun. She hadn't paid any attention to those shadows, not even when Tim had run into the woods moments before.

They quickly packed up the remnants of their lunch and were soon back on the trail.

Nita decided that Tim had given her enough to think about, so she didn't return to the deep subjects that had occupied most of their day. Instead, she talked about the wedding, told Tim some more stories about Joy and heard some of Tim's stories about his large pack of niephews – a convenient shorthand for "nieces and nephews" that Nita had learned from Joylynne who had learned it from Tim who told her he'd learned it from his mom..

Nita wasn't consciously thinking about what she needed to do next, but when she finally gave Tim a hug and a kiss and climbed in her car, she had a plan in mind.

Chapter 6

*A*l was in the kitchen when the doorbell rang. He was expecting Joy and Tim for dinner, but that wouldn't be them. Joy wouldn't ring the bell.

"Sean, get that," he bellowed at the son he knew was in the living room. "And dinner's almost ready!"

He heard the sound of feet from upstairs, heading down the stairs. It almost drowned out Sean's shocked cry.

"Mom!"

Al stared at the stove top, stunned. Danita was at his door?

He heard her voice, but he couldn't understand what she was saying. She definitely was at his door.

Most likely, she was still standing on the porch because Sean probably hadn't thought to step back and let her in.

Al quickly headed to rescue his wife.

When he pushed open the kitchen door, he saw his younger sons, frozen on the stairs, staring at the door. Sean was hanging on the front door. Dani was still on the outside of the screen door.

"Let your mother in!" Al called as he strode across the dining room.

All the boys leapt into action.

Sean quickly pushed the screen door open, while Heath and Chavis clattered on down the stairs.

"Where's Taggart?" Danita asked as she took in the room with a glance.

"He's got a date!" Chavis grinned.

"He's gone to the movies with some friends," Al smiled wryly. He would go with Taggart's assertion that it wasn't a date.

"Friends that just happen to include a girl he's got the hots for," Sean rolled his eyes, then kissed his mother. "Hi Mom. Did you come for dinner?"

Danita was happy to also receive hugs and kisses from her other sons.

"I might have," she smiled slightly. "But I think you boys should go out to dinner, and maybe catch a movie. How much cash do you have, Al? I've only got a twenty and a couple ones."

She lifted her hand which indeed held some bills.

Al was dumbfounded. He could only stare at Dani. His wife wanted time alone with him? Was this good or bad? Was she finally going to ask for a divorce?

Maybe not. She was looking at him in a way that suggested that she might still love him.

Suddenly it dawned on him that Heath was trying to get his wallet out of his back pocket.

"Get your hands off that, boy," he growled as he slapped his son's hand away then fished out his wallet himself.

He also had some ones and a twenty, along with a ten and a fifty.

He was feeling generous. He pulled out the fifty.

"That should cover dinner and a movie," he handed the bill to Sean.

When Dani's face lit up like the Christmas tree in the corner, he knew it was going to be fifty well spent.

"Take my car," Dani held up her keys. "But make sure you put gas in it."

"Aw, Mom," Sean whined though he willingly took the keys.

Al pulled the twenty out of his wallet and mutely handed it to his son. Maybe they would add a joyride to their itinerary. Nita's little Acura was sporty enough to make them think about it.

"I'm drivin'," Heath snatched the keys from his brother.

"No you're not," Sean grabbed them back.

Al reached in and took the keys from both of them before their disagreement could degenerate into a knock-down-drag-out.

"Sean will drive your mother's car," he said firmly, passing the keys to his seventeen year old son.

"Aw, Dad," Heath whined. He'd just passed his road test two weeks before and was eager to have the independence that came with being a licensed driver.

"You could spend the evening in your room," Al arched his eyebrows.

"Fine," Heath grumbled but stomped toward the coat tree by the front door.

Dani had put that coat tree there almost twenty years ago. Now that the boys were so big it was very impractical because they didn't properly hang their coats and jackets on the hooks. Sometimes it tipped over with too much weight on one side from the way they threw their coats at it. Al hadn't had the heart to get rid of it, just like the rest of Dani's touches in his house.

The boys all brushed a kiss on their mother's cheek before they left. Just before the door closed, Sean stuck his head back in.

"I hope you guys do something I wouldn't do!"

The door clicked shut behind him. Al and Dani were alone for the first time in six years.

Al stared at his wife, unsure of what to say or do.

Dani was staring at the floor, biting her lip. Now that they were alone, she looked unsure too.

"Why are you here?" Al tucked his hands in his pockets, just to have something to do, something comfortable and familiar.

"I owe you an explanation," Dani said softly.

Al frowned slightly. Did he need an explanation?

"No you don't, Dani," he gave her a half smile. "All I need is for you to come home."

"But I walked out on you without a word," she stared at him with troubled eyes.

"I'm well aware of that," Al said wryly. "And I'm not going to deny that I haven't wondered why. But that's not what my feeble attempts to pray were about."

Dani tilted her head to the side and stared at him. Al took a few steps toward her.

"I didn't ask God 'why.' I asked him to bring you home."

Dani's eyes were wide, glittering with tears.

Al stepped close enough to catch the first tear as it fell.

"When you come home, really come home, I'll probably ask you why someday," Al shrugged one shoulder and gave her another crooked grin. "But first I just want you home."

"But why?" Nita asked.

"Because I love you and I miss you."

"How could you love me after what I did, walking out like that?"

"I'm not much of a man of God," Al confessed sadly, "but I meant what I said on our wedding day when I promised you that I would love you in God's strength. God hasn't told me to quit loving you, so I haven't even tried."

"Oh!" Dani said in surprise.

"Besides," Al shrugged. "I see you in the children every day. I love them dearly, so they helped me keep my love for you alive."

"I want to come home," Dani said hopefully. Quickly, before the smile finished blooming on Al's face. "But I have to tell you something first."

"You had an affair," Al didn't stop smiling though his eyes were a little sad.

"You know?" Dani gasped. How could he know and still want her to come home?

"Anissa Lunsford told me, not long after you left," Al shrugged. "She divorced Ken."

"You know but you still want me to come home?"

Al nodded firmly.

"I want to come home and be your wife again, fully and completely," Danita said very clearly. She wanted to make sure there was no misunderstanding that maybe she was going to just be his housekeeper and mother to his sons.

47

"Exactly what I want," Al kissed her tenderly.

Dani laid her head on his chest, wrapped her arms around his waist and cried. Al held her and wept too.

She finally lifted her tear-stained face.

"When?"

"When?" Al parroted with a frown.

"When can I move back in?" she asked patiently.

"My dearest wife you are here. You are staying. When? Right now."

"But shouldn't we get married again or something?"

"Renewing our vows would probably be a good idea," Al kissed her again. "But we are still married. I am not waiting until then to be your husband again."

"I don't have my clothes," Dani said. "They're still over at your mom's house."

"And the downside is …?" Al arched his eyebrows.

Dani giggled. "You have a point."

Al picked her up and swung her around, kissing her soundly.

"Mom? Dad?" Joy gasped from the door.

Al set Dani down and grimaced. "I totally forgot that I invited Joy and Tim to dinner."

"We'll leave," Tim laughed happily.

"You don't need to," Dani turned to her daughter and future son-in-law, but she didn't step out of her husband's embrace.

"Does this mean what I hope it means?" Joy's eyes were glowing with delight.

"If you hope it means that your mother has come home to me, yes it does," Al answered his daughter, but his eyes were on his wife.

"I hope it doesn't mean that we're uninvited to dinner," Tim sighed plaintively. "It smells like chili, and I'm hungry."

"You promise to leave as soon as dinner's over?" Al asked almost as plaintively.

"Alfred!" Dani swatted at her husband.

"I didn't send the boys off with a wad of money just to have to share you," Al complained.

"Actually, sir," Tim sighed. "I was counting on you to help me out tonight. We aren't married yet, and your daughter can't keep her hands off me."

"Timothy!" Joy swatted at her fiancé.

Al looked at his young friend and saw the torment in his eyes. Tim did indeed need very serious chaperoning if he and Joy were going to stay sexually pure before the wedding.

"What do you say, dear?" Al asked Dani.

"I guess they won't object if we get mushy," Dani acquiesced.

"That's it? You're back together again?" Joy asked, half doubtful, half joyful.

"Well, your mother did suggest that we renew our vows," Al shrugged slightly. "But we are back together, fully and completely."

"Just before our wedding," Tim said with a broad grin.

"What?" Al frowned. Dani looked as puzzled.

"Perfect!" Joy gasped in delight and threw her arms around her fiancé, giving him a very deep kiss.

"Ahem!" Al cleared his throat loudly. That poor boy certainly did need help.

Joy dropped her arms and stepped away from Tim, her face flaming.

"Renew your vows before our wedding," Tim said a trifle hoarsely.

"That is perfect!" Dani glowed as she smiled up at her husband.

"Yes, it is," Al thought maybe his voice was almost as hoarse as Tim's. He fixed his daughter with a stern stair. "Young lady, you better lighten up on that poor man. You don't want your goal line stance to end in just a field goal."

"I'm sorry, Tim," Joy hung her head.

"I forgive you, sweetheart," Tim kissed her forehead then quickly turned to Al. "Can I help you get dinner on the table?"

"You certainly may," Al reluctantly dropped his arms from around his wife and turned toward the kitchen.

"Did you make real rice?" Tim asked hopefully.

"Yes, and I even have chopped onion and grated cheese," Al said cheerfully.

"You're the best," Tim sighed happily. "I think I'll marry your daughter and take her off your hands."

"You're the best too!" Al laughed as the kitchen door swung shut behind the men.

"I'm so happy, Mom," Joy quickly crossed the room and hugged her mom.

"So am I, darlin'," Danita smiled joyfully.

"You guys are going to get counseling, aren't you?" Joy stepped back with a worried frown.

"Of course!" Danita said confidently. They hadn't talked about it, but she knew that Al was also aware that to successfully re-blend their lives they would need serious help. "In fact, we'll ask your Pastor Charles to help us find a counselor."

"I'm sure he'll know someone."

"Will you mind if we start going to your church?" Danita asked hesitantly.

"Mind? I'll love it!" Joy hugged her mother again.

Danita wanted to just leave it like that, but something was tugging at her heart. She took Joy by the hand and led her over to the couch.

"I need to confess something to you, Joy," she said sadly.

"Whatever it is, I'm sure it doesn't matter, Mom," Joy shook her head.

"It matters to me," Danita swallowed hard and pushed down tears. "When your sister died, I was so upset. I missed her so much."

"So did I, Mom," Joy took her mother's hands. "We all did."

"But I wished it had been you, not her," Danita drew a deep, shuddering breath. "I wished I had never had you so I could've named her Joy."

"I suspected something like that," Joy said sadly.

Danita looked up in surprise.

"I wasn't a baby anymore, Mom," Joy gently touched her mother's cheek. "I was already a young woman. I knew you withdrew from me, but that was okay with me. I wished it had been me too."

"Do you forgive me?" Danita asked, tears shimmering in her eyes.

"Of course!" Joy wept with her mother.

Tim's bellow interrupted their tearful moment.

"Get in here, or we're eating without you!"

"That young man's going to keep you on your toes, Joy," Danita laughed as they popped off the couch and headed for the kitchen.

"I suspect you're right, Mom," Joy laughed. "But Dad will keep you on your toes too!"

They had a wonderful evening, filled with laughter and romance.

They called it an evening about two hours later, well before the Quintanilla boys were expected to return home. Tim left by himself. Al and Danita took Joy home, where Danita packed her bags, kissed her daughter and went home to sleep with her husband for the first time in six years.

Chapter 7

Christmas that year was a very joyous one for the Quintanilla family. The downside for Tim was that he only had a small part of his family with him, but at least they were joined by Uncle Andy, Aunty Rica and Lorna, Stormy's parents and sister.

Tim and Brandon were both glad when the Shepherd-Wolfe ohana began their invasion of Norman the day after Christmas. One of the best parts for Tim was that he no longer had to worry about going too far with Joy before the wedding. With all his family around, he and Joy didn't get more than a minute of alone time the entire week before the wedding.

Tim was particularly pleased to see one couple. Greg's wife Beth was again pregnant with twins. She was due in early March, so it had been iffy whether her doctor would want her to travel that far. The fact that his brother and wife might not be able to attend his wedding had given Tim pause when they'd set the date for the first Saturday in January, but Greg himself had convinced him that their reasons for that date were sound. Since Tim had a very reasonable expectation that he would be drafted to a pro football team in April, which would mean reporting to a very rigorous training camp shortly after he graduated from college, it made sense to have a few months of marriage before that.

Fortunately, Beth's doctor had given her the go-ahead to make the trip to Oklahoma, albeit rather reluctantly. The deciding factor had been that she would be able to fly on a private plane.

Other than his immediate family, Tim didn't know who would be coming to Norman for the wedding. After he'd given Joy the list of invitees that his mother had helped him write, he hadn't thought to ask about who had sent an RSVP. He was excited to see people arriving whom he hadn't consciously expected to see, like Uncle Pena, Aunty Connie, Uncle Kenji and Aunty Hannah, with all his cousins. He was surprised and thrilled when the entire Kurokawa ohana from Hilo arrived, even Cait's husband and their two month old son, Wayland. It was the first time Brian Trask had been in a commercial airport in three and a half years. The whole Kalaau clan also came, including the five siblings whom

Pika and Sarah had adopted after Tim had left Hawaii so he didn't really know them. Ted and Shelly and their crew Tim had unconsciously expected, just like Raul, Lei and baby Buckley.

Derek O'Phelan arrived on New Year's Eve. He and Kendra were obviously together. Tim was excited to see that romance blooming so beautifully. He had been one of the first to see the possibilities there, and to encourage its growth.

After his wonderful success at getting Al and Nita together too, Tim was ready to work on getting someone else into a happy romance. Regrettably, Derek's sister Cari had kindly declined the invitation to his wedding, though she'd sent a very generous wedding gift. That meant Tim couldn't work on getting Brandon engaged. He turned his attention to his little brother Robert, the only one of Joshua and Gloria's children who was not attached to someone.

Unfortunately, though Tim tried hard, he just could not see Robert with Sally, Reylene or any of the other girls who went to Living Stones Ohana Fellowship. He wondered if maybe God had already sent a girl for Robert, but his little brother wasn't confessing. Whoever she was, Tim knew she had to be very special. Robert was a great friend, and Tim knew he deserved the best.

Tim had another friend whom he hoped he could help out with a different family issue, but he needed the help of one of his brothers-in-law. It was a little difficult to get time alone with anyone, but on New Year's Day, he did finally manage to corner Rachel's husband Abe who was a police investigator in St. Louis.

"Do you know that Bill Vogt has a son?" he asked without preamble. He knew they wouldn't have much time before someone intruded.

"No, I didn't," Abe glanced toward the older man.

"He disappeared almost twenty years ago. Bill doesn't even know if he's alive. He does know that Rick got into drugs and has had more than one brush with the law. He served three years for attempted robbery."

"You want me to see if I can find him," Abe said confidently.

"Hey, you're smart! You should be a detective," Tim grinned broadly.

"You think," Abe said wryly.

That was the extent of the conversation because they were invaded by Lori Bryant and Luke's son Jeremy who needed Uncle Tim for a game.

As Tim was willingly pulled away, Abe watched his brother-in-law. He wondered if Tim had any idea how much he was like Greg. He wasn't as goofy or as boldly exuberant, but Tim shared Greg's gift of discernment and love of love, not just romantic love but all love that reflected God's love for his children.

THE NEXT EVENING was the rehearsal for the wedding. With so many of Tim's relatives there, he wanted them all to come to the rehearsal dinner even though they weren't all in the wedding. The multipurpose room at Living Stones

Fellowship wasn't big enough for everyone, so they decided to hold the dinner out on the Vogt farm where the wedding reception would be. Three years ago Bill had turned his old barn into an event center. After dinner, the men would stay in the barn, hold Tim's bachelor party there and then get the furnishings set up for the reception. The women would invade in the morning and decorate.

The rehearsal at the church went smoothly, but out at the barn things quickly turned rowdy, even before dinner could be served.

Tim started the trouble, but he hadn't intended to. He was actually trying to keep things from getting out of hand.

He'd talked about his family a lot over the years, so Joy knew about their infamous 'clash of the titans.' He'd also told her about previous rehearsal dinners and the Shepherd's version of bachelor/bachelorette parties. Joy liked the idea of the parties, and she was also looking forward to seeing a clash, but not the night before her wedding. So, they had come up with a plan to hopefully ward off trouble.

Tim faced the crowd gathered in the barn and tried to implement that plan.

"I have a beautiful and wise fiancée," he started out well. "When she learned about how the evening before a wedding usually goes in my family, she expressed some very serious concerns. I assured her that I would not be hurt if we ended up having a clash of the titans. Not," he raised his voice and a cautionary hand to forestall growls that were rumbling amidst his brothers, "not because I am better than anyone else, but because a few minor bumps and bruises is all anyone gets in our clashes. We wrestle seriously but not viciously."

That took the wind out of his brothers' sails. They nodded in agreement.

"Then Joy pointed out that the weather would be more than a little cold. I don't know if my brothers have had a clash when it was below freezing, but I'm certain that I haven't. Therefore I have no idea how much it will affect the fun and relative safety of our battles. If this evening did perchance descend into a rumble, someone might get hurt.

"So Joy and I decided that we wouldn't wait for Greg to come up with an excuse to have a clash of the titans." Greg frowned deeply, but Tim smoothly continued. "Instead, for your pre-dinner 'entertainment,' we're going to have a fair referee for one-on-one matches. They will end with a pin or after three minutes, whichever is first. Everyone will wrestle only once, then they'll be done."

"I wouldn't bet on that," Steve grumbled.

"Each match will be initiated by a challenger," Tim adeptly ignored his brother-in-law. "If you're between twenty and forty, you cannot challenge someone smaller than you. Anyone under twenty who wants to wrestle cannot challenge someone smaller or younger than you. Of course, any challengee has the right to decline the challenge, if he chooses to."

"Why forty?" Greg asked with a frown.

"What?" Tim frowned back.

"You said we can't challenge anyone smaller than us if we're between twenty and forty," Greg said patiently. "Why forty? What if I want to challenge someone older, like Pika?"

"We wanted to be fair to the old guys," Tim shrugged. "If they want –"

"Try wait," Brian Trask slowly rose and frowned at Tim, his arms crossed over his chest. "Are you calling me *old*?"

Tim stared solemnly at him. When Joy had suggested the over forty part, it hadn't occurred to him that some of his cousins were over forty. They sure didn't act that old.

"Well, no," he tried to explain. "It's just that we didn't think it was fair to make you go one-on-one against a young guy."

"So you *are* calling us old," Mark Kurokawa rose too, glaring at Tim.

Suddenly Tim realized that all his Hilo cousins were glaring at him. Except for Cait, they were all over forty, even Will Garrison, Brian's best friend who'd been adopted by Davin and Monique two years ago. Cait was the youngest of the Kurokawas' children. Doug was the oldest at 51, his wife was Megan, and his children, Mariko, Keith and Hailey, were all now teenagers; Jack was the next brother, just a year younger than Doug, his wife was Kelsie, and his children, Derryl and Morgan were also teenagers; Ed's children were younger, Jesse was the only teenager, but Kira and Gabe were eleven and ten, Ed's wife Sherry was a year younger than his almost 48. Eleanor was the oldest daughter, she and her husband Ryan had two children, Drake was ten and Julie was eight; Mark was next, all of his and Lisa's children were under ten, Ezekiel was just starting kindergarten, Preston was eight and Hazel was a year older. Cait was seven years younger than Mark who was the same age as her husband Brian, who had turned 42 in November. Phil, Davin's son from an affair that had ended even before Phil was born, was a year younger than Brian and Will. Phil's mother had lied to both Davin and Phil about who his father was. Four years earlier when they had discovered the truth, during a series of events that caused quite a bit of trouble for the family, Luke had helped Davin change his name, and Monique had formally adopted him.

"Not old," Tim said weakly, "but older. It wouldn't be fair."

"Would two-on-one make it fair?" Brian asked with deceptive friendliness.

Tim glanced around the room. No one seemed bothered by that idea, so he shrugged.

"Sure, I guess, but it's kind of hard for one guy to pin two."

"How about if you young guys get one of us old guys flat on our back, we're out and our partner is on his own?" Will suggested.

"Sounds fair," Al approved of the idea.

"Sure," Tim shrugged again.

"Okay then," Brian smiled wolfishly. "If the Colonel's game, we'll challenge you."

"Me?" Tim asked in shock. He didn't like the idea. He knew that he was likely to get hurt because he wouldn't want to hurt either Brian or his dad. Not only did he deeply respect Brian, but he would also worry about Brian's bum leg. And Dad really was getting old.

But he also had to figure that they were probably going to work very well together. In the three and a half years since Brian's ordeal, he'd been invited to speak at a couple dozen events, only a few on the Big Island. Since he hadn't set foot in a commercial airport until earlier this week, Tim's dad had transported him on his private jet, which meant that the Colonel had spent a lot of time with the Major. Rumor even had it that Brian was very close to officially becoming Tim's big brother. Like he needed another one!

"Afraid, young pup?" Joshua growled as the silence stretched on.

"No," Tim lied boldly.

"Where are we doing this?" Brian grinned.

"Over here," Bill called.

Everyone turned to where Bill was standing next to a good-sized area that was covered with large mats. The few who had noticed them hadn't thought they would be used tonight. The barn often became a gym.

"Don't tell me he's your fair referee!" Greg exclaimed in shock.

"You think I won't be fair," Bill glared at Greg.

"I think you should be wrestling!" Greg quickly retorted.

He had a point. Bill was seventy, but he was nearly as big as Greg, and strong as an ox.

"I agree," Al spoke up. "If you want, I'll challenge Greg with you."

"Daddy!" Joy gasped in shock.

Tim was shocked too, but for a different reason. Joy was obviously worried about her father getting into it with Greg, but Tim was worried about his brother. Al was a pretty big man too, almost as tall as Greg though not nearly as broad. If he and Bill double-teamed Greg, Tim's brother could get hurt.

"I'm game!" Greg grinned cheerfully.

Tim glanced at Beth but she just sighed sadly and shrugged. Apparently she'd given up trying to keep her husband out of fights.

"We'll have to find another referee," Bill grinned.

"I'll do it!" Grandpa Shepherd was moving toward the wrestling mats.

"Fine," Brian said as he stepped onto the mats with Joshua. "We get Tim first."

"Take off your shoes, belts and watches," Grandpa Connor instructed the wrestlers. "And I guess you should empty your pockets too."

That made a lot of sense. All those things were hazards that could cause minor injuries to be intensified.

The three men stepped to the side, well away from the mats and divested themselves of all their extraneous items.

When they returned to the mats, Connor sidled up to Joshua.

"Hey, Son, you want me to do a McClintock on him?" Connor whispered loudly and tipped his head toward Tim.

"Grandpa!" Tim howled. McClintock was one of Grandpa's favorite movies so Tim had watched it many times, practically every time they visited Bloomington-Normal. He knew that Connor was referring to the scene where McClintock used Fauntleroy to illustrate what wasn't allowed before Fauntleroy fought Devlin Warren.

"So much for a fair referee," Heather giggled.

"No, Dad," Joshua said after some serious thought. "I think Brian and I can handle this."

Tim privately thought they could too. In fact, maybe Grandpa should do the McClintock on them!

Connor stepped off the mats. Joshua circled to Tim's right, Brian to his left.

Tim crouched slightly and shifted his eyes between his opponents. Should he rush them, or let them come to him?

Chapter 8

*F*acing his opponents, Tim realized that Joy's idea hadn't been very good. In a clash of the titans, it was every man for himself. You did the best you could to stay on your feet, but if you went down, you simply rolled with it and got up as quickly as you could. One- or two-on-one was very different. He remembered watching the matches between his brothers on Gavyn Anderson's farm a few years ago. Brandon had been able to avoid Dave's clutches and they'd had to call it a draw, while Dave was taken down by Ted and Greg together even though they had both been handicapped by recent injuries.

For the first time it dawned on Tim that one of the reasons Dave had lost to his best friend and his brother was that he was afraid of hurting them.

As he shifted his position, trying to keep Dad and Brian both in his line of sight, Tim was one hundred percent certain that he was going down. He just hoped that he would make it look good!

Tim feinted to his left, at Brian, but quickly flipped to his right to meet his dad's rush. They collided with enough force to make Joshua grunt.

Wrapping his dad up in a fierce hug, Tim rolled with Joshua cradled to his chest. He angled his roll away from Brian's oncoming attack. Turning as he came up, Tim used his momentum to throw Joshua at Brian.

As if they'd teamed up many times before, Brian ducked and Joshua rolled over him instead of hitting him. He came up slightly behind Brian.

Tim rushed them, hoping to get them both in his arms at the same time.

Instead he went flying through the air when his opponents much too easily clotheslined him! He landed flat on his back. Joshua and Brian both plopped down on his chest.

"That was too easy," Brian sighed sadly. "It was hardly worth taking off my boots."

"You're right. I didn't even break a sweat. Maybe we should let the boy try again," Joshua was mournful too.

"Yes," Tim grunted as loudly as he could with three hundred plus pounds on his chest. He hadn't made it look good at all.

"No!" Joy put her foot down. Literally.

Tim frowned mutinously as Brian and Joshua helped him to his feet. Joy stomped her foot again.

"You will not wrestle again tonight," Joy demanded.

Tim pouted, but secretly he was glad she insisted. A second go-round wouldn't end any better.

"Then I guess we're up!" Greg grinned cheerfully as he stood. He'd already rid himself of his shoes and belt. He dropped a set of car keys on the table beside Beth.

Bill and Al were already on the mats when Greg turned.

Just like the last match, the three men circled warily, watching each other. Suddenly, Al and Bill rushed Greg from opposite sides.

Greg turned to meet Al, intending to wrap him in a great bear hug.

Unfortunately, Bill was either faster or closer than Al. He bowled into Greg before Greg got his hands on Al who dodged at the last moment. Greg went down, but he didn't hit the mat. He tucked and rolled and came up, rushing back at the other two men.

Bill ducked as Al jumped over Greg.

Greg wasn't going to be fooled like his brother had been. He dropped on top of Bill, crushing him face down in the mat.

"Bill's out!" Beth cried gleefully.

"No he's not!" Mama Rey hotly denied. "He's gotta be flat on his back to be out!"

"That's what they agreed to," Connor backed Mama Rey. "Bill's still in."

As Bill rolled to his feet, he wasn't sure he appreciated his wife's so-called defense. The young ox was beyond heavy! He wanted to take an inventory of his old bones and make sure nothing was broken, but he wouldn't give Greg the satisfaction. Though he would pay for it in the morning, he stayed in the match.

They took it almost the full three minutes, but Bill and Al finally timed their hits perfectly. Al went low taking out Greg's legs from the front at the exact moment that Bill hit Greg high enough from the back to knock him face down on the mat. Bill was able to stop his forward momentum and plant his backside firmly on Greg's shoulders before the younger man could rise.

"That one's gonna be hard to follow," Luke shook his head in wonder.

"But I'm ready to try," Will Garrison looked at his adopted oldest brother. "Doug, you wanna take on Luke?"

"With you, brother? Of course!" Doug Kurokawa popped up from his seat with a grin. He was eleven years older than Luke, so when they were younger, he'd picked on his cousin, probably more than he should have, but not for as long as he would have liked to. By the time Luke moved from Africa to stay in Hawaii, not just visit, he was already eleven. Within a couple years he was big enough to give Doug trouble right back. Now Luke was a full foot taller than Doug, but with Will's help, they could probably knock him down to size.

While they were preparing for their match, other matches began to pair up.

"Phil, you game to take on Dave?" Mark asked his half-brother.

"Are you serious?" Phil asked with wide eyes.

"Pretty sure," Mark shrugged with a grin.

"If Ryan will, sure," Phil sighed.

"Three-on-one?" Dave asked in surprise.

"You scared?" Davin laughed.

"No!" Dave sounded like a little boy who couldn't refuse a dare.

"You should be," Brian laughed.

"Did anyone ever mention to the so-called titans that Ryan was captain of his wrestling team in high school?" Ed asked innocently.

"They probably don't know that he went to Nationals both his junior and senior years of college," Ellie said with a proud grin for her husband.

"I think that's cheating," Dave glared at Phil.

"You can always say no," Dei said with a long-suffering sigh.

"Like that's gonna happen," Ted Bryant rolled his eyes and sighed. "Too bad we only get to wrestle once. I'd sure like to see what Brian's got."

"You mean you and me, one-on-one?" When Ted nodded, Brian grinned. "They're Tim's rules so let's ignore them. You're on!"

Luke, Doug and Will were on the mats, but since the challenges were still flowing, they were watching the tables instead of each other. Luke was perfectly willing to wait for what he suspected was going to be a thrashing not unlike Tim's. Though Doug was almost a foot shorter than Luke, Will was right at six feet, and broad too. Proportionately, he was broader than Luke who had been wrestling with Greg too long to trust that his superior height would mean anything in this match.

Ed and Jack debated whether they should take on Steve or Pete.

"Me and my brothers want Pete," Joylynne's brother Taggart spoke up.

"We do?" Chavis squeaked. He was the youngest of the Quintanillas; he would be fifteen exactly a week after the wedding.

"Yeah, we do" Sean said doubtfully. Even though he was almost eighteen, he knew he wasn't big enough or strong enough to take on any of the guys in Tim's family. "And I think someone better help them two with Steve."

Ed and Jack both shrugged, but they didn't argue.

"I will," Abe said boldly.

"No you won't!" Rachel scolded. "That's not fair to Steve."

"To me!" Steve rose, pointing at his own chest with his eyebrow arched.

"You can take 'em, Goliath," Heather assured her husband.

"Sounds to me like the women wanna wrestle," Pika said wryly.

"Too bad Mandy's pregnant," Will sighed. "I'd love to see her take on Dei."

"The women wrestling?" Jack grinned. "Sounds like fun. I bet Kelsie could easily take Nalani."

"These women wresting?" Tim waved his hand around the room, then rolled his eyes. "Sounds boring to me."

He should have checked to see where his sisters were.

"Oh really?" Heather reached across the table and smacked him upside the back of his head.

"Shall we, Rachel?" Jenni was a few feet away and stalking quickly toward Tim.

"I didn't mean –"

Tim turned to flee, but Rachel was blocking his way.

He scrambled over the table on the other side of the aisle, away from Heather, only to find his escape blocked by Stormy.

He went up on the next table and started running.

Suddenly Gloria was on the table in front of him.

"Mom!" Tim wailed, screeching to a halt.

There was nowhere to go. He was surrounded.

He did the only thing that made sense.

"Joy! Help!"

"Oh, please, do not hurt my fiancé," Joy suggested indifferently as she rolled her eyes.

"Joy!" Tim howled at her betrayal.

His mom pushed him off the table, into the waiting hands of his sisters and sisters-in-law.

At least they caught him instead of letting him drop to the ground. Unfortunately, they were carrying him to the mats.

"Joy! Help!" Tim struggled, but with the sheer number of women surrounding him, it was a futile effort.

Joy didn't help. She sighed sadly and turned away. "Can we have dinner before I change my mind about tomorrow? I'm not sure I know what I'm getting into."

"You know exactly what you're getting into," Mama Rey snorted indelicately. "It's that poor boy who's been bamfloozled these past four years."

Without preamble Charles raised his face and his voice to the heavens, "Jesus, please bless this food and keep a modicum of civility in this rowdy crowd until after I say 'man and wife' tomorrow."

"Amen!" a few dozen voices said in hearty agreement.

"We'll be right there," Heather called from the mats that Luke, Will and Doug had willingly vacated.

"He has to take his shoes off," Gloria grinned wickedly.

"No!" Tim howled desperately, but it was pointless. He was soon barefoot, and that was how Joy discovered that his feet were extremely ticklish!

Tim ended up spending a lot of time on the mats that evening. He lost more matches than he won, but that was largely because he was usually outnumbered. His friends Matt, Brad and Russell took him on and went the full three minutes for a draw. Next Taggart and Sean, Joy's brothers teamed up with his cousin Nick and took him down much too easily, in large part because Nick was half Hawaiian and very broad, perfectly built to be a defensive lineman. Even though he wasn't as tall as Tim, he probably could have taken his cousin down by himself, but since he was still in high school he got to wrestle with partners.

Tim's next match was a draw with Robert. After a break for some of the other matches Tim took Will and Ryan almost to the three minute bell before they pinned him, then Carl and Abe wrestled him to a draw, but he finally won when Raul Guerrero decided to risk a one-on-one with him. Probably because Tim was getting very tired, the smaller but well-built street fighter lasted almost the entire three minutes.

After another break for other matches, Tim was back on the mats with Ted and Brian who had wrestled to a draw in their own match. They took down Tim in under thirty seconds.

When Brian and Ted helped Tim to his feet, he discovered a row of grinning teenagers on the edge of the mat. Joy's brothers Heath and Chavis, stood by Tim's cousin Alex, his nephews Linc, Matt, Dave's foster son Gil, Phil Jeremiah who had just turned thirteen on New Year's Day, were shoulder to shoulder with Ted and Shelly's son Gavyn, Danny's half-brother Jared, and the next generation of Kurokawa cousins, Derryl, Keith and Mariko. A wickedly grinning Kara was right next to her Hilo cousin, with Suzie and Brianna on her other side.

Tim stared solemnly at the eleven boys and four girls, not sure if he should laugh, cry or just fall on the mat in surrender.

"You sure you've got enough punks on your team?" Tim foolishly taunted his challengers.

"We'll add some if you think you're man enough, Uncle Tim," Matt taunted back in true Shepherd fashion.

Rather than answer and get himself into deeper trouble, Tim just charged the center of the line.

He should have thought about the fact that Ted's son was one of the two boys in the center. The rascal disappeared just before Tim's arms closed around him and Phil. Unfortunately, Phil took advantage of the extra space and dropped his head and shoulders just in time to plant them in Tim's gut.

This is going to be worse than with Dad and Brian! Tim realized as he instinctively bent over from the force of Phil's hit.

The reason he didn't go down immediately was because he was hit high, low, left, right, front and back. There was nowhere to fall without crushing someone.

He was really going to have to quit wrestling with people he loved!

Tim finally got his arms around Keith and Matt. He rose to his full height, but the boys in his arms had pushed themselves up as Tim lifted. He went up so fast that his momentum kept him going. He was falling backwards toward the mat when a few someones swept his feet out from under him.

He hit the mat hard. What air was left in his lungs was forced out by too many bodies plopping on his chest and belly.

It should have been the worst humiliation of the night, but Kara dropped down on the mat beside him and planted a kiss on his cheek.

"I love you, Uncle Tim!" she grinned happily.

Tim grinned back and winked, then panted, "Get Aunty … Joy. Tell her … can't breathe. … need … mouth-to-mouth."

"Ew!" Keith and Phil objected in disgust.

"Aunty Joy!" Kara sang out gleefully. "Uncle Timmy's dyin'!"

All the youngsters scrambled out of the way as Joy sashayed up onto the mats and dropped down beside her fiancé.

"Oh, you poor baby," she crooned.

Her first aid looked more like a kiss. When Tim rolled over and pulled her into a hug, they were suddenly swarmed by well over two dozen youngsters between the ages of twelve and two. Tim's twelve year old cousins, Hailey, Morgan, Jesse and Brianna rolled Tim over while Sean Garrison, Jeremy, Lori, Clarissa and Jeremiah pulled Joy away from her fiancé. Then all the other children pounced gleefully. It turned out that Joy's feet were ticklish too!

That was the last "wrestling" match of the evening, but it wasn't the last of the fun.

Joy was utterly delighted. She wasn't exactly a stranger to fun, but for almost ten years now, there had always been a shadow over her life. First it was Reybeka's illness and death, then it was her mother's desertion. While the loss of her baby sister would always be a part of her, the intensity of that loss had faded. With her parents together again, there was nothing to darken her enjoyment of this evening.

Chapter 9

*T*he first Saturday of January dawned bright and cold. Joylynne woke up early, even before the sun rose. She tried to be quiet and not disturb the rest of the women who were scattered all over the house, sleeping soundly after a night of partying.

She'd never thought she would have a bachelorette party, and she'd hoped her fiancé wouldn't need a bachelor party. She'd never liked the idea as presented in movies. Why would anyone, man or woman, need a last fling before getting married? What was the purpose? She'd heard all kinds of theories, but they never made sense to her.

Maybe that was because of her parents. By the time she was old enough to really think about weddings, her mom had already left her dad. Joy was pretty confused about love and marriage after that. All her life Mom and Dad had seemed to be in love, but then they weren't. If love was what marriage was all about, then how come her parents' love hadn't kept them together?

When she'd seen her first chick flick with a bachelorette party in it, she hadn't enjoyed the movie. In her teenaged mind, such stupidity seemed to contradict the professed love the bride had for her groom. She'd wondered how strong that love could be, wondered how long it would last.

Now of course, she understood marriage from a more mature Christian perspective. Marriage is not so much about the love of a man and a woman for each other, but about their love for God and a shared commitment. A couple didn't need strong love before they married. The love would grow, as it had with Tim's cousin Madison and her husband Carl Rheese.

Joy knew all about their strange love story because Tim had told her about it as it unfolded. Just a few days ago, Joy had finally met them. They'd been married almost two years, and hadn't known each other even a day before their wedding, and yet they were as happily married as any of Tim's brothers and sisters, some of whom had known their spouses for years before getting married.

Watching the Rheeses, and of course Tim's siblings and parents, Joy hoped she and Tim would be that happy together in two years.

Her more mature perspective on marriage made the traditional bachelor/bachelorette parties seem even more ludicrous. The drinking was bad enough. She knew that from experience. After her mother had left her family, Joy had started going to some of the clandestine parties she was invited to. She'd gotten drunk more than a time or two. Who knows where that would have led her if she hadn't finally started going to church with Sally. Pastor Charles and the youth group had helped her get her life back on track.

Her brief walk on the wild side had assured her that the other part of the last fling parties was even worse than the drinking. More than once, she'd found herself in sweaty embraces, going way too far. She knew from experience that drinking combined with sexual exploration led to lust that was almost impossible to control. In fact, she'd finally gone to church with Sally after a drunken tryst had ended with the loss of her virginity.

Though her family hadn't been to church since shortly after Reybeka had died, Joylynne hadn't forgotten the expectation that as a good girl she would keep her virginity until she was married. When she was seventeen, she'd thought that losing her virginity had ended all her dreams of someday being happily married.

Pastor Charles' teachings about sexual purity had corrected that wrong thinking, and they had also helped her leave behind her degeneration into wanton immorality. It had been hard to tell her friends about what she'd done, but they'd all suspected it. They greatly helped her in her Christian walk, and she helped them too.

It had been much harder to confess her shameful past to Tim. He was such a good man. His family had seen even more troubles than hers had, and yet he had always held his faith. He had continued to live a life that glorified God.

As October drew to a close their freshman year, Joy had accepted the fact that she was falling in love with Tim, and he with her. He already knew about her sister's death and her mother's desertion, and that hadn't affected his attraction to her. She didn't want to wait to tell him about her reaction to her troubles. If that was too much for him to forgive, she would rather know before she was head-over-heels for him. So, after the Harvest Fest out at Bill Vogt's farm, she'd let Tim take her home. He often had a van full of friends to drop off after church events, but she'd never ridden with him before. She suspected that when she did, he would make her stop the last one.

She was right. That night, after Tim dropped off Sally, who lived four blocks from the Quintanillas, Joy climbed in the front seat. She chewed fretfully on her lower lip, trying to figure out how to initiate the conversation she knew she needed to have with Tim. He made it easy.

"You seem pensive," he said as he slowed for the stop sign at the end of Sally's street.

His comment almost stayed Joy's tongue. It highlighted Tim's goodness, his ability to tune in to other people's feelings. She'd seen him do it many times with their friends, and he always helped them work through whatever was bothering them, at least enough to see a starting point to a resolution.

Tim deserved someone like Kendra who, like him, had always been a good girl in spite of her troubles.

But he seemed to have set his heart on Joy, so she had to tell him the truth. If it drove him away, so be it.

"I am," she sighed heavily. "I think we need to talk."

"Oh?" Tim asked warily.

"Everyone seems to think you like me, a lot," Joy stared out the window instead of looking at Tim. "They think that maybe you want me to be …."

She couldn't come right out and say it.

Tim could. "My girlfriend? They're right. I would like that a lot."

"I would too, but there's something I have to tell you first," Joy pushed down tears. Crying now would be manipulative to the max, especially with Tim.

"I'm listening," Tim said somberly.

"I told you about my sister and my mom. I didn't tell you about how I, well, I didn't deal with it very well," Joy hung her head. She took a deep breath to control her emotions.

"You don't have to tell me anything, but I'll listen to whatever you feel you need to tell me," Tim encouraged Joy as he parked in front of her house. He didn't turn the van off because it was much too cold to be sitting outside without the heater.

"I started drinking," Joy confessed. "I went to parties to drink. Of course, with everyone drinking, the boys wanted to … to touch me. I let them."

She risked a glance at Tim. He was staring out the window with a slight frown. She had no idea if that frown was sad, angry or merely troubled, so she finished in a rush.

"I let them go farther and farther. During spring break my junior year, I finally went all the way."

Tim's frown had deepened. Joy sighed sadly.

"Why did you feel the need to tell me this?" he asked after a thoughtful pause.

"Because I thought you should know."

"Why?"

"Because I'm not a virgin," Joy stated it plainly.

Tim sighed sadly. His shoulders drooped and he rubbed his face.

"What have I done that makes you think I would judge you for that?"

Joy was shocked that he sounded ashamed. She'd just told this virtuous man that she wasn't a virgin, and he was ashamed of himself! He thought he'd done something wrong.

"But you're a virgin and I'm not!" She knew he was. He'd publicly declared that to the whole campus back in August when some older guys were harassing Brad and Russell about being virgins. Joylynne had seen Tim in class before, he was impossible to overlook, but it was that moment that she began to fall in love. When Brad and Russell were accused of being virgins, Tim had earnestly stepped in and claimed friendship based on their shared status as virgins by choice.

"Do you really think I'm that judgmental?" Tim asked sadly without raising his head.

"But … but …," Joy didn't know what to say. Everyone knew that Christian boys were supposed to desire virginity in their spouses.

"It has to be me," Tim mused aloud. "Pastor Charles has never even remotely suggested that past sexual acts should be a judging point for future mates. How did I give you the idea that it was a show stopper for me?"

"You didn't," Joy was bewildered. "Don't you want your wife to be a virgin?"

"Heck no!" Tim looked at her in shock. "I want to have sex with my wife."

"I meant before your wedding," Joy snapped angrily. He knew what she was talking about. Why was he being obtuse?

"I want us both to be sexually pure when we get married," Tim shrugged. "But what does that have to do with virginity?"

Joy didn't answer. She had no answer. She hadn't thought about it from that perspective before, but now that she did, she realized that what Pastor Charles taught was that sexual purity is about where you're at, not where you've been.

"My parents raised me to pursue sexual purity for God's sake," Tim explained calmly. "Part of that was keeping my virginity until I got married. Never once did either of them indicate that I should expect my girlfriends to be virgins, just sexually pure. Mom wasn't a virgin when she married Dad."

"Oh," Joy whispered in wonder.

"You aren't still drinking and having sex, are you?" Tim asked with extreme doubt.

"Of course not!" Joy huffed.

"So why should I care if you've already lost your virginity?" Tim's frown was again deeply troubled. "Some of the most virtuous people I know today weren't always sexually pure. My sister Jenni and her husband have a great, God-honoring marriage and neither of them were always sexually pure before they married."

"But that was both of them," Joy said doubtfully.

"Okay. You're right, but my cousin Cait did a whole lot more than you did, but Brian still married her, and he was thirty-eight and still a virgin."

Again Joy had nothing to say other than a soft, "Oh."

"I'm not saying I'm in love with you Joy, but I want to be," Tim said clearly. "I'm going to take things slow because I do want both of us to be sexually pure when we get married, but that's going to be a few years down the road. If we let things heat up too soon, we're not going to make it to our senior year. But don't you even once think that me going slow has anything to do with your past."

The tears that Joy had held at bay all this time finally began to fall.

"Aw, don't cry," Tim groaned. "What did I say wrong?"

"Nothing," Joy sobbed. "Nothing at all. You're a good man, much too good for me."

"Arrgh!" Tim growled as he clutched his hair in both hands. Suddenly he turned toward the back of the van. "Come on and let's do it right now!"

"Timothy!" Joy gasped in shock.

"I'm serious," Tim snapped. "If we do it, I'll be just like you. I won't be too good for you."

"Don't be ridiculous!" Joy snapped back.

"Ridiculous? Yeah, you're right," Tim frowned fiercely. "If *we* do it, then you'll have done it twice, but I'll only have done it once. So I better do it with someone else."

"Tim!" Joy wasn't sure if she was supposed to laugh, cry or smack him. Surely he couldn't be serious, but if he wasn't, she knew he was making fun of her.

"But should it be a total stranger, or one of our friends?" Tim mused out loud but to himself. "I guess I should find out which one of her friends she thinks is also too good for her. Then I can kill two birds with one stone."

"Stop!" Joy buried her face in her hands. She knew for sure he was making fun of her.

She also realized she deserved it. Her line of thinking was absurd.

"Will you stop your nonsense?" Tim glared at her.

"Yes," Joy dropped her hands and nodded without looking up.

"I won't allow this to come between us, Joylynne," Tim said earnestly. He gently pushed her chin up and turned her face toward his. She saw love shining in his eyes. "It's not an issue to me. Knowing this doesn't change my feelings and dreams about you."

Joy wanted to throw herself in his arms and kiss him. That wouldn't be wise, so she just smiled mistily.

"You are indeed a good man, Tim Shepherd," she said. "You're exactly the right man for me."

"This topic is buried?" Tim asked hopefully. Joy nodded. "Then you should probably go in because I'm seriously tempted to kiss you right now."

"Oh," Joy once again couldn't think of anything worth saying. She just smiled happily.

"Would it be okay if I walk you to the door?" Tim asked.

"Why not?" Joy frowned slightly.

"Well, I never walk any of my friends to the door when I drop them off at home," Tim shrugged with a slight smile.

"Are you asking if we can be more than friends?" Joy asked with shining eyes.

When Tim had smiled shyly with a small nod, Joy had fallen completely. From that moment, there'd never been any doubt that Tim was the only man for her.

As Joy woke on the morning of her wedding day to the man of her dreams, she couldn't help but entertain some doubts that she really was good enough to marry her perfect fiancé. She crept quietly into the kitchen, wanting to find a place where she wouldn't disturb the still-sleeping women scattered around the house. Since the kitchen could be closed off from the rest of the house, she hoped she could make a pot of coffee without waking anyone.

She discovered that her dad was already there.

"Daddy?" she gasped in shock as the door swung quietly shut behind her. "You're not supposed to be here! It was supposed to be only women here. You're supposed to be out at the farm."

"Did you really think I was going to sleep without my wife?" Al asked with an incredulous snort. "I've done enough of that for one lifetime. Dani let me in through the window after everyone else was asleep."

"Oh, Daddy, I love you so much!" Joy threw herself in his arms.

"I love you too, sweetie," Al patted her back with a bemused smile. "But I am rather curious. That didn't seem like a logical place for our conversation to go."

"You really don't care about what Mom's done in the past, do you?" Joy smiled at him with shining eyes.

"I'm more concerned with the here and now," Al assured his daughter. "I love her way too much to let the past get in the way of our future."

"Do you think Tim loves me like that?" Joy asked, just to make sure that she wasn't merely seeing what she wanted to see.

"Oh, sweetie," Al laughed softly. "I think Tim loves you like that and then some! You two are perfect for each other."

"Thank you, Daddy," Joy sighed happily and dropped dreamily into a chair.

"Wait a minute," Al also dropped into a chair. He peered carefully at her. "You weren't having doubts about marrying Tim because of your past, were you?"

"Just a tiny bit," Joy shrugged.

"Didn't you tell Tim about it?"

"Before we even started dating."

"And he dated you anyway, so it obviously didn't bother him."

"Oh no," Joy said happily. "He didn't even understand why I felt the need to tell him."

"The more I get to know that young man, the more I love him," Al shook his head in wonder.

"I agree with that!" Joy grinned broadly.

"So," Al spoke thoughtfully as he got up to pour coffee for both of them, "me loving your mom like I do gave you some kind of assurance that Tim could love you."

Joy nodded.

"Why?" Al set the two cups on the table.

"Well, if you can love Mom like that in spite of what she did, why should I doubt that Tim can love me?" Joy blew softly on the hot coffee.

Al frowned at his cup for a long moment.

"I guess you have doubts about God's love for you too," he finally said.

Joy stared at him, her eyes wide. "Not really. I know I'm not good enough for him, but I know he loves me."

"So you think Tim's better than God?" Al asked incredulously.

"Absolutely not!"

"Then you must think that Tim hasn't really been made righteous by God," Al's frown was so deep it was almost a glare. "He's just a really moral unbeliever."

"No!"

"If you've both been made righteous by God, then why wouldn't both of you be good enough for each other?" Al asked softly.

"You're right, Daddy!" Joy's smile lit up her whole face.

"Trust me, sweetie," Al grinned ruefully. "Before the end of the month, your husband will do something that makes you doubt his righteousness. And he'll doubt yours. That's the nature of human relationships. But hold onto the truth – God has made both of you righteous, but you're both also still works in progress. Cling to God so you can cling to each other."

"Thanks Dad!" Joy reached across the table, and Al grasped her hand.

Joy let go of her doubt about marrying Tim. It wasn't worth worrying about. Instead, she sat and talked to her father for almost an hour before anyone else appeared. She was glad he'd violated the rules and slept in the wrong house. She enjoyed one last morning of being Daddy's girl. When she woke up tomorrow morning she would be Tim's wife.

Chapter 10

Joy wished she could peek into the church. She hated hiding back here like she was the prize that Tim was getting. Joy knew that she was the one getting the prize!

"Why do I have to be the one entering to the wedding march?" she grumbled to her dad as Kendra stepped up to the door of the sanctuary. "Why am I the focus of the wedding?"

"That's the way it's done," Al shrugged.

"But why?" Joy pouted. "We sing about the bride waiting for her groom. I should be the one inside watching for Tim."

"You might be right!" Al said in surprise.

"But it's a little late to think about that now," Reylene, Joy's maid of honor, gave her a broad smile and wink, then floated out the door.

Joy was next. She wasn't waiting anymore! She smiled eagerly at her dad.

"I'm so happy for you, sweetie," Al smiled back.

"And I'm happy for you!" Joy hugged him.

The music from the sanctuary paused briefly, then the old familiar notes rang through the old building. Sally kissed her cousin then pushed Joy and Al toward the door. Joy's first choice for her maid of honor had been Sally, but she'd never even asked her. Before she could, Sally had announced that she was going to be Tim and Joy's wedding planner. After graduation in the spring, she would be a full-fledged event planner. A successful big wedding would look great on her resume.

When Joy and Al stepped through the door of the church, all eyes were on them, but Joy only saw Tim.

Her heart swelled with jubilation. He was about to become her husband, and he glowed with happiness. Tim's smile assured Joy that her earlier doubts had been foolish indeed.

Joy floated down the aisle, drinking in the sight of her handsome fiancé. His tux didn't make him look one bit better than he usually did. He was so perfect, and he was hers!

Al and Joy stopped at the front of the church, a few steps away from Pastor

Charles. He grinned broadly as he asked the old traditional question, "Who gives this woman?"

"Her mother and I," Al said proudly and joyfully.

"Yes, you do! Together!" Charles grinned. "And that togetherness is radically awesome!"

"Oh yeah!" Tim agreed.

Joy's heart soared even higher as she stepped over to stand by Kendra while Dani stepped up beside her husband.

"Some of you may not have heard that Al and Nita are going to renew their vows, right here, right now, as part of Tim and Joy's wedding ceremony," Charles explained to the congregation. "When these two couples came to me to discuss how we would do this, they had a few hot debates. None of those discussions were about whether they were going to do it, just about how it would be done.

"Should we tell everyone that Al and Nita's marriage fell apart after the death of their beloved little girl, Reybeka? Absolutely all four said. They also all agreed to tell you that for the last six years, Al and Nita have been separated. She was living in Tucson, and she only returned for a few special occasions, like Joylynne's and Taggart's high school graduations, and even then she didn't fellowship with the family.

"Obviously they are back together again," Charles smiled at the Quintanillas, then sighed. "And that's where the discussions started to break down. Tim was adamantly opposed to telling you all that he was the one who brought them back together again. He did have a point. It was God who worked in their hearts, but Tim was the willing vessel."

Tim was scowling at Charles, but the pastor just ignored him.

"Tim never did relent on his opposition to being given credit, so I won't do that," Charles said with a smirk. "But I will tell you that someone listened to God instead of his own feelings. He wasn't happy about the hurt his ... loved ones were feeling, but he decided to see if he could find out what had hurt Nita so long ago and caused her to hurt her family. Through this nameless person's efforts, God brought the deeper hurt to the surface and healing began.

"All four of these wonderful people want me to encourage everyone here to not let hurts fester. When you're hurt, talk about it with people who can help the hurt heal. There is peace and joy beyond the pain, once you surrender it to God and allow him to work in your life.

"That's what Nita and Al finally did, and now we get to celebrate with them as they renew their vows. It's going to be very simple because Al told me they're anxious to get rid of Joylynne."

"Daddy!" Joy gasped in shock.

Al just shrugged and grinned at his wife, "Not exactly what I said, but I guess it's close enough."

"Al and Nita have written their own vows, and they'll recite the words of the ring ceremony though they won't exchange rings. Since Al never took his off and Nita put hers back on almost two weeks ago, they didn't see the logic in taking them off again even for just a few hours this morning.

"So, now that all the backstory is done," Charles paused for Greg's frown and loud growl, and his family's snickers. "We can get on with these two celebrations of marriage."

Charles nodded to Al who turned fully toward Danita.

"I love you so much, Dani. I thank God that he brought you into my life. Twenty-five years ago I promised to love and cherish you in good times and bad. I didn't do a very good job of it. I lost my way and lost you for a time. But you came back to me. I again promise you that I will love you in God's strength, but this time I have a much better grasp of what that really means. Because my commitment to God is stronger today than it was twenty-five years ago, I have confidence that our next twenty-five years together will be wonderful. Backing that confidence is the knowledge that today our daughter is marrying into a large, crazy, God-loving clan who don't seem to see boundaries when it comes to who they claim as family. If we ever do get stupid again, I'm sure someone will get in our face and get us on the right track. I am very glad because I don't ever want to lose you again."

Danita had tears on her cheeks, but her voice was strong. "You are my beloved, Al. Your vows express my feelings at this moment completely, including the part about the scary family we're gaining today, but especially the part about God's strength. We went to church together when we started our marriage, and that wasn't a bad thing, but now we have something much better. We are choosing to be the church, together with our friends and family. I don't know what the next twenty-five years will bring, but I do know that we have a solid foundation to stand on as we face them. Thank you for loving me, my beloved."

After Al and Nita's ceremony was done, of course they didn't leave the church. Instead they simply turned to sit in the front of the bride's section of the church.

Charles motioned for Tim and Joy to take their place in front of him, then he again addressed the congregation.

"I'm sure that everyone who knows the Shepherds fully expected Tim's brother to have part in this ceremony," Charles said. "Tim and Joy talked about having Greg actually perform the ceremony, but because they're both members of my church and my beautiful wife is Tim's cousin, they decided that they wanted me to officiate. However, I made a suggestion that they both loved.

"What many of you don't know is that another of Tim's brothers expressed to me a secret desire to preach."

"Not what I said," Brandon growled loudly. Most of the family stared at him in astonishment.

Charles ignored Brandon's interjection. "When I told Tim that Brandon had said that someday he wanted to preach, Tim thought it would be a wonderful idea to have Brandon preach the message for their wedding. Joylynne agreed. It took some arm twisting and head thumping, but Brandon finally agreed. So, without further ado, I will temporarily put this celebration in Brandon Wolfe's capable hands."

Brandon rose from his seat in the front pew and stepped up to join Tim and Joylynne at the front of the church, shaking his head.

"Tim, I promised you that I wouldn't complain about not being worthy of this honor, and I won't. I'm not. But I do need to confess that I thought I wasn't worthy. I'm not married and never have been. Who am I to give the message at a wedding? But Stormy pointed out to me that Charles was single for the first ten years of his ministry and during that time he gave many messages at wedding ceremonies. She reminded me that when giving advice, our knowledge of and trust in God are much more important than our past experiences. Everyone has experiences, and if they're in a position to give advice, obviously they lived through those experiences, but living through something doesn't mean a person has truly helpful advice to give.

"This is going to sound bizarre to anyone here who isn't a believer who reads the Bible, but I am the bride of Christ. It is that experience that I am well qualified to talk about, not because I always get it right, but because I messed up big-time for quite a few years. I loved God and I wanted him in my life, but I wanted that relationship to be on my terms, at my convenience. I put on a good show and fooled a lot of people for quite some time, but my relationship with God wasn't growing. In fact, it was sinking fast, and soon that became obvious to my family, and eventually even to the few friends that I had let into my life.

"At the same time, I was still fooling myself that my relationship with God was just fine. Then something happened, and I had to admit that I was at a crossroads. I either had to 'divorce' God, walk away from him entirely, or I had to get serious about living for him.

"I was very fortunate that I'm single. It gave me greater freedom to do what I had to do. From this day forward, Tim and Joylynne, you no longer have that kind of freedom. As of this day, you are bound to each other. The two of you will be one. Your effect on each other will be great. If either of you let your walk with God slip, you'll affect the other one's spiritual walk too. And of course that will affect your marriage.

"Each of you have to live first for God, seeking to know him better, to serve him more faithfully. Of course you have to seek to know each other too, and to serve each other, but if you're living for God, that'll come pretty naturally. That's how God wants a marriage to be, mutual submission to each other.

"There's also a practical aspect to living first for God. He's the only one who will always be with you. You're getting married on this particular day because you both expect that Tim's career will cause you to be separated for a while after graduation in a few months. You won't see each other for days on end. If you're living for each other, you'll mope around all 'homesick' when you're apart, not doing the things you should do, or not doing them well because you're focused on missing each other. If you're living for each other, not for God, when you aren't with each other for any reason, what are you living for?

"Furthermore, if you don't live first for God, when hard times come, and they will come, you won't make it through them without great pain to both of you. Ask Al and Nita if you doubt me. But they'll also tell you how just a fledgling faith, true faith, not the just-going-to-church kind of easy believism, but true I'm-clinging-to-God-as-my-savior-and-guide-and-Lord faith will give you strength to do what you cannot do on your own power.

"That faith isn't going to survive without the love of God, the love for him that gives you an enduring love for each other. The Bible says love is greater than faith and hope. That's because love is God. It's the very essence of God. For six long lonely years, Nita and Al didn't have any faith or hope, but neither of them let go of their love for each other. It wasn't the best love because it was still a little selfish, but it came from the true love of God for his children. It was enough to bring them back to the fullness of life when they were finally ready.

"Learn that lesson early on, and you will have something enduring. Live for God and seek a deeper walk with him. Fall more in love with him than you do with each other, and no matter what storm hits you, you will go through it and be stronger for it."

Brandon looked at Charles with a chagrined smile, and whispered loudly, "I forgot to ask you how to turn this thing back over to you!"

"I guess you just did," Charles whispered back.

"I'm really happy for you two," Brandon turned back to Tim and Joylynne. "I'm going to sit down now so Charles can finish the deed."

It was a beautiful ceremony with no major mishaps. Tim recited his vows flawlessly.

"You are an incredible woman, Joy. I adore you and I am so looking forward to being your husband, but you and I both know that we don't always see eye to eye on things. Our different personalities and backgrounds have already made for some interesting times. That's why I know that I cannot live for you. 'You are my life' is stuff of romantic comedies, but in reality it's not funny at all. Because of our differences our life will be confusing and chaotic if we live for each other. Instead, I promise you that I will live for God, and love you out of the strength he gives me."

Joy only needed Charles to prompt her once during her vows.

"When I first met you, Tim, I was intrigued because you were different than anyone I'd ever met before. Then I met your family and I was scared. Not because they're crazy," more than one person grunted or snickered at that. Joy ignored them all, "but because they live their faith so boldly. I began to understand why you are so different, and I loved you even more. The more I got to know you and your family, the more I realized that I wanted to be like you all. I also realized that I could, if I put God first in my life. I am doing that, and will continue to do it, and someday I hope to be as true a Shepherd as anyone born as one. So, I guess, Tim, that my vow is the same as yours! I will live for God and love you out of the strength he gives me."

When it came time to kiss the bride, Tim gently cradled Joy's face in his hands and kissed her tenderly. Charles pronounced them man and wife, then presented Mr. and Mrs. Timothy Connor Shepherd to the congregation.

As soon as the joyous recessional started, Tim swept Joy into his arms, one hand under her knees the other cradling her to his chest.

"Tim!" Joy gasped and wrapped her arms around his neck, dropping the bouquet that Reylene had recently returned to her.

"Oh, didn't you know?" Tim asked with mock innocence. "This is part of the Shepherd wedding ceremony."

"It is?" Luke asked incredulously.

"I guess so!" Greg grinned smugly at Beth as Tim proudly marched down the aisle.

JOY WAS THRILLED with the silliness that marked the rest of the day. She'd heard stories about Greg and Beth's wedding, so she wasn't surprised when Tim and his dad also "danced" the father dance, stealing the show so Al's tears were shed in relative privacy. Joy and her mom were more than happy to return the favor when it was time for Tim to dance with Gloria.

Tim and Joshua invited all the men to join them in a dance competition. Tim and his dad took turns dancing a few steps. Anyone who couldn't follow them was done. The first couple rounds everyone made it through, even the grandpas, but then the dances got longer and more intricate. For a few more rounds, they didn't lose any of Tim's brothers, but they did eliminate quite a few others. Surprisingly, Pika, Pete's dad hung in through the fourth round. Ted and Brian, in spite of the fact that they both had a bad leg, lasted two more rounds. Taggart and Heath were still standing, as well as Brad, Matt and all Tim's brothers, Joshua's brother Andy, and both his nephews, Kendal and Jared.

Joshua was the one who started adding acrobatic moves, but Tim took it up a notch two rounds later. When he did a double back flip with a twist at the end, he was the last man standing.

After a short break, all the men who'd been at the bachelor party the night before joined Tim for a couple of well-rehearsed line dances. Joy was delighted. Of course she'd seen Tim dance at church before, and she knew he was very good, full of joy and passion. At church his focus was on God, tonight his focus was on his bride!

He was at his bride's side immediately after the second dance was done, but his brothers weren't as quick to clear the dance floor.

"We have a surprise for Tim tonight," Luke announced with a grin for his brother. "We've deeply regretted that for the last three years, we haven't been able to properly celebrate Tim's birthday since it's in early May, so we owe him."

"Oh no," Tim groaned and dropped his head on Joy's shoulder.

She patted his knee but gave Luke her full attention.

"Tonight, the Backyard Braddahs Plus Two have a special number just for you, Tim, to make up for the last three years of no birthday parties."

"You don't need to," Tim begged his brothers.

Of course they ignored him. At least they were using real musical instruments this time. The Colonel was behind the real band's drum set, Dave had a guitar, and Ted at the keyboard was obviously one of the Plus Twos. Brian was the other, but as a vocalist since he had no instrument. The original group had included Tim, Robert, Luke, Greg, Pete and the Colonel for Steve's birthday five years ago. For the Colonel's birthday, Steve was in and the birthday boy was out. Since then, Brandon and Dave had joined them and then Abe after he married Rachel. This was the first time the Braddahs had included someone other than Joshua, his sons and sons-in-law.

Tim again groaned when he recognized the song the musicians were playing. He really liked Kerri Roberts' "Outcast," but he knew this was going to be a parody, and he knew he was going to be the butt of the joke. Joy found it quite funny.

> Since I can remember, guess I been a problem
> Never had a filter, always been the popular one
> To sugarcoat what I know is undeniable
> I just can't hide it, I wear it like a letter
>
> Everywhere I go, everyone is talking
> I can feel them staring, they hope I'm just pretending
> I'm saving all my power, using it to pressure
> I'm not living for them, I know that I am better
>
> I'm just good enough, to be always right
> But let me tell you what, I know who I am
> So just throw me out for not dumbing down
> I will stand my ground and be the smartest

> So what if I'm the smartest?
> So what if I'm the smartest?

Tim was shaking his head and hiding behind his hand, but Joy laughed in delight. The Backyard Braddahs had only changed a few words but drastically changed the meaning of the original song. It was twice as funny because though Tim was highly intelligent, he was very humble about it.

The next verse caused Tim to sink down in his chair, but Joy laughed aloud.

> So what if I don't act the part I'm supposed to play
> What if I don't let her tell me what to do
> She don't know that I am perfect, she waits for me to mess up
> I know she's gonna blow it, the girl should just admit it

The next verse was more of the same, both from the singers and their audience.

> I try to play nice, I don't want to fight
> But I won't be wrong just 'cause she isn't right
> 'Cause I am so smart that I'm never wrong
> If I can be strong, I'll prove I'm dead-on

The final chorus was very different from the previous ones.

> I'm just tall enough, I don't fit the couch

From between two tables, Robert dragged out five chairs that some joker had lashed together to form a semblance of a couch, the three in the middle forming a back and the two end ones turned to make arms. Robert indeed had a very hard time fitting on that couch.

> But let me tell you what, I know I am right
> She can throw me out for not dumbing down
> I will stand my ground an' be cast out t'night

The singers danced their way off stage as they sang the chorus, all except Robert who rolled over to face the back of the couch and pulled his jacket up over his head as the musicians finished with a final flourish.

Thunderous applause filled the old barn. Even Tim rose to his feet with a rueful grin, but when someone, probably one of his Hilo cousins, shouted "Hanahou," Tim replied with a very loud, firm "No!"

Though the premise of the song was way off – he didn't really have that high of an opinion of his rightness – the reality wasn't far off. He would probably make Joy angry more than once in their marriage.

When they did finally get their new home, he would make sure that they had a nice big living room, large enough to easily fit a couch big enough to be comfortable for him.

Chapter 11

Tim woke with a groan. Someone was singing downstairs. Who would be singing at the ungodly hour of – he lifted his head to glare at the alarm clock. Five-thirty-seven! Why would anyone be up at five-thirty, much less singing?

It was Joy, his wife of just over a week. They'd come back from their honeymoon yesterday. During their honeymoon, she hadn't once gotten out of bed before him, but she was definitely gone now.

He growled and burrowed down further under the covers. It was much too early to get up. What was the woman doing? He fervently hoped she wasn't going to be up and singing this early every morning. If she was, they were going to have a problem!

Joy was a morning person, and she did indeed love to sing in the morning. She didn't understand how Tim could sleep until the morning was half over, nor did she appreciate it the first night that he stayed up until nearly midnight before going to bed. Because they truly loved each other, they both kept their annoyance to themselves, but every day the annoyance grew. It finally came to a head the first day of the spring semester, one week after the first time Tim had been annoyed by Joylynne singing.

Once again Tim was rudely awakened by Joy singing early in the morning. He'd somewhat gotten used to it, at least enough to go back to sleep, but that was largely because she'd always been downstairs. This morning she was in the bathroom, right on the other side of the door beside their bed! That was totally unacceptable.

Tim growled loudly and pulled Joy's pillow over his head. He could still hear her.

"Shut up," he growled slightly louder. It didn't work. Joy probably couldn't hear him over that noise. She had a pretty good voice, but not at five-thirty in the morning!

Tim growled again and threw Joy's pillow at the bathroom door. Of course it had no effect on the woman on the other side of the door.

He either needed to throw something heavier or yell. He didn't feel like yelling. He was too tired.

A shoe would be good to throw, but his shoes were all down by the outside door where they should be. A book would be loud enough, but the only book close at hand was his Bible.

Not happening.

He eyed the alarm clock. That would make enough noise, but he would probably break it.

Did it matter? Obviously Joy didn't need the alarm clock to wake up, and if she was already up, she could give him a wake-up call.

He waited a long moment, hoping Joy would shut up on her own.

She didn't.

He hurled the clock at the door. The solid thunk was satisfactorily loud, but kind of crackly.

Joy's song abruptly cut off. Before Tim could sigh in relief, the bathroom door opened rather forcefully.

"What in the world are you doing?"

Tim couldn't see Joy's face because she was backlit by the bathroom light, but her voice sounded rather angry.

"Trying to get you to shut up," Tim muttered.

"Excuse me?" Joy asked incredulously.

"Why you gotta sing at this ungodly hour?" Tim whined. "Why you gotta wake me up?"

"Why do you have to sleep until lunchtime?" Joy snarled.

"If you're gonna gripe at me, you may as well sing," Tim snarled back, then pulled the blanket up and buried his head under his pillow.

"Fine!" Joy slammed the bathroom door.

His bedroom was dark and quiet again.

Sadly that didn't make it peaceful.

Tim turned his back on the bathroom door and firmly shut his eyes. Even so, when Joylynne opened the bathroom door a few minutes later, the light invaded his feeble attempt to go back to sleep.

Suddenly a pillow sailed onto the bed just past his head, then something dropped loudly on one of the dressers.

"I hope you don't expect me to be your alarm clock now," Joy snapped.

Tim snarled wordlessly. Part of his sleepy brain was telling him not to escalate things any further, so he listened to it and kept his unkind comment to himself.

The light was doused then the sound of footsteps assured Tim that his wife had left the room.

Tim desperately wanted to go back to sleep, but the silence downstairs was deafening.

He rolled onto his back and stared at the ceiling. The streetlight shone through the tree outside the window. A light breeze moved the shadows. It was as if the old venerable tree was shaking its wise bald head at him. Why did he want to fight with his beautiful bride?

BY THE TIME Joy descended the steps, she was feeling very bad about her reaction to Tim. Sure he shouldn't have thrown the alarm clock, or even the pillow, but was it that big a deal? She should have been more understanding. It wasn't like she didn't know that Tim was a late riser whenever he got the chance. His friends had been razzing him about it for years.

She really shouldn't have been singing in the bathroom anyway. She'd known Tim was still sound asleep when she'd slipped out of the bed. In fact she'd moved carefully and quietly so she wouldn't wake him! She actually liked alone time in the morning so she always tried to not wake Tim when she got up.

They hadn't had anywhere to go early in the morning this last week, so she'd always come downstairs first off and only gone upstairs to dress after Tim was already up. Since she had to be on campus by seven-thirty today, she'd dressed first, before coming downstairs for breakfast and her devotions. It was business as usual for her. That's what she always did when she had an early class. The song had come naturally, like it always did when she greeted a new day.

She hadn't expected to have a fight with her husband. Now she didn't want either breakfast or devotions. She just wanted to cry.

Suddenly Tim was standing in the door to the kitchen.

"I'm sorry, Joy," he said sadly, his head hanging. "I was way wrong."

"I was wrong first, Tim," Joy confessed. "I shouldn't have been singing in the bathroom."

"You were happy," Tim shrugged and walked over to the table, pulling out the chair around the corner from hers. "Why shouldn't you sing?"

"Because you were happily sleeping on the other side of the door," Joy looked down at the table to hide her tears. "Why should my happiness disturb yours?"

"You have the right to express your happiness," Tim reached for Joy's hand.

"But I should've done it in a way that didn't disturb you."

"And I shouldn't have so rudely interrupted your happiness," Tim snorted ruefully. "If I'd waited a few more minutes, you would've been done upstairs. I could've gone back to sleep after you went downstairs."

"Does my singing downstairs bother you?" Joy was further ashamed to realize that she should have asked that when they first got back from their honeymoon, well over a week ago.

"Not so much anymore," Tim shrugged. "I'm getting used to it. Are you getting used to me sleeping the morning away?"

"Actually I kind of like the quiet time by myself in the morning," Joy admitted with a small shrug.

"And I've always liked some quiet time by myself in the evening before going to bed," Tim said wryly.

"But you've gone to bed with me practically every night," Joy said doubtfully.

"I like going to bed with you," Tim smiled brazenly. He also shivered slightly, partly from the exhilarating thought of going to bed with Joy, partly because it was rather cold in the kitchen.

"You're freezing," Joy gasped, for the first time fully comprehending that her husband was only wearing a pair of pajama bottoms.

"It is a little cold," Tim's grin broadened and he reached for his wife. "You could come warm me!"

"Just for a minute," Joy happily slid into her husband's lap and wrapped her arms around him. "We both have class this morning."

"Yes, we do," Tim groaned and nuzzled her neck. "I guess that means you won't go back to bed with me."

"No, Timothy," Joy giggled. "I'm going to get coffee brewing and breakfast started while you get dressed."

"But I wanna go back to bed," Tim pouted.

"But I have to be on campus by seven-thirty if I'm going to get a halfway decent parking space."

"And I should go with you even though my first class isn't until nine."

"It would be good stewardship," Joy agreed.

"I wasn't thinking about the stewardship," Tim grinned slyly. "I just want to spend more time with you."

"Will you walk me to my class?" Joy feathered a kiss on his bristly chin.

"If you're gonna start that, neither of us are gonna get to class," Tim growled playfully.

Joy popped off his lap. "Go get dressed. Breakfast'll be ready when you get back down."

Joy was pouring her first cup of coffee when she heard Tim singing upstairs. Of course he was destroying the tune, as he always did when he didn't have music to back him up, but whatever it was, he must be destroying the lyrics too because she couldn't quite make it out.

After a few measures, Joy laughed out loud because she finally realized what he was singing. It was the Backyard Braddahs version of "Outcast"!

ON THEIR WAY home that evening, Tim and Joy stopped to get a new alarm clock. The alarm rarely went off because Joy usually woke her husband with a kiss and a cup of coffee. Tim often stayed up long after Joy went to sleep, doing homework, studying his Bible or just relaxing. Sometimes he didn't go up to bed when Joy did, other times he got out of bed after she'd gone to sleep.

Neither Tim nor Joy were foolish enough to believe that having survived that first fight would prevent future ones. They knew it was only a matter of time before their differences clashed again. Their next fight was almost two weeks later, and it ended up being a big one.

Joy started it on Saturday morning when she was doing laundry. She wanted to get to it early because she needed to go shopping too. The sooner she was done with the laundry, the sooner she could get to the store.

Tim was sound asleep when Joylynne's furious howl pierced through the walls and floor.

"Timothy Connor Shepherd, what is this *nasty* mess?"

Tim bolted up in bed. He sat there trying to shake off the sleep so he could figure out what Joylynne was upset about. He was awake enough to realize that angry feet were pounding up the steps.

He wouldn't have to figure out what was wrong. His wife would enlighten him.

She burst through the door and threw something on the bed.

"What in the hell is that?" she exclaimed angrily.

Tim frowned at the object.

"My gym bag," he scowled sarcastically.

She was intelligent enough to figure that out on her own. She had to wake him for that?

"Why does it smell like a sewer?" Joy snapped.

"I sweat when I work out, Joylynne," Tim snapped back. "My clothes start to smell after a while."

"What's it doing in my laundry?"

Joy wasn't calming down. In fact, she seemed to be getting angrier. Tim didn't understand why.

"If they don't get washed, they won't stop smelling! Isn't that the purpose of doing the laundry?" Tim snarled. "Did you need to wake me up to tell me that my gym clothes needed to be washed? I knew that! That's why I brought them home!"

"And threw them in my hamper!"

What was the woman's problem? Tim's temper was fully awake now.

"It's my hamper too, woman! Where was I supposed to put them? Back in my dresser?"

"Well at least then you'd put *something* away!" Joy yelled at him.

"What the hell's that supposed to mean?" Tim yelled back.

A remote part of Tim's brain was appalled that he'd just sworn at his wife. He didn't swear.

Of course, he didn't get angry like this either. What was his problem?

"It means you don't have any respect for where things belong! You leave your clutter all over the house!" Joy's eyes flashed angrily.

She couldn't believe she was fighting with her husband, but she was tired of cleaning up behind him.

"Woman, you're crazy!" Tim finally got tired of sitting on the bed with his wife standing over him like he was a recalcitrant toddler. He swung his legs over the side of the bed and had the presence of mind to keep the sheet firmly clutched in his hand as he rose. It was hard to fight effectively without any clothes on.

Unfortunately, when the sheet came with him it was pulled out from the far side of the bed, Joy's side. The blanket dropped into a heap on the floor.

"Now look what you've done!" Joy howled and pushed Tim with both hands. He was back on the bed, and she was storming from the room.

"Joy!" Tim howled.

She couldn't storm off like that! This was far from over.

"Take care of yourself for once!" Joy shouted as her feet pounded back down the stairs.

Before Tim could decide if he wanted to storm after Joy, the backdoor slammed. She'd taken the decision out of his hands.

Tim laid on the bed trying to figure out what had just happened. So his gym clothes smelled. Surely that wasn't a news flash to Joylynne. How were they supposed to get clean if he didn't put them in the laundry? Besides, she had four brothers, and in the last six years she'd often done laundry for them. Why would she be shocked to find his dirty gym clothes in their hamper?

And what was that nonsense about clutter? Tim sat up and stared at the top of his dresser. It looked pretty well organized to him. He stalked into the bathroom. Maybe his things weren't arranged as precisely as Joy's but they certainly were neat.

As Tim dressed for the day, his anger grew. Joylynne was utterly unreasonable. When he made the bed, he didn't just pull the covers up as he usually did. He tucked the sheets in so tight that Joy wouldn't be able to get in without messing up the bed. He grabbed his gym bag on the way out and stormed down to the laundry room. He certainly could wash his own clothes. Mom had made sure of that when he was still in middle school, and he'd been doing it for three and a half years, without any help from Joy!

He furiously pulled his clothes from the heap beside the washer. No way was he going to try to wash Joy's. He would mess up something, and she would be even angrier than she was now.

After having a bowl of cereal and a banana for breakfast, Tim meticulously cleaned the entire kitchen, making sure there wasn't a crumb left on the counter and every fork was properly nestled in a neat row. When he was done with that, he decided he may as well make sure that everything in the house that belonged to him was either neatly arranged or tucked away so that it couldn't bother his neat-freak wife.

When lunchtime rolled around, the house was totally clean and his laundry was not only washed and dried but also folded and put away. There was no sign of Joy. Rather than trying to scrounge up leftovers, Tim grabbed his keys and coat and left the house. If Joy was going to make him take care of himself then he would go out to eat. That would ensure that he didn't leave a mess in her kitchen.

Chapter 12

Joy stormed out of the house. That man was so infuriating! How dare he talk to her like that? And then he tried to intimidate her with his great size. That was not happening!

She backed the car out of the garage, wondering if she'd let it warm enough.

She didn't really care. If she broke it, Tim would have to fix it. He should be good for something other than lying around the house, eating all their food and dirtying up his clothes.

A voice in the back of her head was trying to tell Joylynne that she was being irrational, but she didn't want to listen to it, so she turned on the radio. She drove for about ten minutes, then she realized that she was heading toward Grandma's farm.

That wouldn't do. Grandma would take one look at her, know she'd fought with Tim and scold her. It was too cold to go horseback riding, the only other reason to go out to the farm, so Joy made a right at the next intersection. She headed back toward town, wondering what she should do. There wasn't anyone she could safely visit. Everyone she knew would tell her she was being foolish and send her back to Tim.

Maybe that should tell her something important.

Maybe she wasn't ready to hear it yet.

She headed to the mall. Her mood was not improved when she realized that she would have to wait fifteen minutes for it to open. By the time the doors did open, she was more than ready to shop.

She and Tim didn't have any money of their own yet. They were both still being supported by their parents, but that was just a technicality. In April, Tim would be drafted. He was one of the dozen or so college players whom sports pundits had already identified as sure-thing first round drafts. In fact, since Tennessee had the first pick and they desperately needed a wide receiver, Tim was the most likely candidate to be the number one draft pick. Within a few months, he would have more than enough money to cover any debt Joylynne racked up today.

She marched through the mall, ready to spend money.

She couldn't find anything she wanted to buy.

Apparently her foul mood was affecting her shopping. Every time she examined something she thought she liked, on closer inspection she found something wrong with it.

The electric kitchen griddle was nice, but where would she put it when it wasn't in use? Once they built their own house down at Gumbwats' Haven they would have plenty of room for it, but not now. Besides, Grandma had left her over-two-burners griddle and it worked wonderfully.

That blouse was the perfect color for her, but when she pulled it off the rack, it had too many fruffly things on the front. She really liked the vertically striped one, but of course it wasn't in her size. One skirt was too long, the other too short.

She found books by her favorite authors in the bookstore, but none of the jacket descriptions intrigued her.

By early afternoon she'd diligently scoured every square inch of the mall. The only thing she'd found that had tempted her to pull out her credit card was a beautiful leather jacket that would be perfect for Tim.

She passed on it too.

Joy finally headed for the food court. She needed a quiet corner and food in her belly. She didn't think well on an empty stomach.

It was far enough into the afternoon that there were plenty of tables to choose from. She took her pretzel dog and soda to a table by the windows. When she bowed her head over her tray, she finally asked God to show her what had gone wrong that morning.

First off, why had she gotten so upset when she'd found Tim's gym clothes? Sure, they were beyond ripe, but that wasn't the first time she'd found that kind of unpleasant surprise in the laundry. She'd even done it to herself once in high school. She'd forgotten to bring her gym clothes home at the end of the week. When she had brought them home on Monday, she'd dropped them in the hamper and forgot all about them until Saturday morning when she started sorting the laundry.

The problem hadn't really been Tim's smelly clothes. So what was it? It wasn't that Tim was sleeping still while she was working. She was used to that too. Her dad and brothers were usually still in their rooms when she started laundry. She actually liked it that way because that ensured that no one would interrupt her or interfere.

Her accusation of Tim leaving clutter all over the house was sheer nonsense. Tim was actually very neat. Sure he wasn't as detail oriented as she was, but not many people were. Most people didn't make sure the front of every label was facing out, or to the right for boxes that were stored sideways. Most people didn't make sure everything – cans, bottles, boxes, bags, books

– were directly lined up and squared off. She doubted most people organized their closets by type, subtype and color.

She knew her near-obsessive neatness probably had something to do with the order necessary in architectural design. She knew she was different, so she didn't expect others to be that neat. Truly, she was rather pleased with Tim's orderliness.

So why had she gotten so angry when she found that gym bag, and then escalated it so ridiculously?

She chewed thoughtfully for a while, exploring her feelings that morning. It had been a perfect day, right up to that moment with Tim's gym bag.

A perfect day.

She had wanted the day to continue to be perfect.

She had expected it to continue to be perfect. When things went awry, she lost her mind.

Somehow, she'd begun to expect that life with her new husband would always be perfect. She would never again have to tolerate the minor annoyances that had been the hallmark of the first twenty-one years of her life.

Suddenly tears clogged Joy's throat. She dropped her pretzel dog and buried her face in her hands.

How had she been so foolish? She knew that marriage wasn't about a perfect life. It was a journey of growth in which two people walked side-by-side, sharing life's burdens and helping each other learn life's lessons. Perfection comes through deepening love, not through trouble-free circumstances. In fact, facing difficult times helps a couple have a better marriage.

Joy gathered up the remains of her lunch and threw it in the rubbish can. She was going home to apologize to her husband.

But first she was going back to that store and getting that jacket. It really was perfect for Tim.

IT WAS PAST five-thirty and the sun was already sitting on the horizon when Joy drove down the street, so the houses were deep in shadows. All of them were well-lit, except hers. She wasn't surprised to see that Tim's van wasn't in the garage.

Of course he would have gone out to eat lunch. He could easily fend for himself at breakfast, but he didn't have the skills to make more than a sandwich and salad for lunch.

But lunchtime had been quite a few hours ago. Where was Tim now? She didn't want to call him. She owed him a face-to-face apology. Besides, he probably wouldn't answer his phone anyway. She wouldn't if Tim had treated her that way.

Joy trudged into the house with her purchases. She'd stopped at the grocery store on the way home, so she had four bags of food in addition to the jacket.

She could easily handle all of them by herself, but they felt heavier than usual. Probably because her heart was so heavy.

She decided to get dinner started. Wherever Tim was, surely he would be home soon.

Joy couldn't fix all the Hawaii dishes that Tim liked because they were too foreign to her, but she did know that he liked chili and rice, so she'd gotten everything she needed for it.

As soon as the meat was browning, Joy went down the hall to start the laundry she'd abandoned that morning. She wouldn't have time during the week, so by next Saturday she would have a mountain of laundry if she didn't do it now. Tim's weekly dirty clothes made up two loads, all on their own. He wasn't exceptionally dirty, just exceptionally large. His clothes took up a lot of space.

Joy was shocked to see that all of Tim's dirty clothes were gone. Her clothes were sorted in neat piles, but obviously Tim had washed his own clothes, just like she'd demanded. He'd probably been afraid to wash hers.

She wanted to cry, but she couldn't. If she started now, she would end up ruining dinner.

Joy returned to the kitchen after starting the only load of clothes she would have to do this week. She resumed dinner preparations, but something was nagging at the back of her mind. She stopped to examine her surroundings.

Everything was very, very neat. The kitchen was never as neat as the rest of the house. When she was cooking, she used and put away things so quickly that she didn't worry about excessive neatness like she did with her desk and her dresser. Today someone had made sure every spice bottle was perfectly lined up, label squared to the front. Every knife in the drawer was neatly placed with the sharp edge to the left, straight edge to the right, bases perfectly aligned. There wasn't a speck of dust or crumb of bread anywhere on the counter. It even looked like the cabinet doors had been wiped down.

Obviously, Tim had taken seriously her attack that morning. He'd tried to correct the faults she had maliciously and erroneously pointed out.

It broke her heart, but Joy was determined not to cry, not until after she got dinner ready.

She didn't really cry. It was just the onion she chopped.

By six-thirty, not only was the chili simmering on the stove, but she also had one of Grandma's top-secret-recipe pound cakes in the oven. Tim still hadn't appeared.

Tim's rice was different from what she'd grown up with. The only time that they'd had his rice here in Grandma's house, Tim had made it, one of the few things he could competently do in the kitchen. Joy knew where the rice cooker was, but she needed to find the instructions to make the rice right. It wouldn't do to make a special dinner for her husband but serve him bad rice.

She found the instruction book nestled among her few cookbooks. She read the directions carefully. It didn't seem too hard, but she still prayed fervently that God would guide her hand.

Joy was standing at the counter watching the rice cooker, wondering what it would do when the back door suddenly opened. Tim stepped inside and watched her warily, his coat still on and his hand on the doorknob as if ready to make a fast getaway if necessary.

Tears filled Joy's eyes. She looked down quickly, trying to hide them. She really needed to apologize before she started crying. She needed to get control of her emotions.

Suddenly she was enfolded in Tim's arms. It was way too late to control her emotions, so Joy clutched his shirt and wept, bitter tears of regret.

"I'm so sorry, Joy," Tim stroked her hair. "I shouldn't have treated you like that."

"No no," Joy shook her head, pushing down her tears. "It wasn't your fault. It was mine. I shouldn't have gotten angry over something so ridiculous."

"I shouldn't have just dumped that gym bag in the hamper," Tim confessed. "I should've asked you what to do with it. It was much more ripe than usual because I forgot about it last week."

"Maybe you should have," Joy acknowledged, "but I blew it way out of proportion. There was no reason for me to lose my mind like that. And you were still sleeping, weren't you?"

"I was sound asleep," Tim shrugged ruefully.

"I'm so sorry! That's a horrible way to be awakened," Joy couldn't stop another sob.

"Singing in the bathroom is way better," Tim acknowledged with a rueful smile.

"I love you!" Joy flung her arms around Tim's neck and pulled him down for a kiss.

The kiss could have taken them to passion, but Tim wisely pulled back from the brink. There would be time for that later. First they needed to talk about what had happened that morning. He wanted some honest growth out of it so that next time he had a little better understanding of what was going on. It also wouldn't hurt to get a little wiser about acknowledging their differences.

By the time the rice was done, they'd agreed that it would be best if Tim did let Joy know when he brought home dirty gym clothes. Even though she assured him that she really wasn't bothered by his minor clutter, Tim extracted a promise from her to tell him whenever something did bug her by being out of place. He would never learn how she wanted things if she didn't tell him.

"I'm not promising I'll always get it right," Tim said with a shrug, "but as long as it's reasonable, I'll try to accommodate your wishes."

"Will you tell me if you think it's unreasonable?" Joy asked earnestly.

"I'm sure I will," Tim smiled ironically. "I just hope I'm not already angry when I do!"

When the rice was done, Tim declared it perfect, and so was the chili Joy had made to go with it.

So was the rest of the evening.

THE DAYS THAT followed were wonderful, trying and busy. Every few days Tim and Joylynne had minor skirmishes, but nothing got out of hand. There were enough good times to far outweigh the bad.

Tim decided that since he was no help in the kitchen and Joy's clothes made him nervous in the laundry room, at least while they were still in college, he could help by cleaning the rest of the house. He daily swept the floors, mopped them weekly and also cleaned the bathrooms. He didn't tell Joy he was going to do it, he just did it.

On February 15, the day after Greg's birthday, they got a call from Tim's mom. Beth had given birth that day.

"I expected Greg to call," Tim was a little disgruntled. Greg always called with his own news.

"Well, Greg's still in shock," Mom laughed happily. "They got three!"

"Three?" Tim didn't get it at first.

"Triplets?" Joy gasped delightedly.

"Triplets," Mom said firmly.

"And they didn't know?" Tim was amazed.

"No, it came as a shock to the doctor too," Mom said. "I guess because Beth wasn't having any troubles with her pregnancy, they didn't do a lot of tests in the last few months, so they didn't see the third baby."

"All boys?" Tim asked.

"Identical boys," Mom replied.

"Poor Beth," Joy moaned.

"Do they have names yet?" Tim asked.

"Greg and Beth had picked out Paul and Patrick, but that was it. I don't know what they're going to name their surprise."

"Triplets," Tim grinned at his wife after the call ended. "It would be cool to have triplets, wouldn't it?"

"Maybe," Joy said doubtfully. "But not while you're still playing football. I'll need you home for that."

"We were already planning to wait until after my first contract expires," Tim grinned. "If God tells us we're going to have triplets, I promise I'll retire early."

The following afternoon, Greg called and proudly told them about Patrick, Paul and Price.

"We heard from Mom that they're three peas in a pod," Tim snickered.

"She didn't say that!" Joy hotly denied.

It was too late. Greg howled gleefully.

"They are! I've got three Ps in a Pod!"

"Bet they keep you busier than a one-armed paperhanger," Tim cheerfully borrowed one of Mama Rey's favorite sayings

"I bet you're right," Greg sighed. "Now I almost wish I hadn't given in to Dave and Abe."

"What did they con you into?" Tim asked.

"Not exactly con," Greg reluctantly admitted. "They both strongly suggested that I become a police chaplain."

"That's a great idea!" Tim exclaimed. "So you did it already?"

"I got my credentials last week," Greg sighed, "but I don't know when I'm going to get to use them now! The Pod's probably going to make me need a chaplain!"

"It won't be so bad," Tim said confidently. "With all the family around, you'll only have to open the window and holler if you need help."

"You're right about that," Greg cheerfully acknowledged. "I guess you and Brandon won't be around until spring break. That's when we'll do the dedication, so plan on being here."

"We already were," Joy assured him.

The next day Brandon called them.

"What's this I hear about you claiming Mom dubbed the triplets 'The Pod'?" he asked suspiciously, though he didn't sound very accusing.

Tim howled with laughter.

"What have you done, Timothy?" Joy sighed sadly.

"I didn't say that," Tim snickered. "Greg may have inferred that, but I did not say that!"

"What did you say?" Brandon snickered too. That phrase was used a lot in their family.

"Just that I'd heard from Mom that he had three peas in a pod."

"Clever, Tim," Brandon chuckled. "Very clever. You know they're The Pod now, don't you?"

"I guess I should've thought about that before I told Greg that," Tim said innocently.

"You are a devious one, Timothy Shepherd," Brandon sighed in mock sorrow. "Hey, Stormy told me to invite you to dinner at their place tomorrow evening. She thinks we're all working too hard and not eating or fellowshipping enough."

"She lives two doors down from us," Tim observed rather petulantly. "Why'd she call you to ask us to her house?"

"I called her. She was planning to call you. I guess you can call her directly to pout and let her know if you're going or not."

"I don't pout," Tim said haughtily.

"Bye, Brandon," Joy said dryly. "I need to go get dinner started before it gets too deep in here."

When Joy left, Tim took the phone off speaker.

"Hey, we haven't talked for a while. How you doin'?" he asked quietly.

"I still miss her intensely," Brandon sighed. "You'd think since I've hardly seen her for the better part of a year it would be getting easier, but I still find myself wanting to call her to share something."

"Have you decided what you're going to do after graduation?"

"I'm going to Africa."

"Permanently?" Tim was shocked.

"No, just to visit Scott and Lindiwe. I'll be back by the end of July."

"And what are you doing after?"

"I'm joining The Project," Brandon said firmly.

"In St. Louis?"

"I'm not hearing anything different from God. I'll do my supervised counseling under Nalani, then in two years I'll get fully licensed."

"That's going to be tough," Tim said sadly. "From what I hear, Cari's even more deeply involved with The Project."

"That's what I hear too," Brandon sighed. "But I've got to follow God, not make my decisions based on what Cari's doing."

"You're right about that. So what time's dinner tomorrow night?"

"I didn't think to ask Stormy," Brandon laughed ruefully.

"We'll find out. How about you come by after class tomorrow and talk story? Then you can walk down with us."

"Sounds like a plan."

Chapter 13

*T*im, Joy and Brandon had a wonderful visit with the Browns. Of course they saw them regularly at church, both on Sundays and Fridays for the young adults' services, but they hadn't fellowshipped together as a family since before Tim and Joy's wedding.

Charlotte was Charles' daughter from a relationship in college, long before he became a Christian. His girlfriend had told him that she'd gotten an abortion, but last fall Charlotte had showed up on his doorstep. He hadn't needed a paternity test to know she was indeed his daughter, but Luke had advised them to get one anyway. That allowed them to amend Charlotte's birth certificate and easily change her name. She was no longer Charlotte Mahurin. She was now Charlotte Brown.

Not only did Charles now have a twenty-one year old daughter, but he and Stormy were also expecting. Stormy was six months pregnant, and glowing with health.

That evening when Joy saw Stormy's gently rounded belly, she was surprised by a tiny stab of envy. It was very small and easily suppressed. When the time was right, she and Tim would also have a baby.

"Do you know if you're having a boy or a girl yet?" Joy asked.

"Yesterday, they said he's a boy," Charles shook his head sadly. "But after what just happened to Greg and Beth, I'm afraid to trust them!"

"They do get it right more times than not, Dad," Charlotte assured him.

"You gonna name him Junior," Tim asked innocently.

Brandon jumped sideways, well out of the way of Charles' fierce glare.

"You're not even funny, Tim," Charles glared at him. Of course he'd never liked his given name – Charles Leroy Brown. There was no way he would saddle a son with either Charlie Brown or Bad, Bad Leroy Brown.

"Just a thought," Tim shrugged.

"Not much of one, Timothy," Joy scolded him.

Tim frowned. "It's odd. Before I married you, no one hardly ever called me Timothy. What's wrong with you Joy? Why you gotta use my whole name so much?"

"I can't take it," Brandon groaned. "Please tell me dinner's ready, Stormy. We need to derail this conversation quickly."

"It is," Stormy laughed happily. "I'll even let you help get it on the table."

Stormy and Charlotte had fixed lasagna with salad and garlic bread. It was delicious.

"This is the best we've eaten since classes started," Joy moaned with pleasure. "I don't have the time to fix homemade anymore."

"We still eat good," Tim defended her. "I'm not starving."

"I'm sorry dearest, but we don't eat as healthy as we should."

"You're probably right," Tim said pensively, then smiled brightly. "But we'd be a whole lot healthier if we ate Spam at least twice a month!"

"Yes, that would be a step in the right direction," Charles said sarcastically.

"I think he has a point," Brandon shrugged slightly.

"Why would anyone want that much Spam?" Charlotte was truly puzzled. "I don't think I've eaten it more than twice in my entire life."

"How could anyone be that deprived?" Tim cried in shock.

"Spam is a staple in Hawaii," Brandon informed his puzzled young friend. "Almost everyone who grew up there loves it, and those of us who lived there for a while usually develop a liking for it, if we didn't have it before we moved there."

"And you did live there?" Charlotte asked.

Brandon nodded. "For almost six years total, three years in grade school and my last three years of high school."

"So you like Spam too?"

"In many ways," Brandon nodded. "Fried and in musubi and sushi are my favorites, but as long as it doesn't come straight out of the can, I'm pretty much gonna like it."

"Spam musubi is onolicious," Tim moaned with pleasure.

"What?" Charlotte giggled.

"Onolicious," Brandon explained with a grin for his brother. "'Ono' in Hawaiian means something tastes good. 'Onolicious' is a combination of ono and delicious, so it basically means 'super delicious.'"

"Surely Aunt Gloria doesn't like it too," Charlotte suggested hesitantly.

"My mom?" Tim exclaimed then laughed loudly. "My dear cousin, how do you think I learned to like it?"

"Well, I guess if Aunt Gloria likes it I'll have to try it," Charlotte sighed. "She's super neat. But one of you guys'll have to fix it for me so it's done right."

"Not me guys!" Tim laughed.

"Unfortunately, frying Spam is the most I can do," Joy shrugged.

"Me too," Brandon grinned ruefully. "Maybe when we're home during spring break, Joy can get Mom to teach her how to make musubi and sushi."

"Whether she does or not is up to her," Tim shrugged and grinned at Charlotte. "But I can guarantee you that Mom'll send us back with plenty Spam musubi and sushi for all of us."

That was the end of that discussion, but Joy filed it away in the back of her mind. Maybe she should get some lessons from Gloria. She was a pretty good cook, so it shouldn't be too hard to learn to make some of Tim's favorite dishes from Hawaii.

Late the next week, Joy made that idea a priority. She even called Gloria and gave her a heads-up.

That came about when she went all-out for a nice Saturday night dinner at home – T-bone steak, baked potato, a vegetable medley and side salad, with French bread. Unfortunately when she put Tim's plate in front of him, he frowned at it.

"Are you ever gonna fix rice?" he complained.

Joy froze. She was crushed. She'd made the quintessential man's meal, and her husband was complaining!

"Mom always served rice at least one meal a day," Tim half growled. "When's the last time you fixed rice?"

It was probably back when she'd made the chili a month ago, but so what? How dare he compare her cooking to his mother's?

Joy's ire rose.

She stood without saying a word, wanting to count to ten but not able to remember what came after three.

When she just stood with her own plate in her hand instead of sitting so they could pray, Tim detected that something was wrong. He looked up with a frown, but his eyes immediately narrowed warily, then quickly went wide.

"Auwe! I'm so lolo!" He dropped his head and clutched his hair in both hands. "Dumb, Tim, dumb, dumb, dumb."

Joy's anger defused.

She dropped into her own chair.

"Oh, I don't know," she said casually. "If you intended to hurt my feelings or make me mad, then that was pretty smart, right on target."

"I didn't," Tim sighed. "I just really like rice. I am part Japanese, ya know."

"Yes, I do," Joy admitted. "But you're also American. I'm sorry, but I didn't realize you valued rice so highly."

"I should've said something instead of just complaining," Tim said miserably.

"Yes, you should have," Joy said calmly. "I really had no way of knowing unless you told me."

"Please forgive me," Tim raised very sad eyes.

"Of course I will, and I'll even fix rice tomorrow," Joy smiled happily, "but only if you enjoy your dinner tonight."

"I can do that!" Tim grinned, then looked down at his plate. "This looks melicious, sweetheart! Thank you for fixing a wonderful dinner."

Joy laughed. She loved her goofy husband!

JUST BEFORE SPRING break, Joy got an even bigger laugh from her increasingly goofy husband. He was done on campus by noon on Thursdays, so he'd already been home for a few hours when she pulled in. She wasn't surprised to hear music as she approached the back door. Nor was she surprised to hear Tim belting out the song, very enthusiastically and slightly off-key.

She was surprised when the door didn't open readily. Tim never locked the door after he came home, not until bedtime.

She had to root around in her bag for her key. She was tempted to grumble, but Tim sounded so cheerful that she couldn't.

As Joy stepped into the kitchen, she realized all the shades were drawn and the lights were on, even though the sun was still hours from setting. She understood why as her husband danced into view, swishing the broom across the living room floor.

His attire was intended only for her eyes!

Joy grabbed the back of a chair to hold herself up as she laughed merrily.

Tim grinned, winked and went right on dancing, sweeping and singing!

When Joy decided to join her husband, they didn't get any cleaning done.

SPRING BREAK WAS an incredible experience for Joy. Of course, she'd met Tim's family many times over the years, but she'd never seen them like this. When she'd spent time with them before, they had always come to Norman to see Tim. There she had a full life that kept her from spending more than a few hours a visit with them, and then she'd always had other friends around too. Now it was just her and the Shepherd-Wolfe Ohana, and she had no other claims to her time.

The family included quite a few people who weren't technically related, like Katie Wheeler, the nanny/tutor whom the family loved as one of their own, the Claybornes who lived at Gumbwats' Haven and helped with the training program, Dillon Washington, the old horse wrangler they'd hired but treated more like a grandfather, and Elton and Sandy Floyd, the couple who had been hired as caretakers at Halelolo after Brandon left the previous year.

The baby dedications were the first Sunday of spring break. Joy was pleased when the family was joined at the church by another couple, a very odd couple whom she had seen at her wedding but hadn't actually gotten to meet, Raul and Leiandra Guerrero. He was tallish, muscular and Hispanic; she was of European descent and average height, but that was the only thing average about her. She was very colorful, from her multicolored spiked hair to her crazy-quilted long skirt over a bright yellow petticoat. Her ears were adorned with more earrings than Joy wore in an entire week.

The Guerreros were dedicating their four month old son. From the way they greeted Brandon, it wasn't hard for Joy to figure out that they were the friends who worked for Carolyn O'Phelan, the woman who'd broken Brandon's heart.

Joy looked around and easily spotted the O'Phelan woman. She hung on the fringes of the crowd of people, looking pretty miserable. She had to love the Guerreros very much to put herself in such close proximity with Brandon. Joy was once again impressed with her brother-in-law's spiritual maturity. He neither avoided Cari O'Phelan nor sought her out. He appeared to be as peaceful and loving as he always was.

Miss O'Phelan was the only one who didn't go back to Halelolo for the party after the church service. It was joyous, with lots of laughter, fun and love.

Joy was proud of Tim when she saw him stealing a few quiet minutes with Brandon in the side yard, then she was frustrated when he picked a fight with his way-too-big brother, Greg.

With Joy, Tim, Brandon and Robert in town for just one week, all of the family who worked in St. Louis took off from work as much as possible. Since most of them worked together, they couldn't all take off at the same time, not so soon after doing it for Tim and Joy's wedding in Oklahoma, but every evening the whole crew gathered at the big estate.

By Friday, Joy was tired of watching the men's clashes. She wasn't tired of the wrestling. She was tired of watching. She picked a fight with Jenni that evening.

"Oh, puh-leeease!" In true Shepherd fashion, Joy sighed dramatically and rolled her eyes when Jenni started telling a story about something her youngest son, Caleb who was nicknamed Roast, had done that morning. "Do we have to listen to another fable about the wunderkind?"

"Excuse me, little girl," Jenni had also seen the start of many clashes. "You think you're woman enough to stop me?"

"More woman than your poor, pathetic little husband could ever handle," Joy said arrogantly.

"Excuse me?" Pete sputtered in surprise.

"Hush up, dear," Jenni waved him away with barely a glance. "I'll handle this spitting kitten."

"You?" Beth laughed aloud. "You couldn't even handle Naomi!"

"And you couldn't handle Zoe!" Rachel snorted.

With shocking ease, Joy had instigated what no one else had ever attempted, a feminine clash, even though there was way too much giggling for it to truly qualify as a clash of the titans.

As Tim watched the writhing mass of estrogen with a bemused smile, Greg propped an arm on his shoulder.

"It's interesting that after all these years of us guys wrestling, someone finally gets the girls in a clash, and it's your wife who did it!"

"And she hasn't even been a Shepherd for three months yet," Luke snickered.

"I think Mama Rey was right," Brandon grinned broadly. "She really has had you bamfloozled. You have no idea what you've gotten yourself into!"

Tim watched his wife take down both Beth and Nalani with one wide-armed flying tackle, then be smothered by Mom and Heather.

He probably didn't know what he'd gotten himself into. She'd already proven she could indeed be a fiery one. On the other hand ….

"You might be right," Tim agreed with a sly smile, "but now that she's started it, do you really think it'll end tonight?"

His married brothers groaned while Brandon roared with laughter.

Tim was tempted to tell Brandon not to laugh too loudly. His time was coming, and Cari was going to fit right in with the rest of the crazies out on the lawn. Somehow, when he'd seen Cari on Sunday, he'd known without a shadow of a doubt that she still loved Brandon. God was going to bring them together somehow.

Tim would keep praying for them. If God gave him the opportunity to bring them together again, he would gladly do it.

Chapter 14

On Saturday afternoon, Joy knew she needed to get some work done before spring break was over. Though she was only a couple months from graduating, she still had plenty to do to earn her diploma. She hid out in the library. She had discovered that during the day, if she was in her bedroom, it wasn't unusual for someone to stick their head in and visit for a while. The library however was a refuge, free from distractions. No one bothered someone who was working in the library.

Tim had told her that the family's unwritten rule about the library had been established out of respect to Greg. Because he gave many messages, he had to have a quiet place to prepare for them, even during family weekends at Halelolo. Because of his learning disability, everyone had developed a healthy respect for the solitude Greg needed to study. That fact made it a great surprise when Greg himself walked into the library and right up to the table she was working at.

"I'm not going to bother you for long," he said as he pulled out a chair and sat across from her. "But I wanted to talk to you about something, and I don't particularly want to run the risk of anyone overhearing our conversation."

"Oh?" Joy was surprised, and a bit wary.

"It's not that big a deal," Greg quickly assured her. "It's just that I don't like getting the other's all excited about something I'm still trying to figure out."

"Okay, but then why do you want to talk to me about it?" Joy was puzzled.

"Because you're the one who brought it up," Greg explained nothing.

"I don't remember bringing anything up to you," Joy shook her head. This was the first real conversation she'd ever had with her brother-in-law. Sure they had talked before, but always in a group.

"You didn't. It came to me via your dad."

"Greg, I'm clueless," Joy sighed.

"Sorry," Greg grinned and shrugged. "I was just following the flow of the conversation. I didn't want to ramble like Heather."

"How about you go ahead and ramble out an explanation of what I brought up to my dad?" Joy said wryly.

"Just before your wedding, you told your dad that you should be the one in the church waiting for Tim, not him waiting for you."

"Of course I did," Joy nodded emphatically. "I guess maybe it was because I'd just started hearing that song, 'Even So Come.' What we were doing seemed to contradict that song, which I'm pretty sure is theologically accurate even if 'like a bride waiting for her groom' isn't a direct quote from the Bible. I think the bride coming to the waiting groom in the church is a foolish custom. What's it all about anyway?"

"I'm not sure either," Greg shrugged. "I never even thought about it until your dad told me what you said. I'm sorry to say that I didn't look into it until earlier this week when you and Tim got here. That reminded me of what your dad had said. I haven't done much checking into it this week."

"That's understandable," Joy smiled slightly.

"Yeah, but I do want to study it. You wanna study it with?" Greg asked.

"Yeah, but when?" Joy frowned slightly.

"I was thinking after you and Tim graduate," Greg said. "By that time we'll have a better routine with the Pod, and you'll have more time too."

"That sounds good," Joy nodded.

"Okay then," Greg pushed his chair back. "I'll let you get back to your work."

He turned and left the library, leaving Joylynne rather bemused.

She had no idea that her father had remembered her rather offhand but very sincere comment, and she would have never guessed that he would have thought it significant enough to talk to Greg about it. She hadn't even thought about it herself since the wedding, though she was pretty sure that she would never be able to go to a wedding again without thinking about it.

Now she was thinking about it, wondering if she had a valid point or not. Greg's conversation had left her hanging.

But she really didn't have the time to think about it now. She had to set it aside and get to the more urgent work that was before her.

She was glad that Derek and Kendra weren't engaged yet. They wouldn't get married before sometime this summer. That gave her and Greg plenty of time to look into her concerns and pass them on if they were valid.

She firmly pushed the thought aside and turned back to the home design she was working on.

MEANWHILE BACK IN Oklahoma, someone else had travelled east. On Friday, Derek O'Phelan arrived in Norman, just in time to attend the young adults' service that evening at Living Stones. He wasn't surprised that Brandon wasn't there. He'd known his friend was going to St. Louis for the week. He'd come to see someone else.

Kendra was very happy to see Derek. They talked a lot on the phone and texted many times a day, but they hadn't seen each other since the Sunday after Joylynne and Tim's wedding when Derek had headed back to New Mexico. She wasn't worried that Tim wasn't there to make sure they got some time together. It had been a long time since she'd needed his help, though without his initial nudge, she might have missed out on Derek entirely.

Of course Tim hadn't been there when Derek first joined the young adults of Living Stones. Tim had been down on the field when Brandon had brought his childhood friend to join the others in the stands. It was Sunday morning before church when Tim met Derek.

His brain must have been on overdrive during the service. Afterwards they were standing with Joy, Sally, Reylene and Matt in the multipurpose room discussing the message when suddenly Tim looked right at Kendra.

"That friend of Brandon's seems pretty cool, doesn't he?" Tim asked her.

Kendra had glanced over at Derek and Brandon who were laughing with Pastor Charles about something.

"Seems?" she asked. "You don't know him?"

"I know of him," Tim shrugged. "Him and Brandon were classmates, but that was way before we met the Wolfes. But I've heard about Derek, from Brandon, Rachel and Cari, Derek's sister."

"He's Brandon's girlfriend's brother?" Kendra had been intrigued. It hadn't taken long for the intrigue to grow to infatuation.

That infatuation could have died an early death when Carolyn O'Phelan broke up with Brandon. Kendra loved Brandon like a brother and she hated to see him hurting. She was tempted to give Derek guilt by association with his sister, but when he was even more deeply upset about the break up than she was, Kendra's infatuation had soared into love. She now gladly spent every minute she could with Derek Gutherie O'Phelan.

The last day of spring break, Derek asked Kendra if she would like to go riding. She expected him to take her out to the Vogt ranch, but he drove right past it. About ten minutes later, he turned down a little-used private drive. A few minutes after that, they emerged from a tree line. In the small clearing sat a pickup truck and horse trailer. Grazing next to the trailer were two saddled horses. An old wrangler was lying in a portable hammock with his hat tilted over his eyes.

"This is where we're riding?" Kendra looked around curiously. Over the years she'd often ridden at the Vogt farm, but rarely anywhere else. She would enjoy covering new territory.

Cover territory they did. Derek set a brisk pace for the horses. Obviously he had a specific destination in mind. Though they rode through many beautiful acres of meadow, field and woodlands, for over half an hour they didn't stop.

They crossed a broad, mostly dry creek bed, passed through a narrow strip of heavy woods and climbed a rather tall lightly wooded hill. Derek stopped in a large meadow about a hundred feet below the crest. They turned the horses to face back the way they'd come.

It was a beautiful vista, even with most of the trees still winter-bare. The hill was high enough to look out at smaller hills rolling in the distance. A few fields were spread below the hill they were on, separated by small creeks and gullies and a few tree lines.

"It's beautiful," Kendra breathed deeply of the fresh spring air. She was glad she didn't have allergies. Sally would have been sneezing her head off.

"It's for sale," Derek said softly.

Kendra's heart began to pound. She was afraid to look at her companion.

"Oh," she simply said.

"There used to be a house down on the creek, but that was years ago, when the current owner still lived here. He's been in a nursing home for almost ten years. He couldn't come home because his house burned down when he wandered outside without shutting off the stove. His grandkids don't want the ranch. They're looking to sell."

"This would be a beautiful spot for a house," Kendra suggested. "With a south face and a nice windbreak on the north, it'll be cozy even in the winter."

Derek suddenly dismounted. He dropped the reins and stepped over to Kendra's horse, offering his arms to help her dismount.

She didn't need the help but she accepted it anyway.

"I want to buy this ranch," Derek told Kendra when they were standing face to face. "Do you think it'd be a good place for a man to build a home for a bride?"

"I think it would be perfect," she said a trifle breathlessly.

"Do you think you'd like to help this man plan that house?"

"I would love to!"

"I'm not asking you to be that bride, not yet," Derek cautioned her. "You still need to finish college, but do you think you'd like for me to take you out for a special graduation dinner?"

"I think that's an excellent idea," Kendra didn't want to wait two months, but it was probably wise to do so.

"It'll take about a month to close on this place," Derek gently touched her cheek then dropped his hand. "Do you think you'd like to find a few spare hours to help an architect start drafting plans so we can break ground as soon as we close?"

"It depends on the architect," Kendra playfully scrunched her nose. They both knew they would work with Joy who was interning at a firm in town.

"I'd really like to move in at the end of the summer, early fall at the latest," Derek stepped back slightly. He needed a little space or he would start kissing Kendra. That wasn't wise out here with no one to chaperone them.

"That's such a long way away," Kendra sighed.

"Not so long," Derek shrugged. "I've got a lot to do between now and then. It's not easy to transfer ranching operations from one state to another."

"Why would you do that?" Kendra asked with a curious tilt of her head.

"I moved to New Mexico because that's where my father's family was from. Turns out the little bit of family I do have left out there aren't that friendly to my mother's progeny."

"Why not?" Kendra frowned.

"I guess my father was supposed to marry someone else," Derek shrugged. "Then when he started having mental problems, they blamed it on Mom."

"So I guess you have no reason to stay in New Mexico," Kendra smiled shyly.

"And very good reasons to move east," Derek shrugged playfully. "With Reed just up in Kansas City and my sisters a few hours farther east, Norman is close enough to see each other more often but not too close to get on each other's nerves."

"I guess that's as good a reason as any to move east," Kendra smiled brightly.

"Right now we should be heading west," Derek made a step for her with his hands. "I need to get you back to Norman."

Kendra couldn't argue with that, so she again accepted Derek's unnecessary help.

Chapter 15

*W*hen Kendra told her friend about Derek's request, Joylynne was delighted to help her, even though she had more than a full plate. During spring break, her in-laws had shown her the lot down at Gumbwats' Haven where Tim's house would be built, and they'd asked her if she wanted to design it since it would be hers too. Of course she did!

If the house was going to be ready for them when football season ended next winter, they would have to break ground in the spring, about the same time Derek's house would need to be started. So Joy had two houses to design, plus a full load at college. She'd worked hard to finish a five-year program in four years, going more than full time most semesters and taking summer classes. It was hard work, but it would be worth it. By the time Tim fulfilled his first professional football contract, Joy would have finished her internship and gotten her license. She would be ready to open her own architectural firm, so they would have excellent options to consider when it was time to decide whether to renew his contract or not.

Of course, Tim needed to be drafted first. That was coming up in April, a month after spring break. In that time, they were both busy. Fortunately, Joy didn't have to fix many meals. After their dinner with the Browns in February, Stormy invited them to share a meal at least once a week. Joy's parents had them over as often, and Mama Rey insisted that they share both dinner and supper on Sundays, and she didn't even mind if Joy and Tim did homework or took a break and went riding between the meals.

Time flew for the newlyweds. The draft loomed larger and larger on the horizon.

Two days before it, Tim's parents called with the news that Tim's cousin had given birth to a boy, Calan Brian Garrison.

"Brian and Will are as bad as my sibs," Tim laughingly told Joy. "Maybe even worse."

"About what?" Joy asked with a small frown. How was having a baby bad?

"Well, their daughters were born two days apart almost three years ago. Now Liam's just over five months younger than Wayland."

"That is taking togetherness to the max," Joy agreed, "but it's pretty cool. Do you think Robert'll get married in time to have his babies with ours?"

"I sure hope so but I don't know," Tim sighed and shrugged. "He's pretty closed-mouth about his love life."

"I wonder why?" Joy asked wryly.

Tim laughed. His family did tease quite a bit, but it was never hateful or hurtful. In fact, when it came to love, they were much more likely to be exceptionally helpful.

TIM WAS EXTREMELY nervous on the day of the draft. He really wanted to be picked in the first round, not because of the prestige, but because waiting these last few months had been agonizing enough. The sooner his name was called, the sooner his anxiety would end.

The pundits were right. Timothy Shepherd's was indeed the first name called. He was drafted by Tennessee. It wasn't the Grizzlies, but at least it was only a few hours from his family in St. Louis.

His whole family celebrated with him, even though they picked on him about going to the wrong team.

Tim and Joy's life had been busy, now it became almost hectic. They would graduate in a little more than a month and have one week before Tim had to report to training camp that would consume much of his time, and leave him exhausted when he was home. Not only did they need to finish their classwork, but now they also needed to find a home somewhere around Nashville.

Fortunately, Tim's parents were more than happy to help them by scouting for apartments. Tim and Joy might eventually get a house in Tennessee, but they would be happy to start with an apartment.

The last weekend of April, Tim and Joy made a whirlwind trip to Nashville where they looked at three places that Joshua and Gloria had found for them. They rented a beautiful third story loft in Franklin, Tennessee. Most of their shopping for furniture they did online. Tim's sisters decided to do a sisters-night-off the middle of the week after Mothers' Day and spend it in Franklin, so Tim and Joy scheduled all the deliveries for those two days. By graduation day, the third Saturday in May, their new home would be ready.

Andrew Raymond Brown obliged his cousins by coming two days after Mothers' Day, so Tim and Joy got to enjoy him before leaving Oklahoma.

Graduation weekend was a bittersweet time, especially for Joy. She would be leaving home, the only home she'd ever known. It would be years before she lived in Oklahoma again, if ever. She was leaving her parents, brothers, grandparents and a host of cousins and friends whom she truly loved.

She wouldn't know anyone in Franklin, Tennessee. Once Tim started training camp, she would be utterly alone for the first time in her life. It was both exciting and scary.

But there were a lot of things going on before that happened.

Since Brandon was going to Africa after Fathers' Day and returning in late July, he decided to minimize his time in St. Louis before his trip, so he was staying in Norman until the first week of June. Robert decided that he would stay with Brandon in Oklahoma and travel east with his big brother. Since Tim had a week before reporting for training camp, he and Joy would stay a few extra days too. They would head east on the Wednesday after graduation.

On Sunday morning, Kendra showed up at Living Stones with a beautiful diamond solitaire on her left hand. To say that everyone was happy for her and Derek was quite an understatement.

As the women crowded around Kendra in the multipurpose room after services, the men offered more subdued but equally as fervent congratulations to Derek.

Since Derek was staying with Brandon as usual, Brandon hung back because he'd already given his congratulations. Of course Derek had told him last night that Kendra had said yes, no surprise there.

Though Brandon was happy for his friends, he still felt regret for what might have been if he'd handled things with Cari differently. Tim knew him well enough to detect his pensiveness, so he sidled up to his brother while everyone's attention was still on the happy couple.

"You're next," Tim whispered in Brandon's ear.

"Sorry, kimosabe, but that'll defy even your matchmaking capabilities," Brandon said sadly.

"Don't bet against me," Tim said slyly.

"I usually don't," Brandon snorted. "But there's no way I'm betting on you this time."

"We'll see," Tim grinned. His mind was already plotting how he could make it happen.

Sally gave him a great idea when she decided that she was going to plan an engagement party for Derek and Kendra on the first Saturday of June. Since they agreed, Tim made two phone calls, the first to his dad asking if he could fly Tim and Joy back to Norman for that weekend. Since Joshua didn't have anything else planned, he was happy to oblige.

That would get Tim in Norman to watch his plan come to fruition, but the second call was the one the plan hinged on.

"Hi Tim," Rachel greeted him cheerfully. "How does it feel to be a graduate?"

"Not very different," Tim confessed. "At least not for me. It's kind of anticlimactic after the draft in April."

"I guess I can understand that."

"You're a pretty smart person, so that doesn't surprise me."

"I know I am, but you don't usually admit it," Rachel said warily. "What do you want?"

"I got a favor to ask you."

"What kind?" Rachel sighed glumly.

"You don't mind lying a little, do you, Tink?" Tim asked slyly.

"For a good cause, I might," she said warily. "How big a lie, and for what cause?"

"The cause is to get Brandon and Cari to both come to Derek's engagement party."

"I'll tell a big lie for that!"

"No need," Tim laughed. "Just a lie of omission will do it, I bet."

"What lie?" Rachel asked eagerly.

"Tell Cari that Brandon's going to Africa in June."

"But that's not a lie?" Rachel was puzzled. "He is going to Africa next month."

"Ah, but you need to avoid telling her what day he's leaving," Tim said with too earnest innocence. "Derek and Kendra's engagement party is the first Saturday of June."

"But Brandon isn't leaving until the Tuesday after Fathers' Day." Even over the long-distance connection Tim could hear the bounce in Rachel's voice. "But if Cari thinks he's not going to be in Norman, she'll go! Brilliant, Tim!"

"I know," Tim agreed humbly.

"Let's keep this to ourselves," Rachel suggested. "The fewer people who know, the less likely the word will leak."

"But what if someone from the fam spills the beans to Cari?"

"They won't," Rachel sighed sadly. "It's just over two weeks away. Cari avoids just about everyone from the family except me, unless she has to see them about the ministry. Then she won't talk personal stuff with them."

"Then yeah, let's keep this on the DL," Tim agreed. "That way, in the off chance that this doesn't work, no one else'll be disappointed."

Chapter 16

After Rachel talked to Tim, she added a detail that ensured that only the two of them would be in on the plot. She convinced Cari to surprise her brother. If Derek didn't know Cari was coming to his engagement party, he couldn't tell Brandon, nor would he tell Cari that Brandon would still be in Norman until the Wednesday after the party.

Rachel passed Cari's travel plans on to Tim. She was flying into Oklahoma City in the early afternoon and renting a car. She would be arriving in Norman sometime between two-thirty and three.

Tim hadn't been released from practice until late Friday night, so Joy, Tim and his parents didn't arrive until nearly lunchtime on Saturday. Sally conveniently drafted the women to help with party prep, so Tim was free to take Derek, Brandon and Robert out riding on the Vogt farm that afternoon. He also managed to palm Brandon's cell phone and turn it off without him knowing. He didn't want any of the women to call Brandon with the news when Cari showed up. He wasn't worried that someone would call Derek because Rachel had told him that Cari was surprising her brother. No one would want to spoil the surprise.

The men had fun on their ride, and of course they were late getting back. The party was in the Living Stones multipurpose room and was supposed to start at six-thirty. They turned onto Baldwin Avenue at six-twenty-nine.

Tim intended to get inside before Brandon because he wanted to see all the action. However Brandon was driving, and he was annoyed with the other men.

For some odd reason, Derek had decided to tell Brandon's younger brothers about a rather embarrassing incident their freshman year of high school when Brandon had tried to prove his physical skill and ended up giving himself a black eye and a mild concussion.

Tim and Robert of course found the story highly amusing. Brandon was more annoyed by their amusement than by the story itself. Little brothers could be more infuriating than anyone else on the planet.

As Brandon parked in front of Living Stones, he directed a particularly disdainful sneer at the rearview mirror.

"At least I left juvenile antics behind when I graduated high school, unlike the little sheep bleating in the backseat."

Those were fighting words! Unfortunately for the Shepherd men, Brandon's finger was already on the lock button of his remote before they even reached for their door handles. He locked their doors after his was open.

Brandon stalked quickly to the building, knowing that if he made it inside, his parents would stop any punishment his brothers decided to inflict. He was already reaching for the church's front door when his brothers finally popped out of the car. He glimpsed them running toward him, with a highly amused Derek trailing behind them.

Brandon walked quickly down the hall. He heard the outside door open as he turned toward the sounds of a party.

He stopped in shock, blocking the door to the multipurpose room. He hadn't even thought about the possibility that Cari O'Phelan would be here! Why hadn't he asked?

Because it had never crossed his mind that she would come to Kendra's engagement party. That was logical because Cari didn't know Kendra, but foolish because Kendra was marrying Cari's brother!

Brandon hadn't thought about Cari coming because in the year that he'd been in Oklahoma, she hadn't visited said brother even once. Since he also knew that she welcomed Derek every time he went east, Brandon had assumed she didn't want to be anywhere close to where he was so she would stay in Missouri, only venturing to Norman for the wedding which she would have to attend, of course.

That wasn't until the end of the summer, so Brandon hadn't decided what he was going to do when he did have to see Cari in a setting that she wouldn't be able to run away from like she had the baby dedication in March.

He needed to decide what he was going to do right now because there she was, coming out of the kitchen of Living Stones Fellowship, and she looked as startled to see him as he was to see her.

Suddenly something hit Brandon from behind. He staggered. Before he could recover, something else collided with him and the parasite that had already latched onto him. He was falling, buried under an avalanche of very long legs and arms.

Brandon forcefully drove his elbow back and heard Tim grunt in pain. At the same time, Tim must have gotten Robert somehow because Brandon heard his youngest brother hiss, "Jerk!"

Brandon swung a booted foot and connected with something at the same time someone put a fist in his side. He was trying to squirm out from under his younger brothers and make some solid connections with fist or foot when a voice scolded from above.

"Boys," Dad sighed sadly, "can't you behave, at least in church?"

Suddenly Brandon was free. He jumped to his feet and straightened his clothes as his brothers also rose.

"They started it," Brandon said with wounded dignity. "I was just standing there minding my own business."

"Standing in the middle of the doorway," Tim growled.

"And you were running in the church," Brandon growled back.

"Could you please grow up?" Mom stood beside Dad, sadly shaking her head.

"Tim should because he's an old married man," Brandon shrugged, "but why should Robert and I grow up?"

"Bet you're married soon too," Robert whispered in Brandon's ear. Obviously he'd also noticed that Cari was here.

Brandon chanced his parents' wrath. He drove his elbow back into Robert's gut.

"I'll take you outside, little man," Robert growled.

"You'll regret it if you do," Brandon said calmly, smiling innocently at Dad who was frowning deeply.

"You're old enough to be a bit more mature, Brandon," Dad scolded. "Even if you aren't going to get married."

"I am more mature than the meese," Brandon said cheerfully.

"The meese?" Kendra giggled from the side. "What's that supposed to mean?"

"Meese are creatures with the size of a moose but the attitude of a scared little mouse," Brandon gladly explained, facing his friend but keeping one eye on his younger brothers.

"I'll show you a meese!" Tim growled.

Robert just swung a punch.

It never landed. Brandon dropped and rolled away from the punch, coming up facing Robert, easily balanced on the balls of his feet. Tim and Robert both looked ready to swing punches so Brandon brought his hands up in front of him, ready to fight.

Except he came up too close to Dad. Joshua's arms wrapped around him. Fortunately Derek, Charles, Russell and Matt were forming a wall in front of Tim and Robert. Brandon hoped it effectively kept them from getting to him. He wouldn't confess it, but he ached after that recent tussle. A thirty year old man probably shouldn't be fighting with guys who were barely in their twenties.

"I'm glad we're sending him back to St. Louis," Charles looked sadly at Gloria. "I thought maturity in Christ was supposed to mellow you. Brandon's corrupting my church."

"Hah!" Brandon snorted defensively as he broke free from Dad's arms and glared at his younger brothers.

"Haven't you met my son Greg?" Gloria looked at Charles with a plaintive sigh. "They're too much alike, I fear."

"I am nothing like the oaf," Brandon said with an aggrieved air, so perfectly in imitation of Joshua that everyone roared with laughter, except Joshua who stared mournfully at his son.

"*That* we are not going to debate," Derek spoke loudly and quickly. "Can we get everyone in the multipurpose room so we can have dinner?"

Brandon turned and marched further into the room, his head held high but his heart quivering like a little boy. What was he going to do about Cari? She'd already firmly rejected him six months ago, but he now knew without a doubt that he still loved her. Was he supposed to open himself up to more hurt, or should he lay low and wait to see if she came to him?

After the prayer, the buffet line quickly formed behind Kendra and Derek. Brandon watched the room for a while, debating whether he should join the line or find a table and wait for the crowd to diminish some.

He didn't actually want to eat. What he needed was fresh air and quiet time with God.

He turned and left the building.

CARI SAW BRANDON leave. She wanted to run after him, but she was scared. She hadn't come here prepared to see him again. Rachel had said he was in Africa this month, so she'd thought it would be safe to come to her brother's engagement party in Norman.

She should have asked Rachel about the specific dates Brandon would be gone. Now that she knew that Brandon was very good friends with her brothers and sister, she should have assumed that he wouldn't want to miss Derek's engagement party. Why hadn't she asked more questions?

"You should go to him," a voice interrupted Cari's private debate.

She turned to face Joylynne, Tim's wife.

"Why?" she asked.

"Because he still loves you," Joylynne shrugged slightly. "I'm not sure why, but my parents-in-law assure me that you are indeed a good woman. But you made some very bad decisions that deeply affected my brother-in-law. You need to do some damage control."

"You assume I still love Brandon," Cari said rather coldly. She didn't think Joylynne Shepherd knew her well enough to be calling her on her past mistakes.

"I don't know if you do or not," Joylynne stared at her, "but I strongly suspect you do. Regardless, you need to either calmly, rationally and in a God-honoring way tell Brandon that you have indeed moved on, or you need to let him back in your life. Go to him, now."

Cari didn't have to decide if she wanted to argue because Joylynne quickly turned and sailed off to join her husband.

Tim smiled with pure pleasure as he wrapped his arm around his wife who gazed adoringly up at him.

Cari watched them for a moment. Her stab of envy of them and longing for Brandon settled any debate.

She left the multipurpose room by the same door Brandon had.

Chapter 17

*B*randon was sitting on the tailgate of his pickup truck, head hanging, feet dangling. He was trying to pray, but his thoughts kept running in circles, back to Cari, standing in the multipurpose room staring at him in shock.

"I didn't know you would be here," a soft voice made his heart jump.

"I bet Rachel told you I was in Africa," he didn't raise his head.

"I should've asked for clarification," Cari said wryly.

Brandon raised his left hand and massaged his forehead, trying to hide the fact that his heart had just shattered into a million pieces, again. How many times could a heart break and still be put back together?

"I'm sorry. I'm going in a couple weeks. Maybe I'll stay there until after the wedding, watch the keiki for Scott and Lindiwe while they come to the wedding." He hadn't yet assumed responsibilities at The Ohana Project. They'd waited years for him to join them, another couple months wouldn't matter much.

"No! Please," Cari stepped closer. "That wasn't what I meant. I didn't mean that I didn't want to see you. I did. I do. But I wasn't prepared. I don't know what to say or how to say it."

"Welcome to the club, Princess," Brandon laughed bitterly. Just because she wanted to talk to him didn't mean she had anything to say that he wanted to hear.

"I'm sorry, Brandon," Cari was close enough that he could see her tightly clasped hands. He refused to raise his head and see her still beloved face. "I was wrong about so many things. I judged you wrongly."

"No, you didn't," Brandon denied firmly. "I was arrogant, opinionated and judgmental. There was no wrong judging on your part."

"Oh yes there was," Cari asserted, equally as firm. "In spite of the fact that you were a deeply wounded man, you were a warm-hearted and faithful friend. You were seeking to grow even before you realized how much you needed to."

Brandon still couldn't look at her. He also didn't trust his voice anymore, so he mutely shook his head, refusing to entertain the hope that was trying to poke up its head.

"After you walked away from me last December, Sebastian was so angry with me," Cari said sadly. "He told me I'd misjudged you and treated you unfairly."

Brandon's heart once again plummeted. Obviously she needed to seek his forgiveness before she could move on with her new love.

"I was absorbed in my own self-pity and came face to face with the evidence that you had loved Papa better than I had." Brandon shook his head. Cari plowed on anyway. "Oh yes you did. How many hours did you spend with him, letting that dear old man remember his Gilly, helping him keep her alive? I never spent more than just a few minutes at a time with him in the conservatory."

Brandon frowned. Cari didn't let him speak.

"Don't say something inane like you didn't hurt as much over the loss of Grammy Gilly. Rachel pointed out what I didn't try to understand before. Grammy Gilly was the only real mother you had growing up. I was much more blessed in that respect. My mother was a good mother, in spite of her faults, and then I had Mama Eugenia, Derek and Reed's mom, and of course Grammy Gilly. Most of my life I had a wonderful, loving mother-figure. You had Grammy Gilly for three years, then nothing until you got your mom five years ago. You went ahead and faced reminders of your greater loss because you had such great love for your Mr. Boo."

Brandon shook his head again, so Cari pressed on.

"You love so much and so well. I know you loved me way back in high school. Your dad told me about your suspension. But Rachel also helped me understand why you were so protective of her."

"My family talks too much," Brandon said with bitter irony. They'd been very tight-lipped when he was trying to figure out what he was missing with Cari.

"Would you quit trying to talk me out of loving you!" Cari stomped her foot, her fists planted on her hips.

Brandon's head snapped up and he stared at her.

"I tried to quit loving you," Cari confessed sadly. "I really did, but it didn't work. And it wasn't just because everyone kept telling me how wonderful you are. When you walked away from me after Papa's funeral, the smallest but truest part of my heart was telling me I was wrong."

Once again Brandon couldn't trust his voice so he just continued to stare at Cari.

"When Sebastian told me that he wasn't romantically interested in me, and he never would be, he just wanted to work with me and be my friend, it didn't hurt. At least not the part about no romantic feelings for me. What hurt was that I knew he was dead right when he said that I'd used him to hurt you."

Brandon frowned.

"I'm so sorry, but I was so angry at you. I didn't understand how you could be so strong and true. No matter how many times I ran away from you, you stood firm. You didn't turn me away when I came back. But you also didn't seem to be hurting either. I had hurt over you for fifteen years and you never felt a minute of pain over me. I wanted you to hurt like I had hurt."

"I hurt, Princess, a lot," Brandon finally found his voice.

"I know that now," Cari nodded with tears in her eyes. "I knew it when you left after Fathers' Day last year, but in my hurt, I convinced myself that you weren't hurting."

"I'm so sorry," Brandon hung his head again.

"Stop that!" Cari was so mad that she did the only thing that made any sense, that would get through his thick skull.

She punched him. Hard. Right on the jaw.

Brandon's head snapped back, half in shock, half because Cari really packed a wallop.

"What the heck?" he jerked his head back down and glared at her.

"Don't you ever again apologize for doing what God told you to do!" Cari snapped, shaking her small fist at him. "There's more where that came from!"

Brandon rubbed his jaw and frowned. He didn't say anything because he wasn't sure what he could safely say.

"You were right to leave, to come here to Norman," Cari insisted. "And you've made very good use of your time. I didn't for the first six months. I just sat around feeling sorry for myself. But after Papa died and Sebastian confronted me, I really started looking at myself. I realized that I hadn't just hidden from you, I'd been hiding from myself too. From the day Dad died, I'd been living the life I thought I should be living, taking care of everyone else and ignoring the hurt that was building up in me."

Cari sighed and hung her head. "I made such a mess of my life. Even Raul and Lei are mad at me. He's especially mad because he's lost the best friend he's ever had. Oh, I know you email and call all the time, but it's not the same as being there. And I don't even know how to fix my mess because I don't know how to show you that I've changed for real. You're here and I'm there, and I saw way back in December that you'd changed but how will you ever be able to trust that I have?"

"You hit me," Brandon said in bewilderment.

"I'm sorry. I shouldn't have," Cari said sadly. "But it was the first thing that came to mind to really get your attention."

"You hit me, Princess," Brandon said in amazement.

"Will you forgive me, please?" Cari looked up through her lashes.

She saw that Brandon's eyes were wide with wonder and her heart stopped. He slowly smiled, and her heart began to gallop wildly.

"Forgive, yes," he nodded, then shook his head with a none-too-serious frown. "Forget, not a chance."

"Meanie head," Cari whispered through tears. They were hopeful tears. Brandon was looking at her like he had before she'd driven him away.

"I'm a little confused, Princess," Brandon said warily. "I thought you were trying to say that you love me, but then you hit me."

"Of course I love you," Cari nodded.

"If I confess that I still love you," Brandon was still wary, "are you going to hit me again?"

"If that's what you want," Cari shrugged with highly believable bewilderment.

"What I want," Brandon choked back a laugh, "is for you to kiss me."

"Okay," Cari stepped toward him eagerly.

Brandon threw up a hand to block her, and for good measure leaned back, way back.

"But you won't," he quickly said.

"Why not?" she sighed heavily.

"I spent six months helping my brother keep his passions at bay before his wedding," Brandon said sternly. "I'm not going to throw caution to the wind for myself and let you kiss me before our wedding day."

"When's that going to be?" Cari asked plaintively.

"When would be a wise time?" Brandon asked with a shrug.

"When are you going to Africa?"

"The Tuesday after Fathers' Day."

"Then wisdom says the Saturday before that," Cari said firmly.

"Oh really!" Brandon's eyebrow shot up. "That's in two weeks."

"You're right. That is a long time from now," Cari frowned thoughtfully. "Next week would be better."

"That's not what I meant, Princess," Brandon said wryly. "I was thinking it was a little quick."

"Not really. We don't need a long engagement, Marine. We're not going to get to know each other any better before we're married. While we both have some growing up to do, if we wait for that we'll never get married because you've got all those crazy family members who have to grow up before it's your turn. We can grow together, and we will grow together because we both love God more than we love each other."

"You're sure of that, Princess?" Brandon asked with a slight smile.

"I am," she nodded. "I saw it in you six months ago. That was one of the things that made me mad. I saw that you were going to live a good life, serve God, with or without me."

"What about you?" Brandon idly pulled on one of her curls.

"If you tell me there is no us anymore, I'll be very sad, but I'll wish you happiness, and mean it," she tilted up her chin with a sad smile.

"Two weeks it is then," Brandon dropped his hand with a shrug.

"Does that mean we're engaged?" Cari asked with a brilliant smile.

"I don't have a ring for you."

"Actually, you do!" Cari smiled brightly and pulled out the chain that was nestled under her blouse. "Or at least I do for you to give me. It was my mother's. Dad kept it all those years we lived on the street. It was such a testament to his enduring love that I've worn it ever since Grammy Gilly gave me a chain for it."

"They were kind of star-crossed lovers," Brandon arched an eyebrow though he took the ring and studied it. "You sure you want to mark our love with a symbol of theirs?"

"Absolutely," Cari nodded. "It'll always remind me that love isn't enough. Mom and Dad both were believers, but they didn't choose to live for God. That's why their life was miserable. I fully intend to live every day for God, not for you."

"Maybe I should have your dad's ring to remind me too," Brandon smiled wryly.

"You can if you want," Cari declared cheerfully. "I've got both their wedding bands back in St. Louis."

"You make me kind of superfluous to this process, Princess," Brandon frowned.

"Oh no! You're the most important part," Cari assured him with wide-eyed innocence. "I've had those rings for nearly twenty years now, and I've never been engaged before."

"Then if I ask if you'll marry me …."

"I'll say yes, and I'll be engaged to you," Cari smiled brightly. "Did you?"

"I guess so," Brandon said hoarsely. That smile was messing with him something fierce.

He held the ring out.

"Then we're engaged!" Cari slipped the ring on her finger. "Should we go in and let everyone know?"

"No," Brandon frowned. "This is Derek's day. I'm not going to steal his thunder!"

"Steal his –" Cari reached in her pocket, muttering to herself as she turned away. "Steal his thunder! We'll see about that!"

"What are you doing?" Brandon jumped off the tailgate.

"Calling Derek," Cari looked over her shoulder with an impudent grin.

"You are not!" Brandon reached over her, trying to get her phone.

He was way too late. Cari had her brother on speed dial, so he was already answering his phone.

What's up, Sis? Where are you?

"Outside, with Brandon."

Oh you are!

"Yeah," she sighed heavily. "He just proposed, but he doesn't want to go back inside."

Why not!?

"Because this is your day and he doesn't want to steal your thunder."

What the heck! You're kidding, right?

"No," she said sweetly. "I would let you talk to him, but he's walking away right now."

Brandon certainly was. His head was hanging and he was moaning softly.

"What have I gotten into, Lord? The woman's going to drive me crazy. But I guess that's nothing new, really. She's been doing it for half my life anyway."

Brandon suddenly realized that people were pouring from the church.

He also realized that he was going to cry. God had given him his heart's desire, and he was going to blubber like a baby.

As the first tear fell, Cari was in his arms. Then Mom and Dad were putting their arms around both of them.

"Praise God!" Tim shouted joyously. "I'm three for three, baby!"

Brandon felt a laugh bubbling in him. Tim certainly was. First Al and Nita, then Derek and Kendra, now him and Cari.

The punk was going to be insufferable, but Brandon would happily live with it.

Chapter 18

*T*im's plan had worked perfectly, but it came with an unexpected troublesome side effect. Brandon asked him to be best man, and Tim wasn't sure he could pull it off.

The first week of training camp had been very intense, with increasingly long days. The second week had truly been "camp." They'd stayed overnight Monday through Thursday, being released very late on Friday. Before he released them, Coach had warned them to not expect another Saturday off, not until the Fourth of July weekend. Tim wasn't sure if that meant working all day but going home in the evening or if they should expect to be there until midnight.

He didn't know Coach well enough to hazard a guess, but he didn't want to ask for clarification. He was afraid it would sound like he was asking for a favor. He didn't want a favor. He didn't want to seem full of himself, expecting special treatment because he just happened to have been the first round draft pick.

Tim told Brandon that he would try to make it, but that was the best he could do. When he explained his predicament, Brandon understood. He asked Dave to be his backup, just in case. Dave didn't have a problem with it.

It was early the week of the wedding before Tim finally worked up the nerve to talk to Coach. He had to do it. The previous Saturday they hadn't been released until four o'clock in the afternoon. The wedding was at six in St. Louis. Even if Dad was standing by with the plane running, they wouldn't make it to the church on time if Coach released them that late.

"Can I talk to you a minute, Coach?" Tim asked as they were breaking for lunch on Tuesday.

"What you need, Shepherd?" Coach growled.

Tim wasn't bothered by the growl. Coach did that a lot, but he was rarely serious. It was mostly for effect.

"Just info, Coach," Tim said firmly. "I'm not asking for a favor. I just need to know."

"Know what?" Coach stopped walking and carefully scrutinized Tim.

"If you don't know, that's okay too. I just need to tell my family something."

"What do you want to know, Shepherd?"

"Do you know what your plans are for Saturday? Not what we're doing. I don't really care about that, but when we're getting released, or if we're even getting released."

"Why do you need to know?" Coach was curious. He knew more about Shepherd than the young man suspected. Before Tennessee's scouts had even looked at him, Coach had known about his connection to Jeremiah and Kalaau. He knew they were all dedicated Christians. Faith and family were very important to them. Coach also knew they weren't strangers to hard work. Shepherd would never try to get out of something he didn't want to do, nor would he ask for favors. That meant there had to be something he really wanted to do for his family or his church. Either was okay. It was good for a man to have a passion other than football. Coach believed that made them better players.

"My brother's getting married on Saturday evening, in St. Louis," Tim explained diffidently. He didn't want to beg like Oliver asking for "some more." Of course he wanted to go to the wedding and be the best man, but whichever way God let it go, he would be content. "I'd really like to let him know if I'm going to be able to make it or not."

Coach stared at the young man standing humbly before him. That was a very good reason to want to have the night off, maybe even two, but he wasn't going to tell Shepherd that.

"Don't plan on making a flight before two," Coach grumbled and stomped off.

Tim was happy with that, and so was Brandon.

Friday just after noon they were even happier. Coach had gotten increasingly irritable throughout the week. Even the returning players were getting on his nerves.

"Y'all are as bad as a bunch of teenagers! Get out of my face!"

Everyone stared warily at him.

"I mean it. I gotta go see my dad and apologize for everything I ever put him through. I'm going home tonight."

Now everyone looked around as if trying to determine if they'd heard Coach right.

"But you all better love on your wife and kids if you got 'em. Give your dads honor, even if they don't deserve it. It doesn't matter if he appreciates it either 'cause you'll be a better man for doing it."

Still no one moved.

"Go!" Coach waved toward the door. "Enjoy your Fathers' Day 'cause it's gonna be the last day you see your family for a long time. You better come prepared to stay 'til the Fourth."

Now that the other shoe had dropped, everyone bolted for the doors

Tim never asked if he had anything to do with that decision, and Coach never confessed.

JOSHUA WAS IN the air before Tim made it back to his apartment. Joy was already in St. Louis, with everything they both needed, so Tim only had to throw together a few hygiene items. By the time Joshua landed, Tim was waiting at the private airport they'd found outside of Franklin. They arrived in St. Louis with plenty of time to join the evening's festivities.

En route, Joshua gave Tim a rundown of the plan for the weekend. Since his return to Tennessee, Tim hadn't had much time to talk to anyone but Joy. As a rookie, his schedule was tightly controlled, and it included a good deal of hazing, on the field, in the locker room and back in the rooms where very little sleeping was done. Some of it was rather hateful, but since none of it was hurtful, Tim wasn't too bugged by it, though some of the other rookies were.

Having so many big brothers and sisters, Tim was used to being harassed, and he'd also never developed an unhealthy sense of his own importance. Some of the other rookies weren't so fortunate. They had arrived at training camp with varying degrees of what Tim thought was a strange and absurd attitude. Since the Hawks had drafted them, that meant they needed the rookies, and therefore should treat them like the "saviors" they thought they were. Training camp needed to knock that idea right out of their heads, and build them up to be teammates.

That meant the rookies barely had time to have a private thought while they were at training camp, much less make calls home. Tim had managed to call Joy at least once a day, but never for more than a minute or two. At home the previous weekend, he'd slept a great deal. When he was alert, he and Joy had plenty of things to do and to talk about rather than be concerned with the wedding the following weekend. But there hadn't been much to talk about anyway. All of the plans that involved Tim had not been finalized until after his brief call on Tuesday, telling her that he would for sure be able to make a flight shortly after two o'clock on Saturday.

Cari and Brandon weren't having a rehearsal. Their wedding was going to be very simple, and everyone involved had been to enough weddings that they merely needed to gather together for a few minutes and verbally run through the logistics. The tweaks that they'd made would be easy for all the participants. The talk-through was planned for early in the evening, at Halelolo, just before supper. Afterwards, they would have the family's traditional bachelor/bachelorette parties. The women would be in the big house, the men in the fort out back. In the morning, the men would invade the lofts for their meals and personal prep for the wedding.

"Try wait," Tim frowned fiercely. "Are you saying I'm not going to get to sleep with my wife tonight?"

"Only if you can find a way to get to her after all of the festivities wind down, Son," Joshua told him solemnly.

Tim nodded thoughtfully. Joylynne had told him about Al sneaking into the house after the parties the night before his and Joy's wedding. Al and Nita had worked out the details beforehand. Tim would do the same with Joy.

Joshua hadn't told him who all was there, so Tim was surprised to see the Trasks. Well before Brandon and Cari had set their wedding date, Brian had planned to be in Missouri for Fathers' Day. Apparently the rumors were at least partially true. Brian was seriously considering joining the Shepherd-Wolfe Ohana. That was the primary topic of discussion between supper and the parties. The children were all outside playing or up in the nursery so the adults could have a serious discussion without interruption.

"Why are you only seriously considering it?" Robert asked Brian.

"It's not as easy a decision for me as it was for y'all, including Dave," Brian explained. "Y'all already had an obvious logical connection."

"I think your connection to us is obvious and logical too," Heather frowned slightly.

"But what does she know about logic?" Tim was thrilled that Joy was the one who muttered the family's normal response to Heather talking about logic.

Heather stuck out her tongue at Joy, who returned the favor.

"That's another thing," Brian shook his head slowly as he looked from Heather to Joylynne. "Y'all are crazy, and rather childish."

"Oh please!" Cait snorted and rolled her eyes.

Brian frowned at his wife.

"Sounds like Cait thinks that's exactly why you belong in this family," Steve said drolly.

"You're also big and scary," Brian shot his frown around the room.

"We're scary?" Robert exclaimed in amazement.

"You out-dad Dad when it comes to the cold stare," Tim agreed with his little brother.

"You do have a deadpan that makes a man think twice," Luke agreed too.

"You can hold your own against any of us," Pete said wryly, "both physically and intellectually."

"Spiritually too!" Greg added.

"You don't have a problem with Mom and Dad, do you?" Rachel asked doubtfully but a little angrily.

"No!" Brian very quickly denied that. "If I didn't love them so much already, I wouldn't even be considering this. But they are pretty young to be my parents." He directed that aforementioned cold stare at Tim. "I'm already old."

Tim sighed heavily but didn't comment. He already knew the answer to "Will you ever forget I said that?" Brian did belong to their family, so of course he wouldn't. That wasn't necessarily bad, because he'd already "forgiven," if it had ever actually been necessary.

"You have a point," Luke nodded. "Dad's almost fifty-five, but you're going to be forty-three in November."

"And Mom'll be fifty-one," Heather frowned thoughtfully. "It'd be pushing it to say she's old enough to be your mother."

"But your birthday's the same day as Mom's, so you'd give her something no one else has, a child who shares her birthday," Rachel said brightly.

"I don't really think the narrow age difference is that big a deal," Nalani spoke up. "It's not as if you need someone twenty years older to be a parent. Experience is what matters. Since Mom and Dad both have a lot of parenting experience, they're knowledgeable enough to be your parents. That's what matters."

"And parents are only part of the deal when we do adoptions," Greg added. "Having siblings is just as important, if not more."

Cait decided it was time to enlighten them about Brian's deepest concern. All that other stuff was really just Brian being silly.

"Brian never had much of a family, even when his parents were alive. He was an only child and so were both of his parents. Not only is it overwhelming for him to think about having this much family," Cait waved her hand around the room, "but he also doesn't understand how it's logistically possible. One problem is that most of you live halfway around the world, but the other issue is, how can there be so many in one family and no one gets lost?"

Everyone looked around the room, staring thoughtfully at each other. They took this question very seriously because they realized that it was actually an issue for them all.

"I think I can speak to part of that," Robert was the first to offer an answer. "For the last three years, I've been the only one in Hawaii full time. Everyone else was living on the Mainland. I can honestly say that I never felt any less a member of the family than I ever did while I was living at Mom's house with the siblings I had from birth. Between phone calls, texts, emails and frequent visits, sometimes I felt like I wished my family would back off a bit."

"I've gotta agree with Robert," Tim nodded. "I was just the next state over, so I had more visits, but in-between times, I never knew when someone was going to pop up in my life through technology. I didn't feel less of a family member because everyone else didn't live in my vicinity."

"I can testify that your belonging is more up to you than the rest of the family," Brandon confessed sadly. "Geographically I was in the thick of things, but mentally and spiritually, I was less a part of the family here in St. Louis than after I moved to Oklahoma."

"They all touch on something that you probably don't understand, Brian," Greg leaned earnestly toward his cousin's husband. "No matter how big,

123

loving, or long-term your family is, there will be times when you don't feel like you belong, for one reason or another. For me, it's that I often feel like a failure. I see my sibs as succeeding at all they do, but I know I mess up everything. But the reality is that they don't see things the same way! I think I can safely say without bragging that every one of my family members admires me for something, and they pretty much have as long as I've known them. I know for a fact that I admire every single one of these people in this room, though I'm never gonna confess it in public!"

Brian laughed with everyone else.

"The sheer numbers in this family aren't a problem," Beth explained the other part of Brian's worry. "If you were still a kid, it might, but I doubt it. Sure it's hard to give attention to every child when you have a bunch, but it is doable. I can safely say that if you care about giving your children attention at all, the more kids you have the more deliberate you are in spending time with each and every one of them."

"Gloria and I kind of like the idea of 'cheaper by the dozen,'" Joshua grinned at his wife who nodded happily. "Sadly, we're still lacking three. We have great hopes for Katie, but she's a tough nut to crack."

"Case in point, she's up in the nursery rather than down here in the living room," Luke frowned up at the ceiling.

"You already belong to us through Cait, Brian. Don't you think it'd be less stressful to become part of our family, who you already know, rather than getting a bunch of new people to have to work into your life?" Gloria asked with a semi-troubled frown.

"She has a point, Brian," Cait agreed with a slightly smug smile.

"It's not like you'll get rid of us by not becoming part of the family," Dave grinned wickedly, but quickly became more serious. "You've been on the fringes of family for way too long, Brian. Sure you had a best friend who was closer than a brother. You've had lots of love in your life, but being in your own family, with your own Mom, Dad, brothers and sisters, having your own niephews, it all makes a difference. It completes you in a way that you'll never understand until you get into it."

"It won't be overwhelming, having this many sibs," Rachel assured him. "I went from Brandon at a distance to everyone but Dave in my face in less than a week. It was actually pretty awesome."

"But that's enough for now," Joshua called a halt to the discussion. "Brian, you've heard your issues addressed by the people you're thinking about becoming family with. If you can't agree with us, then we'll respect you decision. We won't love you any less if you chose to seek a more sane bunch to belong to."

"Though I don't know why you should," Cait muttered.

Brian frowned at his wife who stared innocently back at him.

"Don't take too long to make your decision," Tim sighed loudly. "You are getting old, ya know!"

"On that note," Gloria quickly rose. "You men need to get out of here. Go start your clash of the titans out in the fort!"

OF COURSE THE men did have a clash, but the women had their own version. It started out with just one-up-manship – singing, staring, telling tall tales and such. Joy was amused that it was her mother-in-law who started the dancing, which led to acrobatics, not unlike what the men had done at Joy's wedding reception.

The women ended up in a giggling, heap, which led to some tickling, which in turn led to wrestling. When they were all finally sprawled out on the couches and floor, winded but still laughing, Cari decided that the women were going to prepare a dance for the reception.

It was the wee hours of the morning when a clattering upstairs got everyone's attention.

Joy immediately guessed what it was.

"Oh no!" she cried and raced from the room.

Laughter followed her. Everyone suspected that Tim had just had a mishap trying to sneak into the house.

They were right. Tim and Joy had planned well, except for one small problem.

Trees were abundant around the large old plantation home, and there just happened to be one conveniently located right outside the window of Tim and Joy's room. Joy had made sure the window was unlocked, which wasn't a problem because the alarm system on the house wouldn't be set that night.

The problem was that Tim hadn't done a very good recon of the room that evening. His wife had decorated some in the last few days, making it a more personal space. She'd added a comfortable little reading nook with two arm chairs flanking a single pedestal table with a lamp. That table sat right under the window so that on sunny winter days they could enjoy the sunshine and on hot summer days catch the cooling breeze.

When Tim snuck into the dark room, he knocked over the lamp. In trying to catch it, he fell onto the table, much too close to the edge. The table tipped over, spilling Tim and the lamp on the floor.

The lamp broke but Tim was intact, except for his pride!

He was cleaning up the pieces of the lamp when Joy flew through the door. She wasn't upset about the lamp. She was much too happy to see that her husband was all in one piece.

Joy properly expressed her appreciation of that fact. Tim ardently rewarded her concern.

Chapter 19

Carolyn Maeve O'Phelan's wedding was not a society event. Both she and her groom were sure they could handle it with more peace than they'd ever had at society functions before, but there was no reason to test that theory. They stuck with just the people they really wanted to celebrate with.

Celebrate they did. The wedding was beautiful and joyful. The reception was rowdy and joyful. Most of the events of the day were expected, but there was one big change to a normal wedding ceremony.

A few minutes before the scheduled start of the ceremony, Greg came out the door on the side at the front of the church. Some expected the groom and groomsmen to be right behind him, but he was alone. He addressed the congregation from the steps that led up to the platform.

"We're doing things a little different today, and Brandon and Cari have asked me to explain," Greg addressed the congregation. "The change we made started back in January after Tim and Joylynne's wedding. Al talked to me during the reception. He said Joy had voiced a complaint before the ceremony, and he was wondering if it might be a valid complaint.

"Joy's complaint was that she didn't want to be the center of attention. She thought Tim should be, not her. If she'd left it at that, Al would have never asked me about it, but she added a thought-provoking argument. We sing about the bride waiting for her groom, meaning of course that the Church is waiting for Jesus, so why isn't a Christian bride waiting for her groom? Why is the groom waiting for the bride?

"When Al asked me what I thought, I had to confess that I didn't know. I'd never thought about it before. But it was such an intriguing idea that I had to explore it. I discovered that we don't know much about ancient Judean weddings. There certainly aren't any wedding ceremonies in the Bible. As far as I can tell, the only thing we really know is that the bride was made ready in her father's house, and then they waited for the groom to come and take her to the home he had prepared for them.

"The more I thought about and studied it with Joylynne because it was her idea in the first place, the more I believed that she was right," Greg grinned at his sister-in-law who smiled broadly. "Christians are the bride of Christ. That's very easy to prove biblically but I'm not going to right now because pretty much everyone here already knows that. If you don't, you can talk to me during the reception and I'll show you both Old and New Testament evidence for it. Right now, just bear with me and let's run with the fact that the big-C Church is the bride of Christ.

"That means that every time Christians get married, they are in some small way reflecting the relationship we have with Jesus Christ who is God the Son, our Savior, our Groom. Considering that truth, why do we put the emphasis on the bride in a wedding? Why isn't it on the groom, reminding us of our heavenly Groom? As Christians, aren't we supposed to put Christ in the center of our lives, not ourselves?

"Wedding ceremonies are the traditions of man. All this," Greg waved his hand to indicate the whole room, "is merely traditions. All of it. None of it is in the Bible, except the gathering together part. But all this gives us mental images when we read the Bible. When the epistles talk about 'church' we get a mental image of a building like this. When the Bible says we are the bride of Christ, we get a mental image of a wedding. Since that mental image has the bride as the focal point, it is too easy for us to subconsciously diminish the importance of our spiritual Groom also.

"When Joylynne and I told all this to Brandon and Cari, I'm proud to say that Cari got the point I was trying to make before I could say it. She frowned and said, 'Then why aren't we giving a better mental image for people? Shouldn't a wedding be about the groom coming for his bride, not standing there waiting for her to come to him? That's not what Jesus did, and it's not what he's doing when he comes again!'"

Greg laughed ruefully and shook his head. "I'm sorry to say that my brother wasn't so quick to accept the idea. His growl was something along the line of, 'I'm not going to be the center of attention at the wedding!' I won't detail the entire conversation, but Joy, Cari and I were finally able to convince Brandon that it wasn't about him, it's about Jesus, about living a life that points others to Jesus.

"So, with Joy's help because she suspected something was wrong and then she studied the Bible with me to figure out if her dissatisfaction was biblical, we modified the traditions of man that have become the norm for Christian weddings. Joy and I will explain all our changes, and give you the biblical support for them."

Greg looked up and raised his hands. "Father, we love you and we want to live our lives in service to you. We ask that you use this ceremony today to show your awesome love to everyone who has gathered for this wedding. May we all get a glimpse of what it means to be the bride of Christ."

While Greg was praying, Joylynne slipped from the end of the pew where she had strategically placed herself. Only she, Greg and the wedding party knew what they were going to do. The others knew there were some changes, but not what they were.

After the prayer, the door Greg had come through opened again. Instead of the groom and his attendants, Cari appeared with Sarina and Leiandra.

Cari was wearing a very simple ankle-length white sleeveless shift, but Sarina was carefully carrying a lace garment draped over both arms. They stood beside Greg in the traditional positions for the bride and her attendants.

"The Bible tells us that we are to clothe ourselves with Christ, which means we live in a Christ-like way," Greg said.

"'Rather, clothe yourselves with the Lord Jesus Christ, and do not think about how to gratify the desires of the flesh.' Romans 13:14," Joylynne read Bible passages that supported Greg's statement. "'For all of you who were baptized into Christ have clothed yourselves with Christ.' Galatians 3:27.

"'Therefore, as God's chosen people, holy and dearly loved, clothe yourselves with compassion, kindness, humility, gentleness and patience.' Colossians 3:12."

"Cari has clothed herself in her bright, white gown, but that's not all that the Bible commands her to do," Greg continued. "She, and all followers of Christ, must also allow other believers to speak into her life, to help her grow in Christ, and be more fully clothed in him."

While Joy read the next passages, Sarina and Leiandra helped Cari put on a beautiful lace over garment, with a row of small buttons down the back.

"'I myself am convinced, my brothers and sisters, that you yourselves are full of goodness, filled with knowledge and competent to instruct one another.' Romans 15:14," Joy read. "'Let the message of Christ dwell among you richly as you teach and admonish one another with all wisdom through psalms, hymns, and songs from the Spirit, singing to God with gratitude in your hearts.' Colossians 3:16

"'And let us consider how we may spur one another on toward love and good deeds not giving up meeting together, as some are in the habit of doing, but encouraging one another—and all the more as you see the Day approaching.' Hebrews 10:24-25."

"The Day that approaches, that we help each other prepare for, is of course the Second Coming of our Lord," Greg again picked up the explanation of their rewritten marriage ceremony. "Now, some of you may be wondering if it is right to allow Brandon to come claim his bride as if he was Jesus coming to claim his bride, but let me put your doubts to rest. Both the Old and the New Testaments have examples of husbands being the stand-in for our heavenly groom. The example we have chosen from Hosea is very unflattering to the bride, but we all, Cari included, agreed that it was perfect for our purposes. The truth is that we are all sinful creatures who are unfaithful to God. We're all adulterous wives who can only be redeemed and made pure by the bride-price paid on the cross."

"'The Lord said to me, "Go, show your love to your wife again, though she is loved by another man and is an adulteress. Love her as the Lord loves the Israelites, though they turn to other gods and love the sacred raisin cakes,"'" Joy again provided the passage from the Bible. "'So I bought her for fifteen shekels of silver and about a homer and a lethek of barley. Then I told her, "You are to live with me many days; you must not be a prostitute or be intimate with any man, and I will behave the same way toward you." For the Israelites will live many days without king or prince, without sacrifice or sacred stones, without ephod or household gods. Afterward the Israelites will return and seek the Lord their God and David their king. They will come trembling to the Lord and to his blessings in the last days.' Hosea 3:1-5."

"The New Testament passage that shows husbands 'standing in for' Jesus is probably familiar to many of you, but I think all the men should listen very carefully as Joy reads," Greg said. "If you're married, are you representing Christ in your marriage? If you're single, are you willing to submit your life to such a great act of humility?"

He looked at Joylynne who read the passage slowly, enunciating very carefully: "'Husbands, love your wives just as Christ loved the church and gave himself up for her to make her holy, cleansing her by the washing with water through the word, and to present her to himself as a radiant church, without stain or wrinkle or any other blemish, but holy and blameless. In this same way, husbands ought to love their wives as their own bodies. He who loves his wife loves himself.' Ephesians 5:25-28."

"Today, as Brandon comes to claim his bride, he will finish dressing his bride for the wedding," Greg took up the explanation again. "That's because the Bible assures us that no matter how much we and our believing friends work on clothing ourselves and each other, we will not be fully clothed in Christ's righteousness this side of heaven. Christ himself will clothe us with imperishable eternal garments of righteousness."

"'I declare to you, brothers and sisters, that flesh and blood cannot inherit the kingdom of God, nor does the perishable inherit the imperishable. Listen, I tell you a mystery: We will not all sleep, but we will all be changed— in a flash, in the twinkling of an eye, at the last trumpet. For the trumpet will sound, the dead will be raised imperishable, and we will be changed. For the perishable must clothe itself with the imperishable, and the mortal with immortality. When the perishable has been clothed with the imperishable, and the mortal with immortality, then the saying that is written will come true: "Death has been swallowed up in victory."' 1 Corinthians 15:50-54."

"Jesus is coming soon!" Greg cried triumphantly. "Not humbly, not in a manger, but boldly, victoriously! The Lord of lords and King of kings, is coming for his bride!"

"Revelation 19:11-14," Joy didn't read her last passage. Instead, she looked up, her face awash in wonder. "'I saw heaven standing open and there before me was a white horse, whose rider is called Faithful and True. With justice he judges and wages war. His eyes are like blazing fire, and on his head are many crowns. He has a name written on him that no one knows but he himself. He is dressed in a robe dipped in blood, and his name is the Word of God. The armies of heaven were following him, riding on white horses and dressed in fine linen, white and clean.'"

A heartbeat after Joy finished, up in the choir loft the small band sang the first verse of "Even So Come."

> All of creation all of the earth
> Make straight a highway a path for the Lord
> Jesus is coming soon.

As soon as Stormy's band began "Even So Come," Tim and Dave pushed open the doors to the sanctuary for Jeremy and Danny who pulled a bright white runner down the aisle.

The doors swung shut and Tim looked at Brandon. His brother's face was a little pale and he was shaking his head.

"I can't do this," Brandon whispered hoarsely.

"Yes you can," Tim assured him.

"I can't go out there like I'm Jesus!" Brandon shook his head firmly.

"You're not going out there like you're Jesus," Dave calmly corrected him. "You're going out there like you're Christ-like. That's what you're trying to be, aren't you?"

"Yeah, but this is different," Brandon was still shaking his head.

"We've already been over this," Tim remained calm though a big part of him empathized with Brandon. "You just heard Joy read the passage in Ephesians. God expects us to be Christ-like in our marriages, so there's no reason you shouldn't be Christ-like in your wedding too."

"Oh, like that makes this easier," Brandon growled. "I can't love Cari like Christ loved the church!"

"Of course you can't!" Dave growled back. "No man can. Not on our own, not without God front and center in our hearts and minds."

"Come on, Brandon," Tim snapped. "Quit being so prideful!"

"You're crazy," Brandon snapped back. "I'm not good enough to do this. I'm not prideful!"

"The worst kind of pride," Dave growled. "You're saying that God can't do what he promised to do, make you a new creature worthy to be called his son."

Brandon just stared at Dave, his eyes slightly narrowed.

"Brandon, this isn't about you," Tim said patiently. "It's about you and Cari taking the focus off the two of you and making your wedding day about God."

"You guys really think this is the right thing to do?" Brandon asked. "Would you do it if you were getting married again?"

"Probably not without a lot of the same feelings you're having now," Dave admitted wryly, "but I would certainly do it."

"You're providing a living illustration of what the Bible promises," Tim encouraged him. "That's so biblical. Joy just read one of the things God told Hosea to do to illustrate his prophecy, and I know you know that the prophets did a whole lot of other living illustrations."

"At least God isn't telling you to parade down the aisle naked like he had Isaiah do," Dave grinned.

Tim choked back a laugh, and Brandon smiled slightly.

"There is that," he sighed.

EVERYONE HAD BEEN standing, facing the back of the church since the boys pulled the runner down the aisle, so when the band started playing an extra chorus to "Even So Come," Joy felt free to glance over at Greg. She wasn't worried that Brandon wouldn't come down the aisle. She knew Tim would make sure he didn't back out. She did want to see what Greg thought of the delay.

He was smiling slightly. When Cari looked up at him, he winked at her. He seemed very happy. Cari looked back at the door through which Brandon would come. Her eyes shone with joyful expectation even though her groom hadn't appeared on their designated cue.

Joy wondered why Greg seemed pleased with the unexpected delay, why Cari wasn't even a little bit worried. Maybe it was –

Before she could figure it out, the back doors swung open.

The music swelled as Brandon strode purposefully down the aisle, white garments draped over his left arm. Tim and Dave were only a few steps behind him.

It was obvious the moment Brandon saw Cari. His eyes lit up and his whole face glowed.

More than one person peeked over their shoulder to see Cari's face. She also glowed.

When Joy, Greg, Cari, Sarina and Leiandra joined the singers, the entire congregation also sang. Their voices filled the church with exuberant sound. Tears of joy and awe flowed down many cheeks.

Joy felt her heart swell as the chorus soared.

> Like a bride waiting for her groom
> We'll be a church ready for You

Ev'ry heart longing for our King we sing
Like a bride waiting for her groom
We'll be a church ready for You
Ev'ry heart longing for our King
We sing even so come Lord Jesus come."

She turned her eyes to her own groom. He was watching her with a jubilant smile.

Joy returned his smile and bounced excitedly.

She had no doubt that when Brandon and Cari had decided to abandon the traditional wedding ceremony, they had blessed many people.

Chapter 20

*T*im held Cari's veil as Brandon draped a knee-length cape over Cari's shoulders and fastened it with trembling fingers. He totally understood Brandon's nervousness. He had also been nervous at his wedding, but Brandon had a much bigger reason to be nervous. This ceremony underscored the magnitude of what he was doing like nothing Tim had ever seen before. He knew he felt convicted. In the few months he and Joylynne had been married, he had never once thought about what it meant to love Joy as Christ loved the church. He was thinking about it now.

After Brandon and his groomsmen had arrived at the front of the church, Joy had gone back to her seat. Tim snuck a look at her, but Dave nudged him.

Tim swung his head back toward the front of the church just in time to hand Cari's veil to Brandon.

It wasn't a full veil. It was a wreath of flowers somewhat like hula dancers wear with the veil hanging down the back. As Brandon carefully placed it on his bride, the veil fell to just below her shoulders.

Brandon looked like he was going to kiss Cari, so Tim coughed loudly. Greg grinned broadly.

"This is an awesome day," Greg said. "We've been waiting to add Cari O'Phelan to our family for almost five years, and today it's happening. That was enough to make this day incredible, but then you guys decided that you would do things way different in your wedding. Which isn't too surprising since your courtship and your proposal were rather different too."

Greg paused to let the family's laughter die down.

"You guys chose to start your marriage the way your lives should be lived, in a way that points others to Christ. I know that I for one will have a very different mental image the next time I read about Jesus as the Bridegroom.

"Brandon, I'm pretty sure that the reason we had an extra couple of choruses was that you were back there wigging out." Brandon just stared solemnly at Greg, but Tim and Dave both grinned broadly. "But the Bible says that God will be glorified in every situation. And he was glorified when you started to get cold feet. I see two ways right off the bat. One, every man should take marriage very seriously. The Bible tells us we are to sacrifice ourselves for our brides. If that doesn't scare a man, he either doesn't take the Bible seriously, or he's never stopped to think about what it means to love his bride like Christ loves the church. So your hesitation glorified God because it challenges us all to look at how we are living our lives. Are we taking the Bible seriously, or are we just using it as window dressings?

"The other way your hesitation glorified God is that you didn't come when we expected it. Logically you should have come in no later than the bridge so that you received your bride during the final chorus, but you didn't come. We waited longer than we thought we should have. That's a perfect illustration of the timing for Jesus' return. The Bible says 'soon,' just like the song says, but what does 'soon' mean? We all have our ideas, and pretty much every generation for the last two thousand years has believed that they were the final generation that would see the fulfillment of that 'soon.' They were all wrong. Today, many American Christians believe that they will see Jesus return, because he just has to come. All the signs are right. But that's looking at the world through our own eyes, not through God's. I personally believe that we're going to be waiting through another chorus or two, or maybe even three or four.

"We certainly don't know the time of Jesus' return, but just like you, Brandon, finally came through those doors and claimed your bride, Jesus *is* coming. We need to wait as confidently as Cari did, without losing faith, shining our lights for God even if things get a hundred times darker than we think they should. Especially if things get darker than we think they should!

"You two are beginning your married life in a majorly God-glorifying way. Continue to live your lives that way. You both have already learned the value of honest fellowship, with each other and with family and friends. You know that being a Christ-follower is more than being a believer and reading the Bible. Keep doing the things you've done to grow, and you'll keep glorifying God in your marriage. If you seek to glorify God, nothing will tear you asunder."

When the band started another song, Tim looked toward his own bride. Her eyes were already on him.

He smiled softly. She smiled and nodded, then blew him a kiss.

She understood that Tim was reaffirming his love and commitment to her and to God, and she joined him in that reaffirmation.

THE REST OF the ceremony was quite traditional, up until the very end when of course Brandon carried his bride down the aisle which made her laugh. Then he made her cry when they arrived at the reception in the ballroom of the O'Phelan mansion.

He hadn't intended to make her cry. All he did was ask his sisters to use a rubbish sculpture as the centerpiece on the head table.

Everyone in the family knew that Brandon had been turning rubbish into artwork for many years. Few of them knew that well over a year ago, even before Brandon and Cari had started dating, she'd begun giving him interesting junk for him to work into sculptures. Some of the pieces she'd found she had teasingly told him he should use to make a sculpture for his bride.

Many of the family had received at least one of his sculptures. None of them had anything as magnificent at this.

Everything was framed by wire coat hangers, of course. The backdrop was the front of a castle. Old perfume bottles topped each of the four turrets. Stones and broken bits of bricks filled in the walls. The drawbridge was down. It was a piece of cardboard with logs painted on it. It stretched across a moat which was made with pieces of broken mirrors.

Striding across the drawbridge was a man carrying a woman. The man was dressed in a red jacket and blue trousers with a black ribbon running down the outside seam. The woman was in a ball gown with a princess' crown on her head.

Everyone had to admire the enchanting piece, but there was too much to do for it to stay the center of attention for long.

The groom was roasted cheerfully by his brothers and sisters, but the bride's siblings made sure she was teased as enthusiastically if not as often. By the time the dancing was underway, the best man was beginning to seriously question the wisdom of having accepted the honor of standing up with his brother.

Tim was exhausted. When Joy told him they were going home, he didn't complain, not even when she insisted that she was driving. He was sound asleep before they were half a block away. He slept well that night, then took a nap after lunch the following day. He awoke in time to play some rowdy games with the family, but took himself off to bed shortly after sunset. He had an early morning flight back to Tennessee.

Joy was very glad that she'd decided to stay in Missouri through June. Tim hardly called for the next two weeks. He managed to text her at least once a day, but it was often just luv u miss u. She was glad that she was surrounded by many people who helped her pass the time, and loved her wonderfully.

The construction crew was already working on Tim and Joy's home down at Gumbwats' Haven. They were also working on one for Raul and Lei Guerrero. Neither of them would be officially adopted by Gloria and Joshua Wolfe, but only because technically neither were orphans. That didn't make them any less family to the big, loving ohana that Joylynne had married into, especially since both Raul's and Lei's families had virtually disowned them when they'd become committed Christians.

Other than Tim's absence, the only thing about her time in Missouri that bothered Joylynne was the fact that she had to work with a licensed architect on the two homes she was overseeing. Until she finished her internship and got her license, she wasn't going to be able to work on her own.

That frustration helped Joy make a decision. After the Fourth of July weekend, she was moving full time to Franklin. She needed to find a firm in Tennessee where she could start that internship. Even if it meant lonely evenings, she was going to settle down in Franklin and start working.

Chapter 21

*O*n the first of July, Reylynnda Vogt was in the kitchen already working on her feast for the Fourth. She loved the big old house that Bill's grandparents had built over a hundred years ago. She especially loved the many big windows in the kitchen. It helped her see all the comings and goings of the ranch.

That afternoon, she was curious when an old battered pickup truck pulled into the drive. Reylynnda could see that it was from out-of-state because it had a front license plate, but she couldn't tell what state it was. The truck parked halfway between the house and the barn, and for a long moment, the driver didn't even shut off the engine. Then he sat in the truck. Mama Rey couldn't distinguish his features, but she could tell he was looking from the barn to the house, then back again.

She saw Bill walk out of the barn, staring curiously at the truck.

The man in the truck opened the door and got out.

Bill suddenly clutched his chest and reached for the corral rails.

The man from the truck was running toward Bill, but that barely registered to Reylynnda because she was running also.

When she hit the door, the man from the truck was already at Bill's side, holding him up. She was halfway across the driveway when Bill bellowed at her.

"I'm not havin' a heart attack woman," he sounded joyful. "Rick's come home."

Reylynnda didn't stop running, but she was no longer anxious.

The man from the truck turned toward her without taking his arm from around Bill. He was indeed Rick Vogt!

"Ricky!" Mama Rey squealed joyfully.

He grinned and let go of his father so that he could catch his dear old friend in a hug.

"Greg said you'd been widowed and married the old coot," Rick said after he kissed his father's wife. "I had to come and see it for myself."

"Greg?" Mama Rey asked, at the same time her husband said, "Greg Shepherd?"

"Can't think of another Greg that we all know," Rick shrugged.

"How do you know Tim's brother?" Mama Rey asked with a slight frown.

"He visited me a couple months ago."

It had taken Abe a little while to track down Rick after Tim had talked to him, mainly because he didn't know where to look, and there were a surprising number of Richard Vogts across the country. When he was certain he had the right man, he'd done what everyone in the family did in such a sensitive situation – he'd gone to see Greg.

Greg had decided that they needed to do a background investigation before he approached Rick Vogt. If he knew where Bill's son had been and what he'd been doing, he would be able to get a better feel for who the man was now, and therefore have a better idea what to do. If Rick was only going to use Bill and break his heart even more, Greg might just leave him where he was. He got Dave and Carl to conduct the investigation through TOP. They didn't want anyone wondering why the St. Louis police would be investigating Rick Vogt, originally from Oklahoma.

After months of preparation, early in May, Greg finally went to Iowa to meet Rick, much like he had years earlier with David, who was then called McGarry, and later Ted Bryant. In Rick, Greg had found someone whom he truly liked, but he kept the information to himself because his new friend wasn't sure if he wanted to find out whether or not his father still loved him.

"Why would Greg do that?" Bill asked his son.

"I bet Tim asked him to," Mama Rey declared happily.

"According to Greg, not directly," Rick shrugged. "Don't you think it would be a good idea to sit somewhere to have this discussion? It's going to take a while."

"Oh no! My cookies!" Mama Rey turned and flew back toward the house.

"I bet life's interesting with her, Dad," Rick laughed as he watched her run.

He turned back toward his father and was wrapped in a fervent embrace.

"I'm so glad you're home, Son," Bill cried.

"I am too, Dad," Rick wept with him.

Bill was the one to reluctantly step out of their hug.

"I guess it'd be best if we go and make sure that old woman ain't gonna burn down my house."

She wasn't. In fact, there was only a slight burnt smell in the air when the men stepped into the kitchen. They both snatched a cookie from the cooling racks on the counter before Mama Rey shooed them toward the table. She filled three glasses with ice then grabbed a pitcher of tea from the refrigerator before joining them.

"I would've come home sooner, Dad, but I didn't think you'd want to see me," Rick said after a few minutes of small talk.

"You're my son! Why wouldn't I want you home?" Bill asked with an incredulous frown.

"After what I said to you when I left," Rick stared at the table in shame. "After what I did in the years after that, why would you want me back?"

"Because I love you, Son," Bill said firmly. "The only reason I didn't go looking for you was because I knew it wouldn't do any good. If I dragged you back while you still hated me, I would've only made things worse. I kept hoping and praying that God would get through to you somehow and eventually bring you home."

"He did," Rick smiled. "I'm not sure how long it would've taken me to come home without the nudge from Greg, but God got hold of me more than ten years ago."

"Praise God!" Mama Rey joyfully threw up her hands.

"Indeed," Rick grinned at her then turned solemnly back to his father. "Mom's death wasn't your fault, Dad. I was stupid to say that."

Reylynnda didn't need to ask what he was talking about. Long ago Bill had told her about it. Of course she'd been there when Juanita Vogt had died after an automobile accident twenty years ago. She and Bill's first wife had been best friends since kindergarten. After Rick had disappeared, Reylynnda and Niguel had been the first ones Bill went to talk to.

He'd tearfully told them that his son had called him a murderer because Bill had been driving the car. Rick had loved his mother very much, but his relationship with Bill was already strained.

Bill's father had been a workaholic who was rarely around, and when he was at home, he'd been too strict with his children and utterly unaffectionate. Bill had tried to do better with his own son, but when he was stressed, he often defaulted to what he'd learned from his father. It wasn't until Rick was a young teenager that Bill finally began to understand, largely through his wife's life and her prayers, that he needed God in his life every day, not just on Sundays. Unfortunately, Rick didn't cooperate with his father in his efforts to change. He fought Bill every step of the way.

It had been easy for Rick to blame the father he distrusted for the death of the mother he adored.

Reylynnda and Niguel had been the ones to help Bill see that the accident had just been one of those things that happen in this fallen world. That night the road still had a few patches of snow and ice after the storm three days before, and that deer had jumped out of the woods at exactly the wrong time and place. Though Bill did everything right – he didn't try to swerve, just pumped the brakes – the road conditions caused a skid. Again Bill had responded properly, turning into the skid rather than fighting it, but it hadn't worked. He'd put Juanita's side of the car into a tree. She died en route to the hospital. It hadn't been Bill's fault.

The closer Bill got to God, the more he understood the truth of what his friends had said, but it still took some time for it to finally settle into his soul.

"I know that it wasn't my fault," Bill was able to honestly tell his son. "But I'm mighty glad to hear you say it."

"What've you been doing since you got saved?" Mama Rey asked. She didn't think they needed to dwell on what had gone wrong, at least not now. Bill and Rick could talk more about that later, if they needed to.

"I got into NA and started working as a janitor at a church," Rick said with a small grin. "I ended up working with ex-cons, helping them learn how to live as Christians."

"That's what's going on over on the other side of the ranch," Bill said in shock.

"I know. Greg was pretty excited about that part," Rick took a deep breath. "I also got married and now have three kids."

"What?" Bill looked around the room as if expecting to see his daughter-in-law and grandchildren pop out from hiding. "Where are they?"

"They're back in town at the motel."

"Why?" Bill and Reylynnda demanded in tandem.

"Because in spite of what Greg said, and what my heart told me was true, I didn't want to run the risk with them," Rick said levelly. "Kelly knows why we're here, but the kids don't. They think we're just on vacation."

"Son, I want you in my life," Bill grabbed his son's arm and pierced him with a stern stare. "I want you to join the work we're doing here, if that's what you want. I want to love on my grandkids like I didn't know how to love on you. I love my daughter-in-law even without meeting her because she belongs to you. I want her living right here so I can tell her every rascally story I know about you."

"You shoulda left out that last part, Dad," Rick sighed sadly. "That makes me want to cancel the movers I hired to come at the end of the month."

"No you won't!" Mama Rey crowed joyfully.

Bill just jumped up from the table and grabbed his son in a big bear hug.

In five minutes they were on their way into town to meet Rick's family. In the car, Mama Rey started making calls. Her first call was to her granddaughter in Missouri.

Joylynne was delighted to hear her grandma's news. Tim had said nothing to her about asking his brothers to find Rick Vogt, but it wasn't surprising that he had. It was the kind of loving thing he did for his friends and family.

TIM DIDN'T FIND out about Rick and Bill's reunion until late Thursday afternoon, after Coach had released them with a warning.

"Get on out of here and enjoy the holiday, but you better not lose your edge. If on Monday mornin' at eight, I don't see all the drive and teamwork I been seein' lately, then don't count on seein' your families until after we win our first preseason game."

Tim was happy to take off for a three day weekend. He hoped everyone else was taking Coach's warning seriously. He certainly was.

He called Joy on the way to their apartment to get his things for the weekend. She promised him that they would be in the air within the hour. Tim had time to take a leisurely shower and stop to get something to eat. He made it to the airport before Joshua, but not by much.

Tim was surprised to see that the plane was packed with family members.

"Isn't this a little much for a welcoming committee?" he curiously looked around.

"You complaining punk?" Greg growled.

"Sit down and get your seat belt on so Joshua can take off," Gloria demanded.

"No, I'm not complaining," Tim answered Greg while he obeyed Gloria. Since the seat they'd saved for him was right next to Joy, he stole a kiss, then smiled around the plane. "Why this surprise?"

"Bill got a surprise this week," Joylynne glowed happily.

"Oh, he did?" Tim glanced at Abe who grinned and nodded.

"It took a while to find the right Rick Vogt. When I did, Carl and Dave took over."

"Carl and I just did a background check, then we passed the info to Greg," Dave shrugged.

"I got the fun part. I took a trip to Indiana," Greg grinned broadly.

Tim snorted. When Greg had found Dave five years ago, that was the part that got him in big trouble.

"So," Tim waved his hand around the plane, "does this mean we're all going to Oklahoma for the Fourth of July weekend?"

"Of course!" a half dozen voices confirmed his guess.

It wasn't surprising that they would. Bill and Mama Rey had been two of the first friends that Stormy had made in Norman. Ever since Thanksgiving of Tim's freshman year, whenever family had gone to Norman, they'd stayed out on Bill's ranch. The whole family all loved Bill very much.

When Tim took a second look around the plane, he frowned. None of his niephews were on the plane. Some of his siblings were missing too.

"Your sisters, Steve, Pete, Robert and the kids are already in Norman," Gloria guessed what Tim's frown meant. "We were planning on spending the weekend down at Gavyn & Fiona's farm like we usually do, so they all took off earlier this week. After Joy got the call from Reylynnda yesterday, we changed our plans and they left for Norman."

"I heard that they already love Bill's grandkids," Luke grinned broadly.

"Grandkids?" Tim exclaimed then playfully glared at Greg. "'Lucy, you got some 'splainin' t' do!'"

"What?" Greg gave him a bemused frown.

"Grandma's a big 'I Love Lucy' fan," Joy sighed. "I'm afraid that in the last few years, your brother watched way too many episodes."

"I watched more than once with my mom, too," Dave said wryly. "Isn't that what Ricky Ricardo used to say to Lucy?"

"Almost every episode," Joy nodded then turned to Greg. "You better get to 'splainin' before your brother gets to whining."

Greg jumped right in before Tim could whine about his wife's comment. Greg not only told Tim, but he also filled in some details that the rest of the family didn't already know about his visit with Rick.

As Greg talked, Tim began to get drowsy. He finally dropped off to sleep shortly after Greg's tale was done. Joy woke him just before they landed.

The party that weekend was rowdy and lots of fun. Rick was every bit as big as his dad, so he ended up in more than one wrestling match. Greg's son Danny adored Rick's eight year old daughter, Christy. Five year old Billy was torn between six year old Naomi and the four year old quintet of boy cousins, Chalk, Fleece and the Cubs. Two year old Donovan was enthralled with his sudden wealth of aunties, uncles and grandparents.

At first, Kelly Vogt was more than a little overwhelmed. In fact at times she almost seemed frightened. But Rachel was already well on the way to making friends with her by the time the rest of the family arrived. When Joylynne quickly claimed Rick's wife as if she was a long lost friend, Kelly's fear disappeared in the warmth of her new friends' love.

IT WAS A very good weekend. When Tim reported for training on Monday morning, he was more than ready to get back to work. In fact, everyone was. They got to go home every evening and they didn't work another weekend until the first preseason game, which they lost, but barely. They worked out some problems and won their next two games, then lost their last preseason game.

The weekend between the end of preseason and the beginning of the season was Derek and Kendra's wedding in Oklahoma. Tim and Joy were able to squeeze in a couple days after that to "move in" to their home in Gumbwats' Haven before heading back to Tennessee. Of course they didn't fully move in since they were still living at the apartment in Franklin, but they spent their first night in their own home and unpacked the bridal shower and wedding presents that they hadn't taken to Franklin with them.

Tim saw the house for the first time. He'd made his suggestions to Joy and trusted her to make them work, or discard them if they weren't feasible. He'd picked out the couch he wanted on an earlier trip to St. Louis. He was pleased to discover that it was indeed a comfortable fit for him, but he hoped he wouldn't spend many nights on it.

Some things about the house were rather amusing, like the old fashioned laundry chute and the ironing board hidden in the wall. Neither of them actually elicited a laugh from Tim. The exterior doors did.

"Deadbolts and chains, Joy?" Tim shook his head in wonder. "You know this is a secure estate, don't you, Sweetheart?"

"Of course I do," Joy lifted her chin. "Do you know that all security can be breached by someone with the knowhow and sufficient desire?"

"There's a lot of security to breach before they ever get to our home," Tim stared doubtfully at the door. "But if it'll make you happy, why not?"

"Why not indeed!" Joy gently scolded him.

Part of her knew that she was foolish, but she was a city girl. Practically everyone she knew had deadbolts and door chains. Mom and Dad did, and so did Grandma's house where Joy and Tim had stayed. She hadn't really thought about the necessity when she'd had them installed. It was just something a person did.

Joy really wasn't upset about Tim's teasing. It hadn't been mean. In fact, it had been somewhat playful. Over the last few months, that had become a defining character of their marriage, disagreement expressed playfully if possible but always kindly. She didn't expect that they would never exchange angry words like they had at first, but she also wasn't worried that they would experience lasting hurt when they did get angry again. They were both learning that loving each other often meant they needed to find a compromise by trying to understand each other's point of view rather than always insisting that things be done their own way.

In the two weeks Joy had stayed in Missouri back in June, she'd learned more about cooking Hawaii style. Tim was very happy that he got rice almost every day, and a lot of other foods that Joy found a little questionable. Regular kimchi didn't appeal to Joy, but she really liked kimchi cucumbers. Fortunately she didn't have to make either because her mother-in-law always made enough to share. That was also the case with the takuan – pickled daikon. Joy had never heard of either takuan or daikon before Gloria gave her cooking lessons. Now she knew that daikon was Japanese radish – long, white and very large. In addition to it being pickled, Tim liked it finely grated, mixed with a little shoyu (what people from Hawaii called soy sauce) and served with rice or tofu – a Hawaii staple that she was still debating whether she liked it or not.

Joy had also learned how to make fried rice, chop chae, long rice, kalua pig, lomi salmon, mochiko chicken, saimin, chicken katsu, haupia, butter mochi and lumpia. Now that the weather was turning colder, she was looking forward to making Portuguese bean soup, and of course she was now quite skilled at making Spam musubi and sushi. It was a good thing that Tim made a lot of money. It turned out that Spam was rather expensive!

In addition to her experiments in the kitchen, Joy was enjoying her new job as an intern. Fortunately she'd found an architectural firm right there in Franklin. They didn't have a problem with the fact that she would probably be in Missouri for four months of the year, not as long as she was willing to make

143

at least biweekly day trips back to Franklin.

Time happily flew by for Joy. Though Tim didn't have a lot of time off, they were still able to start exploring Franklin. Tim enjoyed the battlefield at Ft. Granger and looked forward to experiencing it with Robert, along with the numerous other Civil War sites like Carter's Hill Park which commemorated the assault on the cotton gin, and the Carnton plantation and Carter House. Joy and Tim agreed that they would wait to visit the Belle Meade Plantation until both Robert and Katie came to visit; both of them were big time history buffs, so Tim and Joy decided the tour would be more enjoyable with them.

Tim and Joy of course visited many of the restaurants in Franklin, but Tim's favorite was Puckett's Grocery & Restaurant. During the meal their first time there, Tim noticed a can of Spam on display. When the waitress came to ask if they wanted anything else, Tim had to ask about it.

"Yeah, I want to know why you've got a can of Spam up there," he pointed appropriately, "but don't have any Spam on the menu!"

The waitress seemed surprised to see the Spam, and had to confess that she had no idea why it was there. She left to find an answer to Tim's question.

"I've been told that our chef entered and won a Spam competition awhile back," she told Tim.

"Try wait, he won a Spam competition," Tim was surprised but puzzled. "Then why doesn't he have that dish on the menu?"

"I guess we just don't get enough call for it," the waitress shrugged.

"How much would be enough?" Tim asked earnestly. "'Cause I can ask a lot!"

"Yes, he can!" Joy laughed.

And he did ask the next week, and the one after that, but then events conspired to keep them from visiting restaurants for a while.

Chapter 22

The first two weeks of the season were very good because the Hawks won both games. The third week wasn't so good. The fourth week was rather bad. Not only did the Hawks lose for the second time, but Joy didn't feel good all week. The fifth week the Hawks won, but Joy needed to go see the doctor. She told Tim she was going, but since she was overdue for a checkup, she didn't tell him that she was a little concerned.

Since she hadn't already found a physician, she couldn't get an appointment until early the next week. The Hawks lost again on Monday night, and Joy received rather surprising news from the doctor on Tuesday. Since Tim was still grumpy about the loss – they were three and three which was a disappointing start to the season – Joy decided to keep her news to herself, and hope Tim would be in a better mood if they won on Sunday.

They did win, and Tim was in a good mood. Joy told him that evening.

"I'm pregnant," she said casually as Tim lifted his dessert spoon.

He froze, then frowned slightly and dropped his spoon. He slowly turned his head and peered carefully at her.

"You're sure?"

"The doctor told me last week," Joy calmly replied. "I'm due May sixth."

She was a little worried so she watched Tim carefully. They had intended to wait a few years, until he was done with his four year contract. This wasn't in their plan.

"I thought we were gonna wait?" Tim gave her a puzzled frown.

"That's what we'd agreed on," Joy shrugged.

"So why'd you change your mind without discussing it with me?" Tim growled, his frown getting angry.

"I didn't change my mind!" Joy snapped.

"Then why are you pregnant?" Tim snapped louder.

Joy almost screamed at him. Instead she took a deep breath and counted to ten, then twenty.

"I didn't change my mind," Joy calmly restated her assertion. "I thought we were properly protected, but obviously I was wrong."

"I thought you were on the pill," Tim growled, though he was somewhat calmer.

"I was," Joy shrugged. "And I didn't miss any, so I guess the dosage was too low for me."

"How does that happen?" Tim frowned still, but now it was more disappointed than angry.

"I'm not sure, but obviously it does. The doctor told me that after this one comes, he'll up the dosage."

"That's closin' the barn door after the horse is already out," Tim grumbled sourly.

"Do you trust God, dear?" Joy gently covered Tim's hand with hers.

"Yes," Tim sighed sadly.

"Then eat your ice cream and try to be happy."

"I'm sure I will be," Tim picked up his spoon again. "It's just a big shock right now."

"It was for me too," Joy said wryly.

The shock quickly wore off and the joy grew. By the end of the week Tim was excited about having a baby. He felt very bad about his initial response to Joy's news, so he visited a florist and had a special bouquet made.

"Thank you!" Joylynne said when Tim presented it to her on Friday evening. "What's the occasion?"

"I was a jerk," Tim shrugged, then frowned. "But why does there have to be an occasion?"

"Because you've never given me flowers before."

"I should give them to you all the time," Tim shook his head ruefully. "We can afford them, and you deserve at least a bouquet a week for putting up with me!"

"You aren't that bad, Tim," Joy laughed. "And I don't need that many bouquets. Please look in that cabinet over the frig for a vase."

"Here you go," Tim easily found one that was big enough and pretty enough.

"This looks a lot like my wedding bouquet, but different," Joy frowned thoughtfully. "What did you add, and why?"

"Well, I was thinking about how you decided on your bouquet," Tim explained as he filled the vase with water. "I remembered that you were wondering if any flowers mean faith and hope."

"Right. Roses are for love, which is the greatest of these."

"But that doesn't mean faith and hope aren't great," Tim said as he watched Joylynne carefully arrange the bouquet in the vase. "In fact, they obviously are since they're grouped with love, so why do we focus so much on love at marriages and basically exclude faith and hope. Aren't they critical in a marriage too?"

"You remembered all that?" Joy looked up from the vase with shining eyes.

"Of course I did," Tim said almost indignantly, then his shoulders slumped. "But I couldn't remember what all the flowers in your bouquet meant."

"Red roses for devotion, white for new beginnings, yellow for friendship," Joy easily remembered the details about the flowers. "The white calla lilies represent innocence and purity –"

"And we are both equally pure because Jesus makes us that way," Tim remembered that part.

Joy smiled gloriously and kissed him before continuing.

"Violet tulips represent faithfulness, and lilacs represent confidence –"

"Which is what the Bible means when it uses the word hope," Tim knew this part too. "Hope is confidence that what God promised will come to pass. But I don't remember what you substituted and why."

"Well, the florist thought that lilacs would be too big for my bouquet, and I agreed, so she used forget-me-nots instead."

"Which still fits, I guess."

"Of course it does," Joy nodded confidently. "Hope is not forgetting the promises God made!"

"Did you figure out what's different about this bouquet?" Tim asked.

"Yes, all the yellow roses have become pink," Joy wrinkled her nose. "You know that's not a red-head's favorite color."

"I do," Tim nodded. "But I found out that pink carnations represent a mother's love, but I don't like carnations so much because they remind me of funerals, so I decided to compromise. I asked them to make the yellow roses pink."

"It's perfect, Tim!" Joy lifted her face for a kiss. Tim happily obliged her.

THE NEXT FRIDAY, Tim brought Joy an identical bouquet, in part because he'd decided that Joy really did deserve flowers more often, but also to remind them both that they needed to cling to the faith, hope and love they'd discussed the week before. While they were very happy to be having a baby, neither were happy about the pregnancy.

Joy was having a very difficult time. To say that she was having morning sickness was a major understatement. Morning, noon and night she was sick. She couldn't eat more than a couple bites without throwing up. She was always exhausted, so much so that she couldn't do the simplest housework. She didn't have the energy to go to the office, but she was able to do a lot of her work at home. Though it wasn't strenuous work, she found that it was hard to sit up for very long so she couldn't put in nearly as many hours as she wanted.

Tim obviously couldn't stay home with Joylynne, so Danita came to help for a week. When she had to return home, Gloria took her place. Joy hated having either of them there, not because there was anything wrong with them but because she hated being weak. She hated depending on someone else for things she should be doing herself. She hated not being able to work or take care of her home. She especially hated it that she couldn't take care of her own husband.

Danita and Gloria tag teamed for two more weeks, but by the time Gloria arrived for her second visit, Joy was already feeling much better. It was Thanksgiving week. This was Tim and Joy's first Thanksgiving as a married couple, and Joy had intended for it to be celebrated with family in their home in Gumbwats' Haven. Her husband wouldn't let her even leave Franklin, nor would he let the family come to them.

Joy argued that she was doing so much better, and Gloria was there to help. Tim conceded only as far as letting both sets of parents and Joy's brothers come. Joy decided to be happy with that concession. The Christmas season was upon them and she didn't want to overdo things now. If she didn't continue to get better, Tim would probably lock her in their bedroom!

Gloria went home with Joshua the Saturday after Thanksgiving, and all the Quintanillas flew out together too. Joy was again taking care of herself and her husband. She enjoyed it immensely!

Two weeks later, she asked Joshua for a favor. She knew that going by plane would be the only way Tim would let her leave Franklin before the baby was born. Tim's bye-week just happened to coincide with a Christmas festival in Hermann, Missouri that the whole family was planning to attend. Joy wanted to go too, and she was feeling wonderful. There was no reason not to go, except for her overprotective husband.

It took some talking on Joy's part, but she finally won out. She was so happy to be out and about that it didn't even bother her that the whole family watched her constantly.

Joy's parents decided for her that they were coming to see her for Christmas rather than her even thinking about traveling. They even insisted that they were staying in a hotel. Robert and Tim's parents came to, and Brandon and Cari tagged along. They had their own happy news. Cari was expecting in June.

Tim was very happy to spend time with family, but the last game of the season was looming on the horizon. The Hawks had to win it to have any hope of getting a wild card slot. They were seven and eight. Without another win, their season would be done. Even if they did win, the Raptors had to lose for the Hawks to get the wild card.

It was a home game, so all the guys went to see it at the stadium. Since Tim wouldn't let Joy go (though she insisted she would be fine) all the women stayed home with her and watched the game on TV.

It was much too exiting. The biggest margin either team had was when the Wolves were up by nine midway through the second quarter. Both defenses were hot, allowing few yards at a time either running or through the air. Tim never missed anything that came his way, but he also got hit almost every time, sometimes before he even had the ball securely tucked.

The two minute warning had already sounded and the Hawks were down by two. They had the ball on their own twenty-four yard line with over a minute to spare. It was second and two so no one really expected Montero to go to the air, but he did.

He connected with Shepherd who tucked the ball even as he was turning toward the end zone. Tim could see a defender on either side, charging at an angle to stop him before he got to the end zone. Tim ran as hard as he could.

The three paths were on a course to collide just past the five yard line.

It wasn't really a do-or-die situation. If Tim went down, they would still have four downs to make it into the end zone.

Tim decided he didn't want to play four more downs. Just before the collision, Tim dipped slightly as he planted his lead foot. He launched himself up and over the defenders. He smoothly executed a back flip and landed in the end zone where he bowed gracefully to the screaming fans before holding the ball aloft and running toward the Hawks' sidelines.

"You've got to be kidding me!" Nita squealed in delight.

Joy simply grinned proudly.

"Tim was in gymnastics until he got too big to compete," Gloria shrugged happily.

The Hawks hung on to win the game.

Unfortunately, later that evening, the Raptors also won.

Tim's first season in professional football was over.

When Joshua and Gloria left for St. Louis the Monday after Christmas weekend, Tim and Joy went with them. There was no reason to stay in Franklin. They went to Missouri to be with family for the duration of Joy's pregnancy.

Tim's family didn't pick on him about the disappointing end of the Hawks' season. In fact, they convinced him that it had been a very good season.

"You do realize why you were the first draft pick, don't you?" Steve asked.

"Yeah," Tim barely refrained from rolling his eyes. "Tennessee had the first pick and they needed a wide receiver."

"But why did they have the first pick?" Greg did roll his eyes.

Tim merely frowned.

"They not only had a losing record last year, they had the worst record in the league," Pete explained the obvious.

"They only had one win last year," Luke said. "This year, they won eight!"

"That's an impressive improvement," Steve assured Tim with a wise nod.

"I guess you're right," Tim grinned happily.

They were right; his season had ended well.

Chapter 23

The end of the season opened the door for a long-awaited event. Brian Trask legally became the big brother that he'd relationally been since late June. He'd made his decision, but he didn't want to have the ceremony without all his new siblings. Since Tim worked almost every weekend during football season, the family had waited to expand again until after Tim's season was over.

Benton Tatum wasn't one bit surprised when the family who'd written the rules for the adoption ceremony didn't follow them. They were already picking on their big brother when they arrived from the legal proceedings at the courthouse.

"July, August, September, October, November, December and now January," Greg made a big deal of counting the months off on his fingers, then sighed. "That's a ridiculously long wait, Brian. If you'da waited two more months it would've been just be like getting a baby."

"It'll probably be more like getting a baby than you all expect," Will mumbled. As Brian's long-time best friends, he and Amanda had travelled to Missouri with Brian and Cait.

"Oh, but it actually is just like being pregnant," Joy laughed happily. "Most of the time you're already well into the second, or even the third month before you know you're pregnant, so we can say we waited nine months for Brian to be 'born' into the family!"

"Thank God I didn't have to be pregnant!" Gloria sighed in relief.

"But you could be!" Dei suggested.

"I think you should have a baby," Robert sighed dramatically. "Then I won't be the baby of the family anymore."

"No!" Joshua and Gloria both declared firmly.

"That'd be the surest way to get your dozen kids," Tim suggested hopefully.

"We're too old for that," Joshua shook his head.

"Seems you've forgotten about Abraham and Sarah, and Zechariah and Elizabeth," Brian said slyly.

"Bite your tongue, Brian Wayland Trask!" Gloria scolded him.

"Why's it always so scary when your mom or your wife uses all your names?" Brian sighed plaintively.

"What's scary is that I don't know how to keep these people on track," Benton sighed almost as sadly. "Can we get started? I'd like to get home to my wife and see if she wants to make a baby."

"Sounds like fun, doesn't it Dei?" Dave playfully leered at his wife.

"Sure does," Pete hugged Jenni.

"We can try," Heather flirted with Steve.

"Joy and I'll have to wait a while," Tim rubbed his wife's growing bulge.

"A long while!" Joy said firmly.

"Madi and I already did," Carl said proudly. Madison beamed joyfully.

"Really!" Rachel squealed excitedly and bounced over to hug her cousin.

For a few minutes congratulations were the order of business, then Greg spoke over the commotion.

"I'd just like to point out that for all his whining, Benton started this diversion from the rules."

Benton tried to resist, but it was just too much. He had to do it.

"I don't whine," he whined.

Greg's startled look and the roar of laughter from the rest of the family made it worth it. However, ….

"We really do need to get this show on the road," Benton spoke over the noise. "You all know what we're doing, so I'm not explaining anything. If you failed to inform Brian, that's your fault. It'll give him a good reason to pick a fight when we're back at Halelolo. First question," Benton raised his voice to cut off any comment, "Brian, who in your new family added oil to the car through the dipstick hole?"

"Wait a minute! That's not fair," Steve whined. "I'm an in-law! You're not supposed to pick on me."

"Talk to Ann," Benton shrugged. "She gave me the cards, as always."

"But where did she get the stuff on them from?" Steve glared at Greg who merely shrugged.

"So Steve did that," Brian said wisely. "That wouldn't be hard to guess, even if I hadn't already heard that story."

"Next question, when did Brian have a Mohawk?"

"Will! You promised you'd never tell," Brian frowned fiercely at his friend.

"Did I?" Will shrugged. "I don't remember that."

"Never's such a long time anyway," Nalani sighed.

"Since Will had something to do with it, I'm guessing Brian was already fourteen," Greg said thoughtfully.

"But not more than fifteen since he alleges that Will couldn't beat him up after their first year as friends," Luke added his two cents worth.

"Alleges!" Will snorted.

"Wait, is that why you're bald in your seventh grade picture?" Gloria asked, bravely trying to hide a laugh.

"Yes," Brian sighed. "But Will didn't do it. I did, after he dyed both sides of my hair while I was sleeping one night. I thought a Mohawk would be better than looking like a skunk."

"And Mrs. Vaughn shaved the rest of his head when she saw him," Will shook his head. "He looked better as a skunk."

"I don't know," Cait grinned at her husband. "I like the bald look too!"

"But it's not happening again," Brian glared at her and covered his head with his hand, but he really wasn't worried. He still kept his hair at shoulder length, and a three-day growth of beard. Cait liked it, and so did he.

"Moving right along," Benton again interrupted. "Brian, who's been married more times than even her parents can remember?"

"You told, Timothy?" Joy howled and elbowed her husband.

"Maybe it was Brandon," Tim grunted.

"Don't blame me!" Brandon quickly denied.

"So that was Joy," Brian nodded sagely.

"I was in kindergarten," Joy glared at her husband then turned her wrath on Greg. "I'm an in-law too! You didn't have enough crazy stories without your in-laws?"

"The craziest ones gotta come from them," Dave shrugged.

"Why?" Dei frowned up at him.

"Well, duh," Robert said, "You all married into the family!"

"I don't know why you gotta blame me," Greg whined at Joy. "Benton's asking the questions."

"And I do have more! For the family, what did Brian give Amanda for her eleventh birthday?"

Brian and Amanda both looked anywhere but at each other.

"That would've been right after her parents took him in," Joshua said thoughtfully.

"I don't see Amanda wanting a doll at that age," Heather mused.

"At any age," Cait snickered.

"I didn't!" Amanda agreed.

"He wouldn't have bought her something anyway," Greg guessed.

"I'm guessing it'd be something more than a card he drew," Tim suggested.

"Maybe a kiss?" Rachel said doubtfully.

"Not hardly!" Amanda snorted in disbelief.

"A black eye!" Dave guessed.

"I didn't do it on purpose!" Brian defended himself.

"Ha! You yelled 'leave me alone,' and punched me!" Amanda glared at him.

"And you punched me back!" Brian snapped then glared at Benton. "Does that mention that she gave me a black eye too?"

"Um," Benton studied the card. "Nope, it doesn't. But there is another question. Brian, who sang 'Love Me Tender' for a high school talent show?"

"It wasn't a talent show! It was a fundraiser," Pete glared at Greg. "And I'm an in-law too! What the heck?"

"You're not going anywhere," Brandon grabbed his wife who was headed for the door.

"Oh yes I am! You're running out of in-laws," Cari sighed plaintively, but she turned back to the room anyway.

"Y'all are making this too easy," Brian grinned at the in-laws in question.

"Next question, when did Brian get his first tooth?"

"Oh! I know that!" Heather squealed and waved her hand in the air.

"Talk about too easy," Beth rolled her eyes.

"One day last summer when we were talking babies Cait told us women about that," Nalani said.

"When Cecelia was six months old, Brian was worried because she didn't have teeth yet," Cari picked up the story.

"Cait told him there was nothing to worry about yet," Gloria added.

"Then he told her about the story his mom used to tell," Jenni was next.

"Brian was already thirteen months old and they were sitting in the Christmas Eve service when suddenly he started screaming," Joy followed her.

"The lower part of his face was covered in blood which was coming from his mouth," Rachel shuddered.

"His parents rushed him to the hospital, terrified that their baby was dying," Amanda sighed dramatically.

"But he'd just gotten his first eight teeth, all at the same time," Dei grinned.

"And because he was so old and on semi-solid food, his gums were tough enough that the teeth had to really cut through them, so they bled," Madison finished the story.

"I guess if Celi or Whit had followed suit, we would've heard about it," Greg sighed with relief for his brother.

"Thankfully they both had teeth before they were seven months old," Cait nodded happily.

"Next question, for Brian, who got caught smoking during church?"

"Valentine Gregory Shepherd!" Nalani was close enough to punch her brother-in-law's arm. "That's so not right!"

"Thanks, Nalani! I would've guessed it was Dave and Ted," Brian grinned.

"We only got caught in high school," Dave shrugged.

"But I wanna hear more about this," Luke stared at his wife. "Smoking in church?"

"Not *in* church, during church, out back behind the school," Nalani sighed. "It was in second grade. Art had snitched an almost empty pack of cigarettes from his mom's purse. We went out back with Pancho to try them. They were nasty, and we wouldn't have gotten caught if Robin hadn't been following us."

"How did I not know this?" Luke frowned at his wife and his brother.

"Maybe because you were such a rascal that Mom and Dad didn't think to tell you a story like that about me," Nalani raised her chin haughtily.

Luke put his hand on his heart with a wounded sigh. Before he could protest his rascalliness, Benton jumped in with the next question.

"How many times did Brian get beat up when he was fourteen?"

"That's a ridiculous question!" Brian protested.

"Unanswerable too," Dave laughed.

"Unless Will counted. Did you Will?" Brandon asked.

"Didn't know I needed to," Will snickered.

"So let's just go with 365," Tim suggested.

"No, let's add an extra ten, just to make sure we got them all," Robert modified his brother's suggestion.

"Brian, with friends like you have, you need this family," Steve snickered.

"Mom, they're pickin' on me," Brian whined.

"You're the big brother, make them behave," Gloria said with a sigh.

"Sorry, we still have two questions and the vows to get through," Benton quickly gave the last question about the family. "Who at ten was a budding arsonist?"

"Not me," Dei quickly denied when Brian looked her way. "Shelly and I never burned down anything. And don't look at Dave either."

As Brian looked around the room at his puzzled siblings and in-laws, one face had too much deadpan.

"Dad?"

"Why didn't you stick with the in-laws?" Joshua glared at Greg.

"What did you burn down?" Gloria asked her husband with a puzzled frown.

"I didn't burn down anything," Joshua sighed. "And it was actually Sam's fault."

"Don't blame my dad!" Madison quickly defended Joshua's absent brother.

"I got a chemistry set for Christmas," Joshua shrugged. "The explosion wasn't very impressive. I only scorched the inside of the shed, but the table was a total loss."

"Did you get to keep the chemistry set?" Brian asked.

"Yeah, but Dad put it up and would only take it down when he had time to work with me."

"That's not fair," Greg said sadly. "Mom took mine away, and I only did a stink bomb."

"So, last question for the family," Benton cut off further discussion about mishaps with chemistry sets. "When and why did Brian get expelled from Sunday school?"

"You got kicked out of Sunday school?" Tim asked incredulously. "Who does that?"

"How could you possibly know that?" Brian glared at Greg.

"Why does everyone keep blaming me?" Greg asked with almost believable innocence.

"Too many questions and not enough answers," Nalani sighed. "*How* did you get kicked out of Sunday school Brian?"

He simply glared at her with his arms crossed and his lips firmly shut.

"Then we'll have to guess," Jenni sighed. "You were kissing the girls."

"You made the teacher cry with your deadpan," Beth giggled.

"You were passing notes to the girls," Heather snickered.

"This is sounding very familiar," Joshua said sadly. "You better fess up before it gets worse, Brian."

Brian simply stared solemnly at his dad.

"You got in a fight with a girl?" Brandon guessed doubtfully.

"You wouldn't keep your clothes on," Tim grunted slightly when his wife elbowed him.

Surprisingly, Brian's ears started turning red.

"Oh, Tim's onto something!" Greg crowed.

"Did you just moon someone or was it worse?" Joy snickered.

"It was actually very innocent, just curiosity," Brian relented with a sigh. "It started the previous Thursday evening. Mom and Dad were in a Bible study, and that night they met at our house. I'd just turned ten and I was very curious, so I always eavesdropped in the hall when they met at our house. They were studying 1 Corinthians and that week they were in chapter seven, the part about being content with your situation in life."

Greg started snickering, but Brian plowed on.

"I was intrigued by the 'don't seek to be uncircumcised' part. They were all adults, so they talked pretty frankly about what all that meant. I knew what a penis was, but I didn't know what a foreskin was. I just wanted to see if any of the other boys had one."

"You didn't!" Cait gasped. "You got all the boys to expose themselves?"

"I told the girls not to look," Brian pouted. "And we huddled up so they couldn't see what we were doing," he paused for a dramatic, heavy sigh. "Unfortunately the teacher came in before we figured out what a foreskin was. All the other boys blamed me."

Everyone was laughing too hard to comment on that. Even Benton couldn't continue.

Rachel was the first one to get her mirth somewhat under control, but she set everyone off again.

"Oh, Dad! What have you done to me?"

Greg finally waved a hand at Benton.

"Let's move along to the vows," Benton suppressed his laughter. "The parents will start."

"I can't believe we had to talk you into this," Gloria giggled. "You so belong to our family, Brian. We love you deeply, and we've been dreaming of this day for almost five years. Joshua and I hadn't been thinking about looking for another son, but when we spent that first evening with you in the hotel in Atlanta, we both knew that we loved you like a son, and we would continue to do so until death parts us, regardless of what you chose."

The laughter was gone, and tears began to shimmer in more than one eye before Joshua was done.

"We understood your hesitation, maybe even more than you would admit to yourself," Brian's new father fixed him with a loving gaze. "You talked about your concerns last summer, and we let you vent what you wanted to talk about. Now I have to address the rest. You were afraid because as an eleven year old, you were ready to get a family – father, mother, sister – and that family was snatched away from you before it could happen. The little boy who still lives inside you was afraid that family would once again be snatched away from you if you tried to get another. I guess that's why God gave you such a big family this time. You'll lose some of us to death, sure, but you will not lose all of us. You will never be alone again, Brian. The day death closes your eyes, you will be surrounded by family."

Greg stepped up with no prompting from Benton.

"I was asked to speak for all of your siblings, and I'm not going to sugarcoat things. Sometimes, Brian, you're gonna wish you were alone again!" That elicited a few snickers. "Family is scary, especially this one. We are serious about family, probably because every one of us already experienced loss, so we cherish what we still have. We are part of each other's lives, maybe even more so than other families. But that's what your heart longs for, Brian. If you were satisfied with just the average American's idea of family and friends, you would've let Amanda and Will go a long time ago. But you kept them close in spite of distance and difficult circumstances. You're going to do the same with us, and we with you. We don't want you to leave Hawaii and join us here, but we do want you to build a big guest house 'cause we've got kids who need to climb those Trask trees!"

Brian did wait for Benton's nod.

"I've faced a lot of scary situations in my life, so I can honestly say that you all really aren't that scary. You should be. You're large, in numbers and some of you in size, but even when I first met you Shepherds almost seven years ago, I knew that a lot of love resided in your hearts. I envied you for having all that love. Now I am jealous of it. I love you all with an almost shocking intensity, and I'm going to protect that love bond, come what may. Bring it on! I'll build that house, and I'll even put in a few more trees, and if each of you doesn't show up at least once a year, I'm comin' after you! We're family, and that's what family does!"

In the resulting chaos of hugs, Joy was happy to see many other tear-stained cheeks. She absolutely adored this family she'd married into. She privately reaffirmed to God that she too would jealously guard the love she had for them all, not just for her husband.

Chapter 24

*T*im and Joy settled into life in Missouri. She had plenty of work to do, both the architectural kind and in their home. Tim rearranged furniture more than once as Joy tried to decide what arrangements were best. They also got started on the nursery, with help from their family.

Tim finally broke down and got Joy a bouquet of very real looking artificial flowers. He'd brought her an identical bouquet ever week while they lived in Franklin, but Gumbwats' Haven was too rural to be able to easily get a fresh bouquet every week. He wouldn't have thought of it himself, but Joy suggested it when she realized that Tim was driving an hour every week to get her bouquet. She was perfectly happy with a permanent bouquet, especially since sometimes the smell of real flowers irritated her, probably because of the hormonal changes of pregnancy. Tim promised her that as soon as the baby was born, he would give her a huge bouquet of pink roses and carnations, which Joy liked even if Tim didn't.

Of course Tim and Joy spent a lot of time with his family. Though no one else's house was more than a few hundred yards away, Tim rarely let Joy walk over to visit anyone. Not only was it often very cold, but they got snow or rain every few days, and even constant vigilance couldn't guarantee that the sidewalks would be free of ice. Joy tried to reassure him that she'd successfully walked on ice many times without falling. She knew how to do it, and when to avoid it. Tim didn't care; he wanted to eliminate any risk of her getting injured.

Tim's restriction didn't really matter. If Joy got stir-crazy being cooped up in her own house, Tim gladly drove her wherever she wanted to go, whether it was down the street to Luke's house on the other side of the Haven or all the way to St. Louis. But Joy didn't have much of a chance to get cabin fever because every day that she was home, someone popped in for a visit.

Sometimes it was the niephews, with or without parents. Sometimes adults showed up by themselves. Whoever it was, they very rarely let Joy do anything when they were in the house. Even when she stayed home she rarely fixed any meal but breakfast.

All that coddling could have been smothering, but Joy was beginning to have problems again. This time it wasn't nausea, or at least not primarily. Now it was headaches and backaches, swollen feet and dizziness. Toward the end of January, she was again having more bad days than good ones.

The doctor didn't find anything seriously wrong with Joy. Her vitals were good, so her body was probably just not adapting to her pregnancy very well. He advised her to rest as often as her body wanted it, to put her feet up when she sat and to get moderate exercise, but only when her body told her it was okay.

Joy obeyed the doctor pretty well. She didn't really have much of a choice because her husband hovered over her and made sure she rested more than she wanted to.

February crept in, both happy and frustrating for Joy. She enjoyed the good days, was grouchy on the bad, and counted the days until May 6.

ROBERT LEFT HIS last class for the week, Mideastern History. He loved the topic, hated the professor. If it wasn't in his major, he would drop it, but he needed the class to graduate this spring. The problem with going light on classes in the fall for football was that he had to go heavy in the spring if he was going to graduate on time. He had eighteen hours this spring and couldn't drop anything.

Today's class had been better than the last few weeks, but that wasn't because the professor was improving. Most of Robert's other professors he liked a lot, so he'd avoided Dr. Gardner's classes, obviously for a good reason. The professor was the same arrogant, Christian-hating man he'd been since Robert first met him three years ago. That made Robert's thoughts in class pretty funny. The professor had said something that reminded Robert of his pastor's sermon on Sunday.

"It's interesting to think sometimes how one event can be far-reaching, isn't it? What if Mohammed's parents hadn't died? How would that have changed the course of history? Would he still have married Khadija? If he hadn't married Khadija, would he have been in that cave on Mount Hira?"

"That's rather philosophical, isn't it?" one of the girls asked slyly.

"Yes it is," the professor frowned. "But don't you think history and philosophy are intertwined?"

"Philosophy does draw on history, doesn't it?" another student asked thoughtfully.

The conversation continued, but Robert tuned out because he was thinking about Sunday's sermon. Pastor had said pretty much the same thing, but with a different twist.

"Every decision we make has the potential to have far-reaching consequences, even when it seems like something manini. Twenty-five years ago in Portland, Oregon, on a cold, rainy Saturday in February, I was bored so I went roller-skating with a friend, even though I'd never been on a pair of roller-skates. That insignificant decision was a turning point in my life because I met my wonderful wife that day."

Pastor had talked about the decisions we make, but the professor brought up something that Mohammed had no control over – his parents' deaths. While the conversation had flowed around him, Robert started thinking about the turning points in his life that had been out of his hands.

Five years ago, when he was still a junior in high school, Mom and Dad's decision to get married had been beyond his control, but it had definitely affected his life. Being offered a football scholarship the following year had also been out of his control even though he'd worked hard to earn it.

As he left class, Robert thought about the difference between decisions and turning points. The big one, of course was that all our decisions are in our own hands, while we don't have any direct control over many, maybe even most, of our turning points.

He thought about the fact that there are many decisions and turning points in a person's life. Most decisions are conscious on our part, sometimes well-thought out, sometimes spur of the moment, but they can almost always be immediately identified as a decision. Turning points are different. Some we're aware of long before they happen and even look forward to them eagerly. That had been the case when he'd started his junior year of high school, eagerly anticipating getting a father again.

But Robert had also had some unanticipated and unwelcome turning points too. Like when Greg was abducted and held for ransom. That was set up to happen by Greg's seemingly unimportant decision about where to get a burger after landing in St. Louis.

That got Robert thinking about the apparent randomness of decisions and turning points. He was anticipating being drafted by a professional football team and graduating this spring, but how many decisions would he make between now and then that could affect the outcome of either anticipated turning point? And how many people he didn't even know would make decisions that would affect his draft? He dreaded the thought that the wrong people would make decisions that would keep him from being drafted by any team, or get him drafted by the wrong team, like the Berserkers, the long-time rivals of his beloved Grizzlies.

But what turning point might he be facing that he wasn't anticipating or even dreading?

Robert laughed at himself and slowly shook his head. There was no way to know how any single decision would affect a life, or maybe even many lives. If he didn't know that God was ultimately in control, that he already had a plan to work every decision for his glory, then life would be a terrifying endeavor.

"Hi, Robert," Eirian Josephson suddenly fell in step beside him.

"Hi, Eirian. Did you like class today?" Robert was surprised that she was talking to him. Since they were both history majors they'd had a lot of classes together in the last few years, but she didn't talk to him much, only when they were in a group of other students. They had never had a personal conversation before. She seemed a little standoffish.

But she was cute, smart, and she talked about her sister like she really loved her, so she interested Robert. When he'd first met her she'd been a very vocal unbeliever, but in the past year or so she'd sounded a lot like a seeker or a new believer. He'd been trying to figure out how to discover what her current spiritual state was. He would really like to get to know her better, but if she wasn't a believer that might not be a good idea.

"I'd like it a lot better if someone other than Gardner taught it," Eirian replied with a disgusted eye roll.

"Can't argue with that," Robert sighed. "What's up?"

"I've got a favor to ask you," Eirian glanced at him out of the corner of her eye.

"Oh?" The simple answer concealed his confusion. He wouldn't mind doing a favor for Eirian but he didn't know why she would ask one of him.

"I wouldn't normally bother you, but it's for a good cause."

"Okay. Ask. The worst I can do is say no."

"Some of the student groups are getting together and putting on an auction for charity."

"So what do you want?" Robert almost sighed. He'd hoped it would be something like working on a project together. "Autographed footballs from my brother and brothers-in-law?"

"No, I want you."

"Excuse me?" Robert stopped and stared at her.

"I mean I want you to auction off a date with yourself," she almost looked like she was blushing but her calm face and voice belied any embarrassment.

"With me?" Robert frowned. "Why would someone buy a date with me?"

"Get real, Robert Shepherd," Eirian said tartly. "You're almost the hottest guy on campus."

"In a pig's eye," Robert snorted and started walking.

"Oh, come on," she almost trotted to keep pace with him. "You're good-looking, rich, smart and about to be drafted by a pro football team. The bidding will be furious. We'll make a lot of money."

"Nope. Not doing it," Robert shook his head firmly.

"Oh come on, Robert. It's for a good cause," Eirian wheedled. "It's only one date!"

"With whatever girl bids the highest," Robert snorted in disgust. "No thanks, Eirian. I'll pass."

"You can name whatever charity you want," she suggested.

"And I can call my dad and have him drop a wad on said charity without putting myself at risk," Robert shook his head firmly.

"But don't you want to do something yourself?" Eirian asked with a curious tilt of her head. "Don't you ever want it to be something you did, not your family?"

Robert stopped and stared at her.

Maybe it was the fact that just this morning he'd been reading the story of David's census and the resulting plague in First Chronicles. The king bought that threshing floor where the angel of the Lord was stopped because he didn't want to give an offering that cost him nothing.

Maybe it was just because Eirian was cute, and he really liked her.

He said yes.

That decision would become a major turning point in his life.

Chapter 25

*T*im was glad to take Robert's call on the last Tuesday afternoon of February. Joy was having another miserable day. She'd finally fallen asleep about half an hour ago. Tim was more than ready to talk to someone who didn't have anything to gripe at him about.

"Hey, howzit Robert?" Tim cheerfully greeted his brother.

"It's goin'," Robert replied, equally cheerful. "Back atcha."

"Joy's not doin' so well," Tim sighed. "I can't believe we've got almost three more months of this to suffer through."

"That's tough," Robert said sympathetically. "I don't remember Nalani or any of the other ladies having that much trouble."

"Yeah," Tim agreed. "Even Heather wasn't this uncomfortable."

"If she had been, she would've accepted the doctor's restrictions better."

"That's true! But you didn't call to talk about Joy's pregnancy. Wazzup? How's school?"

"Pretty good, but I sure am glad spring break is two weeks away."

"So am I! Joy's already begged Mom to make sure you're here the first possible minute. She thinks I'm hovering and smothering her. She hopes you'll distract me."

"I'll be happy to help my wonderful sister-in-law."

"What are you distracted about right now?"

"It shows, huh?" Robert snorted slightly.

"To me, yeah. So fess up, brah."

"I agreed to do something, but the closer the day gets, the more I'm not sure I should."

"Okay," Tim said cautiously. "What was it?"

"I donated a date with me to a charity auction."

"Seriously!?"

"Seriously."

"What girl asked you?" Tim asked.

"Why'd it have to be a girl?" Robert grumbled.

"Because no guy could ever convince you to do it."

"Eirian Josephson," Robert grudgingly admitted.

Tim thought about that name. "Hey, isn't that the girl who won't give you the time of day even though she's in almost all your history classes? The one that you think is cute?"

"Yeah."

"So you found your Beth!"

"My Beth? She's not …."

Robert hadn't thought about it before, but Tim might have a point. Though Greg had now been happily married for six years, when he'd first met Beth in Bible college, she'd rejected all his overtures to get to know her. It was well over a year before they'd had their first real conversation.

"You sure she's not your Beth?" Tim asked slyly after the sudden silence had stretched on too long.

"No, I'm not," Robert sighed.

"Maybe this is how God's going to finally break the ice between you."

"But she's probably not going to buy this date."

"So what? She'll owe you, so you can claim a real date with her."

"But I'll have to go on a date with someone who might be a total stranger!" Robert complained.

"So what? Take her to a non-romantic comedy and sit smack dab in the middle of the theater."

"I guess that'll work," Robert agreed hesitantly.

"But I would lock Eirian into a date before the auction," Tim snickered. "If she is like Beth, even then you'll have a heck of a time getting her to follow through with it."

Robert wasn't a hundred percent certain of his brother's advice, but he didn't want to talk about it anymore. Instead he asked about the niephews that Tim got to see practically every day. He would pray about the date later. If God told him not to, he wouldn't.

If God didn't say anything, Robert guessed he would worry and pray more, right up to the last minute.

"Hi, Lowri!"

Lowri Josephson looked up in surprise. She knew that voice very well. Half of everyone on campus knew Shariann Delaney. She was only one of the most popular girls. Lowri adored her, but she hadn't thought that Shari even knew her name.

"Hi, Shari," Lowri tried not to be too eager in her greeting.

"Mind if I join you?"

"Not at all," Lowri moved the book she'd been reading and made room at her small table for Shari to set down her drink.

"I heard about what your sister did," Shari whispered excitedly.

"What?" Lowri had no clue what the other woman was talking about.

"She got Robert Shepherd to donate a date for the charity auction tomorrow night!"

"Oh! That!" Lowri grinned. "She sure did."

"Is she hoping to get it for herself?" Shari asked.

"Oh no!" Lowri shook her head firmly. "She's hoping the biding goes way out of her range."

"Would you like to get that date?" Shari asked slyly.

"Who wouldn't?" Lowri sighed. Robert Shepherd was only one of the hottest guys on campus. Lowri didn't know many girls who didn't drool over him, except of course, her big sister. "But there's no chance of that, not even if Eirian and I pooled our resources."

"What if I helped?"

"You'd help *me* get a date with Robert Shepherd?" Lowri was shocked.

"I sure would!"

"What's the catch?"

"It's no big deal, really," Shari shrugged. "Some of the other sisters and I want to 'punk' him."

"Then why don't one of you buy the date?" Lowri asked warily.

"One of us?" Shari laughed. "He wouldn't go out with one of us! If we bought the date, he'd back out of it. He'd get his dad to double whatever we bid so he didn't have to go out with any of us."

Lowri thought about that. Shari was right. Shepherd was boldly Christian. He dated very rarely, and it was always with girls who were at least very moral. He stayed away from the 'bad girls.' Shari and her friends were definitely in the bad girl category.

That gave Lowri momentary pause. She desperately wanted to get into Shari's sorority. What did that say about her?

Not all the girls in the sorority were bad.

"When you say 'punk,' what do you mean?" Lowri was still doubtful.

"He'll probably take you to a movie," Shari leaned toward her and whispered conspiratorially, as if they'd been friends for years. "After the movie, you get him out to the beach, and we'll get to tease him."

"Tease how?" Lowri's frown was a little less hesitant.

"We'll just kiss him and hug and stuff, just to embarrass him. Maybe take off his shirt," Shari shrugged casually. "We'll get pictures with him."

"Isn't a person supposed to laugh after they get punked?" Lowri was more curious than doubtful. "I don't think he's going to laugh about that later."

"Oh, it's not that big a deal. We're not going to post the pictures on Facebook or anything," Shari waved dismissively. "But won't it be so cool? You know he's going to be drafted. Someday he'll be famous and you'll have a picture of him and you together."

"I don't know," Lowri was leaning toward saying yes, but what would Eirian think?

"Oh, come on," Shari purred. "The other sisters are going to love you for this."

"I guess I'm in," Lowri sighed. "But promise me you won't do anything bad to Robert?"

"I promise," Shari smiled sweetly.

THURSDAY EVENING, ROBERT approached the ballroom with mixed feelings. He didn't want to do the auction because he didn't like or want the attention he would be getting. He also wasn't quite sure that it was God-honoring, but since he didn't know it would dishonor God, he couldn't use that as a criterion for judging the rightness or wrongness of selling a couple hours of his time for a worthy cause. In the absence of an answer from God one way or the other, Robert was still conflicted. His brother's advice on Tuesday tipped the scales slightly toward doing it, but only very slightly.

Suddenly Eirian was walking toward him, her face shining brightly.

The I'm-doing-this scale smacked the ground.

"You're here!" she almost seemed like she was going to hug him. Instead she clasped her hands and merely beamed at him. "I was half afraid you wouldn't show!"

"I promised," Robert shrugged. "I wouldn't just not show up."

"But you are tempted to back out," she frowned. "And you would do it face-to-face. Are you going to?"

"If I do this, you owe me," Robert decided that if he was going to follow Tim's advice, he may as well follow all of it.

"Yeah, I guess so," Eirian stared warily at him. "What are you thinking?"

"Dinner and a movie, with you."

"You want a date with me before you'll go on a date with someone else?" Eirian giggled.

"Sounds a little strange when you put it that way, but yeah, I do," Robert nodded firmly.

"What if I buy the date tonight?" Eirian asked with a saucy toss of her head.

"Then I get two dates with you," Robert grinned, absurdly pleased with the idea.

"And if I say no?"

"Then I say no," Robert shrugged and turned to go.

"Wait!" Eirian grabbed his arm to stop his flight. "Okay."

"Okay?" Robert stopped and looked at Eirian but he didn't turn back toward the ballroom.

"I'll go on a date with you," Eirian hissed, but she didn't look unhappy.

"When?"

"After you go on the date with whoever wins tonight."

"I'm gonna shoot for tomorrow night," Robert turned back toward the ballroom.

"Really?"

"I wanna get the charity date over with quickly. So how about you and me plan for Saturday?"

"Fine," Eirian dropped her eyes but smiled slightly. "It's a date."

Robert cheerfully followed her to the ballroom. She led him to the auctioneer. They had a brief verbal scuffle when Robert discovered they wanted him to stand on the auction block and preen. He flat refused, ready to back out, even if it meant losing his date with Eirian.

A little over an hour later, he stood and bowed to the room before taking his seat again.

The auctioneer asked for an opening bid of fifty dollars, which he immediately got from half a dozen voices. Then it took mere seconds for the rapid fire bidding to pass two-fifty. Robert was disappointed when Eirian didn't call another bid as the auctioneer quickly took the bid to five hundred. He was shocked to hear the voice of Eirian's younger sister call out.

"Five-fifty!"

"Six!" The alumnus who had taken the bid to five hundred didn't drop out. She'd already announced her intention to have him clean her carpets for their "date." That was acceptable to Robert. It would be better than having to go out with one of the college girls who were always fawning over him.

"Six-fifty!" That bid came from a trio of senior girls. If they won the bid, Robert was calling Dad to get enough money to buy his way out of the date. No way was he going out with any of them. He knew them too well.

"Seven!" Lowri bid again after a brief pause.

Robert wondered if she was bidding for herself or for her sister.

"It's kind of steep for carpet cleaning, but what the heck," the alumnus cheerfully called out. "Seven-fifty!"

The spokeswoman for the trio didn't hesitate to call, "Eight!"

After another brief pause, then Lowri enthusiastically called, "Eight-fifty!"

"My garage needs cleaning too," the alumnus called. "I'll give you nine!"

"Nine-twenty-five," the trio gave what was hopefully their last bid. The woman who called out sounded a little desperate.

"Nine-fifty," Lowri again called out. Robert wished he could see her, but she was sitting in the back.

"It's for a good cause," the alumnus said cheerfully. "I'll go an even grand!"

The trio didn't bid. The auctioneer looked toward Lowri and asked for fifty more.

He asked again.

Robert shifted in his seat. He didn't care if Lowri bid again or not, but he hoped the senior girls were really out of it.

"Eleven hundred," Lowri suddenly called triumphantly.

The alumnus threw her hands up and deliberately turned away, laughing merrily. "I can get my ex-husband to clean the carpets for that much!"

Everyone joined her laughter.

Lowri won the bidding.

There were more items still being auctioned, so Robert stayed in his seat. He hadn't thought to ask what he should do after the bidding was over. Was he supposed to track down Lowri or wait for her to find him?

Robert had just decided to go find Lowri when suddenly she dropped into the seat beside him.

"It's a done deal," she waved a piece of paper at him.

He didn't need to look at it to know that it said she'd bought a date with Robert Shepherd.

"No," Robert said firmly. "That's just a promissory note. It's not a done deal until after our date."

"When will that be?" Lowri fairly bounced with excitement.

"There's a movie opening tomorrow night," Robert shrugged with a slight smile. "I've been looking forward to seeing it."

"Only a movie?" Lowri pouted.

"If you behave, we can go to dinner after," Robert promised.

"Goody!" Lowri did bounce. "What time?"

"I'll pick you up at six."

As they worked out the details, Robert never once thought to ask her where she got the money. He didn't know the Josephson sisters well enough to doubt her ability to pay that much by herself.

Chapter 26

*E*irian did know her sister very well. She was one-hundred percent certain that Lowri did not have that kind of money. She confronted her sister as soon as she got back to the off-campus apartment they shared.

"Where did you get the money?" she demanded, arms crossed firmly.

"None of your business!" Lowri tossed her head.

"Oh yes it is! I'm the one who roped Robert into this. I know you don't have that much money readily available. You got it from somewhere, and that means from someone with ulterior motives. Who was it?" Eirian was furious. If this went poorly, if Robert got embarrassed he would resent her for dragging him into the auction; he would never talk to her again. That was unacceptable.

"From some friends, if you must know," Lowri kept her nose in the air.

"What friends?" Eirian demanded.

When Lowri didn't answer, Eirian stepped closer, looming threateningly.

She hadn't beat up her little sister in many years, but she was three inches taller and forty pounds heavier than her petite little sister, and when she scowled like that, the scar beside her right eye made her look menacing. Her size, scowl and Lowri's memory combined to great effect.

"Shariann Delaney," Lowri pouted.

"Delaney!" Eirian gasped and sank heavily to the couch. "No no no. This is not good."

"They just want to punk him a little," Lowri still had some misgivings, but she was also excited about the prospect of spending a few hours with Robert Shepherd.

"A little?" Eirian shook her head firmly. "That woman is mean. There's no way she's going to punk Robert 'a little.'"

"She is not mean," Lowri snapped. "She's my friend."

"No she's not! Why'd she pick you anyway?"

"She said she needed someone sweet like me," Lowri tilted her chin again. "She said Robert would back out if she bought the date herself."

"That's for sure," Eirian snarled. She was furious about the whole situation. She was even mad at herself for roping Robert into doing it.

Unfortunately, she knew her sister too well. Lowri had dug in her heels and she wouldn't be moved. She was going on the date with Robert.

Eirian could probably convince Robert to cancel, but that wouldn't work because she couldn't easily get the money to cover the cost of the date so it could be returned to Shariann and her cohorts. She certainly couldn't ask Robert to both cancel the date and pay for it too! She had gotten him into this, and she was going to have to take care of it herself.

She stared steadily at her sister. Any argument would push Lowri farther away from her. The best Eirian was going to be able to do was damage control.

"Where are they doing this?"

"I don't know," Lowri shrugged, somewhat surprised that her sister was dropping her argument. "Shari's going to text me a location after we leave the movie."

"What movie? Where? When?" Eirian snapped out.

She would get as much information as her sister had. She would follow Lowri and Robert. Hopefully if things started getting out of hand, she would be able to stop it.

Robert was past ready for his date to be over. It had started pretty well. Lowri was a sweet girl, and while she wasn't a witty conversationalist, she wasn't an airhead either. Once the movie started, she hadn't needed to be told to be quiet. She'd settled in and watched the action-comedy with apparent enjoyment.

During the movie, she stayed firmly in her own seat. She didn't try to cling to him or share his popcorn. She'd only disturbed him once, a little more than halfway through the movie when she whispered that she wanted some Snowcaps. Since it was during a slow part in the action, he was happy to oblige her.

It had looked like it was going to be a fine evening, but he was starting to feel funny. Maybe he was coming down with something. He felt a little woozy and it was hard to focus on the dialogue of the movie.

When they rose to go after a somewhat confusing ending, Robert was surprised that he was unsteady on his feet. He walked carefully, trying not to stumble. He was happy when the wall was finally close enough to give him some support.

They stepped out of the dark theater and the light in the hall was bright. Much too bright.

Something definitely was wrong.

"So, are we going to have dinner now?" Lowri asked brightly.

"Sorry, but I think I'm gonna hafta pass," Robert frowned in concentration. "I'm not feelin' so good fer some reason. I think I gonna go home."

"You don't look so good," Lowri peered up at him with concerned eyes. "Are you going to be okay to drive?"

Robert thought about that.

It was hard to think that much.

"I guess it'd prob'ly be better if you did. You got a license?"

"Yes, of course," Lowri said happily. She almost bounced with pleasure. She'd been afraid that she would have to argue to get the keys from him.

As they started across the foyer, Robert casually put his arm across Lowri's shoulders. He found it helped to keep him going in a straight line.

EIRIAN WAS IN the parking lot across the street. She'd bought binoculars especially for this clandestine mission. She saw Lowri and Robert exit the building. She focused on Robert's face and hissed.

He was high!

The hypocrite! Spouting his Christian garbage all over campus then getting high on a date with her sister!

She had half a mind to leave him to the untender mercies of Shariann Delaney and her wicked witch sorority sisters, but that would mean abandoning Lowri. Eirian couldn't do that.

Lowri and Robert were crossing the street. Lowri was looking at her phone. She raised her head and kept walking toward Robert's car.

"Come on, Low," Eirian begged, staring at her own phone.

Lowri had agreed that Eirian would follow her and bail her out if things didn't go well. She'd promised to text her the destination as soon as she got it from Shariann.

"Please, Lowri," Eirian pleaded as she watched Lowri help Robert drop into the passenger side of his car.

She needed to know where they were going. She probably wasn't going to be able to follow Lowri, not in the madhouse this area turned into when a movie let out. Besides, she'd decided that it would be better to be in place on the beach before Lowri arrived. She could assess the situation and call off the punking if necessary.

Lowri was walking around behind the car. She stopped and looked at her phone.

As she started walking again, Eirian's phone chirruped happily.

Waimanalo beach park, 1st lot.

"Thank you, Lowri," she cried as she dropped the phone on the seat and threw the car in reverse.

Once she got on the H1, she made good time getting to Waimanalo. She decided she would park down in the second lot and hike back to the first swimming beach. That way Shari and her cohorts would be unlikely to see her car, so they wouldn't suspect they had company. That would work in Eirian's favor if she needed to step in and stop things.

As Eirian ran quietly in the sand along the tree line, she heard laughing voices up ahead. She got close enough to distinguish voices and was dismayed to realize there were some male voices in the mix.

Her binoculars were still hanging around her neck. As soon as she could distinguish figures she tried to bring them closer so she could see who they were.

Finally a face popped into focus. Eirian gasped in dismay. It was Dewayne Bronson!

Bronson was another football player, a defensive lineman like Robert. He'd been recruited from somewhere in California and probably would have been a star here in Hawaii if Robert hadn't overshadowed him in all respects. He hated Robert.

This was way beyond not good. She had to call it off. Lowri needed to just go home. They would deal with the fallout later.

Eirian frantically searched her pockets for her phone. It wasn't there!

She wanted to scream when she realized that it was sitting on the seat of her car, where she had dropped it after getting the text from Lowri.

She couldn't go back and get it. Lowri and Robert would be here any minute. She couldn't do anything to help if she wasn't even here.

She did have her iPod. She could record the whole event. If they crossed the line, even if she couldn't stop it, she could make sure they paid dearly for it later.

ROBERT WASN'T SURE where they were. In fact he wasn't sure of anything. That bottle of water that Lowri had produced from somewhere hadn't helped. In fact, he felt worse. Now no part of his entire body was working right.

If he didn't know that Lowri was so sweet and innocent, he would suspect that she'd given him drugs. But there was no way she would have done that. He must have caught a doozy of a flu bug.

Lowri was parking the car. Robert sighed with relief. Soon he would be safe in his own bed where he could sleep it off. If he still felt bad in the morning, he would call Dave or Greg. They were in town because Greg had been invited to speak at a conference this weekend. Between them and Beth and Dei, they would make sure he got whatever he needed to get over whatever he had.

Suddenly someone was pulling him out of the car. It was more than one someone. They were giggling in a way that Robert didn't like.

His hackles would be rising if his body was working right.

But it wasn't, and he couldn't make it no matter how hard he tried.

Someone was pulling on his shirt and messing with his pants.

He tried to jerk away, but he only stumbled and fell. His attackers were all over him.

He heard Lowri crying and tried to help her, but he couldn't see her. He couldn't even focus on the faces that were right in front of him.

Suddenly Lowri was screaming, and she was coming closer.

Someone else was screaming about cops.

He was being pinned by very strong arms, arms that were much stronger than his in his current condition.

Lowri was being forced on him, but there was nothing he could do to stop it.

He struggled, but he knew his efforts were too feeble.

The blood was roaring in his head.

Suddenly everyone was gone. He was alone.

Not alone. Someone was laughing. Someone was protesting. Someone was screaming.

Lowri was one of the women screaming. Someone was hurting her.

Robert had to stop her from being hurt, even if it meant being hurt himself.

"Leave 'er 'lone," Robert struggled to rise to his knees.

A male voice snarled at him, swearing viciously. "You gonna stop me?"

"Do my darnedest," Robert was trying to get his body to work, but it wasn't listening to him. His brain wasn't right either. He knew that voice but he couldn't peg it.

"How 'bout you take her place?"

Suddenly Robert was face down in the sand.

Now Robert not only couldn't move, he couldn't even breathe. He felt pain, but it was in a fog. He heard voices protesting, felt the weight on him give a little. He was aware of a struggle. Then he was alone.

He laid in the sand, trying to comprehend what had happened to him. Why was he in such agony? What had he done so wrong in his life that God would allow this to happen to him?

He vaguely heard some cars driving off. He heard a sound of soft weeping. He turned his head that way but couldn't make out anything but some shadows. Closer to him he saw something dark laying in the sand. He reached for it.

It was his pants. He pulled them close but it took a lot of effort. Too much effort for such a simple task, but he didn't give up. His phone was in his pants. He needed to call for help.

Suddenly someone was kneeling beside him, helping him find his phone.

"I'm sorry, Robert." It sounded like Eirian. She was crying. He could understand that. He felt like crying too. "I didn't know .... I never would have .... I'm so sorry. I've gotta get Lowri out of here. We're at Waimanalo. I wish I could wait to leave 'til help comes, but I need to get my sister out of here. She was a victim too, Robert. She really likes you. She didn't want .... I'm sorry, so sorry."

Eirian was gone but his phone was in his hand.

He couldn't see anything. He couldn't find the numbers to call 911.

His phone was voice activated.

"Call Greg," he instructed the phone.

GREG WAS JUST slipping out of the nursery when his phone vibrated in his pocket. At this time of night, it had to be family calling. He was ready to talk to someone and unwind. The Pod could be quite a handful at bedtime, but he was able to handle them by himself. He did it as often as he could because then Beth could steal a few precious minutes of quiet time by herself, but whenever he did fly solo, his stress level got a little on the high side. Thankfully the rest of the kids had stayed in Missouri because this was just a short business trip. They'd come for a conference down at the convention center at which The Ohana Project had a booth that had to be manned. He, Dave and some staff from the local office had been there the entire time of the conference, and they'd taught a few sessions too. He and Dave had each done small breakout sessions, but right after lunch today, Greg had spoken for a plenary session.

Beth and Dei had each stayed home a day to take care of the kids, The Pod and little Kenny. Today had been Beth's day with the kids, so Greg had taken care of them when it was time for bed.

He saw his brother's smiling face on the screen.

"Hey, Robert," he cheerfully but softly answered his phone. When the boys were all sleeping at once, he tried not to do anything that might possibly wake them.

I hurt, Robert moaned.

"What's wrong, Robert?" Greg asked urgently, rushing down the hall to the den where he knew Beth was.

They hurt me.

As Robert whimpered, Greg wondered if this was how Steve had felt five years ago when he'd been the one crying on the other end of the phone.

"Who hurt you, Robert?" Greg asked calmly though he felt far from calm.

Beth was jumping up from the couch, rushing to his side.

Don' know. Too fuzzy. Think they drugged me.

"Where are you, Robert?"

Not sure. She said Waimanalo.

"Waimanalo," Greg nodded at Beth who was pushing buttons on her phone. "The beach or the park?"

Yeah, Robert answered unhelpfully.

"Which one, Robert? The beach?"

Sandy.

"Then the beach," with merely a nod at Beth, Greg was out the door.

"What happened?" he kept Robert talking as he raced to the car.

Don' re'lly know. Too fuzzy. I hurt.

"I know. I hurt for you too. How did you call me?"

Phone in pants, but had to find pants.

174

Greg took a deep breath, pushing down the horror that statement brought to mind. Robert needed him calm.

"What happened to your pants, Robert?"

They took 'em. Shirt too. Ever'thing.

Greg continued to talk to his brother, trying to get as clear a picture as he could and still calm Robert. Through the phone, he heard the wail of a siren.

Cops here. Thanks, Greg.

The phone went silent. Greg prayed frantically as he drove the last few miles to the beach park. It was easy to know where Robert was because there were plenty of flashing lights.

As he slowed at the entrance to the beach park, an officer tried to wave him past.

Greg shook his head and pointed at the cluster of police cars.

"My brother called me," for a brief moment Greg thought he was going to have to get in an argument with her, but then another officer was walking toward him.

"You Greg Shepherd?" he called.

When Greg affirmed that he was, the first officer waved him into the parking lot.

"We don't know much yet," the second officer told Greg as he led him toward the small cluster of police officers. "Your brother was definitely attacked, but he's not giving us a coherent account right now. We're hoping that now that you're here you can help him calm down and tell us what he remembers."

"From what he said on the phone," Greg said sadly, "I'm not sure calming down is going to help much."

"What did he tell you?"

"That he thought 'they' drugged him," Greg saw his baby brother and a shudder ran through him. He had to force himself to finish his statement. "But he didn't say who 'they' were."

Greg kept walking. He didn't ask for permission to enter the circle around his brother; he just stepped through and knelt by Robert who was huddled under a too small blanket, shivering. He had on pants but no shirt or slippers. He didn't look up as Greg approached.

"Hey, punk," Greg said softly.

Robert looked up then, but much too slowly. He seemed to have difficulty focusing on his brother, but he suddenly leaned heavily against Greg and wept.

Greg was furious. It hadn't been that long ago that he'd gone to be with Rachel after a similar incident. He couldn't believe God was putting the family through this kind of pain again. What was God doing to them?

He wanted to rage at God, to shake his fist at the heavens.

He held his brother and wept.

In the deepest, truest part of himself, Greg knew that he trusted God to walk with them through the difficult days ahead. Someday he would surrender his anger for the peace that passes understanding. Until that day, God would patiently let him rage and weep. God wouldn't abandon him in this dark time, no matter how angry Greg got.

Chapter 27

*T*he night was very long and dark. Greg stayed with Robert every minute he could. When he had to follow the ambulance that took Robert away from the scene of the crime, he made good use of his time. He called Dave first. He knew Beth would have already called him and that his brother would be standing by, waiting for his call.

What's going on, Greg? Dave asked urgently.

"He's on his way to the hospital," Greg answered. "I'm following the ambulance."

What happened?

"Not now," Greg sighed sadly. "I'll tell you what I know when I get to the hospital."

I'll be there, Dave assured him. *Should I call Brian already, or wait 'til you get here?*

"Wait. We'll call him together. It's probably too late for him to get a flight tonight anyway."

The next call was going to be harder. Luke would need to know everything Greg knew. He was going to have to tell Mom and Dad.

Greg, it's two o'clock in the morning, Luke grumbled into the phone.

Greg hadn't thought about the time difference, but it didn't really matter. He would have called anyway.

"It's Robert."

What happened? Luke asked sharply.

"He was assaulted. We don't know who yet, or even how many. They drugged him."

Is he ...? Luke couldn't say it, couldn't ask if the unimaginable had happened.

"He's going to survive. I don't think he's going to have any physical scars, but the psychological scars will go deep."

I'll get Mom and Dad. We'll call with our ETA. Should we bring anyone else?

"No," Greg said with deep sadness. "Dave's already here. He's the one who'll help Robert the most right now."

Oh, God, Luke groaned.

Greg was glad that Luke understood what he couldn't say. Especially when it's fresh, pain seeks to be known by a similar pain. Robert would need Dave more than anyone else for a while because Dave had been raped by some senior boys when he was a freshman in high school.

LUKE WAS SLUMPED on the floor at the foot of the steps. Even before he disconnected the call, he felt his wife's small hands on his shoulders.

"Robert needs me," he groaned. "I've got to go to Hawaii."

"Of course. I'll help you pack a bag," Nalani simply said.

She started to rise, but Luke pulled her back down, crushing her to his chest.

"Pray for him, Starshine," Luke groaned.

Nalani didn't ask for clarification. She understood that her husband meant now. Pray now because he couldn't do it himself.

"Oh, God, I don't know what's happened to Robert, but I know you do. Please wrap him in your love. Please comfort him and give him the strength to walk through this storm. Give us all strength as we walk with him."

Nalani didn't say amen. She'd spoken her piece, but she would keep on praying.

AFTER LUKE WAS finally on his way with his mom and dad, Nalani started to climb the stairs to return to bed. Of course Luke had told her what he knew before he left. With her foot on the first step, she realized that she was unlikely to sleep again tonight. There was no need to drag herself up the stairs only to lay on her empty bed staring at the ceiling. She turned and went into the den instead.

She spent some time on her knees, but she kept feeling a need to do something useful, something productive. She wasn't sure what she should do. If God was trying to tell her something, she wasn't receiving a clear message.

She got up and wandered into the office. Once there, it was only logical to sit down at the computer. She could start sending some emails, asking for prayer support. Anyone she would want to send a message to would pray without knowing details. There was no way she was telling something like this in an email, not even to the people who did need to know.

Once the computer booted, she opened her email program. It would take a while to fully load, so she went into the kitchen and fixed a cup of herbal tea.

When she got back to the computer, there were a number of new emails. She and Luke both downloaded work emails on their home computer because they sometimes worked from home, though Luke was much more likely to do it than she was. She spent more time with clients than he did, and he had a much heavier burden of paperwork.

The most recent email had come in only minutes ago. It was to Luke from "sorrysister," and it had an attachment.

Nalani clicked on it and found a brief message:

> I am so very sorry. If I had known, I would have prevented it. But I didn't know. I tried to stop it but I couldn't. I hate that this happened, but hopefully this will help justice be served. That's why I recorded it.

Nalani stared at the attachment for a long moment. She dug the headphones out of the drawer and angled the monitor so it couldn't be seen from the door. She didn't want one of her kids to stumble down the steps and see something they shouldn't.

The video was too dark and narrowly focused, but the message came through, loud and clear.

Nalani wept, deep soul-shaking sobs.

When the first wave of the storm eased some, Nalani reached for the phone. She still remembered the number to Luke's old precinct in Honolulu. They would be able to direct her to the right person.

After the video was on its way to Honolulu, Nalani called Greg. She needed to know what the police told them as soon as they knew. She was going to have to tell the rest of the family come sunrise, and she wanted to be able to assure them that justice would be done for Robert.

When she finally started making the rounds on the family farm, Nalani saved the worst for last. She went to Heather and Steve's house first.

She was somewhat relieved when Steve answered the door by himself. She talked to him before he went to get Heather, telling him everything she knew. He went by himself to tell Heather, giving her only the details she had to know immediately. When they returned to the living room where Nalani was waiting, they were both dressed and ready to go with her to make the notifications. Their next stop was Jenni and Pete's, then they told Brandon and Cari. Rachel and Abe would have to wait for later because they were at their loft in St. Louis.

As Nalani, Steve and Heather crossed Tim and Joylynne's lawn, they heard singing in the back of the house. It sounded like Joy was already up and feeling much better than she had in a while. They hated to ring the bell and take that away from her, but it couldn't be avoided.

JOYLYNNE WAS SURPRISED by the doorbell. She'd never heard it ring before. She hurried to the front door, not wanting it to ring again and wake Tim. She still didn't understand how anyone could sleep for ten hours, but she accepted Tim's right to do so whenever he could. Hopefully the bell was just one of the niephews being silly, though it was rather early in the morning for that.

She was immediately worried when she saw Nalani, Steve and Heather. Nalani seemed exhausted and Heather looked like she'd been crying.

"Come in," Joy stepped back so they could accept her invitation. "Tim's still asleep. I guess I should wake him."

"Please do," Steve nodded solemnly.

Joy immediately turned and went down the short hall to the room they were now using as a bedroom. For the first time she was glad that the doctor had said no more steps. Her suddenly shaky legs wouldn't have carried her all the way up to the master bedroom, much less back down again.

"Tim," she called softly as she crossed the room.

He groaned and pulled a pillow over his head. Obviously the bell had disturbed his sleep but he didn't want to wake up.

"Timothy dear," she spoke a little louder. "You need to get up. We have visitors."

"Tell 'em go 'way an' come back at a decent hour," Tim grumbled, his head still under the pillow.

"I can't, Tim," she said sadly. "Something's happened to someone. Nalani, Heather and Steve are here."

"Here?" Tim rolled over and leaned on his elbow, frowning at her. "What's going on?"

"I don't know," Joy shook her head. "They asked me to get you."

"Okay, I'm coming," Tim quickly rose and crossed the room. "Let me relieve myself and get clothes on then I'll be right out."

In two minutes he was standing in the living room, with a worried frown for their early morning visitors. That was the fastest Joy had ever seen him get up and get moving.

"Please, let's sit," Nalani said softly.

Tim's frown deepened, then he abruptly walked over and dropped onto the couch, pulling Joy down beside him.

"Luke got a call this morning around two," Nalani clasped her hands tightly, hoping to stop their trembles. "It was from Greg. Robert was … he was …."

Tim jerked and paled at Robert's name. Nalani knew how much Luke's two youngest brothers meant to each other. They were so close in age. They'd been almost inseparable when they were little. They were best friends. This was going to tear Tim apart.

She began to sob. All the other notifications she'd been able to get through, but this one was too much.

Steve didn't look to see if Heather was going to take over. He didn't want her to. He would carry this burden, even though anger rose in him. He couldn't believe that God was making him do this once again, telling this family that a beloved brother had been hurt horribly.

"Robert's going to be okay," Steve stared steadily at Tim. "He was assaulted on the beach this morning. He doesn't remember much because they drugged him, so the police are still trying to figure out the details. He may have been forced to have sex with an unknown woman. He was definitely raped."

Tim shook his head. Steve stared solemnly, nodding his head once.

Tim covered his face with his hand and began to weep. Joylynne pulled him toward her. He wrapped his arms around her and sobbed harder.

He had to push the tears back. He needed to know more. He slowly sat up again.

"Was it Eirian or Lowri Josephson?"

"Was who Eirian or Lowri Josephson?" Steve asked with a puzzled frown.

"The girl he might have been forced to have sex with? Was it Eirian or Lowri?" Tim asked angrily.

"I don't know," Nalani answered. "Why do you ask?"

"Because Lowri's the one who bought the date with Robert at the auction. Eirian's the one who talked him into it. They're sisters. Were they involved? His date was last night," Tim fairly glared at Nalani.

She merely shrugged. She didn't know anything to tell him, but even if she did, she couldn't tell him. Tears were again clogging her throat. Of course Tim knew more about what was going on in Robert's life than anyone else.

Nalani looked at Steve and shook her head. He was one of the few who would ever know that she'd seen a video of the horrifying event. Greg and Dave knew and they would tell Luke, but no one else would ever know more than that she'd received a video and forwarded it to the Honolulu police.

Steve accurately received Nalani's nonverbal message. He passed it on to Tim.

"Someone who called herself sorrysister captured everything on video. She said in an email that she didn't intend for it to happen but she couldn't stop it either, so she recorded it to make sure justice was done. Right now we don't know if the women you mentioned were involved, but there were two women who were also victimized by what appears to be four men and four or five women."

"Can they identify them?" Tim asked.

"They're working on it, but they're confident they can," Steve nodded.

"They'll be brought to justice?" Joylynne asked.

"Yes," Steve assured her. "Between the video and the DNA evidence, they'll have enough evidence to see justice done."

"Justice?" Tim snarled. "Not hardly. They'll serve their sentence and be released, but when will Robert be released?"

No one had an answer for that. They were all too familiar with how deep psychological wounds can go.

BRIAN HAD ARRIVED on the first flight from Hilo, so he picked up Joshua, Gloria and Luke when they landed just before noon. The only thing Brian would tell them was that Dave and Greg were still at the hospital with Robert who was doing well physically. The only reason the doctor had kept him in the hospital overnight was because of the drug cocktail he'd been given. They wanted to monitor him for ill effects until the drugs were flushed from his system. He would probably be able to go home sometime that afternoon.

Brian wouldn't tell them anything else. Dave and Greg had a much more complete picture than he did, so it would be best to wait and hear it from them.

When they got to the hospital, Dave took them to a private conference room while Greg stayed with Robert.

"They've pretty much figured out what happened," Dave told them. He looked directly at Luke. "Nalani got a video about an hour after you'd left. When she saw what it was, she called your old desk at the precinct and got forwarded to the detective in charge of Robert's case. She immediately emailed the video to him. It confirmed the few details that Robert had already remembered, and filled in some blanks.

"They've already made arrests, and I've been assured that everyone is going to end up accepting a plea, so there probably won't be a trial."

"What happened?" Joshua asked. "Please start at the beginning."

"It actually started before last night," Dave began the tale. "Robert was talked into donating a date with him for a charity auction. The woman who convinced him was Eirian Josephson. Her sister bought the date. The police now know that she received money from some football players and their girlfriends. They told the sister, Lowri, that they wanted to punk Robert, but it would only work if someone sweet and innocent like her bought the date.

"As far as the conspirators know, the other sister didn't know anything about it, but apparently her younger sister told her what she knew. Eirian Josephson must've followed Robert and Lowri because no one knows how she showed up at Waimanalo Beach Park, but she was definitely there.

"Three of the sorority sisters didn't know they were going to do anything other than harass Robert, take off his shirt and get pictures with him. The other two planned something worse with their boyfriends, football players who thought they were bound for the pros until Robert showed up on the team.

"They gave Robert's date, Lowri, a little bit of a date rape drug to put in his drink at the movie. Not enough to incapacitate him, but enough to make him woozy enough to not drive. But they also gave her a bottle of water with plenty more of their date rape concoction to give him after the movie."

Gloria began to weep. Joshua held her a little tighter but he stared steadily at Dave who pressed on.

"The girl Robert was with was a virgin also. The women who got her the date thought it would be funny to make them both lose their virginity. They added Viagra to their date rape mix to make sure that Robert would ... perform whether he wanted to or not. That was why the doctors kept Robert overnight.

They gave him plenty, especially for someone as young and full of vitality as he is. They also added two other football players to the plan because they realized that even drugged it was going to be hard to keep Robert pinned long enough to … finish.

"The other sister, Eirian Josephson, definitely tried to stop them, but she couldn't. In fact, Dewayne Bronson, that's the boyfriend of the mastermind of the whole plot, Shariann Delaney, he was going to rape her when Robert tried to rise to her defense. Bronson turned his attention to Robert instead. That bothered the rest of them enough that they took off, leaving Robert and the two sisters alone.

"The older sister, the one who convinced Robert to auction the date, she must've called 911 because they got two calls, one from Beth and the other from an unknown caller. The Josephson sisters left on an eleven o'clock flight. By the time the police knew of their involvement, they'd already landed in LA and disappeared. Before she left though, Eirian used her laptop in the airport. She opened a new email account and sent one email, with a video attached to it.

"She sent it to you, Luke," Dave nodded at his brother. "She didn't say why, but it was to your Ohana Project address. Nalani got on the computer this morning. When she saw the message come in she forwarded it to HPD. Shortly after that, Robert was cognizant enough to be able to give the police the names of two of his attackers, Shariann Delaney and Dewayne Bronson. With that and the video, they were able to identify everyone involved.

"When they made the arrests, they found more evidence. One of the women was wearing Robert's shirt. A couple others had taken his shoes. Three of the women and two guys had videos of their partying just before the incident. They show Robert's car arriving. One even caught Robert being pulled from the car before it cut off. With all the evidence, they're in the process of working out plea deals."

"So that part's done," Luke sighed sadly. "Now we just need to help Robert get his life back."

Chapter 28

*T*o say that Robert was happy to see his parents and big brother would have been way overstating his feelings when they walked into his hospital room. He would be happy if he could go back and undo that stupid, stupid decision to donate a date.

But while he wasn't happy to see them, he was somewhat comforted by their presence. He knew they would walk with him through this ordeal that was far from over. If his attackers didn't confess and plea bargain, there would be a trial. At that trial, Robert would have to tell what had happened, at least as much of it as he remembered. As the drugs were wearing off, he was remembering more of it with agonizingly clear detail. He didn't want to have to tell anyone about it.

Of course he did have to tell the police. He only vaguely remembered earlier that morning telling a man with a gold shield about the hazy details he'd remembered. The man came back shortly after Mom, Dad and Luke arrived.

When Robert sent Mom out before he would talk to the detective, Dave went with her, but Dad, Brian, Luke and Greg stayed. It didn't take long for Robert to tell what he knew, but it was very hard, both for him and for his companions.

"So you knew nothing about the party at the beach?" the detective asked when Robert was done.

He was looking through his notes so the question almost sounded casual, but it wasn't.

"No," Robert answered angrily with narrowed eyes. "If I had known about it, I would not have gone."

"Weren't you supposed to get your date out there? Did you maybe drink from the wrong water bottle and drug yourself?"

"Of all the –"

Brian threw up his hand and stopped his dad's snarl.

"One of them is trying to accuse Robert of being in on this?" he skewered the detective with a furious stare.

"Yes," the detective closed his notebook with a nod. "His story doesn't add up with what the others are saying, but it had enough credibility to fire up his defense attorney. The prosecutor wanted to make sure Shepherd would be a convincing witness if it comes down to it."

"I suppose you'll assure him he will," Greg growled.

"I most certainly will," the detective nodded at Greg then turned back to Robert. "But I'm relatively certain that it won't come to that. Everyone but Bronson's already talking a plea. With all the others turning on him, he'll plea too. He sure doesn't want what he did talked about in open court, especially not by eight witnesses."

After assuring Robert that the only thing left would be to sign a formal statement, the detective left. Shortly after that, the doctor released Robert.

He'd been staying in Dad's condo down in Waikiki rather than rattling around in the big house in Nuuanu. He would need to go get some of his things from the condo before he, Brian, Luke, Dad and Mom went to the house for the night, but first he wanted to go out to Greg's beach house where Beth, Dei and the kids were. Playing with his little nephews was the only thing that made sense right now.

They of course didn't know anything was wrong with Uncle Robby. They played happily and never once asked him how he was feeling. Even the rest of the family left him alone. They were there if he needed to talk, but they were going to let him deal with it however he wanted, at least for now. If he didn't begin to take steps to heal, the family would begin to push him. They loved him too much to let him wallow for very long.

He didn't want to talk to any of them, not yet, but later that evening, after he was back in his childhood room in Mom's house, he called Tim. He hoped Tim still liked to stay up late, because it was a little past midnight in Missouri.

Tim answered immediately. Robert realized he'd probably been anxiously waiting for his little brother to call, but like the rest of the family, he had let Robert make the first move.

Hey, Robert, Tim said gently. *How you holding up?*

"I don't know. I hurt so bad. Sometimes I can hardly even breathe."

I understand that. Do you want to talk about it?

"Not really," Robert sighed. "I know I need to, but …. Why, Tim? Why me?"

I don't have the first clue, Tim said sadly. *But it wasn't about you, Robert. It was about the people who did this to you.*

"How do you figure?" Robert said angrily.

They decided to do it, not because of who you are or what you've done, but because they're messed up in their own heads.

"Yeah, but before they could do anything to me, God had to allow it. That's what the Bible says, so how is it *not* about me?" Robert snarled.

You have a point, Tim sighed sadly. *But honestly, I don't know anything to tell you that will help right now. You need to grieve now. Answers will come later.*

"Why'd she do it, Tim?" Robert almost sobbed. "That part's the hardest."

Tim didn't have to ask. He knew Robert was talking about Eirian.

They told me that she wasn't part of it, he explained, a little puzzled because he didn't know why Robert hadn't already been told that.

"She wasn't in the planning. I know that," Robert sighed heavily. "But she was there before Lowri and I got there. She knew before it went down, but she didn't stop it. Why?"

I don't think anyone knows, Tim sighed too. *She disappeared without any explanation other than the email she sent Luke.*

Robert didn't want to talk about what was in that email. He hoped it got buried deep and was never resurrected.

"I was dreaming, Tim," was all he said.

I'd figured that out, Tim said wryly. *That's why I gave you the wrong advice.*

"Considering what you had to go on, your advice was solid," Robert said firmly. "Don't you even beat yourself up about it. Did God give you a warning that you didn't pass on to me?"

No!

"Then you've got nothing to be guilty about, so don't you start!"

If you say so, Tim wasn't wholly convinced.

"I'm not kidding you," Robert growled warningly. "If you start blaming yourself ...."

You'll what, punk? Tim said haughtily. *You'll come up here and try to beat me? Oooh, I'm scared, really scared!*

"You better be," Robert laughed in spite of himself. "I love you, Tim."

I love you too, Tim agreed. *So much that I just might let you beat me up when you get here next month!*

When they said their good-byes a short time later, Robert was close to being happy. He fell asleep without much trouble.

Unfortunately, he woke with nightmares a few hours later.

As Robert tried to still his racing heart, he realized it would probably be many nights before he didn't have nightmares. Dad or Brian would probably have an idea how to deal with them, but he didn't want to talk to them right now. They would probably try to turn him toward God, and he wasn't ready for that. God could have prevented the whole tragedy, but he allowed it instead.

It wasn't as if Robert hadn't prayed about the date beforehand. He had. And he'd also sought counsel. Maybe he could have talked to someone other than Tim, but it hadn't seemed like that big a deal. It was just one date, one night.

Except it was a big deal. It had changed his whole life. And God could have warned him, but he didn't.

Robert laid on his bed, staring at the ceiling. He tried to find safe thoughts, ones that helped him find answers. Unfortunately, his thoughts always kept circling back to the same questions.

Why had God allowed that?

What had Robert done wrong to deserve that kind of punishment?

Well over an hour later, Robert's weary brain finally dropped off to sleep again. This time he was awakened by the sound of Mom in the kitchen fixing breakfast.

For one peaceful moment he was a kid again, carefree and innocent. Dad hadn't died of cancer. Heather hadn't gone to war. Greg wasn't abducted. Rachel hadn't killed a rapist.

He hadn't been cruelly and shamefully assaulted.

The moment was gone quickly. His body was still in too much pain for the illusion to remain.

Even after his body healed, his mind would remember. His innocence was finally and firmly lost.

THE NEXT FEW days drifted by. Pain, shame and grief were Robert's most constant companions. As the physical pain drifted into the background, the emotional pain had a shocking tendency to suddenly and violently make itself known. An unseen hand would suddenly clutch his throat or punch him in the gut. A sound or flash of something half-seen out of the corner of his eye would revive unwanted memories. At the most inconvenient times, tears, fear and, worst of all, unrelenting doubts about God's love for him would leap up and demand to be the center of his world.

In the midst of his grief, Robert tried to live a normal life. He dutifully went to church with his family on Sunday, and he accepted the sympathy of his extended family there. It didn't help much, but it didn't really hurt either.

After lunch he played with the keiki until it was time for their naps. The rest of the afternoon he hid out in his room, trying to finish his homework for next week's classes. That's what he told his family, and he did get his books out, but he couldn't concentrate. He ended up playing Spider Solitaire on his tablet until he dozed off. The nap must have helped because when he woke up, he was able to read his textbook until supper was ready.

The following day was pretty much the same, except he didn't go to church. But he didn't go to school either. Instead he tried to study, played solitaire, fell asleep, woke up for lunch and played with the keiki before trying to study again.

On Tuesday, Greg, Beth, Dei and the keiki left as they'd originally planned. Brian left too, but with the promise that he would be back whenever Robert needed him. They did have lives to get back to, so Robert wasn't disappointed.

He almost wished Mom, Dad, Luke and Dave had gone too, leaving him alone like he had been before. But they were staying until spring break started.

They were staying because Robert had some dark days ahead that they thought they could help him get through.

They were staying because Robert was now one of those people who had a before and after, but he didn't yet know how to live in the after.

Chapter 29

*R*obert stayed in his seat though the classroom was quickly emptying. It was the last class of his first day back after his disastrous date. He shouldn't have come back. He should have stayed home.

He'd only come because he'd finally talked to Dave some, and he was beginning to get some peace again. Not much, but enough that he wasn't so mad at God anymore. He wasn't ready to jump and shout hallelujah, but he was beginning to understand that someday he would. It helped a lot that the physical pain was gone.

He was pretty sure that not everyone on campus knew what had happened to him. It was a very big campus with thousands of students. But he was also absolutely certain that everyone who had a class with him did know. If they hadn't known before today, they did now.

In all three of his classes, he'd seen the whispers behind hands, with glances at him. He'd also seen pity in abundance, some of it genuine so-sorry-that-happened-to-you looks, some of it oh-you-poor-wounded-soul-maybe-I-can-help-you-get-over-it ogling. Then there'd been the hateful glares.

He'd thought those were just the product of an overactive imagination until he'd heard two guys come in when he'd been using a restroom stall after his second class.

"He's gotta be so self-righteous all the time, now look what he's done!"

"He knocked a big hole in next year's D-line. How we gonna fill it?"

Robert knew they were talking about him and two of the men who were in prison now instead of college. Bronson and Haslag had been seniors, so their loss wouldn't hurt next year's team, but Stricklin and Tau were only juniors. They should have had another year of football.

It was stupid for anyone to blame him for the loss of two defensive linemen who had assaulted him, but they were obviously doing it.

It was ridiculous for Robert to accept blame, but his shame grew. He'd stayed in the restroom longer than he'd needed to, then finally crept to his next class, staring at the ground in front of him so he wouldn't see whatever looks were being tossed his way.

He'd focused on class as much as he could, but he didn't worry too much. This professor rarely lectured on anything that wasn't in the assigned reading. Robert could skip all the classes, just do the reading, and still pull an A.

In fact, none of the lectures in any of his classes were really all that important. Maybe he should just forget about coming to campus at all. It was Thursday and spring break started next week Friday so he wouldn't miss that much. Maybe by the time spring break was over the other students would have found something else to gossip about.

Robert suddenly realized that the last man out of the classroom wasn't leaving. He was walking to the back of the room where Robert was sitting.

Kaimana Oakes was a local boy who'd transferred to the university after getting his associates at a community college. He was a junior so Robert didn't know him well. They were only casual acquaintances, but Robert knew Kaimana was a Christian. He was deeply involved in InterVarsity Fellowship.

"I'm sorry about what happened to you," Kaimana said when he stopped beside Robert. "That was way wrong."

Robert saw deep sorrow in the other man, but he didn't see pity, anger or disgust. He felt a little more comfortable.

"We don't know each other all that well, so maybe I'm overstepping some boundaries," Kaimana said with a rueful half shrug. "But I really feel like God wants me to encourage you."

Robert just raised his eyebrows.

"People are stupid, Robert. Not just criminally stupid like the people who did that to you, but socially and emotionally stupid. It's a fact of life. Some people are going to act like there's something wrong with you, but there isn't. Well, at least nothing that isn't in us all. We're all natural-born sinners."

Robert knew that Kaimana was speaking truth, and he couldn't think of anything to interject, so he continued to stare at the other man.

"Don't let other people's stupidity shape your life," Kaimana said earnestly. "So what if they point and stare? They used to do it over you as a star football player. It's not really all that different. They point and stare now for the same reason they did then – you're someone different, unusual, a freak. If you live your life for God, then no matter what the reason is that they point and stare, they'll be seeing God when they look at you."

Robert slowly began to nod.

"I see your point. It's something to think about," he stood. "You mind if we walk out together? I could use a friend right now."

"I don't mind at all," Kaimana said, turning toward the door.

"You sure?" Robert asked doubtfully. "We kinda look like freaks."

Kaimana laughed cheerfully. They did indeed look rather Mutt-and-Jeffish. Robert was six-ten and a broad, solid two-sixty. Kaimana was five-six and a very slender one-thirty.

"I don't mind looking like a freak with you," he grinned up at Robert.

As they left the room and walked across campus, Robert decided that he wasn't going to skip any classes. Spring break was only a week away. He could tough it out until then.

But as soon as his last class was over next Friday, he was getting on Dad's plane and going home to his family in St. Louis. A week spent with Tim and the rest of his family would do much to heal his wounded soul and restore his spirits.

JOYLYNNE WATCHED HER husband pacing at the front of the hangar. She was happy that Robert was arriving tonight. Maybe she would get her husband back soon.

She'd always known that Tim was very close to his little brother. Hardly a day went by that they didn't talk on the phone, post on each other's Facebook pages or text. They were worse than she was with her three life-long friends, Sally, Reylene and Kendra.

In the last two weeks, Joy had discovered that Tim and Robert's bond was deeper than she knew. When Robert was hurt and Tim couldn't go to him, it tore him up. It was a deeper grief than any of his brothers or sisters had. It was even intruding in their marriage. Tim seemed to have withdrawn from her.

He was still in the house, still slept with her, still took care of her during her sometimes difficult pregnancy, but she was beginning to feel emotionally disconnected from her husband.

Joy suspected that Tim was feeling guilty, but she wasn't sure about what. She knew that he'd been the one to advise Robert to go ahead and do the auction. The same evening that he'd initially talked to Robert, Tim had told Joy about it. She'd thought his reasoning was sound. She remembered laughing cheerfully at a sudden thought.

"What?" Tim had asked her with a curious grin.

"I was just thinking about a date I had in high school," Joylynne had enlightened him. "I broke his nose and gave him two black eyes because he got a little too frisky."

"That's not funny," Tim had frowned.

"No, *that* wasn't funny, but my next thought was," Joy snickered. "I thought, 'At least Robert won't have to fight off the woman if she gets too frisky.'"

"No he won't," Tim laughed. "Not unless an Amazon princess wins the bidding."

As it turned out, they'd both been wrong, but who would have guessed that something like that would happen?

Maybe it wasn't just Tim's own guilt that was bothering him. Maybe he was disturbed by her guilt.

Now that she thought about it, maybe he hadn't actually gotten over his anger about her getting pregnant. Maybe he'd just buried it and it had sprouted again in this time of trouble. If she hadn't been pregnant and having so much trouble, Tim would have gone to his brother two weeks ago when the attack first happened.

Joy sighed heavily. She prayed that this time with Robert would be a time of restoration, both for her brother-in-law's wounded spirit and for her own marriage.

Suddenly Tim stopped pacing. The plane was arriving.

Robert was the first to disembark. Tim was running to him.

They were holding each other, crying together.

Joy carefully pushed herself off the chair. With a small smile and slight shake of her head, she declined the help Steve stepped over to offer. Pain had settled in her back again. She well knew how to handle it. Steve's help wouldn't alleviate it.

She was slow enough that she was bringing up the rear as everyone surged toward the new arrivals. All the adults were here since the Guerreros, Rose, Faith and Dillon were staying with the children. Because they were already teenagers, Matt, Linc, Kara, Gil and Phil had complained loudly when they were told that it was too late in the evening for them to come, but their parents had stood firm. Joy knew that the main reason for only adults tonight was the fact that even though Robert loved his family, this was going to be a rough homecoming.

Standing in the back of the large crowd, Joy felt out of place. She loved Robert dearly, but she didn't know him well since he'd stayed in Hawaii for college while she and Tim had been in Oklahoma. With football practice and the season taking up the better part of nine months, and classes in the other three months, in the past five years Joy hadn't seen Robert more than a half dozen times, and that included the wedding last year. Those two weeks last June were the longest time she'd seen Robert. She didn't feel like she was really part of his family.

Apparently Robert felt differently. As soon as he saw her, his eyes lit up and he reached for a hug.

"Good grief, Sis. You're huge!" he looked at her rapidly expanding abdomen in surprise. "You got a future member of the brute squad in there?"

"We don't know," Joy rubbed her belly, smiling softly. "We didn't ask yet. We kinda want to wait, but I'm seriously leaning toward finding out at my next appointment."

"I think you should find out, but I'm not sure you should listen to me. I always tried to peek at my Christmas presents before Christmas Eve," Robert shrugged ruefully.

"Only tried?" Joy grinned.

"Yeah, Tim wouldn't let me," Robert sighed.

"He doesn't want me to peek either!"

"Is he taking care of you?"

The way Robert was looking at her told Joylynne that he saw signs of stress and was concerned.

"Mostly," Joy shrugged slightly then burst into tears. "But he's been so worried about you!"

She flung her arms around Robert, as best she could and sobbed.

Suddenly Tim was beside her, wrapping his arm around her.

Robert leaned back slightly and lifted Joy's chin.

"Hey, no worries now," he smiled sadly with misty eyes. "I'm home and mostly healthy. Luke and Dave assure me that I'll be much better after I find a good counselor, but I don't know how I'm gonna do that."

When Robert sighed dramatically, Joy had to laugh. Of course there were three counselors in the family, Nalani, Beth and Brandon, and The Ohana Project had a few others on staff too.

"You're staying with us," she declared. She hadn't thought about it before, hadn't talked to Tim about it, but suddenly it seemed right.

"That's an offer I can't refuse," Robert grinned at his brother.

"That way Tim can worry about you *and* take care of me at the same time," Joy said brightly. "Maybe you can also rescue me from your brother's feeble attempts to help me in the kitchen."

Tim laughed with everybody else, but he knew that Joy's light-hearted tone hid more than a grain of truth. He hadn't been taking care of her.

He stepped closer to her and leaned down to kiss her, partly to show his appreciation for her love of his brother, partly to apologize for having been distant. When Joy turned her face to him, beneath her happy smile he saw sorrow, pain and exhaustion.

"Joy's right, of course," Tim said as he raised his head from the kiss. "She's also exhausted."

He scooped Joy up in his arms and started for the car, speaking to Robert over his shoulder. "We're leaving for home now, so grab your bag if you're coming with us."

THE NEXT WEEK was an emotional yo-yo for Joy. She was very happy that Robert was staying with them, and the first couple days she was delighted that Tim seemed to easily give both her and Robert equal attention, but then she was disappointed when he again began to ignore her. By Tuesday she was getting miserable. In the early hours of Wednesday morning, she was furious when she woke up alone.

The last two nights she'd woken up alone, which of course wasn't unusual. Tim often didn't come to bed before midnight, but when he did, he always woke her. With her increasing girth and a very active baby, falling asleep was difficult, especially after having gotten a couple hours of sleep already. Having to go to the living room and wake up her husband and his brother made it even more difficult to get a good night's rest.

That was one of the reasons for her anger. She'd of course woken up alone shortly before midnight but this time she was too tired to go get Tim. It had been well over an hour before she'd fallen asleep again. Now she was waking at four-thirty because her husband was in the bathroom, finally getting ready for bed. She knew she wasn't going to fall asleep again, but he would sleep until ten or eleven.

No he wouldn't. With his brother here, he was getting up at eight, ready to spend the day with Robert who was a much earlier riser than Tim was.

Tim would get up at eight and go running with his brother, but when it was just his wife, he slept the whole morning. That fact really ticked her off this morning.

"Did you have fun sleeping with your brother last night?" Joy snapped as Tim walked out of the bathroom.

"I'm sorry," Tim shrugged, not very apologetically. "We fell asleep in the living room."

"Again!"

"So sue me," Tim growled as he dropped down on his side of the bed.

"You spend more time with your brother than with your wife," Joy glared angrily.

"He needs me right now, Joylynne," Tim tried to speak calmly, to defuse the situation.

"I need you too!"

"If you're so jealous of my time, why'd you ask my brother to stay with us?" Tim snarled.

"Because I thought you could love both of us at the same time," Joy snapped as she pushed herself off the bed. "Obviously I was wrong!"

She grabbed her robe and stalked from the room.

Tim glared after Joylynne for a moment, then dropped his head in his hands and groaned.

Why was he fighting with his wife again? He loved her so much, but she was right, he hadn't been loving her the way she deserved. He certainly hadn't been loving her as Christ loved the church, like Paul said in Ephesians. Yes, his brother needed him, but his first responsibility was to his wife.

God, I'm messing up my marriage. Why am I having such a hard time loving Joy the way she deserves? Please help me. I don't know what I'm doing wrong.

*I'm so lolo, God! I do too know what I'm doing wrong. I spent two weeks worrying about Robert, fretting to **myself**. I should've been talking with the rest of the family. But I had this stupid idea in the back of my mind that no one would really understand how I feel because Robert's **my** brother. But they don't love him any less because they didn't have exactly the same birth parents. They love him different, sure, but I don't love Brandon less because we share* *no blood connection. I'd be tore up for him if this had happened to him. I'd be tore up if it was one of Joy's brothers!*

Please help me get things back on track, God. Remind me that I need to talk to the incredible family you've given me. Right now, please give me the right attitude and words to make things right with Joy.

JOY WAS CRYING in the corner of the couch when her husband walked into the living room, his head hanging, shoulders slumped.

"I'm sorry, Joy," Tim said as he dropped on the floor in front of her.

The anger and pain in Joy's heart melted immediately. His attitude was more powerful than his words. He was humbling himself before her. He wanted to make things right.

"I haven't been treating you right these last few weeks," Tim wasn't going to be satisfied with a simple apology. He was going to make a full confession. "I let my worries about Robert be a priority over you. But you should be my number one priority. Not only is that the way God wants it to be, but I love you way more than I love Robert. He was the best friend of my youth, and he'll always be very special to me, but you are my best friend now. Your heart is my heart. One of the reasons I worried so much about Robert was that I didn't let you share my pain. Because I shut you out of the pain in my heart, I started shutting you out of my life too.

"I think one of the reasons for that is that subconsciously I was angry at you. You backed my advice to Robert about the date. If you'd told me that it was wrong, that he shouldn't do it, then I would've called him and advised him to cancel. None of this would've happened. But we both dealt with it the best way we knew how. Robert did too. None of us were wrong. Being angry with you was very wrong. Will you forgive me, please?"

"Yes, I forgive you, but you need to forgive me too," Joy knew she also needed to confess if they were truly going to get back on track. "When my heart started hurting, I didn't tell you. I told God, pretending that was enough, expecting him to somehow show you what I was feeling. I wanted him to get you back on track. But God wanted me to tell you how I was hurting over your actions. He wanted us to develop a deeper intimacy through me being vulnerable. But I was afraid that I'd hurt worse if you didn't change. I was wrong to treat you like you were untrustworthy because you are very trustworthy. Please forgive me?"

"Of course," Tim sat on the couch and pulled Joy into a hug. "I love you, Joy."

"I love you too," Joy willing went into his arms where she cried tears of sweet release.

Tim wept awhile too, but the resolve forming in his heart was too strong to allow many tears.

He would learn to love his wife better. He had plenty of people to help him.

Joy's tears tapered off, and her breathing became deeper. A few minutes later, she sighed and shifted, trying to put her feet on the couch. Tim scooted down toward the other end to give his wife room to curl up with her head on his lap and her pregnant body as comfortable as it could be. Soon she was fast asleep. Tim was right behind her.

ABOUT THIRTY MINUTES later, Robert crept quietly down the stairs. He'd heard angry voices coming from his brother's bedroom shortly after he'd gone upstairs. He felt really bad. He'd been so certain that he would make sure he and his brother went to bed instead of falling asleep talking in the living room again. He'd been shocked to find that it was after four when he'd suddenly awakened.

He didn't hear voices anymore, but he wasn't sure that was a good thing. He wanted to know if things were good between Tim and his wife. He was going to move to Mom and Dad's place today if Tim was sleeping on the couch.

Because the lamp was still on, Robert could clearly see the living room when he peeked in. He grinned broadly.

He didn't have to move to the Lodge even though his brother was indeed sleeping on the couch. Joy looked very comfortable, curled up with her head on Tim's lap. There was no way Tim was comfortable. His long legs were wedged between the couch and the coffee table. He'd had to scrunch down to make enough room for Joy's head to fit comfortably on his lap. His upper body was twisted sideways and down because his head had fallen onto the back of the couch. The way it was tilted told Robert that Tim was going to have a serious crick in his neck when he woke up. But his arm was around his wife and a smile was on his lips.

Obviously Tim had made up with his wife and was willing to do what it took to make things right between them.

He was going to have help from his brother, at least for the next few days. Robert wasn't going to let Tim neglect Joy. In fact, he was more than willing to help take care of Joy. She was a very special woman, the perfect wife for his brother. If Tim was going to turn his brother into a stumbling block in his marriage, then Robert would leave. It would be the best way to truly love his brother.

AT ABOUT SEVEN-THIRTY that morning, Joy awakened to the smell of Portuguese sausage frying in the kitchen. She was startled to discover that she was sleeping on the couch with her husband who looked extremely uncomfortable.

When she lifted her head, he muttered and frowned but didn't wake up. Joy eased his head down on a pillow and lifted his long legs, one at a time, to place them on the big couch. She covered him with a light blanket, then strolled into the kitchen to see what her brother-in-law was fixing for breakfast.

About thirty minutes later, Tim wandered into the kitchen. He was barefoot and bare-chested, wearing nothing but his lounging pants and the blanket wrapped over his shoulders and clutched tightly in one hand. With his sleepy eyes and tousled curls, he looked like a little boy who'd woken up in an oversized body. He looked wonderful to Joy.

Tim dropped into the chair at the end of the table without a word. He stared at the place mat, blinked his eyes a few times and frowned.

Joy started to rise, but Robert waved her back down.

"Sit. I'll take care of the poor boy."

A few seconds later, a cup of coffee materialized in front of Tim. He wrapped his hands around it and lifted it to his lips. He silently sipped his coffee for a bit.

"Thank you," he said when the cup was half empty.

Robert had given Tim his coffee, but Tim's eyes and smile were directed at his wife. That didn't bother Robert at all.

Robert placed a plate with Portuguese sausage, rice and eggs in front of Tim.

Tim frowned at the plate.

"You guys brought back Portuguese sausage and I'm just now getting some?" he growled.

"Monku monku monku," Robert rolled his eyes. "Shut up and eat it or I'll give it to Joy."

"Do you want it?" Tim looked at his wife with concern. "You can have it if you do."

"No," Joy smiled happily. "Robert already gave me more breakfast than I needed."

"Good," Tim grinned boyishly. "'Cause I really want this sausage."

Robert was thrilled to see that Tim and Joylynne were back on the right track, but he was still a little worried. As he watched his brother pour shoyu over his eggs, Robert decided that he may as well bring into the open what they all knew.

"I'm going to move down to the Lodge," Robert said calmly as he dropped down into the chair he'd vacated when his brother had stumbled in.

Tim and Joy both frowned.

"If," Robert calmly stared back. "If you start neglecting Joy again, Tim. If you ignore your hurt over his neglect, Joy. I will leave this house and move in with Mom and Dad if you two can't be husband and wife while I'm here."

Tim looked at Joy with love and longing.

"I really am sorry that I've been so lolo lately," he said sadly.

"I already forgave you," she smiled sweetly.

"I'm going to help out this morning by going out to find another breakfast and leave you guys to have some alone time," Robert frowned slightly. "I realized this morning that since I got here, you guys haven't been alone except when you go to bed at night, and the last few nights you haven't even had much of that."

Joy thought about that and realized he was right. When he left the house to visit other family members, Tim always went with him, and often she did too.

"Enjoy your morning together," Robert said as he rose from the table. "I'm sure you can figure out something to do, but just in case, I'm gonna suggest that Tim might need a neck massage, Joy. I'll be back for lunch. This afternoon, Joy, you're in charge. We're going to do what you want for a change."

Robert turned and strolled from the room.

Tim rubbed his neck ruefully and Joy smiled proudly.

Her husband certainly did need a neck massage. When she'd cried herself to sleep, he'd assured her comfort with no thought of his own.

Of course his legs had been rather cramped and his torso somewhat contorted.

"I think you need more than a neck massage," Joy brazenly smiled at her husband.

"Woman, you're six months pregnant," Tim frowned playfully. "You need to behave."

"I will," she promised. "I won't do anything to hurt the baby or make me uncomfortable."

And she didn't, but they still had a very intimate morning.

Chapter 30

*T*he next few days were glorious, the best Joy had known in a long time. Tim and Robert both spoiled her, and she loved it. She wasn't one who normally enjoyed that kind of attention, but having so many difficult days in her pregnancy had finally made her realize that she needed to accept all the help that anyone offered her.

Robert was a pretty decent cook, though nowhere near as good as Steve, but then few people were. That evening, he made real mashed potatoes to go with Joy's meatloaf, and on Thursday he made macaroni and cheese from scratch. She had to ask him about that because that was one dish she'd never before had with her husband's family.

"I visited Brian and Cait quite a few weekends in the last few years," Robert shrugged. "Brian loves mac and cheese. Cait didn't mind help in the kitchen, and she even let me do all the work a time or two."

"You like cooking?" Joy asked.

"Not as much as Steve, but yeah, I do."

"You're the only Shepherd who does, aren't you?"

"Greg's pretty good in the kitchen, but I don't think he really likes it. The real good stuff takes too long for him," Robert said.

"That's why he came up with his quick Portuguese bean soup," Tim snickered.

"There's a quick version?" Joy asked in surprise. "Your mom's version takes a good twenty-four hours."

"Greg can whip up a pot in less than an hour, but I don't know how," Robert shrugged. "Maybe you can get his secret. It's actually not bad."

"You want us to beat it out of him?" Tim boldly asked Joy.

"As long as Robert's going to help you, sure! Why not?" Joy grinned cheerfully. "I've got a hankering for some tonight!"

The brothers didn't get the recipe, but Greg did invite them over for dinner Friday night, and he made a pot of his soup. He even let Joy in the kitchen, after swearing her to secrecy.

The next day a late snow storm descended, dropping big downy flakes that quickly blanketed the ground that had been mostly bare for a couple weeks since the last snow had been in February. Tim, Joy and Robert sat around the fireplace roasting hotdogs and marshmallows. They debated the merits of different baby names, all three of them mindful of the fact that Greg could spot a bend in almost any name and turn it into an unusual, corny nickname. Joy had picked up a baby name book back in Franklin, but she hadn't looked at it very much. They brought it out that afternoon.

Robert had it first. Of course he found lots of obscure names that Tim and Joy quickly rejected like Aphrodite, Etelvina and Laquinta for a girl, Calixtrato, Karuntunda and Nokonyu for a boy.

Tim took the book away from him.

"Hezekiah's not bad," Tim suggested. "It means 'God gives strength.'"

"Hezekiah Timothy Shepherd?" Joy said doubtfully.

"HTS," Robert snickered. "What will Greg do with 'Hits'?"

"Why Timothy?" Tim frowned.

"That's how we do it in my family," Joy said firmly. "Taggart's middle name is Alfred. Dad is Alfred Niguel, and Grandpa was Niguel Callan, his dad was Callan something that was probably his dad's name."

"Callan Timothy doesn't sound bad," Robert suggested.

"Do you think Greg can do anything with that?" Tim asked warily.

"I don't see what, but if something comes up before the baby's born, we can always change our minds," Joy said firmly. "I really like Callan Timothy."

"Okay, then how about a girl?" Robert reached for the book again but Tim pulled it back out of his reach.

"Are we keeping your family's Rey – Lynne tradition?" Tim asked Joy.

"It would be nice to, but I've always kind of liked the name Gabriella."

"I like it too," Tim said, but a little hesitantly. "Doesn't that usually get shortened to Gabby?"

"Or Ella?" Robert shuddered.

"That'll make Greg call her Cinderella," Tim snickered.

"Gabri," Joy said firmly. "With the 'ah' sound, not a hard A. That's how we'll shorten it."

"Sounds good, and maybe we can give her a middle name with Rey or Lynne in it," Tim nodded and turned back to the book.

They tried Nia and Neena, Shea and Sasha, Leia and Lora, but no combination with Rey or Lynne sounded quite right.

Suddenly Tim grinned happily, "Hey, according to this book 'Ani' is Hawaiian for beautiful!"

"Reyani! I like it," Robert agreed.

"It's a little too different for a first name, but for a middle name? I think it's fine," Joy agreed.

"Gabriella Reyani Shepherd," Tim said proudly. "That has a nice ring to it."

"And it has the added benefit of basically giving her Grandma Reyanne's name too," Robert grinned and nodded.

"Sounds good to me too!" Joy grinned happily. "Now I can't wait to find out which we're having, a boy or a girl."

"Yes, you can," Tim scolded her. "Don't you dare ask to peek when we see the doctor Tuesday morning!"

Joy didn't argue; she simply laughed.

Sometime during their baby name discussion, the snow had slowed considerably. They could again see the houses around them, but they were now blanketed with eight inches of snow.

Steve, Heather and their kids were the first ones out in the newly fallen snow, but others were not far behind them. Tim didn't even think about keeping Joy inside, but he did make sure she bundled up, and extracted a firm promise that she wouldn't walk one step without him or one of the other guys right beside her.

Joy was happy to walk down to the Lodge and sit on the porch with Gloria and Cari, who complained that Brandon was being way too protective. The swing was covered with blankets to provide a barrier from the cold and they shared lap blankets too. Foot warmers filled with hot coals from the fireplace in the Lodge made them quite cozy.

The rest of the family quickly divided into two teams. Each team built a snow fort and got a good supply of snowballs, then the war commenced. The men were quickly walking, falling, laughing snowmen. Neither side technically won the war, but they all had so much fun that no one cared.

The sun briefly peeked through the cloud cover, promising that soon the sky would be clear. That meant a cold night, but the evening was still relatively warm, so the men built a fire in the big campfire pit and big pots of soup came out of a half dozen houses. Sandwich fixings, cookies, chips, marshmallows, hot chocolate and hot cider completed the evening meal. Some of the sandwiches were toasted in the fire while others were eaten cold. Few of the marshmallows were eaten cold.

Between their exertion, the cold and their full bellies, the children soon began to get drowsy. Parents took them off to get them ready for bed. The teenagers grumbled when they had to go home too, but they went.

The fire was still burning merrily when all the children and their parents had disappeared. The only ones left to enjoy the fire were Brandon and Cari snuggled together under one blanket, Tim and Joy with another, and Gloria sandwiched between Robert and Joshua with two blankets. They happily shared stories about the day. Too much had been going on for anyone to see it all, so there was a lot to tell.

"You gonna miss this back in Hawaii?" Tim asked Robert after a while. He didn't envy the aloneness that his brother would endure, but it sure would be nice to have warm weather again.

"I'll miss the family, that's for sure," Robert sighed. "Too much. I'm not going back tomorrow."

Joy wasn't sure what to say. She would be very happy to have Robert stay a while longer, but it was too sad to think about why he wanted to stay.

"Are you sure that's wise?" Gloria asked.

"I talked to Dad about it earlier," Robert assured her. "I haven't missed any classes except those few days right after …. I can wait another week, or even two and not be in trouble with the university."

"He's used his time with the family wisely," Joshua explained further. "If he'd been sitting around moping and hiding, I'd be worried, but another week will do him good. I can take him back any time he's ready."

"I think it's a good idea," Brandon nodded.

"So do I!" Tim quickly agreed.

"I do too, if he promises he's still going to stay with us," Joy said firmly, then sighed and frowned playfully at Robert. "But we might have to revisit that idea if you decide to stay a second week."

The next day when the rest of the family found out that Robert wasn't leaving after church, they were all happy too, but every adult had the same mixed feelings that Joy had felt. Everyone was determined to do whatever they could to help Robert be ready to resume his life in Hawaii soon.

JOY'S DOCTOR'S APPOINTMENT on Tuesday was at eleven in St. Louis, so on Monday evening, Tim, Joy and Robert went up to Halelolo to spend the night. The weather forecast was for an overnight low in the upper forties. Robert observed that they would have good weather on Tuesday morning, and since Monday's high had been the mid-fifties, the snow would already be mostly be gone on the jogging trails. A morning run on Tuesday would be perfect.

"Where are you going to jog? How far?" Joy asked a trifle crossly. She didn't mind them jogging, but they needed to be back in plenty of time for Tim to shower and change before their doctor's appointment.

"Even in morning traffic, Forest Park is only a thirty minute drive," Tim said. "We'll leave at eight, no later than eight-thirty. If we run no more than forty-five minutes at the Park, we'll be back here with time to spare. Your doctor's only twenty minutes from here."

"I guess that'll be okay then," Joy sighed, "but only if you go to bed at a decent time tonight."

Tim played it safe. He went to bed at the same time Joylynne did.

Of course she was up long before he was. She walked into the bedroom singing at exactly eight o'clock. Many months ago she'd begun to wake Tim with a song, but only when he turned off his alarm and overslept as he had this morning.

"Come here, woman," Tim playfully reached for her, but Joy easily evaded his long arm.

In the last couple weeks, her physical discomfort had seemed to lessen, and Joy relished being able to move without pain. This morning she was delighted that she could almost nimbly dance back away from the bed.

"Not a chance, little Shepherd boy," she teased her husband. "You've gotta get up now."

"Maybe you should come back to bed," Tim pouted.

"No can do," Joy pulled the covers off him. "You've got to get out of here!"

"You're trying to get rid of me!"

"I want to make sure you leave home soon enough that you get back in time to go to the doctor with me," Joy explained patiently. "You do want to go to the doctor, don't you?"

"Of course!" Tim swung his legs over the side of the bed. "If I don't, you'll peek!"

"There's that!" Joy laughed as she headed for the door. "I'll get your after-run snack ready, so stop by the kitchen before you leave."

It was almost eight-thirty when Tim and Robert left Halelolo. It was indeed a beautiful morning for a run, so when they parked the car at Forest Park a few minutes before nine, they decided they could still get in a forty-five minute run.

They timed it almost perfectly. Their phones said 9:46 when they jogged up to the car. They would be home by ten-fifteen. That was more than enough time to shower and still be out the door by ten-thirty.

"You drive," Tim tossed the keys to Robert. "I hate St. Louis traffic."

"You think I like it?" Robert tossed the keys back.

"You're still used to driving in Honolulu," Tim snorted wryly and tossed the keys again. "St. Louis is a breeze compared to that."

"You have a point," Robert grumbled and headed for the driver's side. "Why can't we just stay in the country?"

"I used to wonder why Greg let Beth drive all the time," Tim said as they both buckled their seat belts. "Now I understand. It's hard to focus with so many things going on around me."

"I kinda understand too, and that's scary!" Robert sighed.

"Why?"

"'Cause that means we're a lot like Greg!"

"You're right! Pull over and let me drive!" Tim cried in alarm.

"Not a chance!" Robert threw out his right arm to block Tim. "I don't wanna be like him either!"

They both laughed, but then Tim sighed.

"I actually do, you know."

"Want to be like Greg? Yeah, me too," Robert nodded. "But I'll never tell him that."

"At least not before he's on his deathbed," Tim agreed.

"You know what's one of the coolest things about Greg?" Robert asked after a moment.

"I've got some ideas, but they might not be what you're thinking," Tim shrugged.

"I'd be willing to bet that there are ways that Greg wishes he was like us."

"Yeah, you're right," Tim agreed thoughtfully. "What's even cooler is that he probably doesn't envy us the football, but it's something more personal that's part of us that we'll have long after we're done playing football."

"You're probably right!" Robert was pleased with Tim's thought, especially since it wasn't a surprising idea. It was more like Tim was verbalizing something Robert had subconsciously known. "I wonder what – Oh man!"

The thunk-thunk of the tire was not a good sound.

"No!" Tim stared at his brother in alarm. "We do not have a flat tire."

"Don't worry about it," Robert said reassuringly. "I'll bet we have it changed in five minutes, tops."

"Pop the trunk," Tim said as he reached for the door handle.

It only took them about thirty seconds to get the spare tire out, but they weren't going to make Robert's five minutes. The spare was flat.

Tim called the travel service, thankful that he'd followed Steve's advice and become a member of the nation-wide network even before they'd left Norman, back when the van he had owned was way less reliable than his current car. He prayed that by some miracle they had someone right around the corner.

They said they would have someone there within the hour.

Tim's heart sank. There was no way they were going to make it back to the house in time for him to go with Joy. The best he would be able to do was meet her there.

Tim knew there were many ways Joy could blame him for this. If he'd gotten up on time instead of sleeping late once again. If he'd been doing proper maintenance on the car. If he'd preferred to spend time with his wife rather than his brother. If, if, if.

There was no avoiding Joy's ire, so he went ahead and called her. He immediately broke the bad news about the tire.

Did you already call the travel service? Joy asked with a sigh.

"Yes," Tim was rather puzzled. She didn't sound angry or upset, just disappointed.

Then I guess you'll join me as soon as you can.

"I certainly will!" Tim agreed happily. "So you're not angry?"

Just a little disappointed, Joy sighed again. She did that a lot when she talked to her husband. *It's not like you're trying to avoid going with me.*

"No, I'm not!" Tim said emphatically. "I love you."
Love you too, dear. Don't drive Robert crazy while you're waiting.
"Me?" Tim asked with innocent disbelief.
I'm hanging up, Tim, Joy laughed. *I've got to get ready to go.*
"Okay, see you there!"

Tim did drive Robert crazy, but that was only because it took the tow truck an hour and twenty minutes to get there. He apologized for the delay and explained that traffic was snarled because of an accident on the freeway. He also told them they'd picked up a nail so they would have to take it to a tire shop, but their spare was simply out of air. Five minutes later, they were on their way.

Half a mile down I-55 they realized they should have asked more questions about that snarl on the freeway.

"No, no, no!" Tim groaned and clutched his head with both hands as Robert slowed behind a solid river of cars. It was already quarter after eleven. Even if the doctor was running late, Joy would be in and out before they even got off the freeway!

He texted her – You in yet?
Walking now. They just called me.
Traffic jam on 55!
I guess I get to peek!
Better not!
Can't stop me, can you? ;)
Call me when u pau.
Will do.

Robert inched closer and closer to the next exit. Once they got off the Interstate, the GPS would recalculate a new route to the doctor's office. Hopefully it wouldn't be too much farther than the 17:43 that it now said was time to destination.

Almost thirty minutes later, when the GPS said their destination was now 16:59 away, Tim's phone rang.

Hi, Daddy! Joy greeted Tim happily.

"Hi, Mommy," Tim's heart swelled with love to hear her happy voice. She really wasn't upset that he hadn't been able to make the doctor's appointment with her. His wife was one special lady. "So what's the verdict?"

I thought you didn't want to know, Joy teased him.

"I changed my mind. Isn't that a guy's prerogative?"

That's a woman's prerogative! Joy snickered.

"But why shouldn't it be a guy's too?" Tim insisted.

No reason.

"So, what's our baby's name?"

Gabriella Reyani Shepherd.

"It's a girl!" Tim shouted even though Robert was sitting close enough to hear him whisper.

It's a girl, Joy assured him needlessly.

"You're heading back to Halelolo now, right?"

No. I thought I'd go dancing and drinking to celebrate.

"You what?" Tim's voice rose an octave.

Ask a silly question ...! Joy laughed. *Of course I'm on my way back to Halelolo.*

"Then we'll change course too," Tim sighed in relief. "We can see the exit now, so we should make it back shortly after you do."

That sounds great, Joy said happily. *I've got another picture. She's really grow – Oh God!*

Tim heard squealing tires and the sound of a crash.

Joy's world went black.

Chapter 31

"**J**oy!" Tim yelled in the phone. "Joy, are you alright? Joy? Talk to me."

Though Joy didn't speak, Tim knew they still had a connection. He heard sounds he couldn't distinguish, then a voice in the background.

Is she okay?
I'm not sure. I can't quite reach her to check for a pulse.
I called 911.
So did I. I hope they get here soon. She doesn't look so good.

Tim sobbed into the phone and called Joy's name again.

It looks like her phone's still on! Can you get it off the seat?
Yeah! a female voice said, then after a few seconds added, *I got it. What do I now?*
Just talk in it and see if there's anyone on the other end, someone close to her said.
Hello? she said hesitantly.

"What happened to my wife?" Tim cried in agony.

She's your wife? I'm so sorry.

"What happened?"

Some guy blew through a red light and hit her.

"Oh, God," Tim groaned. "Is she ...?"

She doesn't look good, but I think she's still alive, was the answer.

"Please, God," Tim sobbed. "Don't let her die!"

Robert took the phone from Tim's suddenly lifeless hand, putting it on speaker so Tim could hear too.

"Where are you?" he barked at the phone.

Where are we? the woman on the other end had to ask someone before she could answer Robert's question.

"We probably won't be able to make it before the ambulance gets there," Tim groaned.

"Will you stay on the phone and tell us where they take Joylynne?" Robert asked.

That's her name? Joylynne?

"Yes," Robert tried to control his impatience at the very dumb question. Who else would he have been calling Joylynne? "Will you stay on the line?"

Yeah, sure.

Robert handed the phone back to Tim and dug out his own phone.

Through a haze of agony, Tim realized that Robert was calling Mom or Dad. He also realized that they were parked on the left shoulder of the freeway, and that he heard sirens over the phone but saw flashing blue lights behind them.

A motorcycle patrolman was approaching Tim's side of the car. He began to panic. He didn't know what to say. The only thing he knew was that Joy might be dying and he wasn't with her.

"Is there a problem with your car?" the officer asked from slightly behind Tim.

Tim just stared at Robert in agony.

"I'm sorry, officer," Robert leaned across the car and spoke loudly. "We just found out my brother's wife was in an apparently serious accident. We needed to pull over for a few minutes, just long enough to call Dad and to figure out what we need to do next."

"Where was the accident?" the officer asked.

When Robert told him, he walked to the back end of the car and talked on his radio.

Tim was grateful for the updates the woman on Joy's phone was giving him. The police were there, and an ambulance and fire truck were approaching.

The motorcycle patrolman walked up to Robert's window.

"I'm going to help you get out of this mess. Dispatch will keep me updated so we can get your brother to his wife as soon as possible."

Robert didn't like the solemnness of the man's tone. He knew more than he was saying, but Robert didn't ask. Tim was already worried enough.

"Thank you, officer," Robert simply said.

"I'm going to get in front of you then cut across traffic. You stay close behind me."

They had an agonizing creep across the freeway, then they were free and flying. Soon a rear guard joined them.

Wherever Joy was, Tim would soon be at her side.

GREG WAS SITTING in stalled traffic, praying. He knew that the most likely cause of the sudden snarl was an accident. Somewhere ahead someone was in need. He didn't know who it was, but he knew God did.

His phone interrupted his prayer.

Joylynne's been in an accident, Dad said immediately.

"Where?" Greg's heart sank. Even before Dad told him the intersection, Greg knew that it was up ahead. It was a block and a half away.

"I'm there!"

He didn't pull his car to the side of the road. He simply turned off the engine, pocketed his keys and ran.

He saw Joy's Dodge SRT. There was an Escalade buried in the driver's side.

"Oh, God!" Greg moaned. "It's bad, Dad. Very, very bad."

I'll send out the alert, Joshua's solemn but calm tone belied his horror. *Call me back when you know more.*

"Yeah," Greg said distractedly. He disconnected and slipped his phone back in his pocket. He was intensely glad that he'd followed Dave and Abe's suggestion to become a volunteer police chaplain. His badge would get him access to the accident without any argument.

"How many are hurt, Sgt. Brodbeck?" he asked as he walked up to an officer he'd met a few times before.

"Hi, Chap. Just the one," Kirk Brodbeck said. "The woman in the SRT. It's bad, and to make matters worse, she's pregnant."

"I know," Greg said with tears in his eyes. "She's my sister-in-law."

"I'm so sorry," Brodbeck groaned. "She's unconscious, but if you want, you can pray with her."

"Of course," Greg immediately started for the car. He knew he was walking quickly, but he felt like he was swimming in molasses.

The only access to Joy was through the passenger side.

"Can Chap get in and pray with her for a minute?" Brodbeck leaned in and talked to the paramedic who was in the front seat working on Joy. "He's also her brother-in-law."

"I guess," the paramedic answered as she left the car. "There's not much else we can do until the firemen get her out."

Greg's heart howled as he crawled into the mangled front seat of Joy's car.

The side airbag had already deflated, but it hadn't done Joy much good. Her right arm was hanging limply, her head sagging over it. The rest of her body was pinned between the seat and steering wheel. Her door had crumpled around the grill of the Escalade and pushed onto the seat, pinning Joy's left leg.

Her face was amazingly free of any signs of the impact, but her legs were covered in blood.

Greg wedged himself into the car, clasping Joy's limp hand in his left hand and tucking his shoulder up under her head. He covered her pinned abdomen with his large right hand and threw himself whole-heartedly into the fervent but intermittent prayer that he'd been praying since Dad's horrible call.

He prayed that God would be glorified and that he would give the family, especially Tim and Joy, the strength they needed for this difficult journey.

TIM FEVERISHLY PACED the hospital waiting room, trying to form a prayer other than, "Oh, God, no! Please don't take her. Please don't take Joy."

They had been working on Joylynne too long.

Tim had barely even glimpsed his wife when she'd been whisked into the hospital and immediately surrounded by urgently efficient doctors and nurses.

Tim and Robert had arrived an agonizing five minutes before the ambulance. Initially, Tim had been consoled when his unnamed comforter had told him that a big man who claimed to be Joylynne's brother-in-law was with her, praying. Tim didn't ask how Greg got there so fast. It was just one of those God-things that seemed to happen to Greg.

When Greg had entered the waiting room shortly after Joy had gone back to treatment, all Tim's comfort had fled. His big brother's face had been much too solemn and sad.

Tim didn't know how long it had been since Joy had arrived at the hospital. He knew he had looked at the time, but he couldn't remember what the clock had said. It felt like it had been an eternity, but maybe it was thirty minutes, maybe two hours.

Suddenly Greg was leading him over to an empty couch.

"Sit, Tim," Greg demanded.

Tim sat. Greg dropped down next to him. Mom sat on his other side.

That was when Tim realized a very somber doctor was approaching.

"The baby seems to be fine," the doctor said as he sat on the coffee table in front of Tim's couch. "We'll monitor her very closely until she's born so we can make sure she stays healthy."

"And Joy?" Tim asked, gripping the hand Greg offered him.

"We have her on life support but if it weren't for your daughter, she wouldn't be," the doctor said gently. "We're only prolonging her life to save the baby."

Heat rose in Tim's chest and burst like a fist in his head. He couldn't have heard right.

Mom was sobbing, and the sound was echoed around the room. Greg had his arm around Tim.

"No!" Tim cried. "No, no, no! Not Joy, God! Please give her back!"

As he howled in agony, Tim didn't realize that his grip on his brother's hand was bone crushing.

He distantly knew that when he tried to rise, he fell to his knees and was cradled in his brother's arms. His mother was hugging him from behind. Sobs and prayers surrounded them. He grasped at straws.

"But she is still alive?" he asked with hopeful agony as he lifted his face to look at the doctor.

"Technically, yes," the doctor nodded. "But the chance of her recovery is so remote that I cannot even suggest it."

"But she is still alive," Tim said firmly. "I want to see her."

"They're moving her to a room," the doctor sighed and nodded at a nurse. "Cindy will take you to the floor. As soon as she's settled in, you can see her."

As he rose unsteadily to his feet, Tim was only vaguely aware that Robert slipped under his arm and walked with him, giving him strength. Mom was on his other side, holding his hand. Someone was behind him.

He was glad they were with him because the hall was a long dark tunnel that he wouldn't have been able to navigate on his own.

No one realized that Greg didn't follow the rest of the family. He was on his knees in the waiting room they'd abandoned, sobbing, praying more fervently than he'd ever prayed before.

JOY'S FAMILY ARRIVED later that day, Brian and Cait early the next. Everyone took turns sitting with Tim in Joy's room.

Anyone who walked into the room with the thought that they would console Tim was soon disabused of that notion. Tim would have none of the fearful solemnness that had characterized the first few hours after Joylynne's accident.

"Joy and the baby are both going to be fine," Tim firmly told all visitors. "They need to hear laughter and happiness, not tears and fear."

No one argued with that. It was certainly better for Tim's baby to be surrounded by hopefulness and joy. For the first week after the accident, no one realized that Greg didn't join in the positive talk. While he never contradicted anyone, he also never joined in the affirmations about when Joy woke up.

Almost a week after the accident, Brian showed up at Greg's office in The Ohana Project. The family members who lived in St. Louis kept to their daily routines as much as possible. It made sense, not just because the work they did was important, but because there were too many family members for everyone to be at the hospital at once. Rather than sitting around doing nothing but moping or praying, they may as well be doing God's work. Brian envied them the work.

Greg's secretary Ann assured Brian that Greg was alone in his office, so Brian went right in.

Greg was sitting at his desk but staring out the window. He turned in surprise when Brian walked in. Ann hadn't warned him that someone had come to see him.

He stood as Brian walked up to his desk.

"Joy's already dead," Brian declared calmly.

"Why do you say that?" Greg asked, careful to keep his tone neutral.

"I had a dream last night that confirmed a conviction that started pretty much the first day I was here."

"That confirms my conviction," Greg sighed sadly and motioned toward the couches. "I thought God wanted me to tell you too."

"How long have you known?" Brian asked as they sat.

"I knew as soon as I crawled into the car with Joy."

"Was she already gone then?" Brian asked in shock.

"No, but there was barely any life left in her," Greg said sadly. "She died in surgery."

"Tim's not going to handle it well when he finally has to let her go."

"How well would any of us handle our wives dying?" Greg shrugged. "Just thinking about that being Beth in that room tears me up."

"I hear that," Brian sighed sadly.

"I'm trying to hold out for a miracle," Greg's eyes filled with tears. "God hasn't told me to quit praying, but he also hasn't told me Joylynne will be restored to Tim. I haven't tried to tell Tim she's already gone."

"And I don't think you should," Brian said sadly. "It'll be harder for him if we try to convince him to let go of her before he has to, before the baby's born. Does anyone else know?"

"I think maybe Brandon does, but he won't admit it to himself. He's really close to Tim and Joy."

"That year they spent together in Oklahoma," Brian nodded. "But he'll support us when it's time to let Joy go."

"Are you still glad you joined the family?" Greg asked sadly.

Brian frowned. "Do you wish you had a different family?"

"No! I love my family."

"There's your answer," Brian said firmly.

"But we've had some awful things to deal with since you joined the family," Greg sighed and shook his head. "I never thought about that when I started this ministry."

"You don't really think I'd be better off alone rather than walking through times of suffering with a family, do you?" Brian asked incredulously.

"No," Greg frowned thoughtfully. "But I guess some people would."

"Your process is long enough that by the time you pair orphans with families, they're ready for whatever comes their way."

"I hope you're right."

"I am," Brian grinned slyly. "I'm the big brother. I'm always right."

Greg laughed. "You most certainly are the big brother!"

Brian arched an eyebrow as if waiting for an agreement on the rest of his statement.

He knew that agreement would never come, so he changed the subject.

"I want to do something physical and productive. Do you think anyone would mind if I did some work on the grounds at Halelolo?"

"I don't see why not," Greg shrugged. "Ask Steve. He manages all the properties."

Brian did, and Steve was happy to confirm that he was free to do whatever he wanted on the grounds of any of their properties, Halelolo, the TOP complex and Gumbwats' Haven, but he did need to work with Elton who was their head groundskeeper. Of course Cait worked with him. Back in Hilo, Brian owned a nursery and Cait had a landscaping business.

Brian and Greg didn't tell anyone else what God had revealed to them, but the rest of the family began to have their own subtle revelations, including Joylynne's parents. None of them clearly understood that Joy was already gone, but they did lose their confidence that she would recover.

When the calendar flipped up to reveal April, everyone but Tim and Robert already privately knew that they had lost Joy, but no one spoke about it.

Chapter 32

*L*uke shot up in bed, suddenly fully awake. That dream had been too real.

He turned on the light and reached for his phone. He didn't have to worry about waking Nalani because, as usual, she was already up, probably out on the back porch with a cup of coffee enjoying a beautiful morning.

The phone rang before his hand touched it. It was Steve.

I had a dream, Steve said without a greeting.

"So did I," Luke sighed. He hadn't needed the confirmation that the dream hadn't been just a dream. It had been a vision.

The baby's coming today, Steve said.

"Yes," Luke's phone interrupted him with a beep. He looked. "Greg's calling me."

And Dave's calling me, Steve said. *We have time. Tell Greg to come over here for breakfast.*

When Steve sent Heather and the kids to join Nalani and her children for breakfast, neither of the women thought anything of it. The boundaries for fellowship times were quite fluid in their extended ohana, especially since they all lived so close. More than once Steve, Dave, Luke and Greg had shared breakfast while their wives and children were breakfasting with other family members.

Heather was still getting Shaky ready to go when her brothers arrived for breakfast. They of course had to greet her as if it was just another day.

As soon as the men were alone, Greg dropped heavily into a chair.

"Today's the day," he sighed. "Brian called me. He had the same dream. He'll alert everyone in Halelolo after we're on the road."

"The baby's coming," Luke nodded, sitting also.

"And Tim's going to have to say goodbye to Joylynne," Dave finally said aloud what they all had suspected. He was helping Steve prepare breakfast. It was very light by their usual standards, just scrambled eggs, toast and fruit.

For a long moment no one said anything. Lost in private grief, they didn't even look at each other. Finally Luke sighed heavily.

"We have to tell Dad and Brandon," he said firmly.

"I understand Dad, but why Brandon?" Steve asked. He wasn't opposed to adding Brandon; he was just wondering why in their big family Luke chose him as the other addition.

"Because he and Greg are the ones who Joy gave medical power of attorney to," Luke said sadly. That had been one of the things Luke had helped every adult family member do.

"We're going to have to make the call to shut down the machines after Gabriella is born," Greg's eyes filled with tears.

"Call them now," Dave nodded at Luke. "But we only tell them about this morning's dreams that the baby's coming today."

Within fifteen minutes, Brandon and Joshua joined the other men. They were quickly convinced that Tim's baby would be arriving that day, but it took a little more work to convince Brandon that they needed to terminate Joylynne's life-support. They used the same arguments that Greg and Brandon would present to Tim – Joy's life was in God's hands, not in the hands of the doctors and their machines.

Both Greg and Brandon knew that to shut off the machines they didn't need to have Tim's agreement. They would like to have it, even if it was grudging. Regardless of whether or not Tim agreed, they would follow through with what they knew was obedience to God.

TIM SLOWLY AWAKENED. Once again he was sleeping in an awkward position. It had been two weeks and two days since he'd slept in his bed. Thankfully he'd never had a hard time sleeping any time he got the chance, whether or not he was comfortable.

He'd hardly left his wife's side since they'd allowed him into her room the afternoon of the accident. Someone brought most of his meals to him in the room. The only time he ate outside of the hospital was every few days when a couple of his brothers would virtually drag him to Halelolo to take a shower and change his clothes. He was never gone more than a few hours. He slept in a chair beside Joy's bed. While it was a recliner, it hadn't been created for someone as big as him.

He talked to Joy, read to her, held her hand and cried. Sometimes he laid his head on her abdomen and talked to the baby. Thankfully his daughter was doing well.

Tim continued to pray fervently for a miracle. Two or three times a day, a small group of family members would gather in Joy's room to pray with him. As little Gabriella Reyani grew with no signs of stress, hope continued to grow in her father.

Robert was Tim's most consistent companion. Without an immediate family of his own, he didn't have any other claims on his time. Sometimes he went back to Halelolo to sleep, sometimes he spent the night out in the waiting room. He was almost always the one who brought Tim breakfast.

Tim stood carefully and worked some kinks out, then he gently kissed his wife.

"Good morning, Joy," he said cheerfully. "This would be a fine day for you to wake up. I sure miss those beautiful green eyes."

He stroked her hair for a bit, then gently laid his hand on her abdomen.

"Morning to you too, baby girl," Tim had decided that he would not call his daughter by her name until his wife woke up and spoke it. "I'm looking forward to seeing you someday soon. I bet you're beautiful, just like your mommy, but I'm happy to wait awhile longer since you've still got some growing to do in there."

"I see you're up already," Robert walked in with two breakfast trays. "This is turning you into a morning person."

"I think not," Tim said wryly as he took his tray. "I'm sure I'll be back to a nine o'clock walk-up call when Joy and I are home with the baby."

"Not for a while, you won't," Robert was even more wry.

"You have a point," Tim laughed. "I'll have to work out a deal with Joy where every other day I get to sleep in."

"Has the doctor been in yet?" Robert asked as they started eating.

"Not yet. The nurses came in and did their thing, but I didn't wake up enough to talk to them."

"Any change," Robert asked hopefully.

Tim desperately wanted to say yes, but he couldn't honestly do so. His wife hadn't twitched, moaned or groaned in over two weeks.

That did not mean he had to accept the doctor's assessment.

"Not yet," Tim answered his brother.

While they were eating, they turned on the television to watch a morning news program. Neither of them were avid TV watchers, but they'd long ago exhausted the only topic of discussion that Tim really cared about – Joy's recovery.

The show was halfway into its second hour and Tim was idly rubbing Joy's abdomen. Suddenly he jerked his hand back and stared at the place his hand had been.

"She moved!" Tim gasped.

"It was the baby," Robert said rather doubtfully.

"No. It wasn't the baby. I've felt her move many times," Tim carefully laid his hand back on Joy's abdomen. "That was Joy. I think it might've been a contraction."

"Should we call the nurse?" Robert stood on the other side of Joy's bed.

"It wouldn't hurt," Tim shrugged. They could wait for the doctor who could come through on his rounds any minute now, but why?

Tim was surprised when Dad arrived just before the nurse. Since the family was so large and they couldn't all be in Joy's room at the same time, they came in shifts. During visiting hours, there were always two or three family members around, and everyone came every day, but they worked around each other's schedules. His parents and Joy's parents usually came midmorning and midafternoon so that the siblings could visit during the lunch hour and before and after work. Tim thought his mom and Danita were supposed to be coming later this morning; Dad and Al weren't due until afternoon.

"Greg said your baby's coming today," Joshua told Tim as he crossed the room to give his son a hug.

"How does he know?" Tim asked, not as a challenge but for clarification. The family members knew better than to doubt Greg when he made a firm declaration. He always had some special insight from God, and he'd never been proven wrong.

"Brian, Luke, Dave, Steve and Greg all woke up with dreams this morning," Joshua said as he accepted a hug from Robert who'd gone around Joy's bed, not just to hug his dad but also to free up space for the nurse to work. "Dreams that were apparently visions because they all dreamt exactly the same thing."

"All of them?" Robert was surprised. As far as he knew, Heather was the only one in the family other than Greg who'd ever had a vision-dream. That was when God revealed to her that he was sending Phil and Becca to join the family.

"All of them," Joshua nodded firmly. He didn't object to his son's question. He'd been shocked too when they'd first told him. "Everyone's on their way."

"Your father might be right about the baby coming today," the nurse told Tim. "We'll get the doctor in here right away to check on your wife."

The doctor must have been close because he arrived in just a few minutes. He confirmed that Joy definitely was in labor. Quickly they got her ready to move into surgery because she of course would have a C-section. Tim followed his wife's bed as she was wheeled through a maze that included an elevator and innumerable halls.

The hospital wouldn't allow Tim to follow Joy into surgery. When he stepped into the waiting room, he was surprised to see that his whole family was there, minus the children.

Greg had indeed gotten a word from God.

Tim didn't think anything was amiss when Dad led him over to a small cluster of chairs where Greg and Brandon were waiting. Their somber looks as they sat with him finally raised an alarm.

"After they get Joy back in her room, we're going to have them disconnect her from life-support," Greg didn't bother with small talk. If they beat around the bush, the C-section would be over before they convinced Tim that letting Joy go was the right thing to do.

"What?" Tim glared. "No, we're not!"

"It's the right thing to do, Tim," Brandon said calmly.

"It is not!" Tim denied. "When she comes out of her coma, then we'll disconnect life-support. Not before."

"Do you know with one-hundred percent surety that she will come out of the coma?" Greg stared steadily at him.

Tim opened his mouth to say "Yes," but he couldn't do it. Though he'd hoped and prayed and spoken confidently of Joy's return to awareness, he'd never received confirmation from God that his heart's desire would be granted.

"Tim, if it's God's will that Joy lives, it won't matter if we terminate her life-support," Brandon explained earnestly. "If God has willed that her time on earth with you is over, then life-support is making Joy one of the living dead."

Brandon's choice of words was deliberate. He knew that Tim despised the popularity of zombies, the living dead.

Tim angrily glared at Brandon. He would not try to keep Joy alive if she was dead, but she couldn't be dead. They had a baby girl who needed her mother. He needed his wife.

"They're not talking about killing Joylynne, Tim," Steve said gently. "They just want to take the measures necessary to let her body go if her soul has already gone to be with Jesus."

"We just want you to put it in God's hands alone, Tim," Greg urged him gently. "Let him either give you the miracle of a restored life, or show you that you need to let go of the shell of a body that we'll all someday leave behind."

Tim looked around the room at his family. He saw varying degrees of acceptance on almost everyone's face. Some were resigned, some slightly fearful, only a few were hopeful. Robert was the only one who frowned fiercely.

Al and Nita were sitting on the couch at a right angle from Tim's. He stared at them, wanting to know what they thought but afraid to ask.

"She's your wife now, Tim," Al said firmly. "It's not our decision."

Nita nodded, then buried her face in Al's chest and wept. Joy's brothers stood behind them, weeping also.

"We don't have to go into the room with a negative attitude, Tim," Brian advised. "Surround her with the love and happiness you've insisted on these last couple weeks. If there's a spark of life left in her, she will keep breathing when the ventilator's turned off. If her spirit's still there, she won't leave the people she loves."

Tim couldn't find a hole in their arguments. If she was alive, she would breathe on her own. If Joy was gone, he did need to let her go.

"Fine," he hung his head. "Do it."

With the decision made, the wait for the doctor was agonizingly long, but he came much too soon.

"You have a healthy girl," the doctor told Tim with cautious cheerfulness. "She was big for a month early, seven pounds three ounces. If you go down to the nursery you can see her in just a few minutes."

"And Joy, my wife?" Tim asked.

"They're taking her back to her room, but it'll be a good fifteen minutes or more before she's settled in. Why don't you stop and see your daughter on the way?"

Some of the family followed the doctor's advice, but not Tim. He paid little attention to who followed him and who joined him later in the other waiting room. He knew Robert was by his side the whole time, but at this point it didn't matter who else was. Emotionally, Robert was the only one firmly in his corner.

Tim, Robert, Gloria, Danita and Brian were in Joy's room when the doctor walked in with Greg and Brandon right behind him.

Tim grabbed Robert's arm as he rose. The time had come.

"Your wife gave medical power of attorney to your brothers, Greg Shepherd and Brandon Wolfe," the doctor said solemnly.

"I know," Tim nodded.

"They've signed the order to terminate life support."

"They talked to me about it earlier."

"Would you like to speak with her before we do this?"

Tim shook his head. He knew the doctor meant say goodbye, but it wasn't goodbye. Joy wasn't dead.

"Would you like anyone else to be in the room?"

Tim looked around. "Her dad and brothers if they want to come in."

"We're here," Al stepped into the room, trailed by Chavis and Heath. Taggart and Sean stayed at the door beside Greg and Brandon.

"Okay then," the doctor nodded to the nurse. They went to work.

Tim didn't watch them. He kept his attention focused on his wife. With Joy's hand clutched firmly in his, Tim stared at her chest. Its gentle swell and decline with the rhythm of the ventilator was the only visible sign of life in her.

Please, God, please, please, let her live! Let her keep breathing on her own when they turn off the ventilator. Please, God! I don't want to live without her!

Chapter 33

The ventilator went silent. Joy's chest rose. It fell.

Tim stared at her chest, willing it to rise again.

It didn't. Instead, the flat tone from her heart monitor pierced Tim's soul.

"No!" Tim wailed, dropping to his knees beside Joy's bed. He howled at the ceiling, "Please, God, no!"

He lunged up, wrapped his wife in his arms and clutched her tightly to his chest. He kissed her feverishly, begging her to wake up.

Her lips were too cold. Maybe it was his imagination, maybe it was a revelation, but suddenly he knew what he had denied for two weeks now.

His Joy was gone.

She had been gone long before Greg and Brandon signed the order to terminate her life-support. The life-support had been for the baby Joy had so looked forward to seeing.

Tim's eyes were blinded by tears as he gently lowered the lifeless body back to the bed. He stroked Joy's hair and kissed her one last time.

Slowly he rose. Pain was mushrooming in his chest. It was going to explode and shatter him into a million pieces.

It didn't explode. It kept building.

He couldn't breathe.

Why should he?

Someone touched his arm.

Tim jerked away and fled the room.

He was dimly aware that he bounced off a couple walls and ran into a cart of some kind, but he finally made it outside.

He ran until he could run no more, then he trudged wearily on, not aware of where he was going, or why.

This was living death. It had to be. He knew that somewhere out there was life, light and love but it was gone from him. Darkness shrouded his heart.

How could a man feel such pain and not die? How did his heart keep on beating when his chest was crushed in agony? How did breath fill his lungs? Why didn't his throbbing head rupture into a thousand geysers?

After a very long time, Tim was aware that someone was following him. He trudged on, not really caring who was behind him. Maybe it was some gangster who was about to mug him.

If it was a gangster, would Tim submit to a beating death or would he take out his agony on a would-be attacker?

He couldn't answer that question.

He turned a corner and glanced down the sidewalk.

It wasn't an issue. Robert was the person following him.

Tim walked another two blocks then suddenly stopped. Robert walked up to him.

"Why are you following me?" he asked. He wanted to be angry but he was too tired.

"To make sure you get home safe," Robert replied.

"Maybe I don't want to go home," Tim sighed and started walking again.

"I understand," Robert sighed too.

Tim rubbed his forehead.

Of course Robert did. They'd talked a lot about Robert's feelings after the attack. Though their situations were very different, their pain was agonizingly similar.

"I guess it wouldn't be fair to you to just curl up and die," Tim said sadly.

"No, it wouldn't, but who said life was fair?" Robert snorted derisively.

"Why?" Tim whispered hoarsely. "Why did Joy have to die?"

"I don't have the first clue, Tim," Robert said bitterly. "Right now, I'm inclined to believe that God is a harsh taskmaster."

"It does seem like that, doesn't it?" Tim agreed, even though a tiny voice, deep in his soul whispered, *God loves you. He will carry you through this difficult time.*

Tim wasn't ready to entertain that voice, so he quashed it.

"Sometimes I think our family would be better off without God's 'blessings,'" Robert growled resentfully.

"I know I should argue with you but I can't think of a good reason why," Tim replied after they'd trudged on a few more steps.

Robert had no response. He felt bad because he knew he couldn't offer his brother any comfort. He was too in need of comfort himself. All he could do was walk with Tim and hope to help him bear his agony.

They walked a couple more blocks in silence.

Suddenly, without warning, like a fist in the gut grief once again punched Tim, hard.

Tim keened in wordless agony, dropping to his knees and clutching his hair in tight fists.

Robert helplessly stood beside him, with an angry look directing other pedestrians around them. Tears streamed down his cheeks.

"How am I going to live without her?" Tim finally lifted his ravaged face, grabbing his brother's forearm, begging him to help.

Robert didn't have an answer for him.

Tim was trying to decide if he should stand and try to go on, or curl up in a ball right there on the sidewalk and let life flow by him. A car stopping at the curb beside him interrupted his inner debate.

He lifted his head, half angry because he was expecting it to be one of his irritating family members here to drag him home.

It was a police car.

"What's going on?" the patrolman on the passenger side asked with wary concern.

"Nothing the cops need to be concerned about," Robert growled. He had a bad taste in his mouth when it came to cops. The first ones on the scene back in Waimanalo had treated him like he was the criminal. One of the detectives had interrogated him as if he was complicit in his attack.

"You're creating a public disturbance," the first cop's partner was going around the back of the car.

"Disturbance?" Robert snarled. "What kind of bull is that?"

Tim suddenly realized that his little brother was dangerously close to having an altercation with the police. They'd talked enough about his experience in Hawaii for Tim to suspect his feelings without too much effort. He didn't care if he lived or died, but he did still care about Robert.

Tim couldn't think of anything to say, so he reached up and grabbed Robert's arm. When his brother looked down at him, Tim frowned and shook his head.

Robert glared. Tim glared back.

Robert sighed and shrugged, tension draining out of him. When he looked back at the cops, they were both out of the car, one on either side of him and Tim. They were both very wary. Their hands weren't on their weapons, but they looked more than ready to draw them.

Having released his anger, Robert realized that it was certainly a worrisome situation – two very big men acting strangely on a city sidewalk.

"I'm sorry, officers," Robert drooped. "My brother's wife died this morning. We're struggling to deal with it. We didn't give a thought to where we were."

"Maybe somewhere private would be a better choice," the shorter one, the passenger, suggested kindly. He was no longer wary.

"You should head on home," the other officer was bigger in height and girth. He was much less wary than before, but still cautious.

Robert looked around and shrugged. "I have no idea where we are. I just moved here from Hawaii last month."

"Hawaii?" the big one was surprised. "You related to Chaplain Greg?"

Neither of Greg's brothers were surprised or bothered by the question.

It could have been annoying, the assumption that just because this St. Louis police officer knew someone from Hawaii, they should be related to him. There are over a million people in Hawaii, and not all of them are related. But they knew that they looked a lot like their brother, not just in size but in appearance too. And they were well aware that between Greg's brush with the law five years ago and the street work he'd been doing in St. Louis since then, both informally and as a chaplain, many St. Louis police knew their brother by sight and reputation at least. It also helped that their brother-in-law, Abe Lawrence, was a detective on the force.

"Our older brother," Tim was the one who finally answered.

"Then I probably know where you live," the bigger officer told them. "Are you in the warehouse by the offices or at the big house?"

"The big house," Robert said.

Tim sighed and used his brother's arm to pull himself upright. Even though it hadn't been someone in the family who'd stopped next to him, they were still going to drag him home.

Thankfully the officers didn't talk about Greg on the way to Halelolo. Normally Tim loved hearing stories about how Greg had impacted people's lives. Today wasn't a normal day. Today Greg had ended Tim's life. Today, Tim detested his big brother.

TIM'S EXISTENCE BECAME a mosaic of pain and anger. Life kept trying to intrude, but he pushed back, hard.

When the police dropped him and Robert off at Halelolo, Tim trudged in without looking around, heading straight for the steps. Mom's voice followed him.

"Tim, would you join us for a few minutes? We really need to make funeral arrangements."

"Ask Al and Nita," Tim snarled bitterly without breaking stride. "Joy was their daughter way longer than she was my wife."

Without thinking, Tim walked up the steps and down the hall to the room he and Joy had shared when they were in St. Louis. He took one look at the obvious signs that Joy had intended to return shortly – the nightgown laid neatly across the foot of the bed, the bottle of lotion on the reading nook table, right beside a tray which still had the empty dishes from Joy's midmorning snack two weeks ago – rinsed in their bathroom and neatly stacked. It was all mute testimony to the fact that Tim's neat freak wife had learned that economy of motion was more important than absolute lack of clutter. If putting things away took her off her planned route, she left things out, but they were always neatly placed. Tim often helped her by putting things away for her.

In the last couple weeks, Tim had never straightened up anything in his few trips here. He'd just showered, changed and headed back out. He'd hoped to bring Joy home and tease her about the "mess" she'd left. Obviously no one else had been in here to clean either. That wasn't surprising. The one cleaning person the family had hired didn't do the private rooms unless specifically asked.

That meant there would be rather large piles of dirty clothes in the bathroom, and a hamper with Joy's clothes from the night before her accident. Joy's personal hygiene things were all in the bathroom still, neatly lined on the vanity or the small shelf in the tub. They spent enough time at Halelolo that Joy had decided they should keep their bathroom fully stocked. That way there was no need to pack much, either coming or going.

Tim turned and left the room. He couldn't bear to see evidence of the life he used to live with his wife. He walked down the hall and around the corner, back to the very last guest room, small and rarely used.

He threw himself across the bed and stared at the ceiling. It was white and smooth. The ceiling in his and Joy's room had a pattern, even arcs swooping out from the light fixture in the center of the room. He knew because more than once he and Joy had laid with their heads together staring up at the arcs.

"They're myriad mini rainbows," Joy had observed the first time they'd examined their ceiling.

"Not hardly, sweetheart," Tim had snorted. "They have no color."

"Shows what you know, little Shepherd boy," Joy had corrected him with playful condescension. "White isn't colorless. It's the presence of all colors. So they're rainbows that are so infused with light that you can no longer see the separate colors."

"Oh really?" Tim had laughed. "Does that mean that rainbows are actually all around us every day, but we can't see them because they're too infused with light?"

"I guess it does!" Joy had giggled.

Staring at the white ceiling above him, Tim found it appropriate that there were no rainbows on that ceiling. There would be no rainbows in his life, ever again.

Tim curled up on his side and began to weep. It didn't take long for him to cry himself to sleep.

His grief combined with many nights of too little sleep and the exertion of a three hour walk after two weeks of inactivity. His sleep was deep and long. It wasn't disturbed when his father found him later that evening and covered him with a light blanket. Not even dreams disturbed him that night, but it would be his last peaceful sleep in a long time.

THE SKY WAS almost to its zenith when Tim finally awakened the next day. He was disconcerted by his unfamiliar surroundings, but reality quickly cleared his confusion.

Joy was gone. Life would never be familiar and comfortable again.

Tim wept again, and dropped off to sleep again. But this was a fitful sleep that didn't even last thirty minutes. As consciousness again returned to the grieving man, he wished that he could fall asleep and never wake up again.

Better yet, he would wake up and discover he'd had a horrible nightmare. He would awaken and it would be the morning of Joy's appointment. Tim wouldn't run with Robert. He would not leave his wife's side, ever again.

He wasn't going to wake up. He was going to have to live through the nightmare that his life had become.

As Tim slowly swung his legs over the side of the bed and sat, he realized that his head and gut both ached.

He was hungry. How could he possibly be hungry?

Tim stumbled into the small bathroom that was attached to the guest room. As he relieved himself, he decided he may as well see if he could eat something. An aching stomach was the only ache he had that he could actually do something about.

He briefly thought about brushing his teeth. All the guest rooms were stocked with the basic essentials, so he could do it without having to go back into that other room.

Who would he be brushing his teeth for? If anyone got close enough to discover his lack of oral hygiene, they'd just have to deal with it.

Leaving the room, Tim discovered that he was rather unsteady on his feet. Was that from grief or hunger? He had no idea, but he stayed close to the wall and used the hand railing as he descended the back stairs to the kitchen.

He hadn't heard any voices so he was surprised to see the kitchen occupied. Cari, Beth and Brandon were there.

Emotions he couldn't quite identify flashed across their faces, but before any of them could say anything, Tim turned and left the room.

He didn't want to see Brandon, now or ever.

He hadn't taken his clothes off yesterday, so he checked his pockets. His keys and wallet were right where they were supposed to be. He climbed in his car, only briefly wondering who had brought it back from the hospital. He drove to the nearest fast-food joint. It was too late for breakfast, so he just got a shake.

He drove aimlessly for a while. He seriously thought about finding one of the Interstates and following it to its terminus. He drove back to Halelolo instead. Yesterday's incident of the cops finding him without even knowing he was lost told him that running would be useless. Hiding would be a better option.

Again he mounted the steps without looking around. Even though he was on the back staircase, someone still attempted to arrest his flight before he'd gone far.

"Tim, your daughter needs a name for her birth certificate," Heather called.

"Ask Greg," Tim snarled. "He knows everything."

"He can't sign it," Heather sighed heavily.

"Have Robert bring it," Tim sighed too. "I'll sign it."

As Tim dropped onto his bed, he realized that he hadn't yet seen his daughter. She was a day old and he didn't know what she looked like.

He didn't care. He didn't want a daughter. He wanted his wife back.

He cried himself to sleep again.

The next day he signed the birth certificate application, not caring enough to check the name. He didn't leave his room for it.

The day after that, he had to leave his room. It was Joy's funeral.

Robert brought him clothes from that other room, and he made sure Tim showered and brushed his teeth before getting dressed. He even tied Tim's tie for him. He also never left his brother's side through the whole long ordeal.

When Tim walked into the church and saw Joy in the casket, his life shattered anew.

He wanted to run, to escape, but he couldn't breathe. Something was crushing his chest. Blackness descended.

The next thing he knew he was stretched out on the floor. Robert was right next to him and there were faces in the background, but Tim didn't try to focus on any of them. He clung to Robert.

"Should we step outside and get some fresh air?" Robert asked gently.

"Won't help much," Tim moaned. "Take me t' Joy."

Robert helped him to his feet. Tim dropped his arm across Robert's shoulders and let his brother lead him to the casket. Tim stared at the ground until Robert stopped walking.

He slowly raised his eyes to behold the face of his beloved.

His chest constricted with that all-too-familiar fist of pain. His eyes filled with tears, but he remained upright, leaning heavily on his brother.

He stared at the face he had loved for so many years now. Then he saw that she was wearing a green dress that they had both loved.

He saw the pink bundle in her hands and frowned. Joy didn't like pink. He looked closer, and his tears fell fast.

Joylynne's lifeless hands clasped the bouquet of pink roses and carnations that he had promised to give her after their baby was born.

Tim and Robert stayed beside the casket even though Tim was virtually blinded by his tears. They stayed because Tim couldn't make his legs work. The finality of death had imprisoned him.

That wasn't his Joy in the casket. He knew without a doubt that others would claim she looked at peace, but she didn't. She looked without life.

Because she was.

The mind and soul that had inhabited this beautiful shell was gone.

Tim finally gained enough strength to turn with his brother. He allowed Robert to lead him to the front pew. He made Robert sit beside him. He couldn't let go of his lifeline.

The service was interminable. Tim heard and saw everything but nothing registered, not until a slide show began.

Tim just stared blankly at Joy as a baby and a child, but the teenaged Joy was both terrible and wonderful to behold. When short video clips were interspersed with the pictures, Tim was comforted and destroyed. This was his Joy, full of life, love and laughter. When he showed up beside her, knives stabbed his gut, but he couldn't look away.

He remained dry-eyed throughout the presentation, but as soon as the last picture of Joy – very happily pregnant – faded from the screen, Tim dissolved in tears.

Though he was still deeply devastated by his loss, for the first time a tiny voice of hope whispered deep in his soul. Joy had indeed left this world, but she'd left behind many blessings that would sustain her grieving husband in the days to come. Once he was strong enough to search out those blessings, he would be able to live again.

The rest of that day, Tim was barely strong enough to do what he knew was expected of him. He'd hidden out in his new room the day before, so if there had been a visitation the previous night as was the custom in the Midwest, he'd missed it. Back at Halelolo after the funeral, he had to greet a seemingly endless parade of fellow mourners. Some were easier to face than others.

Nita, Al, Joy's brothers, Mama Rey, Bill and the rest of Joy's friends and family from Oklahoma, Tim welcomed with open arms, weeping with them, consoling them as much as they comforted him. His own family was a struggle.

Maybe it was irrational, but he felt like his family had betrayed him. Except for Robert, every one of them had backed Brandon and Greg when they terminated Joy's life-support. The best Tim could manage with his own family was stiff, half-hearted hugs. For everyone except Brandon and Greg. He turned away from them without even a nod.

He didn't see how distraught his brothers were over his rejection, nor did he notice that some of the others in the family were infuriated at his cold treatment of Brandon and Greg. He never became aware of their anger because no one got the opportunity to voice it to him. The two brothers he loathed intercepted and diffused all of the attempted angry assaults on Tim.

Long before the last mourner left Halelolo, Tim climbed the steps to his room at the back of the house. Once again he cried himself to sleep.

Sometime in the early hours of the morning, Tim was awakened by the cry of a newborn. Still more than half asleep, he rolled over to ask Joy if he should get the baby. When he realized that Joy wasn't there, and never would be, but there was indeed a newborn baby crying somewhere in the house, Tim was angry.

God had cheated him. He took Joy away from him after little more than a year of marriage, and now he expected Tim to be a single father. God was cruel.

Tim rolled out of bed and grabbed clothes from the floor. He quickly dressed and ran from the house.

He didn't have the energy to figure out how to disappear forever, but he did have a place where he could be completely alone for a little while, long enough to figure out what to do next.

Chapter 34

*T*im pointed his car south. Just over an hour after leaving Halelolo, he was pulling into his garage down on the family farm. It was still early enough in the morning that maybe no one noticed his arrival. Of course yesterday all the family had been up in St. Louis at Halelolo or the lofts, so he wasn't sure who was even here.

He dimly remembered seeing most of the staff at the funeral too. Of course the ones who were way more family than employees, like the Guerreros and Katie Wheeler, had been there. But even the ones who rarely left the farm were there, Dillon Washington, Rose and Faith Clayborne. Maybe they'd spent the night in St. Louis too.

Tim wasn't taking any chances. Even if he was alone down here now, the great return would soon begin. He checked all the downstairs windows and the doors, securing them with Joy's ridiculous dead bolts and chain locks that didn't seem so ridiculous anymore.

After the house was secure, Tim dropped face down on the couch and fell into an exhausted sleep.

He didn't sleep long. The pain of his loss kept his sleep restless and finally pulled him back up to reality.

Tim rolled onto his back. It was still dark but the windows were a bit lighter.

He realized that the curtains were all open. Anyone could see in and know he was here.

But if he closed the curtains now, it would advertise his presence.

He would close them later, after the first time someone pounded on his doors.

Tim was rather shaky as he pushed himself up off the couch. That was probably because he didn't remember when the last time was that he'd eaten. He vaguely remembered a large buffet table at Halelolo yesterday, but he had absolutely no recollection of putting even one bite of food in his mouth. Maybe he should go see if there was any food in the kitchen.

He opened the cupboard where he knew Joy put the cereal. Sure enough, there were two boxes, his favorite and hers. Tim grabbed the granola-like cereal that Joy preferred. He opened it and took a handful. It was still fresh.

He got a bowl then turned to the refrigerator for milk. Of course there was none. It had been almost three weeks since anyone had lived in this house.

He frowned. He remembered having milk on cereal their last morning here. Robert had complained about just cereal and fruit, and Joy had told him he could make his own breakfast. He'd decided to eat the cereal then go out and find a second, bigger breakfast. Tim had gone with him. They'd gone down to Greg's where two more mouths were hardly noticeable with seven boys between nine and one, but extra pairs of hands preparing food and taking care of troublesome triplets were always welcome.

Tim didn't want to think about that morning, so he frowned harder at the frig. Someone had cleaned it out. The milk and juice were both gone. The leftovers were probably in the freezer. If he had any bread, that was where it would be too, along with any lunch meat.

He had a wandering thought that maybe he should go ahead and open the freezer and retrieve the bread at least. He wasn't going to be able to fix himself anything other than a sandwich later.

The thought wandered right on out of Tim's head because something else caught his eye.

Joy's two bottles of cooking wine were in the back on the bottom shelf, where they always sat. Normally they weren't noticeable because there was usually plenty of other things on that shelf. They were very noticeable now.

Tim stared at them. Joy called them cooking wine, but they were just regular wine. Tim knew they were because he'd been with Joy when she got them when they'd been in Gasconade County in December. A whole bunch of them had gone to visit the Bryants and go to the German-style Christmas market in Hermann. When Joy had discovered that there was a winery right in town, she wanted to see it. They'd ended up with two bottles of white wine and three reds.

When Tim had teased her about turning him into a drunk, she'd lifted her chin and arched her eyebrows.

"They're for cooking, Timothy," she'd said haughtily.

"How much do you use in a recipe?" he'd looked at the five bottles in surprise.

"Since I can't taste them today," Joy had gently rubbed the bulge of her belly, "I don't know which will be best. After I try them, I'll know which ones I want to stick with."

So they'd brought home five bottles. Tim remembered a delicious macaroni and cheese casserole that Joy had used white wine in, and every time she made marinara sauce or chili she added some of the red wine. She probably didn't use much, because the bottle of white wine was nearly full and the red was half-full.

Tim looked at the box of cereal he'd set on the counter. What kind of wine went with granola?

He grabbed the bottle of red wine and closed the frig.

He sat on the floor, in part because he didn't have the energy to sit in a chair but also because it seemed more appropriate to his intentions. He'd heard that alcohol dulled the senses, and his senses could sure use some dulling. He didn't want to feel anything anymore.

He took a swig of the wine.

It was different from anything he'd ever tasted before. It wasn't bad or good. Tim didn't know what alcohol was supposed to taste like, but maybe that was what made the wine rather strong, gave it a bit of a bite. It was way more … potent than grape juice.

He took another swig. The wine was a little fruity. Another big swallow. Maybe next time he should put it in a glass so he could taste it better.

Tim ate a handful of the granola cereal. It wasn't unpleasant. He didn't know if a wine connoisseur would pair that particular wine with that cereal, but it worked for him.

Another three swallows, another handful of cereal.

This probably isn't a very good balance of food and wine, Tim thought idly. He'd heard somewhere that two glasses with a full meal was the max a normal person could eat and still be under the legal limit.

He was a lot bigger than the average person, so he could drink more.

But he probably should be eating more. He'd never drank before so he had no idea how much alcohol he could handle. He was also stressed and exhausted, which undoubtedly affected the way he handled the liquor. And just how much was "a glass" anyway?

He didn't really care. In fact, by the time the bottle was down half of what he'd started with, Tim was wondering about what had happened to those other three bottles. Had Joy already used them, or were they somewhere in the cupboards?

He got to thinking about what else might be in the cupboards. There should be a bottle of vodka somewhere. When they'd been on the Big Island during their honeymoon, they'd visited the vanilla farm up in Paauilo. One of the things Joy had bought was vanilla beans. After they had settled into their temporary home in Norman, she'd asked him to pick up a bottle of vodka so she could soak the beans and make vanilla extract.

He knew that his very frugal wife wouldn't have tossed the remaining vodka when they moved. She would have packed it with her other kitchen supplies. But it might be at their house in Franklin.

Even if it was, that wasn't the only alcohol Joy used when she cooked. It had been right here in this house that she'd made a rum cake, so there had to be a bottle of rum somewhere.

And there was probably a bottle of whiskey sitting beside it because he remembered Joy telling Steve that the secret to her baked beans was whiskey.

Last month she'd made baked beans for Robert, then complained because he wanted hot dogs chopped into it.

"My baked beans are not Beanie Weenie beans!" she'd scolded him with hands on hips.

"But Sis, they're so ono! It'll be the best Beanie Weenie ever!" Robert had begged.

"Don't you buy like gourmet hot dogs?" Tim had suggested hopefully. "It'll be malicious over rice."

It had been. In fact, that should be some of the leftovers that were probably stored in his freezer.

More importantly, even though they weren't drinking people there should be enough alcohol in this house to bury Tim's sorrows for a while. If it worked, he would get some more bottles on his way to wherever he decided to disappear to.

Tim's bottle was empty. He stared at it, wondering what he should do now. It would be interesting to find out if white wine went as well with granola as red did.

After a few minutes, Tim grabbed the edge of the counter and pulled himself up. He was halfway up when his head began to swim. It was rather surprising, but not entirely unpleasant. In fact, it made him want to sleep.

Since oblivion was what he was going for, Tim sank back to the floor, rolled into a ball and let the darkness overcome him.

TIM DIDN'T KNOW how long he slept, but bright sunlight filled the kitchen when he woke up with a groan.

His sorrow still sat on his chest like a hundred pound weight. His body ached and his head hurt, but that was business as usual so Tim wasn't sure if he had a hangover or not. He didn't worry about it since it wasn't making his life any more unpleasant than it had already become.

He did however have a very urgent need that would make him feel slightly better once it was met.

When Tim came out of the bathroom, he went ahead and pulled the curtains shut in the living room. The kitchen curtains where fluffy, frilly things that weren't meant to close, but they did have window blinds. He dropped them then went right to the refrigerator and pulled out the bottle of white wine. He wondered if he should hunt up the other bottles of wine and refrigerate them. Was wine better cold?

He didn't know, but he could find out later if he left those bottles in whatever cupboard they were hiding in.

Before he sat back down by the box of Joy's granola cereal, Tim picked up the empty wine bottle and put it in the sink. There was no need to degenerate too far too quickly.

He also found a juice glass. A wine glass would probably be better, and he was pretty sure they had some somewhere, but he didn't know where. If he found them on his hunt for the hidden bottles, he would use one, but that would be later.

Tim discovered the red wine was probably better with the granola, but white wine went okay with it too. This time he was very careful to eat a handful of cereal between every drink from his glass.

He drank and ate steadily. The box had been a little over half full when he'd started. After he poured the last of the wine into his glass a little more than an hour later, he discovered that the cereal was almost gone too. He popped the last handful into his mouth then chased it with the last of the wine from the glass.

That was as good a time as any for another nap.

TIM DRIFTED SLOWLY up from oblivion. The first thing he was aware of was that he missed Joy, then his body started complaining. This time in addition to a headache and a full bladder, he also had a sour taste in his mouth. He was pretty sure that was from the wine. It was kind of like the bad taste he got when he had a cold and slept with his mouth open.

While he was in the bathroom, he brushed his teeth, but without toothpaste because he was slightly nauseous too.

Returning to the kitchen he decided that the descending darkness wasn't full enough to require him to turn on the lights to search for Joy's stash of cooking liquor.

It wasn't hard to find it. The bottles were on the top shelf of the cabinet, right above the rest of Joy's cooking supplies. Obviously she had wanted them to be easy to get to but out of the way.

Tim put all the bottles on the counter – rum, whiskey and three bottles of wine. No vodka so it was probably in Franklin. He would stick with wine for now, but the other bottles would be ready if he wanted them.

If? When would probably be more appropriate.

Since the pantry cabinets were right there, Tim looked for something to eat. His box of Cocoa Pebbles wasn't going to go well with the wine. There was some Spam but that would require frying, or at least heating in the microwave. He didn't feel like any kind of cooking.

That pretty much eliminated everything in the pantry except for the can of mixed nuts and the bag of cheese curls. They should go well with the white wine.

Before he sat on the floor, Tim decided to see if the wine glasses were in the same cabinet as the rest of their everyday dishes. If they weren't there, they were probably in the china hutch in the dining room with the rest of Joy's special occasion china.

There they were, again on the top shelf because they were so rarely used. In fact, Tim didn't think they'd ever been used before.

He looked in three drawers before he found the corkscrew. It took him awhile to figure out how to use it, but that just gave him a head start on the nuts and chips.

Once again he fell asleep shortly after the wine and food were gone. Once again he awoke feeling no better but no worse. Again he relieved himself. Again he searched for food.

He still didn't feel like fixing food. It was too early for breakfast anyway. He opened the freezer and found the bread and lunch meat that he'd suspected would be there. There was also one of the frozen strawberry yogurt bars that Joy really liked.

He set the bread and lunch meat on the counter to thaw and sat on the floor with the fruit bar and a bottle of the red wine. After he was done with the frozen yogurt, he would check to see if the bread and meat were thawed enough to make a sandwich.

TIM DIDN'T GET around to the sandwich. This time when he awakened well into the afternoon, he knew he had a hangover.

His headache stretched from the back of his skull all the way across his head and down to his teeth. The light hurt his eyes. His mouth was dry, sour and fuzzy. His stomach rolled dangerously. All of his physical agony only underscored the pain in his heart.

As he slowly pushed himself up, Tim snorted scornfully. Guys actually bragged about their hangovers? That was even stupider than Tim had previously imagined.

He was thirsty beyond belief. He didn't bother with a glass. He drank straight from the faucet. He promptly retched in the sink.

It was beginning to seem like drinking really wasn't a good idea. Sure he wanted something to distract him from the emotional agony of his loss, but was intense physical agony really the way to go about it?

Tim retrieved his wine glass and filled it with water. He grabbed a box of crackers from the pantry and staggered into the living room where he dropped onto the couch. With a cracker in one hand and the water in the other, he carefully nursed the nausea.

There had to be a trick to this drinking thing. He wanted the oblivion it brought, but he didn't want the hangover. Maybe if he controlled his drinking it would help. He pondered his dilemma. He finally came up with a plan of attack.

When he thought he could move without getting sick, Tim again made a trip to the restroom. Back in the kitchen, he found one of Joy's serving trays. On it he put the juice and wine glasses he'd used earlier, then grabbed another small glass from the cupboard. He put the remaining three bottles of liquor on the tray along with the bread, lunch meat and cheese from the frig. He thought about mayo, but that would take too much effort.

This time he sat on the couch in the living room. It had a more civilized feeling to it, not quite as desperate as sitting on the floor of the kitchen.

First Tim made two sandwiches, then he carefully poured three drinks, wine in the wine glass, whiskey and rum in the juice glasses. He would make sure that he ate both sandwiches before he finished all three drinks.

For some reason sitting on the couch intensified his loneliness. He looked at the TV and thought about turning it on, but they didn't have cable or satellite. To watch television, he would have to get up and choose a DVD then wait for it to load. That was too much work. Maybe when he had to get up the next time. He didn't really need to look at their collection to know what was there, so while he ate and drank, he could think about what movie he wanted to watch.

When he was about two-thirds done with his first sandwich, he put down his now-empty wine glass and picked up the rum.

Wow! That was strong! But it was also smooth. It was a spiced rum, and it tasted a lot like Joy's rum cake. Go figure.

The memory of Joy's cake made him drink the rum too fast. He started the whiskey right after the first bite of his second sandwich.

He gasped for breath and grabbed his throat. Now that was strong! It burned all the way down. There it sat, radiating warmth out to his body. No wonder so many people were whiskey drinkers.

When Tim finished the whiskey and sandwich, he had a light, pleasant buzz going. It wasn't enough to drown his sorrows entirely. He was a long way from oblivion.

He decided to just have one sandwich with his next round of drinks. He also decided to save the rum for last. It would be like a dessert.

Chapter 35

When Tim woke up some time in the morning, he guessed he should have had the extra sandwich. Half a day after that, he knew that even two more sandwiches didn't make the difference. He still had a hangover that intensified his longing for Joy.

In fact, physically he was feeling much, much worse. He spent a long time in the bathroom as his body tried to purge itself of the alcohol he'd consumed in ....

How long had he been drinking? He had no clue. It hadn't just been hours. It had been days, but how many?

As Tim sat leaning against the bathroom wall, he began to accept the utter foolishness of this endeavor. He would drink himself to death before he drank enough to forget the pain of his loss.

There had to be a better way to deal with his grief.

Tim sighed. There was a better way, and he knew how to get there.

God, help me. I don't know what to do. I miss Joy so much. I'm really angry with you. If you really do show us a way out of our temptations, please help me, because right now I'm very seriously tempted to follow Joy.

Nothing. He felt nothing except the pain and grief that had been his closest companions for too many days.

Tim rose slowly and walked from the bathroom, leaning against the wall.

He was halfway back to the living room when he realized he smelled something bad.

He stopped and sniffed. It smelled a little like the gym clothes Joy had thrown a fit over so many months ago, but maybe even worse.

Tim sniffed his shirt and realized that he was smelling himself.

He turned around and made his way back to the bathroom. A shower might help him gain some perspective on life.

When he reached for his soap, he picked up Joy's bottle instead. He just wanted to smell it. It reminded him of his wife, but it was lacking the warm muskiness that was pure Joy.

He slumped against the shower wall and sobbed.

The bottle fell from his hand. He left it there. It wasn't Joy. It had only been a small part of all that his wonderful wife had been.

The water was growing cold when Tim finally pulled himself together and turned it off. He toweled himself mostly dry, then wrapped the towel around his waist and stumbled into the bedroom. He'd intended to get dressed, but he fell across the bed instead. Soon he was deep in the first truly good sleep that he'd had in many days.

When Tim woke up, he had a very slight headache and a powerful heartache. All things considered, he felt better than he had since he'd gotten back home. He rolled onto his back and assessed where he was.

It was fully daytime, but he had no idea what day it was, or if it was late morning or early afternoon. Though he'd briefly entertained the thought, killing himself was not an option. He now knew for certain that he wasn't going to be able to drown his sorrows. He would have to find a better way to face the rest of his life.

He rose from the bed and stumbled into the hall.

He heard someone pounding on the door, and a voice called. It sounded like Heather, and maybe Robert.

"Go away," he growled. His voice was hoarse, so they probably hadn't heard him.

Since he vaguely remembered some pounding on the door in the past few days, they were probably getting ready to break down the door, just to make sure he was still alive.

He would let them know he was alive.

Tim turned and faced the door, then bellowed as loud as he could.

"Go away! I'm not dead. Just leave me alone!"

He couldn't understand the discussion on the other side of the door, but when the pounding didn't reoccur, Tim figured they'd left.

It was only a matter of time before he had to face his family, and probably not much time. He needed to take care of some things before that time came.

First, he washed his face, brushed his teeth and hair, then got dressed. In the living room, he retrieved the tray from under the couch where he'd shoved it when it was in his way. He piled up the remnants of his drunken disaster and carried the tray to the kitchen, which also needed some cleaning. The empty bottles he rinsed and put in the proper recycle bin. The last wine bottle he put in the back of the bottom shelf of the frig. The seriously depleted whiskey and rum bottles went back up on the shelf where Joy had stored them. The glasses went in the sink, the empty packaging from both the living room and the kitchen went in the rubbish, along with the last of the cheese which was now completely dried out because he hadn't properly wrapped it.

He wet the dishrag and wiped down the counter and the coffee table, then he got a rag to clean the floor where he'd been sitting.

That was that. He'd cleaned up his mess. The only other room he'd used since he'd returned home was the bathroom.

Now that he thought about it, that room could use some cleaning too. He needed to at least pick up his dirty clothes.

When his clothes were in the hamper, he decided he might as well clean the entire bathroom.

As he scrubbed away, tears trickled down his cheeks. He remembered how tickled Joy had been the first time she'd caught him cleaning the bathroom. She'd been properly appreciative every time he'd done it, especially the times when he'd given her an extra special surprise and cleaned with nothing on.

After the bathroom was clean, Tim wasn't sure what to do next. He stared at the hamper for a long moment, but he couldn't do laundry, not yet. He knew that beneath the very dirty clothes he'd just thrown in there were some of Joy's clothes. He wasn't ready to deal with that yet.

He turned and wandered out of the bathroom.

He felt a pull to go upstairs, but first he unlocked the doors and opened the curtains downstairs. He wasn't exactly ready to face his family yet, but he wouldn't turn them away again when they did come.

Upstairs, Tim's feet became leaden. He and Joy had moved their room downstairs months ago, so there was only one destination for him up there. The nursery.

He stepped to the door and crumpled to the floor.

The room was more Joy than their bedroom was. Rachel had helped Joy decorate it, but as he well knew, Rachel was adept at knowing people's needs and tastes better than they did themselves.

The part Joy had been proudest of, the crowning glory that brought the whole room together in one exuberant celebration of life were the laughing, playing, singing creatures that cavorted over every flat surface, not just the walls, but also the ceiling, floor, dresser and changing table. Joy had imagined it. Heather had sketched it, and Tim and Heather had painted it. There were lambs and bears and horses, dogs, birds, fish and dozens of other animals. But life and laughter also flowed through happy trees and dancing clouds. It wasn't bright and garish or pastel and placid. It was more like a real meadow with a brook running through it.

Everything they had painted was a celebration of the Creator, alive with joy.

All because of his Joy.

Tim was still sitting in the door to the nursery, crying, when someone knocked on the door again.

"Come in," he called, but his voice was so hoarse that he knew whoever it was hadn't heard him.

It didn't matter. They would soon discover that the door was open and they would come in anyway.

AFTER HEATHER AND Robert had left Tim's house a short time ago, they'd called for a family conference down at the Lodge, Mom and Dad's house.

"This has got to stop," Heather announced when everyone had gathered. "He's still got the doors bolted from the inside. Who knows what he's doing in there?"

"He did talk to us this time, Heather," Robert tried to calm his sister.

"Yelling at us to go away isn't talking!" Heather crossed her arms and glared at her little brother.

"But it's a step in the right direction," Joshua had to agree with Robert. "All anyone else has heard was incoherent mumbling."

"It's not a step," Heather protested. "It's barely a nudge."

"I think it's about time he got some real nudges," Luke growled.

"It is getting extreme, shutting everyone out for all this time," Beth agreed.

"He hasn't left the house in five days," Jenni worried. "What's he eating? I know there's not enough food for him. We didn't restock it because we didn't expect him to be back so soon."

"Tim has to get his head on straight," Gloria said firmly. "He has a daughter he needs to take care of."

"Who are we to judge Tim's grief?" Greg suddenly spoke up, though he addressed no one in particular.

Everyone stared at him in shocked silence.

"Are you saying we should just let him go?" Joshua finally asked with a deep frown.

"No." Greg said firmly. "That is not what I said. I asked, who are we to judge Tim's grief?"

"Greg's right," Nalani sighed. "We're sounding very judgmental right now. We aren't going to help Tim at all if we go in there angry at him for how he's handling his grief."

"Handling it?" Heather snarled. "He's not hand–"

"Heather!" Steve snapped. She glared at him. He glared back. "How would you handle the first week after *I* died?"

Heather turned pale and tears pooled in her eyes.

Everyone but Robert stared at their spouse. Shock, fear and compassion flooded every face.

Robert was suddenly acutely aware of something that had been gnawing at the back of his mind for quite some time. He was an outsider in his own family.

"So, how do we help Tim carry his grief?" Luke asked carefully. "He's not letting us help him, and that's what family is for."

"We don't go kicking the door down," his wife said sarcastically.

Luke hung his head as his skin turned darker. Nalani knew him well.

"But we can't continue to let him shut us out either," Joshua said firmly. He sadly smiled at Gloria. "Your mother's right. Tim does have a daughter who needs him."

"While we can't kick the door in," Rachel smiled ruefully at Nalani, "we do need to get in and talk to him."

"If it comes down to it, I can pick the lock, even on his deadbolt." Everyone stared at Dave in surprise. He shrugged. "Ted and I had some very interesting adventures."

"Dad's bolt cutters will work on the chain locks," Brian added.

"Okay, but who will go?" Beth asked. "We shouldn't all descend on him."

"I'll go," Greg shrugged. "He can't get any madder at me. No one else needs to run the risk of driving him further away. He needs family whom he loves right now."

A deeper sorrow descended over the group. Greg had spoken very matter-of-factly, but everyone knew he felt the pain of Tim's rejection very deeply.

"I'm going too, for all the reasons Greg just said," Brandon suddenly joined the conversation. "And I'm taking Gabriella with us."

Chapter 36

"**T**im?" a voice called from the apparently open front door.

Tim was surprised to feel a surge of joy at his brother's voice. He'd missed Greg, much more than he'd realized.

"Upstairs," Tim called, hoping his voice carried to his brother.

It must have, because he heard footsteps coming up the stairs and down the hall.

"I guess you're ready for visitors," Greg said cautiously as he dropped to the floor in the hall. He leaned against the wall on the other side of the doorway, facing the other wall instead of looking at Tim.

"Visitors no, but family's okay now," Tim said sadly.

"That's good because your family's beyond worried about you," Greg still seemed wary. "That's why they sent me."

"I'm sorry, Greg," Tim propped his elbow on his knee and covered his face with his hand.

"There's no need to be," Greg said gently. "You were dealing with an impossible situation in the only way you knew how."

"I'm talking about the way I treated you after … after Joy died."

"So am I," Greg sighed sadly. "I was hurt, but your hurt was considerably greater."

"So did you come to drag me back into life?" Tim asked after a long pause.

"I came to see if you were ready to be reminded that God is still worthy of your praise," Greg replied.

"I don't know, Greg," Tim sighed.

"Fair enough," Greg nodded.

"Fair enough? That's all?" Tim arched his eyebrows.

"No, that's not *all*," Greg smiled wryly. "But it's enough to start with. It wasn't a flat 'no.'"

"Where do I go from here?" Tim asked miserably. "I don't like where I'm at, but I can't see my way to a better place."

"I guess a good place to start would be to remember your wedding day."

"Why?" Tim was puzzled.

"As I understood it, you and Brandon didn't exchange notes about what you were going to say."

"No, we didn't."

"But you both said something that was critical to your situation now. Do you remember it?"

Tim thought carefully but came up with a blank. He shrugged.

"Brandon said that you and Joylynne wouldn't make it through the hard times that would come to you if you were living for each other. You have to live for God, because he's the only one who will always be with you."

Tim nodded. He remembered now. "And I'd already written my vows that included, 'I know that I cannot live for you, Joy. Our life will be confusing and chaotic unless I live for God, and love you out of the strength he gives me.'"

Tim sighed and stared out the window that faced the slowly sinking sun.

"I truly believed that when I said it, Greg, but I'm wrestling with it now."

"Keep on wrestling, and I know you'll eventually prevail," Greg assured him with a slight smile, then asked seriously. "For now, would you like something a little easier to handle?"

"I'd love something easier to handle," Tim snorted bitterly.

"I said easier, not easy," Greg warned him.

"I don't think anything's going to be easy for me for a long time," Tim said sourly.

"Okay then," Greg turned to face him squarely. He frowned sternly. "You have a child. You don't have the right to wallow in grief. Deal with it, yes, but you better start putting your child first."

Tears filled Tim's eyes. "Thank you, Greg. I guess I subconsciously already accepted that."

He motioned toward the room.

Greg peeked around the corner and grinned. "I guess you did! That's why you're up here."

Suddenly Tim heard a soft noise on the steps. He frowned.

"You didn't come alone?"

"No, Brandon came too," Greg replied as the man in question emerged from the stairwell. "And he's got something for you."

Brandon knelt beside Tim and placed a blanket-wrapped bundle in his arms.

For the first time, Tim saw his daughter's face.

He wept, but this time his tears were more about his love for his daughter than about the loss of his wife.

She was beautiful with dusky skin, dark red hair and a dimple on her left cheek. She was sleeping soundly, so Tim couldn't see her eyes, but at her age they would be dark blue. Tim hoped they ended up green, just like Mommy's eyes.

"Hi, Gabriella," Tim said softly. "I'm glad to finally meet you. I'm sorry that I got a little lost for a while, but I'm here now."

Without waking the baby jerked an arm free of the blanket and waved it happily, mewling softly and turning her head toward her daddy. Then she sighed and settled into a deeper sleep.

"She knows my voice!" Tim whispered in awe.

"Of course she does," Brandon said proudly. "You talked to her before she was born. Why wouldn't she know your voice?"

Tim gently stroked the tiny hand resting on the blanket.

Suddenly fear reached out and grabbed him.

"What am I going to do?" he raised anguished eyes to his brothers. "I can't do this!"

They both knew that Tim wasn't talking about the basic mechanics of baby care. He'd been changing diapers and feeding babies when he was still a child himself. But he'd never had a baby that was *his*. When the lights went out, the babies were always safe and sound with Mommy and Daddy.

"You aren't alone, Tim," Greg softly assured him. "You'll have as much help as you want."

"More than you want if you don't send the women home when you want them gone," Brandon said wryly.

"You'll only be alone when you want to be alone." Greg shook his head at Brandon, then whispered, "Don't scare the poor man like that."

"This poor man is already scared," Tim shook his head and smiled sadly at Greg. "Were you scared when your babies were born?"

"Terrified!" Greg quickly acknowledged.

Brandon and Tim both groaned.

"But it does get better," Greg comforted his brothers. "You get a little more confident after every crisis that you survive. It also helps to realize that you can't save your baby from anything, only God can. Sure he expects you to do your best, to love the babies with all your heart, but the results of everything you do are always in his hands."

"That doesn't comfort me a whole lot right now," Tim said sadly. "I don't like what God's hands did with my 'best' last month."

"What do you mean?" Brandon thought he knew what Tim was talking about, but Tim needed to say it.

"I thought it was no big deal if Robert and I went running that morning, but I wasn't home to take Joy to the doctor. I didn't even make it there late. If I'd been with Joy, she wouldn't have died."

"You don't know that, Tim. You don't know what would've happened," Brandon said gently. "You still may have been in that intersection at that same moment, and you might have been killed instead of Joy."

"That would've been better!" Tim asserted.

"Really?" Greg said in surprise. "You would wish this on Joy so you didn't have to go through it?"

"No!" Tim said in shock.

That wasn't what he'd meant.

But it was the logical result of what he'd been thinking.

"Do you love Gabriella?" Greg asked softly.

"Of course!" Tim hugged his daughter tighter. She whimpered slightly and Tim eased his hold a little.

"You hold onto that love and it'll bring you back to your faith," Greg assured him.

"How do you know?" Tim frowned doubtfully.

"'The greatest of these is love,'" Brandon said with a soft smile.

"Three things remain, the apostle Paul said, faith, hope, and love," Greg nodded as he explained. "Your faith is in tatters right now, Tim. Your hope is nearly dead – you have no confidence that God is faithful to his promises. But you have love for your family, especially your daughter. God is love. You cling to your love, and it'll lead you back to faith and hope."

"When you're ready to look, you will see that God was glorified in this terrible event," Brandon promised him.

"I don't see how," Tim felt tears welling in his chest again. It frustrated him. He didn't want to cry. He was tired of crying.

"Do you still believe that Jesus is your savior and that he earnestly desires that all should come to saving knowledge?" Greg asked earnestly.

"It's about the only thing I do believe without a shred of doubt," Tim confessed sadly.

"It's enough for now," Brandon assured him.

"If Joy hadn't been in that intersection, the guy behind her would've been," Greg declared. "I met him at the scene. Trust me, Joy's in a much better place than he would've gone to."

"And I suppose you witnessed to him," Tim said wryly. He hated that Joy had to die, resented that someone else would benefit from it, but he was also realistic enough to know that someday he would be comforted by that.

"I planted some seeds," Greg nodded with a small grin.

"Luke brought in the harvest after the funeral," Brandon said. Both of his brothers stared at him in surprise. "I was with Luke when a guy walked up to him and introduced himself. His name's Gino. He came because he saw the obituary in the paper. Between what happened out at the scene and the funeral message, he was ready to know more."

"What happened at the scene?" Tim asked Greg, who merely shrugged.

"I planted seeds."

Brandon snorted in disbelief. "According to Gino, the part that really got to him was when you talked to the kid in the Escalade."

"The Escalade?" Tim suddenly realized that he didn't actually know what had happened. He knew people had talked about it around him, but he hadn't paid any attention. Joy was hit in an intersection. That was all he knew. "What happened? How did Joy get hit?"

"The kid is Travis Schroeder," Greg said sadly. "He's nineteen, a soldier who'd just gotten back from training. He was on his way to see his girlfriend. He borrowed his dad's Escalade because he wanted something nice to pick her up in. He was going to take her to lunch to propose to her. He was texting, and didn't see the light turn red."

Tim stared at his brother in shock, his mind in turmoil.

He'd lost the wife he'd loved more than his own life, but he still had his daughter, his life. Travis Schroeder had lost everything. He'd killed someone. And he'd done it in a way that hurt his father and his girlfriend. Would they still love him and support him, like Tim's family would love and support him?

"What's going to happen to him?" Tim finally asked.

"After Gabriella was born last week, he pled guilty to one charge of vehicular manslaughter," Brandon said. "They were waiting to bring formal charges until after they knew if the baby would make it. If she hadn't, there would've been two charges."

"What does that mean? What'll they do to him?"

"We don't know for sure," Greg shrugged sadly. "His sentencing is tomorrow."

"He'll spend time in prison." Brandon carefully kept his tone neutral. He hated the idea of the poor man being made to suffer more, but he didn't know what Tim felt. No way was he going to add to his brother's pain at this time.

"Prison? Why? Isn't living with knowing what he did prison enough?" Tim frowned.

"Are you sure?" Greg asked calmly, though his heart leapt.

Tim hadn't lost his faith. In fact, it was much healthier than he knew.

"You met him," Tim challenged his brother. "Is he a bad man?"

"No worse than anyone in our family."

"He's a believer?" Tim easily understood Greg's deeper meaning.

Greg nodded.

"If I advocate for him, will that make a difference?" Tim asked urgently.

"We should ask Luke, but I'd bet that it will," Greg grinned.

"Call him," Tim ordered Brandon then turned back to Greg. "What time is his sentencing? Do we need to go to St. Louis tonight?"

"Nah," Greg happily shook his head. "The sentencing is at ten, so if we leave here by eight, we should get there in plenty time."

"Let's make it seven-thirty," Tim sighed and stared sadly at his infant daughter. "Just in case something goes wrong."

From Brandon's end of the conversation, it sounded like Luke thought Travis Schroeder would have an excellent chance if Tim advocated for him.

"Thanks, Luke," Brandon said into the phone.

"Hey, before he hangs up," Tim said.

"Wait a sec," Brandon told Luke, then gave his attention to Tim.

"Ask him if he's got some food. There's nothing here to fix." Brandon grinned. Tim quickly added. "But just him and Nalani tonight. I'm not ready for a total invasion yet. Maybe tomorrow, after we get back from St. Louis."

Brandon passed on Tim's request.

Of course Luke said they would bring supper over.

"Is the diaper bag downstairs?" Tim asked his brothers while he was gazing at his daughter. "I think you need to be changed, don't you, Gabriella?"

As he said his daughter's name, sorrow welled in Tim again. He'd been so sure that Joy would say that name to their daughter before he did.

"You want me to go get it?" Brandon asked as he started to rise.

"Let's go downstairs," Tim lifted his daughter. "One of you guys better carry her down. I'm not sure I safely can yet."

Brandon took Gabriella then Greg rose and offered Tim a hand getting up.

"Too weak or too sad?" Greg asked as Tim pulled himself up.

"Both," Tim sighed. "Sometimes it hits me like a fist and I can't get my breath."

When they got downstairs, Brandon was already spreading out a blanket to lay Gabriella on.

"I'll do that," Tim quickly moved in and sat beside the blanket, reaching up for his daughter then laying her tenderly on the blanket.

Brandon handed him wipes and a fresh diaper.

When Tim pulled down Gabriella's dirty diaper, he was surprised to see the umbilical cord.

It brought a memory that made him cry.

He and Joy had started birthing classes after moving to Missouri. Part of the instructions had included care of a newborn. When they'd talked about the umbilical cord drying up and falling off, Joy had wrinkled her nose.

"That sounds disgusting!"

"You've never seen an umbilical cord?" Tim had asked in surprise.

"On whose baby?" Joy had asked tartly.

"I guess you have a point," Tim was surprised to think that he knew more about babies than his wife did.

"Dried up umbilical cords falling off and nasty tarry stuff," Joy made a gagging noise. "I think I'll let you change all the diapers for the first two weeks."

"I won't have any trouble getting my family to help!" Tim had assured her.

As it turned out they'd both been right, but even more than they'd suspected. Joy never changed even one of her daughter's diapers, and Tim's family had changed a whole week's worth before he'd even touched her.

"Tim?" Brandon said gently.

Tim shook his head and wiped his tears with his sleeve.

"I'm good. I'll do it," he focused on his daughter again. Soon she was in a fresh diaper and snuggled in his arms again.

"Is that better, Gabriella?"

Of course his daughter didn't answer, but his brother did have a comment.

"Gabriella's quite a mouthful. You aren't going to call her that all the time, are you?" Greg frowned.

Tim smiled down at his infant daughter. "Don't worry about Uncle Greg. Your mommy already took care of this."

He looked up and stared sternly at Greg. "Gabri. That's the only nickname she needs. Joylynne anticipated you, Greg. No Gabby, no Angel, no other silliness that you might dream up. She's Gabriella or Gabri."

"Okay," Greg said meekly.

"You make sure everyone knows," Tim fixed his glare on Brandon. "No matter what the goofus tries to saddle her with, she's Gabri."

"Gotcha," Brandon grinned broadly.

Suddenly the front door popped open and Nalani breezed in, followed by Luke who was carrying a box.

"That was fast!" Tim exclaimed.

"I had supper already cooking in the Crock-Pot," Nalani shrugged.

Tim sniffed. "Is that perchance chili?"

"How'd you guess?"

"How'd you know you'd be feeding me tonight?" he asked with a little laugh.

"I guess I'm psychotic like that," she said brightly.

"She's been hanging around Tink too long," Luke groaned.

"Oh no!" Nalani waved a hand dismissively. "I was psychotic the day I said that I'd marry you. Rachel just made me understand it was safe to admit it."

Tim's laugh was a little heartier. It felt strange, but right.

"She didn't start the rice yet," Luke walked toward the kitchen. "Do you have any?"

"Of course!" Tim snorted. "In the pantry. The rice cooker's on the counter."

"Hapa rice?" Luke cried in disgust a few moments later.

"What can I say?" Tim said wryly. "My wife was a health nut. Be glad it's not just brown."

Luke had no trouble getting the rice started. Since Nalani already had the grated cheese and chopped onion, they didn't have anything to do to prepare dinner until the rice was done. While they waited, they planned what they would do the next day.

Tim wanted Mom, Dad, Brian, Luke, Greg and Robert to go with him to the courthouse. He decided that it would help mend fences if Heather, Jenni,

Rachel and Dei took him shopping afterward. He and Joy hadn't stocked the nursery yet. They'd still had plenty of time for that, and Joy had known that her sisters-in-law would probably throw her a baby shower.

"Sounds like a plan," Brandon approved, with a caveat, "but Nita would probably like to do both, if you don't mind."

"She's still here?" Tim exclaimed.

"Al took the boys home on Sunday so they could get back to school," Nalani said. "But Nita decided to stay and help with the baby a while longer. She's down at the Lodge."

"Of course I don't mind if she goes with us tomorrow," Tim sighed guiltily. "In fact, she can come up tonight if she wants, Mom and Dad too."

They were there in ten minutes. Tim cried when they walked in.

There were a lot of tears that evening, but there were smiles too, and even some laughter.

Tim refused to give up Gabri for anyone, not even her grandmas. He decided that since it was his house, he was going to eat in the living room, sitting on the floor with his bowl on the coffee table.

He let Nita and Gloria stay with him that night, but since he'd had Greg bring Gabri's cradle downstairs, every time the baby cried, he got to her before the grandmas made it downstairs.

They were happy to help him fix bottles, hand him wipes and fresh diapers and dispose of the dirty ones. They were so glad to see him getting back into life and loving his daughter that they couldn't resent him hogging their grandbaby.

Chapter 37

A surprise was waiting for Tim when he arrived at the courthouse.

"When Dani told me what you were doing, I hopped the first plane," Al greeted him with a hug and an explanation.

"And I told him he couldn't keep me from going too," Taggart grinned and offered his own hug.

"You guys know I'm going to stand up for Schroeder, don't you?" Tim thought he knew the answer, but he didn't want there to be any doubts.

"Of course!" Both men declared.

"And we're beside you a hundred percent," Al added.

"Are we all set?" Tim looked at Luke.

"There's nothing to be 'set'," Luke shrugged. "As the spouse of the victim, you're automatically listed as a potential witness. Al, Nita and Taggart will be too."

"Then let's do this."

Their small contingent was already in place in the courtroom when Travis Schroeder came in. He didn't look around so he didn't see them, but even if he had, he probably wouldn't have known who they were.

Things proceeded quickly. The charges and the plea were read, then the judge asked about witnesses.

"Yes, your honor."

Tim was surprised that he recognized the prosecutor who turned toward him. He was Greg's friend Alan Zimmer.

"Mr. Timothy Shepherd, the victim's husband is here. I believe he would like to speak."

Tim rose with his daughter in his arms. He thought about handing her to Nita, but decided to keep her. She was a very important part of this.

Witnesses in the sentencing phase are given a lot more leeway in their testimony than in a trial. Tim was free to explain what he thought Schroeder's sentence should be, and why.

"I want you to know something up-front, sir," Tim addressed the judge. "What Travis Schroeder did was very bad. I know because it was my wife that he killed when he ran that red light. My daughter will grow up without knowing her mother. And my wife was a very special woman. She was full of light and life and laughter. In one careless moment, that man cut off Joylynne's life.

"But it was one careless moment. Schroeder wasn't driving drunk which would be a different story. He hasn't lived a life of wanton violence. He doesn't commit random acts of violence. In fact, he's a soldier, someone who chose to serve his country. That's got to count for something. Sure, he ended my wife's life, but why should the one decision that he made that caused the accident be the defining moment of his life?"

"Let me get this straight," the judge frowned slightly, but it was mainly for effect. He knew something about the Shepherds and their ministry. This wasn't the first time one of them had showed up in his courtroom. "You're asking for leniency for the man who killed your wife?"

"Yes sir, I am," Tim said firmly. "Why should he be punished severely for something that a few thousand people in the St. Louis area are probably doing right now?"

"Maybe so he can serve as an example to those few thousand people," the judge said wryly.

"That's a bogus argument," Tim snorted, then grimaced apologetically. "Sorry, sir. I know that's the theory behind some of our laws about how we administer what we call justice, but I don't get it. How many of the citizens of St. Louis will ever hear about Travis Schroeder and Joylynne Shepherd? And of those who do, how many will make a connection between their own behavior and that of Schroeder? The way I see it is that we don't obey laws because of the punishment we might get, except maybe speeding because that's the most likely law we're going to get caught breaking. No, we choose to obey laws for one of two reasons. We either respect the law too much to break it, or we think we have a high probability of getting caught ourselves. The fact that someone else got caught and punished never enters the average American's mind when they're 'considering' whether or not to break the law."

"So, would you have us discard punishment entirely and just give leniency to everyone?" the judge asked.

"No, sir. Not at all!" Tim denied rather incredulously. Why would the man even ask such a thing? "I'm not testifying about all lawbreakers, just this one. I only said that to address your suggestion that this one man serve as an example. His value as an example isn't enough to outweigh the harm you will do if you punish him to make him that example."

"Excuse me?" the judge was highly intrigued.

"Sure, Joy is gone, but what good will it do her family if Travis Schroeder goes to jail? Absolutely none. Joy will still be dead whether he serves five minutes, five months or fifty years. But won't it do tremendous harm to

Schroeder's family if he goes to jail? How will he 'pay his debt to society' if he's behind prison bars? It'd be one thing if he was a cold-blooded killer, or even if he'd run that red light with deliberate disregard for the law, but he didn't. He just happened to glance down at his phone at the wrong moment. It only took a few seconds of distraction to take one life. Those seconds shouldn't also take his life."

"So what would you have me do?"

"Best case scenario would be to let him go back to his life."

"No punishment at all?" the judge asked in amazement.

"No punishment? Not hardly!" Tim shook his head sadly. "He will never be able to forget what he did. For a good man, that's a lifetime of punishment. I hope he eventually learns to let go of his guilt and accept God's forgiveness. I know he already has mine." Tim looked right at Schroeder. "I hope you know God as well as my brother thinks you do. I hope you give your guilt to God and learn to live free from it. I hope you choose to live a life that glorifies God. That's what I'm choosing to do. That's why I have to forgive you. I hope the state forgives you too."

Schroeder bowed his head and wept.

"You want leniency for Travis Schroeder, but does your wife's family feel the same?" the judge asked.

"Yes, sir!" Al jumped to his feet. "I'm Joylynne Shepherd's father, Alfred Quintanilla. My wife Danita and our oldest son Taggart are with me. We all agree with Tim wholeheartedly."

The judged looked at Nita and Taggart, sitting beside Al. They both nodded emphatically.

"Absolutely," Nita said firmly.

"Yes, sir," Taggart said.

"Do you have anything else to add, Mr. Shepherd?" the judge looked back at Tim.

"Just one thing," Tim smiled sadly at his infant daughter, sleeping peacefully in her daddy's arms. "Joylynne's life was ended, but nothing has been ruined. Joy's in heaven with her savior. My life, Gabriella's life, they're still books yet to be written. Sure they'll be written without the wife and mother that we should have had, but our lives aren't ruined, just different. If our lives get ruined, it's because we choose to let them be, not because of what Schroeder did."

As Tim went back to his seat, the judge stared thoughtfully at the guilty man.

"Mr. Schroeder, I hope you understand the magnitude of what just happened this morning. I very rarely get pleas for leniency from a victim's family. I agree with Mr. Shepherd that there will be no benefit to you, your family, your victim's family or society if you go to prison. However, the law must be served. Therefore, I am sentencing you to ten years in prison," he ignored the gasps of horrified shock and smoothly continued. "I am suspending that sentence. What that means is that if in the next ten years you run afoul of the law in any way, you will immediately find yourself behind bars for this crime. I wish I could make the Army keep you because service to your country is the ultimate community service, but that's outside of my power. However, I can give you five hundred hours of community service, which will be waived if the Army does not discharge you. I am also ordering you to seek counseling."

The judge dropped his gavel then rose to leave.

Schroeder stared in shock at the suddenly empty bench.

Tim turned to Greg. "Please talk to him before you leave. I wish I could, but it's still a little too hard."

"I can understand that," Greg nodded solemnly.

"This doesn't mean I don't forgive him," Tim declared earnestly. "I'm just too early in the process."

As Robert trailed his brother from the courtroom, he was deeply troubled by what had happened. How had Tim forgiven like that, and barely a week after his beloved wife had been buried?

Robert wasn't even close to forgiving the people who had attacked him well over a month ago. He knew he should forgive them, but he didn't care.

AFTER LUNCH BACK at Halelolo, all the women dragged Tim off to go shopping. He hated to be separated from Gabriella for however long they would torture him with an endless parade of stores, but his daughter was a week old. She'd already been to the courthouse that morning, which was more outing than she should have at her age. Tim left her in care of her grandpas and uncles.

The afternoon was a jumble of laughter and tears. Shopping for his daughter was much more enjoyable than Tim had expected, especially with these women. But every now and then, the fact that there should have been one particular woman at his side hit Tim.

When Jenni held up a tiny green dress, Tim cried because he'd almost turned to Joy to tell her it matched her eyes. Heather wondered how many boxes of diapers they should get in the size Gabri was in now, and Tim wanted to congratulate Joy on her plan to keep Greg from nicknaming her daughter.

Any time Tim needed to cry, the women let him, offering him a shoulder to cry on if he wanted one. His tears quickly turned to laughter in Baby Gap when Rachel grabbed his hand and pulled him toward the entrance.

"Let's go find somewhere for you to sit," she sighed dramatically. "That'll be better than kneeling so you can get your head on my shoulder."

Tim stopped, laughed and pulled Rachel back toward him. He lifted her well off the floor when he wrapped her in a big bear hug and kissed her soundly on the cheek.

"I love you, Sis," he whispered.

"I love you, too," Rachel had tears in her eyes. "I'm so sorry."

"Thank you," Tim kissed her again, then he easily shifted her onto his back and turned back to the other women.

"Put me down, you brute," Rachel pounded on his arm with her tiny fists.

"Not yet," Nalani grinned wickedly. "It's so easy to tickle a child when they're captive like that!"

"I'm not a child!" Rachel protested.

Beth and Dei just closed in with broad grins.

"No!" Rachel squealed and squirmed but remained firmly anchored to Tim's back.

Tim's grin broadened when he notice half a dozen people staring their way. They were a rowdy bunch, his family. They lived life joyfully, and that got attention. It was also the lifeline he would cling to in the coming weeks and months. They would let him cry, encourage him to laugh and lead him deeper into love – eventually his faith and hope would be stronger than it had been before.

WHEN THEY WERE done shopping, some of the cars went directly down to Gumbwats' Haven, but a few went back to Halelolo first to pick up the family members there. Of course Tim went to get his daughter.

Once he got home, Tim stayed in with Gabri, but before bedtime, every single family member had come over to see them. Of course the women helped get all the day's purchases put away. They even did laundry for Tim, not just Gabri's new clothes, but also the hamper of dirty clothes that Tim still didn't want to face.

That evening, Tim asked Robert if he wanted to move back to the room he'd been in for almost two weeks before Joy's accident. That didn't keep two of the women from staying too, Jenni and Cait. They were superfluous since Tim got to Gabri first every time she cried.

That Saturday was their monthly Childless Saturday, when all the siblings and their spouses got together. The children were with big brothers and sisters or Grandma and Grandpa, Uncle Dillon, the Guerreros or Aunties Rose and Faith. No one objected when Tim showed up with Gabriella, but Katie did object when Tim wouldn't let her change the baby's diaper.

"It took us the better part of two years to convince you to join us as a family, and you still only do it sporadically," Luke backed Tim. "You're not going to act like a nanny now!"

"In fact, we're about to fire you as nanny," Greg frowned fiercely at the young woman they all loved as a sister.

"Except it better be someone other than Greg," Dave sighed. "He doesn't know how to fire someone and make it stick!"

Greg "fired" his secretary, Ann Lindeman, whenever she called him "Mr. Shepherd," but she never left, and Greg always eventually apologized, with a can of macadamia nuts. Every time anyone went to Hawaii, they brought back at least a dozen cans for Greg's stash.

"We *should* fire you, Katie!" Nalani said in amazement. "Why didn't I think of that before?"

"Of course," Beth groaned. "Why would you think you're family if we're paying you?"

"You're going to fire me?" Katie asked incredulously.

"There's no 'going to' about it. You are fired, effective immediately," Luke said clearly and distinctly.

"That's the way firing usually works," Heather snickered at Greg.

"You are no longer our nanny/tutor," Brandon said firmly.

"But that doesn't mean we won't get you a job," Dave told Katie, then turned to Steve, the administrator for their family ministry. "Do we have one for her in The Ohana Project, like most of us have?"

"We've been talking about starting an after-school program," Steve nodded.

"We originally hired her because she has a degree in elementary education," Pete said a little crossly. "Maybe she wants to work at the elementary school. Rebecca Bray might not be back after her baby comes this summer."

Pete was the only one in the family who was employed outside of The Ohana Project. When he'd retired from professional football, he'd gotten his dream job as a third grade teacher at the school where all the elementary-aged children who lived at Gumbwats' Haven attended.

"Excuse me, people," Katie said loudly. "I'm in the room. You can talk to me."

"She's so your sister," Beth laughed and leaned on Greg's arm.

"I am not like the oaf," Katie deadpanned.

Everyone roared with laughter. Katie had done a perfect imitation of Joshua.

"If Brian had to join the family because of his deadpan, Katie does too!" Cait finally gasped.

"Definitely!" Brian nodded emphatically.

"I don't know what you're talking about," Katie turned cool eyes on Cait and lifted her chin.

The laughter was redoubled.

"Make her stop," Dei begged Dave.

Katie looked around the room, shaking her head then she looked up at the ceiling, and whined, "Why you do this kine stuff to me, God?"

Greg laughed so hard he slid off his chair. Luke cradled his arms on the table and buried his head in them. Rachel clung to Abe, gasping for air. Except for Katie, Tim and Robert, everyone was pretty much incapacitated with laughter.

"I thought you agreed to pray for a *little* sister," Robert sadly mourned to Tim.

"Well, she is smaller than either of us," Tim sighed sadly too. "I guess God misunderstood. We should've been specific about a *younger* sister."

"I don't recall saying I want to be your sister," Katie elevated her nose slightly. "Maybe I don't. You all are crazy."

Which set everyone off again.

Katie had quickly grown to love this family that she'd first started working for almost five years before. They loved her and encouraged her in her Christian walk, but she'd been holding back. She hadn't understood why. Nalani's revelation had come as a shock to Katie. She had hit the nail on the head. Katie was an employee, a beloved employee, but nevertheless an employee. She had long known she would always belong to this crazy bunch, but she'd never seen herself as one of them. Suddenly she knew that one day she would be.

Tim was thrilled to see Katie's moment of understanding dawn on her, overjoyed to see her boldly step into the place that he didn't doubt she would officially accept one day.

His fresh, raw grief intruded. Joy had firmly and undeniably claimed her place in a similar way last summer when she'd started that feminine clash. She hadn't known Katie well, but she had liked her. This moment would have tickled her funny bone as much as it did the rest of the family. It made Tim ache for what he'd lost.

Robert worked hard to bury anger as he watched Katie step into her place in the family. It wasn't that he didn't love Katie. He did. He loved her as a sister. He'd even been one of the first ones to recognize that she belonged with them as more than just the tutor who needed them to find her a family. Since she was only five years older than him, Katie was closer in age to him and Tim than any of their other siblings. When he'd first met her, he'd realized that she filled in the gap that he sometimes felt so strongly. He'd wanted her to be his sister. He was happy to see the evidence that one day she would be a formal member of the family.

But why now? Why in this time of grief and sorrow? He hadn't had the time to properly process his own loss before Tim had abruptly lost his wife. This kind of laughter didn't fit with his grief. It seemed indecent, a callous disregard of the agony that was his constant companion. The fact that he couldn't wholeheartedly join in the merriment of his family increased his pain and fed the anger that laid beneath it.

Chapter 38

Rachel and Heather went home with Tim, Robert and Gabriella that night. They were supposed to be helping Tim take care of the baby.

Earlier that day, the guys had all helped Tim move his things to the upstairs bedroom that he and Joy had only slept in a short time before the doctor had restricted her from climbing stairs. Of course Gabriella had also moved upstairs to the nursery.

Somewhere around one o'clock when the baby woke up, Tim was once again the first one to get to her. He got a scolding from Heather.

"Timothy Shepherd, you need to let me help you with that baby! That's what I'm here for. How are you supposed to get any sleep if you get up every time she does?"

"Leeme 'lone, Boss," Tim grumbled just like Greg. "She's my daughter. I'll take care of her when I want."

"If you're not going to let us help you, then what are we doing here?" Heather persisted.

"You're here for the same reason that I take care of her whenever I can," Tim confessed sadly. "Sometimes the grief is crushing, Heather, and I can hardly breathe, much less take care of Gabri. I've had a couple good days, but the grief isn't gone. I don't want to be alone with her if it comes back with a vengeance."

"Oh," Heather sighed. "I guess I'll go down and make a bottle."

"Thanks, Sis," Tim kissed her on the forehead. "I'll wait for you to get back."

As Heather made the bottle for her infant motherless niece, she wept. She didn't want to try to imagine the pain Tim must feel, but she couldn't block those thoughts. If she lost Steve …. Tim's pain had to be intense.

Before she went back upstairs, Heather wiped the tears from her cheeks. Right now Tim was happy so she would be happy with him. When she got upstairs, Rachel was sitting on the floor beside the rocking chair, chatting quietly but cheerfully to her brother.

Robert heard Heather and Tim's conversation but stayed in his room. It hadn't been a good night so far. He'd been in the grip of another nightmare when Gabriella's cries had awakened him. He'd been on the beach again, and he'd tried to call Tim, but he'd gotten Joy instead, and he'd heard her die. When he'd awakened, he would have gladly taken care of his baby niece but he was too weak to rise from his bed. He understood why Tim was afraid to be alone with Gabriella right now.

He didn't understand how Tim had managed to have two good days, especially as emotionally trying as Friday morning had been. Why did Tim have the strength to face his grief head-on, but his brother was drowning?

It was a long time before Robert fell asleep again, but his brother and sisters were sound asleep fifteen minutes after Gabriella was back in her cradle.

BRIAN, CAIT AND their children were returning home the next day, so everyone went to church in St. Louis then over to Halelolo for a family dinner before it was time for the Trasks to head to the airport. Since Brian had rented a car when they arrived, no one needed to drive them. The goodbyes were hard. Even though the circumstances that brought it about had been dreadful, it had been good to have the whole family together for those few weeks.

It was a fine spring day, so the party spilled out onto the lawn. Of course there were lots of rowdy games. About midafternoon, while Gabriella was up in the nursery napping, Tim and Robert were horsies for noodle jousting, a particularly exhausting endeavor. When Knights Chalk and Fleece were finally eliminated, their horses found two chairs over by the Guerreros. Tim dropped into the lawn chair next to Raul.

"You do know that's Dave's chair, don't you?" Raul raised his eyebrows.

"He doesn't scare me," Tim waved a careless hand, though he did look carefully around the yard and sighed in relief when he didn't see his big brother. He jumped right into his reason for sitting in Dave's chair. "Did you already apply to a master's program?"

"No," Raul said rather cautiously. "Andie and I decided I would take a year off before graduate school."

"Good! Then maybe my idea wasn't so hare-brained."

"What idea?" Raul was definitely wary, but Leiandra leaned forward eagerly.

"I'm going to be reporting to training camp next month, but I can't leave Gabriella," Tim explained. "I'm looking for a nanny and housekeeper for the next year or two. I don't think more than three because I'm not planning to renew my contract when it expires, not unless God makes it clear he wants me to. I don't want Gabriella growing up with an absentee dad."

"You want us to go with you to Tennessee?" Raul asked in surprise.

"Yeah, if you think you can part from Brandon and Cari for that long," Tim said hopefully.

"They've got to grow up some time," Leiandra said facetiously.

257

Tim grinned. Both Brandon and Cari were a few years older than Lei and Raul.

"Of course it's only during training and the season. I'll be back here in the offseason," Tim added details that would hopefully make the idea more attractive to them. "And when I'm on the road, you can bring Gabri back here, or even go to the games too. She'll be big enough by then to travel fairly well."

"We'll have to pray about it," Raul said wisely. Lei frowned, so he quickly added. "But we're both very much in favor of the idea."

"It's okay if you don't want to. I'll figure out something else," Tim shrugged. "Or maybe you can go with me but for the purpose of helping me find a nanny and/or housekeeper. Of course, since I travel so much, I really like the idea of a couple, but if it's God's will, I don't think we'll have a problem finding someone."

"We probably will do it," Raul sighed. "Cari said last night she's firing us."

"You too?" Tim laughed. "They fired Katie, probably for the same reason. What job are they giving you at TOP?"

"Raul is going to be a counselor," Lei said proudly.

"I gather there's some talk about opening an office in the Nashville area," Tim said thoughtfully. "You can help with that and help me take care of Gabri, then when we find your replacement, you can come back here. If I recall correctly, and I usually do, Lei's crazy for kids, and we've got a bunch in this family. If you're in St. Louis full time, you'll both have plenty of work that you love since we don't have a nanny/tutor anymore. Brandon and Cari, Dave and Dei, Madison and Carl are all just getting started still. Since Katie and Robert are both probably gonna get married someday soon, you'll have her keiki, and in the offseason Robert'll be here with his wife and babies."

WITH A HEAVY heart, Robert half listened to Tim, Raul and Lei plan their future. When Tim first presented his idea to the Guerreros, Robert had been deeply hurt. He'd planned to go to Tennessee with his brother. Sure they hadn't talked about it yet, but he'd thought Tim would want him. Realizing that Tim didn't want him there had hurt.

When Tim mentioned the offseason, Robert realized why it apparently hadn't crossed Tim's mind that his brother would be around to help him. Tim expected Robert to be drafted, to go to another professional football team. Even if he didn't graduate from college, he could still be drafted.

Robert didn't know if he wanted that. He hadn't thought about it since Joy's accident.

He had to think about it now because the draft was this week!

The monitor said a baby was crying upstairs, so Tim got up to go see who it was. Lei went with him. A few minutes later, Brandon called to Raul, probably to get him involved in some hijinks. He was almost as bad as Greg.

Suddenly Robert was alone. He sat in the lawn chair watching his rowdy family playing in the huge lawn.

It was business as usual this fine spring day. Someone on the outside looking in would think they didn't have a care in the world.

Tim walked out of the house, Gabriella cradled carefully in his arms.

Business as usual for his brother was now being a single father, without his beloved wife.

Robert's heart ached for Tim. One month ago he was happily looking forward to the birth of his first daughter, expecting to bring her home with his wife at his side. In the blink of an eye, a fool texting behind the wheel of a car destroyed that happy future.

Suddenly, Tim wrapped one arm around Heather and laughed heartily.

Robert was shocked. How could his brother laugh like that?

He'd seen the evidence that Tim was handling his grief very well, but this was too much. It had been almost two months since Robert had been attacked and the best he could manage was a smile and a weak chuckle. Tim's tragedy was a month younger, and here he was, laughing as if all was right in the world.

Robert rose quickly and walked toward the side yard which was empty for the moment. In his peripheral vision, he saw some concerned looks. He ignored them. Everyone knew he was struggling, trying to deal with this fresh round of tragedy that he'd been in the center of.

He paced in the side yard for a while, trying to form a coherent prayer, but his guilt kept rising up to block his efforts.

He wasn't just at the center of it. He was the cause of it.

If he hadn't been trying to flirt with a woman whom he had no business getting involved with, he wouldn't have agreed to do that stupid auction. If he hadn't done that auction, he wouldn't have been assaulted on the beach. If he hadn't been assaulted on the beach, he wouldn't have been in Missouri after spring break. If he hadn't been in Missouri last month, Tim would have gone with Joylynne to her doctor's appointment. If Tim had been with Joy, they wouldn't have been in that intersection at that moment to be hit by another hapless fool whose life Robert had ruined.

So many people affected by one stupid decision.

Robert saw Greg coming around the corner of the house.

He walked the other way, toward the tree line.

It only took a few minutes to come to the huge stone fence that surrounded the estate. Robert walked along the fence. He wasn't paying attention to where he was. When the pedestrian gate loomed beside him, he turned and went through it.

He trudged through the streets for quite some time. He wasn't sure how long he walked, but he began to realize that it was cooling, and the shadows were getting quite long.

He stopped and looked around. He'd never been in this part of town. He had no idea where he was.

He was lost.

He didn't really care. He started walking aimlessly again.

A few minutes later he turned a corner and noticed a bar about halfway down the block. Suddenly that seemed like the right destination.

He stepped through the door without hesitation and walked up to the bar as if he'd done it a hundred times before.

"What can I get ya?" the bartender leaned on the other side of the bar.

"I'll take a beer," Robert nodded toward the row of spigots under the big mirror.

"I'll need to see some ID," the bartender said with a rueful smile.

Robert snorted softly as he pulled his wallet out. It was a good thing he had it on him.

"What kinda beer you want?" the bartender asked after examining his ID.

Robert had no clue. But he'd been to see the world famous Budweiser Clydesdales, both here in St. Louis at Grant's Farm and out at Warm Springs Ranch in Booneville.

"Budweiser," he said confidently.

"Bottle or tap?" the man asked.

Robert stifled a sigh. Who knew it was so hard to just get a beer?

"Tap," he correctly assumed that meant from the spigots behind the bar.

He cautiously sipped the foamy glass the bartender set before him.

It wasn't too bad, but if he hadn't had many glasses of root beer over the years, the foam would have given him pause.

He sipped again. It was strong, and there was a slightly bitter taste to it, but it wasn't totally unpalatable. On the other hand, it wasn't 'woo-hoo, this is malicious' good either.

He sipped his beer for a few minutes, staring at the television. It was set to a sports channel, of course. Thankfully it wasn't football season. In this town, baseball was the hot topic now. The football draft was coming up, but there was a baseball game in progress so it was on.

It was probably a good thing that the sound was off. Though a baseball game was airing, with the football draft this week, the commentators might mention it during some downtime. He stood a fair chance of winning a hefty sum if he bet that his name was coming up in talks about the draft – would he put his name in even though he'd disappeared and apparently wasn't going to graduate?

He hadn't "disappeared." He'd only gone to his family's home in St. Louis.

Now that he thought about it, disappearing seemed an attractive option.

Suddenly a woman sat down at the bar next to Robert. There were plenty stools, but she chose the one right next to him.

He wondered if he was supposed to talk to her. Though he'd never been in a bar before, he'd seen plenty movies with bar scenes. Men and women usually went to bars by themselves to either get drunk or pick up someone. He was contemplating the former, but maybe the latter would be a better option.

He needed to say something to the woman, even if she also wasn't looking to pick up someone. Of course the only thing that would come to his mind was one of the worst lines he'd ever heard in a movie. He modified it slightly.

"The world's going to come to an end unless we don't have sex right now," he said casually taking a sip of his beer.

"Excuse me?"

He risked a glance out of the corner of his eye. She was shocked but intrigued.

"Didn't lie, did I?" He shrugged. "We're not having sex, and the world isn't coming to an end."

"Does that line usually work for you?" she asked with a laugh.

"Never used it before." Robert took another sip of his beer and tried not to grimace. No wonder people guzzled beer. It didn't take long for it to lose the little flavor it had.

"What usually works?" She turned fully toward him.

"Never used any line before," Robert said casually. "Never tried to pick up a woman before, but since I've never been to a bar before either, I figured what the heck. In for a penny, in for a pound."

"You can't be serious," the woman stared at him as if he'd grown two heads. "You've never drank or had sex?"

"Didn't say that," Robert said abruptly. This wasn't going the way he'd expected it to. But then again, he hadn't really had any expectations. "You extrapolated from what I said."

"So you have drank and had sex, but not with women?" She seemed both repelled and attracted by the seemingly obvious conclusion.

"You're extrapolating again," Robert growled and glared down at the bar. "I've never done either by choice before."

"Oh!" She gave a soft gasp of sympathy and laid her hand on his arm. "That's terrible."

"You're still extrapolating," Robert shook his head slightly, "but at least you're on the right track this time. It was terrible. The stuff nightmares are made of."

"And now you want the stuff dreams are made of?" the woman leaned slightly toward him.

"It doesn't seem like such a good idea anymore," Robert set his beer back on the bar.

"Oh, come on honey." She slid off the barstool and rubbed his back. "I'll take you where you wanna go."

"I want to go back to the time before it happened," Robert turned toward her, his eyes intense. "Do you know how to get there?"

She just stared at him.

"I didn't think so." Robert pulled a ten out of his pocket, slapped it on the bar, then left.

The woman stared after him, hurting for the big man. She watched for him many nights, determined that she would give him something to help him forget the past, but she never saw him again.

Robert walked out into the night. It had gotten cold again. He kind of liked it. There weren't going to be many more cold nights before summer smothered the land with sweltering heat. He decided to walk and try to enjoy the beauty of the night. Whenever he was done walking, he could hail a taxi that would easily take him home. He'd made a point of remembering the physical address after the cops had taken him and Tim home a couple weeks ago.

He walked with his head bowed, his hands in his pockets.

God was majorly unfair. His family had served the Lord for many years, long before Robert was even born, but God kept punishing them. He took Kalea from her children, then he took Joylynne from the daughter who had been taken from her dead womb. He took Dad through cancer, but only after he took Heather's health over in the desert. Then he took Greg's memories and even after five years, there were many he still hadn't given back to Greg. But he wouldn't take the memory of one horrid night from Robert, a night that did to him what Rachel had interrupted when her frantic hand found a broken beer bottle.

Suddenly the thought of going home, back to Halelolo, back to his family, was overwhelmingly oppressive. He couldn't face their irrepressible faith, their confidence that somehow God would work out even this, even Joylynne's death. They believed it would work for his glory and their good.

It wouldn't happen. There would always be this aching emptiness whenever he saw Tim without his beloved wife, an overwhelming sorrow that Gabriella would never know the mother who loved her so much.

Robert would always carry around the memory of his own pain and shame.

He looked up and saw the bus station. He wondered if there was a bus heading out of town tonight. He had plenty money. Eventually Dad would cut off his credit card, but there was more than enough money in his checking and savings accounts to see him through many nights on the road. He would find a job somewhere before the money ran out.

He walked inside and discovered that in fifteen minutes a bus was leaving for Kansas City. He bought a ticket and found a seat toward the back. He was asleep before they hit the city limits of St. Louis.

In Kansas City, he hopped a train bound for Arizona.

Midmorning his phone rang. He contemplated not answering it, but that would be cruel beyond measure, disappearing without any word at all.

It was Dad.

"Robert, where are you? Did you come home last night?"

"No, I didn't. I'm on a train."

"A train," that shocked the old man. "Where are you going?"

"Nowhere," Robert sighed sadly. "I'll call you when I get there."

He disconnected the call, smiling bitterly.

That wasn't cruel beyond measure, but it almost filled the cup.

Dear Reader,

This was a hard story to write. Many times I tried to change the way things happened, but it didn't work. This was the story I believe God wanted me to tell.

Bad things happen to Christians. That is one of the few guarantees we're given in the New Testament. "In this world you will have trouble" Jesus promised his disciples, but he didn't leave it at that – "But take heart! I have overcome the world" (John 16:33). Those were some of the last words he spoke to them before being taken in the Garden. Jesus not only suffered for us, he also promised us that we would get to suffer for him, and that he would always be with us.

In this story, Tim and Robert represent two of the types of soil that Jesus talked about in the Parable of the Sower and the Soils. After writing twelve books about this family, I was surprised that Robert's soil was a rocky place that hadn't allowed him to grow deep roots. Trouble caused him to fall away instead of standing firm in his faith. Tim's soil was on the edge between the thorns and the good soil. Thankfully he let his family help him pull out the thorns when they became obvious. While he had a short season of unfruitfulness, he did indeed produce an abundant crop, which will continue to grow. (See Mark 4:16-20.) At this time, I can't tell you if Robert will regain his faith.

Some people might reject this as a "Christian" novel because of Tim's drinking, but that was the story I needed to tell. Really, it shouldn't disqualify this story from Christian markets. If it does then the Bible needs to be disqualified too. Noah not only got drunk, but in his drunkenness he was laying naked for his whole family to see (Genesis 9:21). Lot got drunk too, and his daughters had sex with him, but he still ended up in Jesus' family tree (Genesis 19:30-38; Ruth 4:10; Matthew 1:5), through the sons he had with his own daughters.

I believe that sometimes we try to sanitize "Christian" literature too much. We want to keep the darkness of life on the outside, but the reality is that Christ-followers aren't always good. If you have read many of my books, you probably will have realized that occasionally a curse pops out of a true believer's mouth. (But I only use "hell" and "damn." When Ted used something stronger in *A Cord of Three*, I didn't specify it in the book.) That's because I believe that's how Christians really live. Most of the time they're good, moral people, but occasionally their sinful flesh rises up.

I hope you don't mind, but Robert will be wandering alone out West for a while. Katie's story is next – *From the Rooftops*. She steps into her place in the Shepherd-Wolfe Ohana just in time to have the strength of family help her deal with her realization that Tyler Reynolds is infatuated with her. I hope you'll join me to see how that works out.

Until then, you can find me on Facebook, at www.cherylokimoto.com or email me at cheryl@cherylokimoto.com.

Mahalo and God bless,
Cheryl Okimoto

Characters

Primary characters, by book, in chronological order:

Heather (Shepherd) & Steve Jeremiah, *Seasons of Change*

Beth (Harrison) & Greg Shepherd, *A Gilded Sky*

Jenni (Jeremiah) & Pete Kalaau, *After the Storm*

Gloria (Shepherd) & Joshua Wolfe, *Always a Sunrise*

Rachel (Wolfe) & Abe Lawrence, *The Blessed Winter*

Cait (Kurokawa) & Brian Trask, *Shadows in Light*

Shelly (Mitchell) & Ted Bryant, *A Cord of Three*

Amanda & Will Garrison, *Flames of Hope*

Stormy (Wolfe) & Charles Brown *Living Stones*

Dei (Bryant) & Dave Jeremiah, *A Piece of Dust*

Madison (Wolfe) & Carl Rheese, *Foolish Things*

Cari O'Phelan and Brandon Wolfe, *Secret Righteousness*

Secondary characters, in alphabetical order, appearing in this book:

Alfred (Al) Quintanilla, Joylynne's father

Andy Wolfe, Joshua's brother, Stormy's father

Ann Lindeman, Greg's secretary

Alex, Tim's cousin, Kenji & Hannah's son

Benton Tatum, Greg's friend and fellow minister

Bill Vogt, Mama Rey's husband

Brad, friend of Tim's from church

Brianna, Tim's cousin, Kenji & Hannah's daughter

Chalk (Thomas), Luke & Nalani's son

Charlotte Brown (Mahurin), Charles' daughter from a college relationship

Chavis, Joylynne's brother

Connie Minatoya, Pena's wife

Connor Shepherd, Joshua's adopted father; James Shepherd's father

the Cublets, James and Hosea, Greg & Beth's twin sons

Danita (Nita, but Al calls her Dani) Quintanilla, Joylynne's mother

Davin Kurokawa, Cait's father

Derek Guthrie O'Phelan, Cari's adopted brother

Derryl Kurokawa, Jack & Kelsie's son

Dillon Washington, horse wrangler at Gumbwats' Haven

Doug Kurokawa, Cait's brother

Drake, Ellie & Ryan's son

Ed Kurokawa, Cait's brother

Elanor (Ellie) Franco, Cait's sister

Elton Floyd, Halelolo caretaker, Sandy's husband

Ezekiel, Mark & Lisa's son

Faith Clayborne, Gil's aunt

Festus, Reylene's father, Al's cousin-in-law

Fiona Anderson, Gavyn's second wife

Fleece (Gideon), Pete & Jenni's son

Gabe, Ed & Sherry's son

Gavyn, Ted & Shelly's's son

Gavyn Anderson, Shelly's grandpa, Fiona's second husband

Gil Clayborne, Dave's foster son

Hailey, Doug & Megan's daughter

Hannah Minatoya, Kenji's wife

Hazel, Mark & Lisa's daughter

Heath, Joylynne's brother

Jack Kurokawa, Cait's brother

Jared Jackson, Danny's half-brother, son of Thomas Jackson

Jared Wolfe, Joshua's nephew, Madison's brother

Jeremy, Luke & Nalani's son

Jesse, Ed & Sherry's son

Julie, Ellie & Ryan's daughter

Kara, Jenni & Pete's daughter

Katie Wheeler, nanny/tutor for the Shepherd-Wolfe Ohana

Kendal Wolfe, Joshua's nephew, Madison's brother

Keith, Doug & Megan's son

Kelsie Kurokawa, Jack's wife

Kendra, Joylynne's friend

Kenny, Dave & Dei's son

Kenji Minatoya, Gloria's brother

Kira, Ed & Sherry's daughter

Leiandra (Lei) Guerrero, Cari's friend, Raul's wife

Linc, Heather & Steve's son

Lindiwe O'Phelan, Scott's wife

Lisa Kurokawa, Mark's wife

Lorna Wolfe, Stormy's sister

Mama Rey, Joylynne's grandma, Bill's wife, unofficial grandma to all of Living Stones Fellowship

Mariko, Doug & Megan's daughter

Mark Kurokawa, Cait's brother

Matt, friend of Tim's from church

Matt Shepherd, Luke & Nalani's son

Megan Kurokawa, Doug's wife

Monique Kurokawa, Cait's mother

Morgan, Jack & Kelsie's daughter

Naomi, Luke & Nalani's daughter

Nick, Tim's cousin, Kenji & Hannah's son

Niguel Quintanilla, Mama Rey's late husband

Pika Kalaau, Pete's dad

Pena Minatoya, Gloria's brother

Phil, Heather & Steve's son

Phil Kurokawa (formerly Chung), Cait's half-brother

Preston, Mark & Lisa's son

Raul Guerrero, Cari's friend, Lei's husband

Reed Guthrie O'Phelan, Cari's adopted brother

Reyanne Shepherd, Joshua's adopted mother; James Shepherd's mother

Reybeka, Joylynne's deceased sister

Reylene, Joylynne's friend and cousin

Roast (Caleb), Jenni & Pete's son

Rose Clayborne, Gil's grandma

Russell, friend of Tim's from church

Ryan Franco, Ellie's husband

Sally, Joylynne's friend and cousin

Sandy Floyd, Halelolo caretaker, Elton's wife

Sarah Kalaau, Pete's mom

Sarina O'Phelan, Cari's sister

Sebastian Murphy, Cari's friend

Scott O'Phelan, Cari's brother

Sean, Joylynne's brother

Sherry Kurokawa, Ed's wife

Suzie, Tim's cousin, Pena & Connie's daughter

Taggart, Joylynne's brother

Family groups before this book begins:

Central characters:

Joshua and Gloria (Shepherd nee Minatoya) Wolfe. Children: Luke Shepherd, Jenni (Jeremiah) Kalaau, Heather (Shepherd) Jeremiah, Dave Jeremiah, Greg Shepherd, Brandon Wolfe, Rachel (Wolfe) Lawrence, Tim Shepherd and Robert Shepherd.

Luke and Nalani (Kawada) Shepherd. Children: Matt, Jeremy, Naomi, Thomas and Azariah.

Pete and Jenni (Jeremiah) Kalaau. Children: Kara, Ana (Jenni's, father Bill, adopted by Pete), Gideon and Caleb.

Steve and Heather (Shepherd) Jeremiah. Children: adopted Lincoln, Alyssa, Phillip and Becca; Connor.

Greg and Beth (Harrison) Shepherd. Children: Danny (Beth's, father Thomas Jackson, adopted by Greg) twins James and Hosea, and Nathaniel.

Abe and Rachel (Wolfe) Lawrence. Children: Ethan Allen (No Deal) and Zoe.

Dave and Deidra (Bryant, adopted into Ted's family, born Collins) Jeremiah. Child: Kendrick.

Katie Wheeler, nanny/tutor for Shepherd & Jeremiah children.

Brian and Caitlyn (Kurokawa) Trask. Children: Cecelia and Wayland

Carl and Madison (Wolfe) Rheese. Child: Ester Rose (stillborn).

Charles and Virginia "Stormy" (Wolfe) Brown.

Ted and Shelley (Mitchell nee Anderson) Bryant. Children: Gavyn, Lori, Shay (all three Shelly's, father Frank Mitchell, adopted by Ted), and David Michael.

Will and Amanda Garrison. Children: Sean, Duncan and Carlotta

Other family, friends and relationships before books began:

Alfred and Laura Jean Sullivan. Children: Rodney, Alan and Eryn.

Alfred and Danita Quintanilla. Children: Joylynne, Taggart, Sean, Heath, Chavis and Reybeka (deceased).

Andrew and Ulrica (Perez) Wolfe (divorced, remarried in *Living Stones*). Children: Stormy (Virginia) and Lorna.

Ann Lindeman, Greg's secretary.

Benton and Joanna Tatum. Benton, pastor of a homeless mission in St. Louis; Greg's friend; works with The Ohana Project.

Bill Vogt, wife Juanita deceased.

Blake Maloney, friend and former partner of Carl Rheese.

Cari O'Phelan, woman who broke Brandon's heart.

Calvin and Natalie (Wallace) Bryant. Children: Linda [Dennis – Don, Gill, Bruce, Lucy], Evie, Rikki [Craig – Kylie, Jason (deceased), Ruthie, Dustin, Mark], Jodi [Farrell – Isaac], Ted [Shelly – Gavyn, Lori, Shay, David] and Dei (adopted, born Collins) [Dave – Kenny].

Davin and Monique (Emmet) Kurokawa. Children: Doug [Megan – Mariko, Keith, Hailey], Jack [Kelsie – Derryl, Morgan], Ed [Sherry – Jesse, Kira, Gabe], Ellie [Ryan – Drake, Julie], Will Garrison (adopted) [Amanda – Sean, Duncan, Carlotta], Mark [Lisa – Ezekiel, Preston, Hazel], Phil, Cait [Brian – Cecelia, Wayland]

Dillon Washington, horse trainer/caretaker at Gumbwats' Haven.

Edward and Lida Jean (Reagan) MacDougall. Children: Carl Rheese (adopted), Reagan, Lloyd, Donovan, Fowler and Hoyt.

Gavyn and Fiona (Halloway) Anderson, Shelly's grandfather and his second wife.

James and Kalea (Nakanishi) Shepherd. Children: Luke, Heather, Greg. Kalea died when Luke was 12. J and Gloria (Minatoya) Shepherd. Children:

Timothy and Robert. Kalea's three children adopted by Gloria. James died the year before *Seasons of Change*.

Joshua and Patricia (Jefferson) Wolfe. Children: Brandon and Rachel. Patricia died before *Seasons of Change*.

Kenji and Hannah Minatoya. Children: Malia, Nick, Alex and Brianna.

Nathaniel Pierce and Maggie Wilson, not married. Child: Jeremiah Wilson – changed name to Wilson Jeremiah. N and Mandy Sue (died) Pierce; no children. N and Lucy (died); Children: Sophia, Grace, Tabitha, Martha, and twins, Phillip and James. N and Ms Mimsie Pierce; married in *A Piece of Dust*.

Niguel (died) and Reylynnda Quintanilla. Children: Alfred [Joylynne's father]. Other family members not named at this time. R and William (Bill) Vogt, married in *Living Stones*.

Pena and Connie Minatoya. Children: Suzie, Jeremiah and Leilani.

Pete and Alicia Kalaau, no children. Alicia died before first anniversary, which was before *Seasons of Change*.

Pika and Sarah Kalaau. Children: Pete [Jenni – Kara, Ana, Gideon, Caleb]; adopted Delroy, Saralyn, Culver, Hardy and Lanae.

Ralph and Sophie (Pierce) Harrison. Children: Beth, Debra, and Kyle.

Raul and Lieandra Guerrero. Child: Buckley

Raymond and Jocelyn (Gandry) Brown. Children: Ray [AnnMarie – Landon, Jonathan], Austin [Leann – Kamile, Geoff, Perry, Vance], Charles [Stormy – Charlotte], Mitch [Clarissa] and Travis [Sharene – Wesley, Luis, Robynne].

Rose Clayborne, husband died in earthquakes; daughter Faith, husband died in earthquake [Anita, Cypress]; grandson Gil, father died in earthquake, mother died years ago.

Samuel Jr and Evangeline Wolfe. Children: Samuel III [Jacquiline – Kendal, Jared, Madison}], Joshua [Patricia (died); Gloria – (children all main characters)] and Andrew [Rica – Stormy, Lorna]. Samuel Jr and Evangeline died before *Seasons of Change*.

Samuel III and Jacqueline Wolfe (divorced and remarried). Children: Kendal, Jared and Madison [Carl].

Scott and Lindiwe O'Phelan.

Stan and Elizabeth Lawrence. Children: Abraham [Rachel – Ethan, Zoe], Catherine (deceased), and Kevin.

Ted and Lynne Jeffers; Ted is Joshua's friend, also a pilot.

Thomas and Melissa Jackson. Children: Jared, Clarissa and Shannon. Thomas is father of Beth's son Danny.

Trenton and Cerise Halloway – Children: Barrett, Evonne, Hanley and Dara Lavena.

Wilson and Eryn (Sullivan) Jeremiah. Children: Jenni [Pete – Kara, Ana, Gideon, Caleb], Steve [Heather – adopted Linc, Aly, Phil, Becca; Connor] and David [Dei – Kenny]. Eryn and Wilson died before *Seasons of Change*.

Tyler Reynolds, friend and teammate of Steve and Pete.

Vince and Trinidad (Kerrigan) Cypriano. Child: Rafael; Vince, detective, Abe's friend and partner; Trinidad, psychologist with St. Louis PD.

There is a complete list of the characters from each book on my website, www.cherylokimoto.com.

Notes

Auwe – an exclamation of dismay; "Oh, no!"

Guaranz ballbaranz – guaranteed

Gumbwats' Haven – the Shepherd-Wolfe Ohana's farm south of St. Louis. It was named for a fictional character created by Greg's mentor in college. Gumbwats are Christians, new creatures, and we need to discover how to care for these new creatures so they can grow.

Halelolo – the Shepherd-Wolfe Ohana's home in St. Louis. Hale is Hawaiian for house or home, and lolo is not too bright and a little crazy.

Keiki – children

Kine (da kine) – kind; kind of. Da kine is also a general catch-all word when the specific word escapes you. "Did you get da kine?" Amazingly, most locals very easily figure out what is being talked about

Lanai – balcony

Living Stones Fellowship – church in Norman, Oklahoma that Bill Vogt and Mama Rey founded when the board of their old church, White Stone Community Church, became more interested in keeping their church the way it had always been instead of trying to follow God. Charles Brown is the pastor.

Living Stones Ohana Foundation – the ministry Bill Vogt and Mama Rey started on his old family farm. As its name suggests, it is closely tied to both Living Stones Fellowship and The Ohana Project. They provide life-skills and employment training for homeless, ex-convicts, etc.

Lolo – someone not too bright, even a little crazy

Mahalo – thank you

Melicious – (mom-ism) extraordinarily delicious

Monku – grumble, complain

Musubi – Japanese rice balls. In Hawaii it has come to mean a block of rice with a piece of meat on top, usually Spam, and a strip of nori (seaweed in sheets) wrapped around it

Niephew – (mom-ism) niece or nephew

Ohana – family

Ono – delicious

Try wait – in Hawaiian pidgin "wait" is rarely used as a stand-alone word. Usually it's "try wait," something like "back up a second," or "wait wait wait" (sounds more like "way-way-wayt" with a very soft t-sound), something like "hold your horses."

Gloria's Chop Chae

*T*he most obvious recipes to include here would be either Mama Rey's top-secret pound cake, or Greg's Portugese Bean Soup, but neither are willing to share them yet, so I had to get something from the list of things Gloria taught Joy to make (page 149). This is a dish that a lot of the people at our church in Salem, Missouri really like.

16 oz. long rice (bean threads)
2 Tbsp oil or bacon grease (depends on how healthy you want it to be)
1 Tbsp minced garlic
1 Tbsp minced ginger
3 or 4 veggies, cut in strips as much as possible, a cup or two of each, depending on how many veggies you want, for example:
    julienne carrots
    broccoli
    cabbage (bok choy is best)
    baby corn
    bamboo shoots
    zuchinni
    or any other vegetable that stir fries
Can of Spam, cut in strips (optional)
Salt and pepper to taste

Sauce:
    1 cup shoyu (soy sauce)
    1 cup brown sugar
    4 cups chicken or veggie broth
    1/2 cup sesame oil

1/2 cup chopped green onions
toasted sesame seeds

SOAK BEAN THREADS for 20 minutes. Drain.

In a large pan, heat the oil/grease to briefly sauté the garlic and ginger. (Not too long or they might start to burn when you add the vegetables). Add the vegetables, starting with the ones that will take longest too cook. For example, if you're using carrots and zuchinni, put the carrots in a couple minutes before the zuchinni. Salt and pepper as much or little as you want.

When the vegetables are all tender, remove from pan.

Add all the ingredients for the sauce. Bring to a boil, then add long rice, cooking until the threads are translucent and tender.

Remove from heat. Return veggies to the pan and stir well.

Put in 9x13 pan or large platter for serving.

Sprinkle with green onion and sesame seeds just before serving.

Some of these ingredients will be unfamiliar to many Mainland cooks. You might be able to find them in the Asian foods section at your local grocery store, at an Oriental market, or you might have to shop online for them. Take the time to find them. It's worth the effort!

A Novel Approach to Discipleship

Discipleship is one of the most important aspects of Christian living and yet it's often neglected. One of the reasons for that is that it's hard to disciple people. A Novel Approach to Discipleship is a fun, interesting tool. It's also very comprehensive, encompassing both Christian living and Bible study. Find a good novel (like this one) and you have the start of a discipleship plan.

A Novel Approach is based on two premises:

1. Good fiction shows what Christian living looks like as opposed to non-fiction which tells how it should work.

2. Most people are more comfortable talking about other peoples' problems and mistakes rather than their own.

There are four basic steps to A Novel Approach:

1. *Pick a scene from a book.* This scene should illustrate a principle of Christian living, present a question that you want to explore or provide a starting point to discuss God and the Bible. (E.g., remaining sexually pure; what does a good apology look like?) Read the scene with your group.

2. *Discuss the scene.* Start with specific but not overly leading questions. Explore the positive and negative aspects of the scene. Don't worry if you can't get a consensus. This is the opinion stage. You'll search for the truth in the next step.

3. *Go to the Bible and see what it says.* This is the heart of A Novel Approach to Discipleship! This is where you will spend the bulk of your time. Use this to teach the basic rules of good Bible study:

    Context. Read entire paragraphs, not just a select verse or two. Read the whole passage. Read the passage before and after. See how they relate to your subject passage. How does your passage fit in the greater context of the book of the Bible that it's in? What about the Testament it's in? Filter Old Testament passages through the grace found in the New Testament.

Cross-references and concordance. Find other passages that address similar topics. As you find them, go back to the previous step and read them in context. Look for more cross-references when you find passages that do apply to your topic.

Commentaries and Bible dictionaries. When the meaning of a passage is hard to discern from context (or when you can't agree on the meaning from the context), always refer to commentaries. Two is better than one, three is better yet. Bible dictionaries help bridge the gap of a different culture, different time.

4. ***Process what you have learned.*** This is a *discipleship* exercise, so make sure you take your studies all the way to their application to real life. In the study in this book, I'll sometimes give you an application step, sometimes I won't. When I don't lead you in processing what you have learned, please don't skip this step!

Let me clearly state what I hint at above (e.g. your group, consensus, agree on the meaning): This is *not* a solo activity. A person cannot disciple him/herself. While each individual will do some "homework" on their own, you must have a group to process with. As the word "discipleship" implies, at least one in the group should be a more mature Christian.

You can go to my website, www.cherylokimoto.com, for more detailed information on how to use A Novel Approach to Discipleship. I have included some studies here, but there are even more on my website. Go to the "Resources" tab then pick "A Novel Approach to Discipleship." In "Bible Study Help," you will also find more information about the kind of Bible study used in A Novel Approach to Discipleship.

If you're having trouble finding scripture references for the studies below, please email me at cheryl@cherylokimoto.com.

STUDIES:

1. A couple weeks before the wedding, Tim thinks about the difference between virginity and sexual purity. He thinks that "their virginity wasn't that big a deal." Do you believe that's a proper attitude toward virginity for a Christian? Why or why not? Consider the whole paragraph on page 28. Now look at what the Bible says about sexual purity, and one of the opposites to it – adultery. Do you think you've had a good attitude about sexual purity, or do you need to develop a new thinking process about it?

2. Tim talks about Jesus as creator (pages 41-42). When most Christians think about biblical creationism, they only think about Genesis. Find other passages about creation, in both the Old and the New Testaments. What is the Bible's main emphasis on creation? How does this help you see God and mankind?

3. On page 74, Brandon talks about the difference between "the just-going-to-church kind of easy believism" and "I'm-clinging-to-God-as-my-savior-and-guide-and-Lord faith." Do you understand the difference? What does the Bible say about believing without the full commitment of accepting Jesus as Lord? What does it say accepting Jesus as Lord truly means? What's required of believers? Are you ready to make that commitment? If not, why not?

4. When Robert catches up with Tim after he leaves the hospital (page 221), Tim realizes that "though their situations were very different, their pain was agonizingly similar." Do you think he's right? Much of our current teachings about sharing grief/pain can lead one to the conclusion that if you're suffering, you need to find others who have suffered like you when you want someone to help you deal with it, but the Celebrate Recovery program doesn't function on that principle; it brings together people who are facing a wide variety of issues. On page 178, Greg observes that "when it's fresh, pain seeks to be known by a similar pain." Does that conflict with Tim's observation or can both be true? Explain your answer. What does the Bible say about recovering from grief/pain? Can you find any indication that you need to find people who have gone through the same type of circumstances you have? Carefully consider Hebrews 2:18 (in context). Is it possible that for true healing, we need to begin to see that our grief/pain isn't all that unique?

5. In Chapter 34, Tim tries to deal with his grief by drinking. Some people think that any alcohol consumption, much less drunkenness, is inappropriate for the hero of a Christian novel. What do you think about that chapter? Can a person who has shared his faith like Tim did with Danita in Chapters 4 and 5 really respond like that to grief? Defend your answer. Can you find examples in the Bible where a true believer didn't handle trials very well? What does that tell you about whether or not it's "okay" to fail? Have you faced similar temptations? How did you deal with them? How could you prepare yourself to make good decisions the next time you face difficult circumstances?

6. Tim testifies in court in Chapter 37. Do you think that a real person would have defended Schroeder under similar circumstances? What do you think about what Tim said? Do you think he was right? Why or why not? Can

you defend your position with Bible passages? Can you find anything in the Bible that opposes your position? (Don't just assume there isn't anything. Earnestly try to find something that might change your mind. Don't be afraid to have what you already believe challenged.)

Also by Cheryl Okimoto

The Shepherd Series

THE SHEPHERD SERIES is inspirational fiction with characters who are real friends. These books show what Christian living looks like. Through their relationships, both romantic, friendship and with family, the characters are challenged to change, but they also learn that when we study the Bible properly, it gives us a truly transformational knowledge of God.

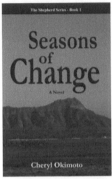

Book 1: *Seasons of Change*

Steve Jeremiah has everything he needs, except a family. In the Shepherds, he finds the family he's dreamt of having, but his growing attraction for Heather may not allow him to stay in his newfound family. (Available in hardcover.)

Book 2: *A Gilded Sky*

In a moment of weakness, Beth Harrison agrees to work with Greg Shepherd. That opens the door to her heart, but they both have hidden issues to deal with.
(Available in hardcover.)

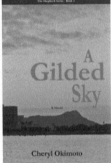

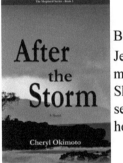

Book 3: *After the Storm*

Jenni Jeremiah has made a lot of mistakes and been hurt many times. She's afraid to love again. Pete Kalaau seems like the perfect man for her, but he has a dark past too.

Book 4: *Always a Sunrise*

When Joshua Wolfe finally faces his tragic past, he can begin to woo Gloria Shepherd, but tragedy strikes her family and they must put their love on hold.

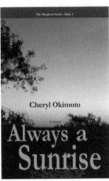

Book 5: *The Blessed Winter*

Abe Lawrence takes in Greg Shepherd when he's forced to stay in St. Louis. Greg's annoying sister, Rachel Wolfe, moves in next door and turns Abe's world upsidedown.

Also by Cheryl Okimoto

The Ohana Project

AS THE SHEPHERDS settle into St. Louis, Missouri to build their family ministry, they reach out to many people. They also reach across state lines. Join them as they meet new friends and help them learn the importance of family.

Book 1: *A Cord of Three*
Ted Bryant runs away from his tragic past. During the long dark winter, he successfully keeps away from his neighbors in Owensville, but spring brings new life, even for Ted.

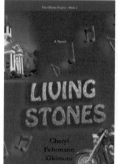

Book 2: *Living Stones*
Stormy Wolfe is looking for a place to use her new Master's in Music Ministry degree. Pastor Charles Brown is looking for someone to bring a little life to his rather old-fashioned congregation.

Book 3: *A Piece of Dust*
Dave Jeremiah and Dei Collins don't hit it off at first, but with their best friends getting married, they try to like each other, and find it surprisingly easy.

Book 4: *Foolish Things*
When Greg and Nalani Shepherd get independent messages from God for the same idea, they know they have to pursue it. They find two volunteers who are willing to follow God, and the foolish adventure begins.

Book 5: *Secret Righteousness*
Brandon Wolfe had actively disliked Cari O'Phelan for many years, but his family's love for her has finally pushed him to carefully consider why. The answer spritually exposes both of them.

Also by Cheryl Okimoto

Hilo Suspense

Book 1: *Shadows in Light*

When Caitlyn Kurokawa discovers she has a stalker, the only person she trusts is her brother Mark. Even with his help, she can't solve the mystery, so they seek the help of two friends from church. It doesn't take long for their problems to multiply.

Book 2: *Flames of Hope*

As Brian and Cait return to Hilo, they run into a bit of difficulty. God uses their troubles to touch many lives, including Brian's best friend who long ago turned his back on God.

Historical Fiction

By Any Other Name

This novella is based on a stage play by the same name. It's about the naming of Owensville, Missouri. It includes the known historical facts, which are greatly fictionalized.

CHERYL'S BOOKS ARE available through Lulu.com or the author's website, www.cherylokimoto.com.